PRAISE FOR SHIFTING SAND

"This is some of the best new crime writing in the West."

— W. MICHAEL GEAR, *NEW YORK TIMES* BESTSELLING AUTHOR

"This story takes off like a shot...Jefferson Glass has staked out a significant place in the modern Western novel, between the traditional Western and the contemporary Western. We can expect more good stories to follow."

— JOHN D. NESBITT, SPUR AWARD-WINNING AUTHOR

"Jefferson Glass harnesses his love of Western history and sparse landscapes into an action-packed mystery that will leave you guessing until the end."

— JENNIFER KOCHER, AWARD-WINNING JOURNALIST AND AUTHOR

SHIFTING SAND

ALSO BY JEFFERSON GLASS

Conor Armenta Mystery Series

The First Light of Dawn

SHIFTING SAND

A CONOR ARMENTA MYSTERY
BOOK TWO

JEFFERSON GLASS

WOLFPACK
PUBLISHING
— EST 2013 —

Shifting Sand
Paperback Edition
Copyright © 2024 Jefferson Glass

Wolfpack Publishing
1707 E. Diana Street
Tampa, FL 33610

wolfpackpublishing.com

Paperback ISBN 978-1-63977-545-3
eBook ISBN 978-1-63977-544-6
LCCN 2024944776

To all of the veterans of what was then called The War to End All Wars, and later became known as World War I.

Among those patriots were both of my grandfathers, William Foster Ranney (1896-1975) who served in the United States Army and Walter Maxwell Glass, Sr. (1901-1952) who served in the United States Navy.
There were thousands of others, some like the fictional character George, who appears in this story and suffers from what is now referred to as post-traumatic stress disorder (PTSD).

Though many are forgotten, I sincerely thank them all for their sacrifice and dedication to our country.

SHIFTING SAND

1

SUNDAY, JUNE 1, 1930

Harvey Rae leaned all of his weight on the railway spike-puller as an eyebrow of sunlight glimpsed over the eastern horizon. Nick Logan and another coworker performed the same task on other ties a few feet apart down the rail. A weak timber on the trestle between Dry Lake and Crystal gave way during the night causing the rail to break and resulting in a severe jolt for the midnight Union Pacific freight train to Salt Lake City as it crossed. The engineer and fireman felt it when the locomotive crossed, then watched the cars progressively jostle more violently behind them. The engineer poured the steam to the engine in an effort to hurry the train across before the trestle collapsed. By the time the caboose crossed, the condition had worsened sufficiently to toss the brakeman from his seat, but a derailment had been avoided.

Amos Browne rousted his track crew from their bunks at three o'clock in the morning. They hurried to the location with tools, timbers, ties, and rails before daylight. When Harv moved to the next tie, he spotted a nearly new deerskin glove resting on a timber below. Dropping to his knees, he reached for it. There was something inside. As he took a closer look to identify what this dark purplish-black stuff could be, he unexpectedly pitched it into the air with a yelp as if it had burned him.

"What was it, Harv?" Logan asked, staring at Rae, still on his knees and looking suddenly pale.

"A hand."

"A what?"

"Someone's hand...in the glove," he said shakily. Then abruptly became ill.

* * *

Shortly before eight o'clock, Sheriff Conor Armenta and Deputy Jesse Slater pulled up alongside the graveled highway known as Arrowhead Trail. The road from Las Vegas to Salt Lake City paralleled the tracks intermittently. Armenta blocked the rising sun with his light-brown Stetson as he peered up at the gang of men silhouetted atop the trestle.

Amos Browne agilely descended the loose-ballast-covered shoulder of the railroad bed at the end of the trestle as easily as if he crossed a smooth and level dancehall floor. He met Armenta as he stood beside his pickup truck. "No one has touched any evidence since we discovered the hand, Sheriff. I sent a couple of my men up the track to see if the owner of the hand was laying out in the brush bleeding to death. He wasn't that lucky. Pieces of him are scattered along the track for a quarter mile."

County coroner, Dr. Harold Martin pulled up behind Slater's sedan a few minutes later and walked up to hear the sheriff's discussion. At a pause in the conversation, he turned to the young deputy. "Have yourself a big breakfast this morning, Jesse?"

"No, sir," he replied somewhat quizzically. "When the sheriff called, I jumped into my clothes and raced to the office. I grabbed a cup of coffee there."

"Good. You won't have much to lose that way," the old doctor concluded as he turned toward his sedan delivery. "I'll grab some sacks." When he returned with a fistful of clean flour sacks and his camera, Browne was leading the officers to the hand a few yards from the track.

"How did you happen to discover it clear out here?" Sheriff Armenta asked the foreman.

"One of my crew noticed a new-looking deerskin glove laying on a timber up there," he pointed up to the trestle. "He picked it up. Then when he figured out what was in it, he hurled it in fright...right before he hurled last night's supper." He winked. "Harv found it right there on the first span." Browne pointed again to the north end of the trestle above them.

"Harvey Rae?" the sheriff asked.

"Yessir. That's him and Nick on the fourth span, there." Browne nodded toward the track above.

"Nick Logan?"

"That's them. You must know them, Sheriff."

"I met them in court a couple of months ago."

"I'll bet they're hoping you've forgotten about that. They've become the best of friends since then. Been no trouble at all." Amos Browne paused for a moment remembering the two fistfights the men had had with each other that brought Deputy Slater out to the work camp at Arden twice one Sunday a couple of months earlier. "They work well together now. No drinking. They're two of my best hands."

"That's good to hear." Armenta recalled the incident. It stemmed from a drunken vulgar remark about Rae's sister. "I'm glad it worked out," he added as he watched the coroner snap a photograph of the gloved left hand. "Jesse, go up and get a statement from Harvey Rae," he said. "Talk to Nick Logan and the rest of the crew. See what they know. Finish up with Mr. Browne, then catch up with Hal and me down the track."

The sheriff turned back to Mr. Browne. "Any idea why someone would be walking across the trestle in the middle of the night?"

"None. Maybe he was sleeping on the trestle. Afraid of snakes in the desert or something."

"Never thought of that. Even if he heard the train coming, could have tripped trying to run to the end of the trestle before it got there. I suppose it's a possibility. Thanks."

Dr. Martin wrote and drew a map with estimated distances in his notebook. Then he methodically penciled #1 on a manilla tag from his pocket, dropped it into a sack and dropped the sack near the hand. When he turned to Conor and the foreman, Jesse was slipping and sliding his way as he scrambled up the ballast to the track. "There an easier way up than that?" he asked Browne.

"Couple hundred yards up, the bed's only three feet higher than the road," Amos answered.

"Worth the walk," the aging coroner surmised and headed in that direction.

"Hold up, Hal," Con spoke. "It'll be really warm by the time we're finished here." He turned back to the foreman. "Any trains coming our way soon."

"Not until we repair the trestle and I telegraph that the track is clear. That'll be at least a few hours. This is quite a job replacing that broken timber."

"Follow me in your car, Hal," Conor told him and climbed into his pickup.

They left the sheriff's truck alongside the road about where Amos Browne had suggested the carnage ended, then drove back in Hal's car and parked a short distance from the trestle. Con picked up the bundle of flour sacks and led the way through waist-high brush toward the tracks. Just a few feet from the foot of the railroad bed, he noticed an unusual-looking rock under a scraggly clump of rabbitbrush. Nearly round. Somewhat oblong. Like a light-brown, fat football. Dark-colored veins, perhaps some mineral wove around it, and dark lichen covered one end of it. As Conor got closer, he could see sand stuck to it as if it had been damp and rolled across the desert to rest there. As he bent down to get a closer look, "Egad!!" escaped rapidly from his throat as he bolted upright in disbelief. He forced himself to swallow the acidic vomit that wrangled its way to the back of his mouth, then took a long deep breath.

"What is it, Con?" Hal anxiously blurted from behind him.

"The head." Conor stood there for a moment regaining his composure. He could not blame the river of sweat running down his back on the still reasonably cool morning. In fact, the slight breeze against his now-damp shirt nearly brought a shiver up his spine.

Conor's tracking experience took over his train of thought. On closer examination, a slight indentation across the sand indicated the trajectory the skull had taken as it rolled from the point of separation from its owner. About thirty feet from the rail, he guessed, as he sighted up the trail back to the tracks. He swallowed again, wishing he had a drink of water to wash down the nasty taste in his mouth, then turned back to the ghastly source of his churning stomach.

The visible half of the disfigured face stared blankly through a waxy dark brown eye at the base of the rabbit-brush. Most of the observable ear was missing. The complexion must have been swarthy, but now was much paler. What had seemed to be lichen was short-cropped black hair. The victim may have been Hispanic or Asian, but based on the near proximity to the Moapa River Indian Reservation, more likely Paiute. The short hair nearly guaranteed a male. Even though many native men wore their hair long, those attempting to blend into Caucasian society often cut it short. The facial features were mutilated beyond any possible recognition.

Hal snapped photographs, scribbled in his notebook, wrote #2 on a manila tag, placed it in a flour sack and dropped it near the bush.

Con ascended the railroad bed to the tracks and proceeded toward the trestle, counting the ties as he went. "A hundred and three," he called back to Hal, who noted the figure on the map he had drawn for #2.

Jesse joined Conor at the trestle. "The two guys that walked up the track said that half of him is just past where Hal is standing, and the rest of him is a couple hundred yards past that. That's about all they saw."

The track ran straight from the trestle in a northeasterly direction for several miles. "You take the left side," he told Jesse. "Check the track, the roadbed and the nearby brush.

Look for anything that might be connected with our victim. I'll check the right."

Within a few yards, Jesse spoke up. "What do you think of this?" he asked, pointing to a small scrap of light-blue fabric. It clung to the sharp mushroomed crown of a spike securing the inside of the left-hand rail. "Chambray shirt maybe?"

"I think you're probably right," Conor added as he took a closer look. "Nineteen ties," he mumbled as he counted back to the trestle. They left the cloth in place and continued on after Con noted it in his tally book. The duo found two more similar fragments of the blue cloth by the time they reached Hal's position. These others appeared to be a darker shade and denim.

"It looks like he might have been dragged by the train," Conor told Hal as they neared him.

"That would explain the distance," Hal stated without further comment.

Conor picked up a flat rock and leaned it against the right-hand rail marking the spot. "We know how far it is to here."

Before the three had progressed more than a dozen yards, Conor noticed a rumpled pile of blue denim along the foot of the roadbed. It turned out to be most of a jean jacket. Hal shot a photograph before Con checked the remaining pocket. Empty. #3, the coroner marked the tag as he dropped it into the flour sack and left it near the jacket.

"Twelve ties from the head," Conor told him, as Hal made his notes.

"From the what?" Jesse exclaimed, still standing between the tracks.

"The skull," Con answered. "It's right below where the doc was waiting for us."

Jesse turned paler and bent over to grab his knees. He took

deep breaths, but remained standing and kept from losing whatever might be in his stomach.

"You all right?" Conor asked as he and Hal regained their position between the rails.

"I'm okay," Jesse replied as he stood back up straight. He was beginning to appreciate Dr. Martin's comment earlier about eating a large breakfast.

They next found the remnants of the victim's chambray shirt. Jesse spotted it about halfway down the embankment on his side. Again, Hal took a picture and Conor checked the pockets. And again, both were empty.

As Hal completed his documentation, Con watched Jesse standing further up the track. He was looking at something about the same distance below the track as Conor stood presently. Some rounded sand-colored object. A large boulder maybe. Suddenly Jesse bent over, vomiting. *It must be more of the victim*, Conor thought to himself as he ascended the bank and advanced toward his distracted deputy.

The ghastly sight below was the naked, decapitated torso of the victim. A dark purple gash of meat and bone marked the armless right shoulder. The bare left arm, the only extremity, ended at the wrist. Bits of entrails protruded from the waist where it had been rent apart from the pelvis just below the navel by the massive steel wheels of the train. A flat, muscular chest confirmed the victim's sex. Scarcity of body hair, a common trait of many natives, and tan complexion supported Conor's suspicion of the man's ethnicity.

Jesse had just begun to regain himself as the coroner approached.

"Well now," the old man surmised, "The parts seem to be getting larger."

The coarse remark nearly brought back Jesse's retching, but he managed to force the reflex into submission.

Conor carefully examined the rail in search of the exact place the train had cut the victim in half. He found a spot in a likely location that was slightly discolored, but nothing to conclusively identify it.

"Fifty-two ties from the skull, Hal," Con told him as the coroner snapped photos of the torso. "We're moving ahead."

"Okay, boys. I'll be along."

Two hundred sixty-four ties farther up the track, an ankle-high, lace-up right boot, lay scuffed and tattered between the rails. Conor noted the distance in his tally book. Another large, dark object lay between tracks in the distance. "Wait here for Hal," he told Jesse. "I'm going on ahead."

As the sun rose higher in the sky, heatwaves danced from the ballast, ties, and rails of the track. Con had to force himself to continue looking for clues along the way, as he kept glancing at the object ahead. The motion of the mirage made it look like the dark object was dancing on the rippling surface of a distant lake. He found a sock and began seeing tattered bits of denim between the rails. He suspected the object to be the rest of the body, the man's jeans being shredded by the sharp rocks of the ballast amid the tracks. He stared at the object, noting to himself that he had covered a fair distance, while he advanced several more steps. Suddenly a black explosion erupted before him as two large turkey vultures burst into flight. The object nearly submerged into the sea of the mirage. Conor continued on.

At two hundred fourteen ties past the boot, the lower half of John Doe lay between the tracks. Like the glove, it had the appearance of just a pair of jeans laying on the ballast, until the shape brought to reality that they were occupied. The right foot was severely damaged from being dragged the relatively short distance from the boot. The left leg pointed straight ahead up the track, while the right, trailing behind, appeared dislocated at the hip. Parts of entrails protruded from the waist where the vultures had dined. The man wore an expensive-looking silver belt buckle. Conor had seen similar buckles before, but rarely. He didn't know much about the fine art of native jewelry making. Navajo sand casting, maybe. Turquoise and red stones adorned it. It had been scraped from the violence of the incident and a stone was missing, but still quite valuable, he thought. Damaged and dirty, it still gleamed in the sun. Careful not to move anything, Con kneeled to check the front pockets. Empty. Hal would check the rear pockets during the autopsy.

Conor rose to his feet and looked back down the track. Hal and Jesse were just turning to walk toward him. They're at the boot he thought and turned back toward the victim. That's when he saw it. A length of twine trailed from the left ankle. About three feet long and frayed at the end. Like it had been stretched until it broke. Conor kneeled down and inspected the twine. He raised the pant leg. The twine had a slipknot that looped around the ankle. It had pulled too tight for Con to loosen it. The ankle was chafed from the twine. He moved to the right ankle. It, too, was chafed in the same area. The victim had been tied up. Maybe held hostage...or prisoner some-where. How did he end up here?

"Go ahead and document what we have, Hal. This is prob-ably the end of our work here, but we're still missing the right arm. Jesse and I will continue up the track a bit farther, just in case. We might have overlooked it, or some coyote might have packed it off." Then Con added, "I counted 633 ties from the trestle. At about two feet per tie, that's pretty close to the quarter mile Mr. Browne estimated."

Conor and Jesse found no more evidence along the track and cut over to the highway and the sheriff's pickup truck. After having a swig of water from Conor's canteen, they drove down the road to meet with the coroner. Conor carried the water as they walked back to the tracks.

"Notice that twine around the left ankle?" Conor asked as he handed Hal the canteen.

Hal nodded before taking a drink.

"What do you make of it?"

"I'm not sure, but it appears that someone didn't want Mr. Doe here to get away."

"Kidnappers, maybe?"

"That's certainly a possibility," the doctor surmised.

"There's something else that's odd about this whole horrific situation," Con noted.

"What's that?" Jesse interjected.

"No blood. Or almost no blood, anyway," Conor replied. "Shouldn't there have been blood sprayed all over the place where the hand was amputated? At say, thirty or maybe forty miles per hour it would have only been a few seconds before he was decapitated. Then cut in two. And the last of him would have landed here in less than a half a minute from the start. I've not found a single drop of blood anywhere except on the victim's wounds and clothing. Even that is minuscule."

"Must have been dead before the train hit him," Jesse concluded.

"Walked out onto the trestle and died? Then got hit by the train?" Conor questioned. "That seems pretty far-fetched."

"What if he was already dead and someone tied him to the

trestle?" Hal suggested. "The trestle crosses right over the road. Not too far to carry a dead body. No one out here in the middle of the night to see you. And that would explain the twine."

"It would have been easier just to dump the body right where we're standing than to lug him all the way up onto the trestle," Conor countered.

"Nobody said that whoever hauled him out here was smart," Hal offered.

Conor grinned at Hal's dry humor, even at a grizzly time like this. "Let's start picking up the pieces," Con responded. Jesse jumped into the back of the truck while Hal climbed into the passenger seat and they drove down the road to the coroner's delivery.

"You've got all of the pictures we need?" Conor asked Hal.

"Sure do."

Conor grabbed a handful of large envelopes from the coroner's supplies and handed them to Jesse. "Start at the trestle and walk the track," he told him. "Pick up each piece of cloth we found and write down how many ties from the trestle it was on the envelope. Put the shirt and jacket into the sacks when you get to them and bring them along. We'll meet you at the torso."

Jesse headed toward the tracks.

"I'll go down and get the hand while you pick up the head," he told Hal. "Then we'll drive up and meet Jesse."

The railroad crew had significantly disassembled the trestle and begun installing several new timbers. Conor placed the hand in the sack Hal had left for it and approached Amos Browne.

"Quite a mess, isn't it?" Browne commented more than asked.

"Did you go up there?" Con asked.

"I went as far as the first half of him," he answered. "That's all I cared to see."

"Have you noticed any twine tied on the trestle anywhere?" Conor questioned.

"No sir, Sheriff," Browne replied. "And I've inspected every timber on it. We're changing a few more than the one that failed, as you can see."

"How hard of a jolt was there when the train hit the broken track?"

"Well, the engineer felt it, but the locomotive cleared it okay. By the time the caboose got there, it was severe enough to toss the brakeman clean out of his seat!" Browne explained. "When we got here, the track had dropped a couple of inches in front of the break. That'll rattle your dentistry when a car hits it," he grinned.

Con grinned in return. "Thank you for your help, sir," he responded, offering his hand. Conor liked this man. He and his team were hardworking laborers in an unforgiving environment. Even as the sweat dripped from his nose on a day with a gruesome beginning, he could find a little bit of humor to raise his spirit and most likely that of his crew.

* * *

It was early afternoon when Conor stepped into the sheriff's department. He had sent Jesse to assist Hal with bringing John Doe into the coroner's examination room. Hazel Corbyn fulfilled several roles in the department from office manager to daytime dispatcher. A generation older than Sheriff Armenta, she occasionally overstepped her authority by imposing on her supervisor the skills of a matchmaker and surrogate mother. This rare digression usually drew her boss's indignation. He felt that his own mother and especially his younger sister were perfectly capable of sufficiently irritating him regarding matters of his personal life without further assistance.

"How did it go out there, Sheriff?" Hazel asked when he came in.

"Okay, I suppose. What are you doing here on Sunday?"

"The operator called me around ten this morning. She said no one was answering the telephone at the office. She thought you and Jesse were out along the railroad somewhere investigating a dead body."

"Where's your husband?"

"Frank? He's out at Boulder City building a barracks or commissary or something military sounding. Seven days a week right now. Contractors are in a big hurry to get workers for the dam settled in. This sounded more interesting than staying home and cleaning house." She tried to be serious but chuckled.

"I can understand that." Conor smiled as he turned toward his office.

"Sheriff Andrew Neilson from Beaver, Utah, called about an hour ago. He said that you knew him and asked that you call back as soon as possible. He said it was important," Hazel informed him. "The number is on your desk."

"Thanks," Con replied. "I wonder what he wants?" he asked himself aloud as he entered his office and closed the door.

A pleasant female voice answered the telephone on the second ring. "Beaver County Sheriff's Department. How can I help you?"

"Sheriff Conor Armenta returning a call from Sheriff Neilson," he responded.

A moment later, a cheerful male voice came on the line, "Con Armenta, how the heck are you?"

"Howdy, Andy. I'm fine. Hazel said you called. What's on your mind?"

"I got a call this morning from the railroad over at Milford. They said you were working on a John Doe that got hit by a train."

"Word travels fast. You know who he is?"

"No. I sure don't. But I have his right arm."

2

MONDAY, SEPTEMBER 3, 1923

Gary and Katherine Wagner owned the most successful trucking company in Las Vegas. A half-dozen years earlier Wagner Trucking Company was a struggling two-truck operation of which Gary was the driver of half the fleet. The discovery of oil in the Circle Cliffs region of southern Utah a couple of years later had caught Gary's attention. He and Katherine gambled everything they owned on the new opportunity and moved their company there. The boom that followed flung the fledgling company ahead, and the business soon blossomed into a prosperous ten-truck operation. The result was not without a lot of hard work and determination by the owners. As that successful venture declined, they returned with their company to their hometown of Las Vegas where the enterprise continued to flourish, though at a much slower rate.

This morning Gary received a telephone call from the

Starlight Mining Company, their largest customer. Starlight had experienced a major breakdown over the weekend and would be shut down several weeks while awaiting the arrival of replacement machinery being assembled in Kentucky. In three weeks, Gary and his good friend, Brice Campbell, were leaving for Switzerland on a mountaineering expedition. The trip they planned was what both men considered an opportunity of a lifetime. They were meeting four fellow climbers from France and Austria. Their goal? To conquer the north face of the Eiger, a rugged peak among the Alps and a feat yet to be accomplished by anyone.

Gary Wagner contemplated his circumstances. Though not wealthy, the temporary reduction in income would not be a significant setback. Katherine, his wife of twenty-plus years was more than a lover and business partner, they were best friends and had been since elementary school. She balked at the proposed climbing expedition, convinced he still considered himself a teenager, though he would turn forty at the end of next week. He had attempted consolation with a new Oldsmobile coupe. His gift to her for his birthday he joked. This temporary respite in business offered up the opportunity for Gary to further recruit her tolerance of his mountaineering hobby.

"My dear Katherine," he began as he emerged from his private office.

"Yes?" She suspiciously glanced up from the work on the desk before her. "What are you buttering me up for, Mr. Wagner?"

"How would you like a vacation?"

"I'm not sure that I know what that might be like."

"Exactly! How would you like to spend two weeks

exploring the Navajo Lands? The ancient pueblos? Shopping in the old trading posts? What do you say?"

"I say, you're leaving in three weeks for Europe, and we have a business to run," she replied with a knowing smile. "You're just looking for a diversion while you plan your escape. Who's going to run this place while we're gone?"

"Well, as it turns out, Starlight Mining is shut down for a few weeks. Agnes can run the office, and Dutch can keep track of the few trucks we'll have working."

"Dutch? You can't be serious. He may be twenty-one years old, but he's hardly mature enough to run his personal affairs let alone the company that you've spent your entire life building. He'll have us bankrupt in a week!"

"All he'll need to do is make sure the trucks get repaired if they break down and that someone drives them to where they need to go. How difficult can that be?" He knew the answer and Katherine's skepticism. Their son, Dutch, was a spoiled brat, who had no concept of a work ethic. He had been on the payroll of Wagner Trucking since he became a teenager. Gary had tried to utilize him in a number of positions at the company without success. He was too lazy to even sweep the shop floors effectively and too conniving to trust with any sort of responsibilities. His only attribute when it came to money was a natural instinctive ability to cheat someone else out of theirs. "He'll be fine," Gary went on, trying to convince his wife...and himself. "Agnes will control the checkbook."

Agnes Spencer was a few years older than the Wagners and split the office duties with Katherine. She was a solid employee and the two women made a good team.

Katherine Wagner finally agreed. They had never had a real vacation since they were married. They worked hard and could afford it. They spent the rest of the day planning and making business arrangements for their absence. Tuesday, they packed and planned their vacation.

* * *

WEDNESDAY, SEPTEMBER 5, 1923

In the wee morning hours, Gary and Katherine Wagner motored down the gravel highway in the darkness toward Searchlight. As they approached, the lights came on in the café on the corner, and Gary wheeled the coupe to a stop out front. Katherine had napped intermittently on the drive thus far and forced back a yawn with a smile as Gary opened her door to step out into the cool darkness. The café served a homestyle menu, and they enjoyed a pleasant breakfast and coffee. A young friendly waitress kept their cups filled and shared in cheerful conversation...a joyful premonition they hoped for the days ahead.

Gary started the car, and they turned east toward the Colorado River just as the pink tint of dawn's first light appeared on the horizon. Sunrise glinted off the maroon fenders of the dove-gray Oldsmobile as Gary eased it onto the Searchlight Ferry. The loading and unloading process took far longer than the short passage across the river.

"What a beautiful morning," Katherine commented.

The breeze on the water put a chill into her, while she and Gary stood against the rail listening to the river lapping at the side of the ferry as they crossed.

"The air smells so fresh and moist along the river," Gary observed in response. He wrapped his arm more tightly around her as she shivered against his side. Katherine snuggled against him and watched a bird in flight, skimming for insects upstream. The warmth of her husband's body comforted her in the cool morning air.

They climbed back into the car when the ferry landed on the far bank. The V-8 rumbled as the car climbed the twisting road through the Black Mountains. They topped the grade over a thousand feet above the river. In a gradual descent, they broke out into the Detrital Valley and were again in the desert. What a change of scenery from the heavy vegetation along the riverbanks a short time ago to the spiny Joshua trees and yuccas, Katherine thought. As the sun rose high enough to reduce the blinding glare they had been staring into, the road turned southeast into the arid landscape.

"The coolness of the river didn't stay with us long, did it?" Katherine stated rhetorically as hot air blasted through the open windows. They chuckled to each other sharing in the amusement of a roadrunner darting ahead as they continued down the road at a brisk pace.

At noon, the coupe rolled into Kingman. Conversation had waned as the temperature of the day rose. The town bordered the Atchison, Topeka, and Santa Fe Railways. There, a more well-traveled thoroughfare than they had been on, paralleled the railroad to the east and west. After a light lunch with glasses of iced tea, they continued on. The road began northeast from Kingman, then made a sweeping turn around the end of the Peacock Mountains at Antares. From there, they began the ascent up Truxton Wash to the southeast.

"It's amazing how quickly the scenery changes," Katherine marveled as they passed through Hackberry, a small town resting below the mouth of Truxton Canyon. The road again turned northeast and continued to follow the railroad as they gradually climbed.

"Are you ready for a cold drink?" Gary asked midway

through the canyon as they approached the community of Valentine.

"Sure, I would enjoy a cold sarsaparilla."

Gary purchased sodas from a refrigerated machine at the gas station, as Katherine found shade at a picnic table beneath a scraggly cottonwood tree. A slight breeze carried through the canyon and lightly blew her hair. At an altitude of nearly four thousand feet, the heat of the afternoon was less severe than it had been in Kingman. There was a small hotel there, but a large two-story brick schoolhouse dominated the little town and looked out of place to Katherine in the landscape between the Music Mountains to the north and the Cotton-wood Mountains to the south.

"Indian trade school," Gary told her, noting her gaze toward the building when he returned with their drinks. "Guy in the station said it's a boarding school. Supposed to assimi-late the younger natives into the *American* way of life. The main Indian Reservation begins a few miles on up the road."

Feeling refreshed after their short interlude, Gary checked the car over, and they were soon back underway. They emerged from the canyon and continued along the upper portion of Truxton Wash. After passing through Cherokee, they entered into the Hualapai Indian Reservation. There the road veered east through Peach Springs and traversed the southern edge of the reservation through Yampai Canyon. In the dozen miles through the canyon, they left the reservation, crossing Yampai Divide at over a mile above sea level.

The route opened into the broad Aubrey Valley and ran almost perfectly straight for twenty miles where it rounded the southern end of the Red Mesa. Turning east again for another twenty-five miles of nearly straight road they pulled up to the Hotel Escalante at Ash Fork, Arizona that evening.

Katherine had read about the extravagant hotel in a magazine several months ago and had shown the article to Gary at the time. The magnificent establishment had been built in the tiny Arizona town by Fred Harvey to accommodate the elite clientele of the railroad. Little had Katherine imagined that she would ever be staying there, but Gary had remembered how awed she had been over it.

"We aren't staying here?" Katherine flinched at the thought of squandering their hard-earned money. "We can't afford this," she continued as he got out of the car. But Gary rented an elegant suite in the luxurious Hotel Escalante, and the couple each soaked in the tub of the well-appointed bathroom before dressing for a late supper.

"We never had a honeymoon when we got married," he told her as they were seated in the elegant dining room, "and scant opportunity to enjoy ourselves since. This is our honeymoon now. I want this vacation to be memorable in every way."

The dining room of the Grand Harvey House offered gourmet cuisine far beyond their familiar fare. They feigned their worldliness effectively enough to not feel terribly out of place among the crystal goblets, fine china and sterling silver dinnerware that bejeweled the linen covering on the table. Both ordered the squab. The waitress served hors d'oeuvres, followed by a creamy oyster soup that pleased Gary, but disappointed Katherine. On the other hand, she was delighted with the main course while he was less impressed.

"It's probably just a tough old chukar or quail hidden in the fancy sauce," Gary scoffed, though they had a wonderful time.

"What's this?" Gary asked in surprise as the maître d' filled champagne glasses from a large bottle without replying. They were shocked that the hotel would be so brazen to serve alcohol to their guests, considering prohibition regulations.

Katherine nearly spewed the beverage from her mouth as she snickered.

"What is it?" Gary asked.

"Taste it!" she said, as the man finished filling his glass and left the table.

Gary cautiously took a small sip. "Cider!" he burst out, and they chuckled over the restaurant's substitution of sparkling cider for champagne.

By the time they finished their crème brûlée dessert, both had consumed far more food than was comfortable, and they opted for an evening stroll before retiring. The night air of Ash Fork was cool and comfortable. They ambled along the dirt street under a star-filled sky.

"Remember Circle Cliffs?" Katherine asked.

"How could I forget? We worked our tails off up there."

"Remember when the drilling rig broke down, and I rode with you in the truck to Green River to get the part they needed?"

"Yes?"

"While you went to the trainyard to load the truck, I went to the mercantile and bought the first real groceries we had had in months. When we got back, the oil company was so pleased with how quickly you had made the trip they gave you a bonus."

"Yes, I remember all of that. What brought it to mind?"

"I made us a special celebration supper that night from some of the newly acquired delicacies I'd bought in Green River. As usual, you got back to the shack after working a long, hard day, and it was nearly midnight when we finished our feast." Gary was lost in the memory as Katherine recalled the story. "We went for a walk down the road in the darkness afterward. It was a night very much like this."

"Yes it was. Those were hard times," he recalled.

"But good times too..."

Slowly wandering the empty street from end to end had scarcely expended a half hour when they returned to their room. It had been a long day. Two hundred fifty miles from home, many new sights and a wide variety of scenery all capped by an epicurean meal. Katherine felt as if she were in heaven.

* * *

THURSDAY, SEPTEMBER 6, 1923

Gary and Katherine awoke late in the large, soft, comfortable bed. They had never before experienced such luxury and neither could recall a time when they felt so unencumbered and relaxed. They lazed about the hotel enjoying a late break-fast in the courtyard before leaving. Their drive for the second day of their tour consisted of a mere twenty miles to Williams, though the climb of nearly two thousand feet in elevation surprised them. The Oldsmobile lumbered easily up the slopes past scattered ponderosa pine trees that began to decorate the landscape. A broad departure from the Joshua trees they admired a mere twenty-four hours earlier. They planned their short trek today to accommodate an early departure the following morning by train to the rim of the Grand Canyon.

The Fray Marcus Hotel at Williams was also owned by the railroad, but less luxurious than the Escalante had been at Ash Fork. Still, they enjoyed an afternoon dinner far more sophisti-cated than their usual menu in Las Vegas, and again, Gary and

Katherine took a stroll down the main street of Williams afterward. The cooler air prompted Katherine to grab a sweater as they left the hotel.

They leisurely walked the length of the street. In the shadows of dusk, they could still see window displays in several of the stores. "Quite a few businesses," he commented.

"And most of them seem to direct their inventory toward visitors to the Grand Canyon," Katherine added.

They continued on their leisurely jaunt that ended under the moonlight back at their hotel. They did not have the luxury of a private bath in their room. The one down the hall was shared with three other rooms, but it appeared that only one of them was occupied this night. They both used the facility before dressing for bed and hoped it would sustain them until morning.

* * *

FRIDAY, SEPTEMBER 7, 1923

Katherine and Gary rose early.

"Breakfast will have to be pastry and a quick cup of coffee if we're going to be ready for the six o'clock departure on the train to the canyon," Gary told Katherine as he carried their bags behind her down the stairs.

"We'll make it in plenty of time and can have a more substantial meal when we get to the canyon."

The porter took their luggage from Gary with a smile and a pleasant, "Good morning, sir," in the early morning light.

They had barely taken their seats when they heard the, "All abo-oaard," droned by the conductor from outside their car. The train whistle blew, and with a slight bump, they were underway. The chuff, chuff, chuff of the steam locomotive gradually picked up cadence as the caboose cleared the platform. The sun glinted through the open pine forest where the tracks made their gentle turn north.

"Good mornin' folks! I hope you're headin' fer the Grand Canyon this mornin'," the conductor chuckled as he approached their seats.

"Yessir," Gary replied with a grin. "We certainly are," as he handed the man their tickets.

"What would you do with a couple of wayward passengers if we were not?" Katherine asked wryly as she tried to hide her grin.

"Well, ma'am. I'm afraid I'd have ta' toss ye' off as gently as I could on the first slow grade," he replied in as serious of a tone as he could muster.

"Well sir, then. I'm glad we have our tickets." She giggled.

"And so am I." He laughed with a roar.

"It surely is a wonderful morning, my love," Katherine cooed, reaching through Gary's arm as the conductor continued down the aisle. "Thank you for this beautiful adventure."

"And I could not be sharing it with a more beautiful lady," he replied as he raised her entwined hand and gave the back of it a soft kiss.

They thoroughly enjoyed themselves as the train wound its way through the hills at a relaxing pace. The scenery changed to nearly flat open country, and the train picked up speed. When they had covered some twenty miles of it the conductor appeared at the front of the car. As he stood looking out the window the train began to slow.

"Where are we?" Katherine asked him, unable to see any resemblance of civilization.

"Willaha," he answered. "Get ready, George," he called to a man at the back of the car. The man picked up a knapsack and slung it over his shoulders, then tugged a large canvas duffel bag from under the seat. It was like those the soldiers who came home from the war had, Katherine noted to herself as she studied the situation in silence. George dragged the bag out the rear door of the car, and Katherine watched him through the window as he stood on the little walk outside the car. The train slowed to nearly a stop as unexpectedly two or three small stone buildings appeared through the window. When she turned back, George was gone, and the chuff, chuff, chuff began picking up its rhythm as they rolled ahead.

"What happened to George?" she asked as the conductor turned to exit the car.

"He got off."

"Just like that? The train didn't even stop?"

"We can't stop out here except in an emergency. Not authorized."

"So, he just jumps off a moving train?"

"Yep. We slow down enough so he won't get hurt." The conductor looked at Katherine's still questioning face. He walked back to the seat in front of hers. Flipping it over to face rearward, he kneeled on the backward seat toward her.

"Ye' see, George was in th' war. A real hero from what I hear. When he come home, back east somewhere, he had a hard time bein' around a mess o' people, so's he comes out here." He looked at Katherine's eyes. Her gaze was intently glued on his. "He's got hisself some sort o' shack out there somewhere," he motioned out the window into the vast expanse of desert. "An' that's where he lives. Ev'ry month 'er two he stuffs that empty war bag inta' the knapsack an' waves a red bandanna tied to a long stick fer the engineer when we're still about a half mile back an' flags us down. When the engineer blows the whistle, George knows we're slowin' down. He ditches the flag, throws that knapsack o'er his shoulder, an' gets ready fer' th' footrace. Ain't missed the passenger car but once't an' still caught the rail of the caboose. He rides inta' town loads up on grub an' books an' whatever else he needs. In a day or two, he drags that big ol' bag full as Santa Claus could stuff it an' heads back home."

"How does he pay for his food and books?"

"Don't know. Might get a pension 'er has folks back east that sends to 'im."

"Doesn't he ever talk to you?"

"Been near four years now. Few months ago, he got on board out here. I came by his seat a while later. Said, 'Howdy,' when he looked up at me. He says, 'How have you been?' I says, 'Good, an' you?' Then he says, 'Good,' an' looks away. That half-dozen words 's the first he ever spoke to me."

"How does he pay for his ticket?"

"Never asked him fer' one." Then he turned and left the car.

Katherine sat in silence staring out the window. Gary had heard every word of her conversation with the conductor. He had not felt inclined to intrude. Katherine needed time to absorb the conversation. Neither was he inclined to interrupt her thoughts. A few more miles and they were back in mountains and canyons. In one such canyon, the train entered a horseshoe-shaped turn that nearly turned it completely around.

"I thought the hound was going to bite its own tail there for a bit." Gary finally broke the silence as the train began another U-turn in the opposite direction.

His voice broke her trance. "Sorry, I kind of got lost in my thoughts."

"I noticed that."

"That George. He must have had some dreadful experience during the war that he can't get out of his mind."

"I've heard of that happening to some of those guys over there. The trauma of war can be a terrible thing. Hopefully, George and men like him will be able to overcome their demons."

"I hope so too...my word, what beautiful scenery," Katherine quickly noticed the view from their car. "I must have been staring right past it in my daze."

"I think we made the right choice in taking the train. The vistas are splendid. I can hardly wait to see the canyon. It must be spectacular."

They did not have long to wait. The train soon began a sweeping turn into Bright Angel Wash to begin a nearly straight course of a half-dozen miles to the Grand Canyon Station and El Tovar Hotel, perched on the south rim over-looking the panorama. Their feet had hardly hit the platform when Gary spotted the porter bringing their luggage.

"El Tovar, sir?"

"Yes...thank you."

"Right this way, if you please folks," came the reply as he sped toward the broad stone steps leading to the lobby. The building was magnificent. Katherine gazed in awe at the array of taxidermy adorning the high log walls of the lobby while Gary followed the porter to the manager who stood behind the registration desk. The luggage was transferred to the care of the bellman, and Gary tossed the porter a half-dollar as he returned toward the station.

"All of these different animals live here?" Katherine asked him as he came toward her.

"Yes, ma'am," he paused to look around the room. "A'cept for the buffalo. They're mostly gone now," then continued his rapid pace out the door.

Upon discovery that he and Katherine would again share their bathroom with three other rooms, Gary opted for the indulgence of a small suite. He knew Katherine would never complain of the inconvenience, but he wanted her to feel pampered on this trip. The luxury of privacy seemed worth the added expense.

"Your suite, Mr. Wagner, is at the far end of the north wing, overlooking the canyon," the manager was explaining when abruptly they heard from the dining room, a loud female voice.

"Ohhh, my..." came Katherine's long exclamation. "I've seen plenty of canyons before, but nothing even close to this!" Nearly vacant in midmorning, she had seen her first view of the Grand Canyon through the expansive windows of the large room.

Gary followed the sound of her voice and was equally awestruck by the view beyond his wife as she stood staring at the grandeur.

"It truly is spectacular, is it not?" the manager remarked from behind them as he approached.

"It is all of that," Gary answered, unable to turn his gaze from the landscape.

"...and more," Katherine added as she turned. "I didn't catch your name?"

"Palmer," the manager replied with a slight bow. "At your service, Mrs. Wagner."

"Mr. Palmer? Thank you," she quizzed as she offered her hand.

"Just Palmer," he replied, graciously refusing her hand by keeping his behind his back. "It is my pleasure, ma'am," as he again bowed his head.

Gary and Katherine followed the bellman to their suite, but did not linger beyond another momentary glance at the view through the window. They rushed outside to the deck overlooking the canyon.

"The view is simply amazing!" Katherine gasped.

"I couldn't agree more. Let's get a closer look." They nearly ran down the stairs as if they were half their age and out to the rim of the canyon.

"Completely breathtaking! I'm at a loss for words," Katherine uttered as they gazed into the expanse.

"It is definitely worthy of its name," Gary responded. "Grand."

After a few minutes, they began to stroll eastward along the rim, pausing often to take in the vast scene as it gradually changed along their route. Gary took in the terrain with the eye of an experienced mountaineer. The multitude of spires and pinnacles protruding from along the rim and in the distance far below appeared as a mecca of adventures. The slightest wisp of smoke occasionally escaped over a small rise in the depths below only to disappear again. He could see the raging Colorado River intermittently, and the source of the smoke did not seem close to it.

"I wish now, I had taken time to unpack my field glasses when we were in our room," he told Katherine as he pointed out the subject of his interest.

"Oh, I see it now," she pointed joyfully. "What do you suppose it is?"

"A campfire, I imagine. It doesn't appear to be close to the water, though."

"Cooking lunch?" Katherine asked, unexpectedly realizing that their early morning snack had long since been displaced by her body. "I could use something to eat myself," she added. They had meandered along the trail for over an hour.

"I am pretty hungry too. We should head back toward the hotel."

As they turned and began their stroll toward El Tovar the sun was high, but an irregular breeze churned by the updrafts along the face of the canyon and the high altitude provided pleasant walking conditions. Though their pace was less leisurely than it had been earlier, they still made systematic stops, absorbing the beauty surrounding them. Gary and Katherine had seen plenty of massive rock formations and an array of color between the Circle Cliffs of southern Utah and the railroad at Green River during the four years they had lived and worked there. All of that was far surpassed by the massive display God created within the Grand Canyon.

They took their seats in the cool El Tovar dining room just after noon. Overwhelmed by the beauty of the canyon, both had squelched their hunger longer than either noticed. Seated before the windows, they glimpsed the magnificent view between bites as they devoured sandwiches and lemonade.

Suddenly realizing that her dining manners did not appear very ladylike, Katherine blushed and wiped her mouth with a napkin, "I guess we're both hungrier than we thought."

Taking a cue from his wife, "I suppose I kind of look like a hobo attacking his first meal this week. Is that what you're saying?" Gary chuckled and also took the moment to wipe his face.

"I'm afraid we both do."

When finished with their lunch, they stopped by the front desk and spoke again with Palmer.

"We thoroughly enjoyed our walk along the rim to the east earlier," Gary commented. "We would like to manage our time here as effectively as possible. What do you recommend we should try to see before our departure on the train tomorrow?"

"Perhaps you would like to take the afternoon coach out to Hermit's Rest. It is the furthest accessible point along the rim in that direction. The coach is open-sided like a surrey for good viewing. The driver will stop at several overlooks along the way...and anywhere else you ask him to, as well."

"That sounds splendid."

"He leaves in about twenty minutes and will be back in time for supper."

"Where do we need to go?"

"He will be pulling up right out front anytime now."

"Thank you," Gary replied and turned to Katherine. "What do you think?"

"It sounds like a good way to see quite a bit in a shorter span of time. I need to change shoes. These were great on the train, but less suitable on our little hike."

"I would like to get my field glasses too. We have enough time to run up to our room."

When they descended the stairs returning to the lobby, a young Native American man stood talking to Palmer. He turned when he heard them and greeted, "Good afternoon! You must be Mr. and Mrs. Wagner. I am Freddy, your driver... here to serve you," he concluded with a slight tip of his broad-brimmed hat.

"Good afternoon, Freddy," Gary replied. "We look forward to seeing what sights may be in store."

"You and Mrs. Wagner will be pleased, sir. There is much

to see. I have just filled the keg on the coach with cool, fresh water, and we can begin whenever you are ready."

"There are no other passengers?"

"No, sir. Not going out. The coach will be full coming back though."

The coach was a nine-passenger affair including the driver. Customers sat on three forward-facing seats that snuggly accommodated three riders each. Canvas stretched across a wooden frame that protected travelers from the sun. Additional canvas curtains rolled up and fastened to the sides of the top to be lowered for moderate protection in the event of inclement weather. Freddy directed them to the second-row seat, where Gary helped Katherine up and followed along behind her. Freddy climbed aboard in front, loosened the reins and with a click of his tongue the team of agile horses quickly brought the conveyance to a trot. When they left the hotel Gary thought to himself, the beautiful four-horse team must be a show for urban guests. Surely two horses could handle the light-weight coach with ease.

A short distance from the train station, Freddy turned in his seat. "This next stretch is a little rough," he told them in a slightly elevated voice. As he returned his attention to the team, they slowed slightly and began the descent into Bright Angel Wash. Freddy pulled back on the reins with a feather-light touch and began applying the brakes on the coach. Gary was amazed at the young man's finesse with the team. He looked less than twenty, but must have been driving wagons since he was six, by Gary's estimation of his experience. The wagon trail crossed the bottom of the wash one hundred feet below the rim. On the far side, it was an additional fifty feet higher. The need for the four-horse team soon became apparent, but they scampered up the slope hardly breaking a sweat.

All the time, Freddy guided the coach around a myriad of obstacles, providing his passengers the smoothest possible ride.

At the top, the trail turned north along the circuitous edge of the canyon. Freddy slowed the team to a fast walk and returned his attention to his guests. "Everyone still with us?" he asked with a broad grin. "It's mostly pretty good the rest of the way. There's a good place to see Garden Creek and the canyon a little ways up here," he told them. "I'll stop there and let them blow," he nodded toward the team, "and you folks can get out and walk around a bit."

True to his word, Freddy brought the team to a halt a few minutes later on the trail. Katherine and Gary scrambled from their seat and crossed the few yards to the edge of the canyon.

Looking through his field glasses, Gary spotted eight riders followed by four pack animals working their way up a series of switchbacks on a trail across the side canyon below them. "There's a dozen horses and riders down there on a trail!" he exclaimed.

"Mules actually," Freddy remarked. "They're coming back from Phantom Ranch across the river."

"There's a ranch down there?" Katherine asked.

"More like a camp. Cabins and a cook-house. A few chickens and rabbits. A milk cow, no cattle. A few peach and plum trees...and willows and cottonwoods," he narrated to his guests. "That's Garden Creek below us." He pointed to the bottom of the side canyon. "Those mules are about two thousand feet below us where they are now. They will get to El Tovar about the same time we get back there."

"We saw smoke down there earlier," Katherine commented. "It didn't look like it was very near the river."

"That was probably them," he pointed to a copse of trees

along the creek in the distance to the northeast. "They eat lunch at the Indian Garden,"

Gary pulled his attention away from his field glasses momentarily. "So, who are those people?"

"Two are guides. The others are guests…like you."

Katherine saw Gary's face light up when he heard this. "How long does it take?" she asked.

"It's about half a day to the Indian Garden, then another couple of hours to the bridge. From there it's about a half mile." He looked at Katherine quizzically. "How fast do you walk?"

"We don't ride across the bridge?"

"It's a suspension bridge," Freddy answered. "Mules don't cross it."

"This sounds so exciting!" Katherine burst out to Gary's surprise.

"You know that I'm game." He beamed in anticipation. "The views from here are magnificent, but I would love to get a closer look."

"Palmer can make arrangements when we get back to El Tovar," Freddy offered as they returned to the coach.

They continued west along the rim, and Freddy stopped the coach at Hopi Point. From there he brought to their attention Powell Point just east of them. "They built a memorial to John Wesley Powell out there on the point about ten years ago," he told Katherine and Gary. "When they made the canyon a national park, that's where they held the dedication ceremony."

"And where were you?" Katherine asked.

"I was right there, Mrs. Wagner, driving my coach," he beamed with pride. "They actually made it a national park the year before. I was in France, then. But when they had the ceremony, I had just come to work here. It was really something to see." Freddy drifted into a momentary reverie recalling the occasion. "This is called Hopi Wall," he said as he brought the rim ahead to their attention. "Over fifteen hundred feet almost straight down, before it starts to taper off very much down there." He pointed to a still severe slope below.

Even though the views were amazing, Gary had difficulty keeping his mind on the scenery. His thoughts constantly drifted ahead in anticipation of a trip to the bottom of the canyon.

Freddy stopped again at Mohave Point. "The Great Mohave Wall," he told them, pointing along the rim ahead of them. "It's not quite as high as Hopi Wall, but it runs two miles south to The Abyss where the rim sweeps west again."

"The Abyss?" Gary asked as he visualized technical climbs at several of the many fissures in the distance.

"It's the head of this canyon." Freddy indicated the side canyon below them. "Kind of a hole, where Monument Creek starts. From the top, you can look straight down it almost all the way to the river. You'll see."

Gary gazed through his field glasses at the hodgepodge of outcroppings and terraced rows of vegetation along the far wall. "What's that?" he suddenly exclaimed in excitement.

"I don't know," Freddy answered, trying to spot what caught Gary's eye in the distance. "I can't see what you're looking at."

"It looks like a bird, but it can't be. It's just hanging there. It must be over a mile away."

"Ahhh," Freddy responded, smiling while bobbing his head in understanding even though it still had not caught his keen eye. "A condor. They're very large."

"Like an eagle?"

"Bigger. Eight, maybe ten feet," he said, holding his arms out indicating wingspan, but Gary kept his watch on the huge bird, nearly stationary in flight, riding an updraft near the far side of the offshoot canyon. "Like a giant buzzard," Freddy added. Suddenly, the bird's buoyancy changed. Without any movement of its wing, a gust swept it nearly straight up above the far wall, silhouetted momentarily against the blue sky, it gradually descended back to its approximate previous altitude.

"Yes! I see it!" Freddy called out.

"Oh! Me too!" Katherine joined in unexpectedly. She had been staring relentlessly, shading her eyes with her hand, in search of the quarry for several minutes.

"That's definitely a condor," Freddy confirmed.

"Holy smoke!" Katherine blurted out. The urgency in her voice drew Gary's attention away from his field glasses. "Look!" she continued, pointing to their left. A second condor had rounded a bend in the rim on their side a quarter mile away. The massive bird glided effortlessly slightly below the edge and three hundred yards out from the wall.

"It's enormous," Gary marveled, watching it float motionlessly as it gradually grew nearer. "I sure don't need these at this distance," he added, indicating the lowered field glasses in his hand. "I never imagined anything like this existed. Are they hunting?"

"Scavengers. Looking for dead animals. A deer in the bottom or maybe a sheep along the cliffs."

Gary's daydreaming of descending the canyon completely escaped his thoughts upon sighting the condors. The wrens that flitted about the brush nearby looked like horse flies in comparison to these Goliaths of the sky. Surely the acute eyesight of the powerful aviator had not missed their presence as it casually passed. If alarmed, Gary could not detect it.

"We should be going," Freddy suggested soon after the condor disappeared around the point. "The guests should be arriving at the rest from the Hermit Camp pretty soon."

"I have seen many eagles up close while climbing," Gary commented as they returned to the coach. "These birds are close to double in size. Thank you, Freddy, for bringing us here."

"It is not only my job, Mr. Wagner, it is my pleasure." He spread his arms and faced the canyon. "I love sharing all of this with our visitors."

Beyond the moving landscape of the canyon to their right, the coach ride to Hermit's Rest was uneventful. Freddy kept his team at a quick trot and ably navigated them around obstacles along the marginally smooth trail. After brief introductions, Gary and Katherine moved forward to share the front seat with the driver while the new passengers sat three abreast on the other two seats. Two of those seated on the middle seat were a couple from Saint-Étienne, France. They spoke English quite well, and Gary turned in his seat to engage them in conversation. He spoke a little French from his association with French mountaineers over the years, and the couple chuckled at his harsh American accent when attempting their language. The awkwardness of their seating made the conversation short, but the four agreed to dine together when they returned to El Tovar.

At the hotel, Gary immediately approached Palmer with questions about the pack trips to Phantom Ranch. There was no problem booking the trip for the next morning. Only one other couple was planning to make the trek. Palmer told him that the hotel was lightly booked, and they could leave their belongings in their room for the night they would be in the canyon without any charge. For the trip they would only be allowed one small valise for the two of them. Palmer gave Gary a suggested packing list of items they should bring. Cargo space on the pack mules was at a premium. They would have breakfast in the dining room at five o'clock in the morning and depart at six. Gary booked the excursion, then headed to their room to share the news with Katherine and freshen up for supper.

Gary and Katherine were joined in the dining room by Jean and Rosalie Garnier, the couple from France they had met on the coach earlier. The four shared in pleasant conversation. Jean was impressed with Gary's planned ascent of the Eiger. Though not a mountaineer himself, the famous peak was less than five hundred kilometers by road from their home in France. Its reputation and news of many of the expeditions far surpassed that.

As they finished their dessert, the Garniers asked to be excused as they had very early plans in the morning.

"We, too, have an early adventure and should retire," Gary responded. "We're heading into the canyon by mule to the Phantom Ranch across the river."

"So are we!" Jean exclaimed.

"So, you're the other couple we're sharing the trip with?" Katherine glanced back and forth between Jean and Rosalie. "That is fantastic!"

3

MONDAY, JUNE 2, 1930

"There's a crate at the depot for you, Sheriff," Hazel called to Con as she hung up the telephone.

Conor Armenta gulped down the second half of his first cup of coffee for the morning, donned his cowboy hat, and walked out the door. He drove his County Sheriff's pickup truck the four blocks to the train station, where the ticket agent directed him to the expressman.

"Right over here, Sheriff," the expressman commented as he towed a steel-wheeled cart across the wooden timbers that decked the platform. "She's full of ice," he added as he noticed Conor's skeptical gaze at the fluid oozing from the wooden box as they approached it. "Oh!" he exclaimed. "Almost forgot. This goes with it." The expressman stopped to extricate a wrinkled envelope from his pocket and handed it to Con.

The sheriff noted the return address imprinted on the envelope:

Beaver County Sheriff's Department
Beaver, Utah

Scrawled across the center of the envelope in handwriting barely more legible than his own:

Sheriff Conor Armenta
Las Vegas

The envelope had something thick inside it. More than a simple note. It was sealed, and Con began to open it when he realized the expressman stood waiting for him beside the box. It was about eighteen inches square and three feet long. The rough crate had no handles and contained over a hundred pounds of melting ice. Both men managed to find finger holds on the rough exterior and hefted the box onto the cart. The expressman then turned the cart and dragged it toward Conor's truck backed up to the platform nearby. After they transferred the box into the pickup, the expressman turned away.

"No paperwork?" Con asked.

"No, sir," the expressman turned back to the sheriff. "Sheriff Neilson personally helped me load it at Milford. Handed me the envelope. Then he told me to give it to you myself...only you, Sheriff Armenta. I know who you are, sir, and the railroad's paying the freight. That's good enough for me."

"And me too, sir."

"Whatever is in that crate must be pretty special."

"Yes, it is. Thank you."

Conor climbed behind the wheel of his pickup truck and

drove to the morgue. The strong smell of disinfectants over-powered the fresh morning air as he entered the cool hallway. Bold lettering on the window of the door to the right read CLARK COUNTY CORONER'S OFFICE followed below in smaller letters with Dr. Harold Martin, MD. Hal sat behind the desk poring over pages of a journal of some kind. He looked up as Conor entered.

"Morning, Sheriff. I was just refreshing my memory on the characteristics of blood coagulation." He assessed Con's facial expression. "It's only a guess because we weren't present to evaluate his condition when Mr. Doe lost his hand, but based on the blood loss we discussed yesterday, it seems he had already been dead for a few hours when the train hit him." He waited for Conor to question his theory, but he didn't. "Based on that and decomposition of the body when we brought it in, I estimate the time of death between eight and eleven o'clock Saturday evening."

"I don't think the train hit him," Conor replied.

"Well, sure it did! We picked up the pieces for a half mile."

"Closer to a quarter mile," Con corrected.

"It felt more like a half mile when I walked it," Hal countered. He continued before Conor could reply, "So what do you mean, the train never hit him?"

"I think it dragged him."

"All the way from town? There'd be nothing left of him long before they reached Dry Lake."

"I've got something outside we need to look at."

"What is it?"

"Another piece to the puzzle," Conor answered. "Literally," he added, leading Hal outside to his pickup.

"So, what's in the box?" Hal asked, peering into the truck bed.

"I'm pretty sure that it's John Doe's right arm."

"Where did you find that?" Hal asked skeptically.

"It was tied to the brake linkage on a boxcar with a piece of twine. The same train we thought hit our John Doe. Someone discovered the arm when the train arrived in Milford, Utah, on Sunday morning. They called the sheriff in Beaver who sent it down to us."

The crate was noticeably lighter as Con and Hal toted it into the morgue. A steady stream of ice-water now flowed from its seams, creating dubious footing on the asbestos floor tiles in the hall. They sat the box on the concrete floor of the examination room. Hal rummaged through the utility closet in search of a hammer and crowbar while Conor grabbed a mop and began herding the river of water they left, running down the hall toward the drain in the center of the examination room.

They soon had the top pried off of the crate. A bundle of oilcloth nestled among several chunks of melting ice were the only contents. Hal placed the bundle on a steel table and began carefully unwrapping the object of interest. As they suspected at first glance, the arm appeared to belong to the other body parts concealed beneath an assortment of sheets placed at various points around the refrigerated room. The oilcloth had, for the most part, served its purpose of keeping the appendage dry during transport while submerged in a boxful of melting ice.

The right hand protruded from the sleeve of a denim jacket. The cuff of the jacket remained buttoned and pulled tightly up around the forearm. A length of twine ending in a slipknot created a noose around the wrist. Stretched nearly to breaking, the cord had embedded deeply into the flesh. The other end appeared to have been cut with a sharp knife by whomever separated it from the railcar. Conor studied the evidence before him. Most of the right front portion of the jacket remained attached to the sleeve, including the unbuttoned flap and pocket. The remainder of the jacket was missing and Con anticipated they had retrieved most of it from the scene yesterday.

"Well, we know now that John Doe was dead before the train left Las Vegas. The question is, who tied the body beneath the railcar and when. It couldn't have been a simple task," Conor surmised.

"This guy was kind of small, but stocky," Hal contemplated. "He must have weighed in at one-thirty or so at the very least."

"Could one man hold up that much weight and tie the victim to the belly of a boxcar while working on his hands and knees? There must have been an accomplice." Conor considered the possibilities. "Have you found anything else of interest, Hal?"

"Well, I did a couple of decomposition tests before I left yesterday. Otherwise, I just got started this morning. I do know Mr. Doe was very scared before he died. Probably knew what was coming, or at least suspected it."

"What makes you say that?"

"He defecated himself."

"Couldn't have occurred after he died?"

"Not likely."

"Cause of death?"

"No idea right now. Might be difficult to figure out." As the old doctor looked around the room, Conor noticed a hint of that familiar wry smile appear. "Lots of pieces."

"Let me know," Con concluded and started to leave. "Where's that silver buckle?"

Hal led the way. "I took it off his belt yesterday and locked it in my desk. That's when I found the deposit in his drawers." Hal turned and winked.

Conor could not contain himself and chuckled. How could this old man find humor under such morbid circumstances? "Do you make a joke out of everything you stumble across?" he asked rhetorically. "If you ever find me in that condition, I sure hope you will curb your wit."

"Oh, I don't think that would ever happen. A couple of months ago I recall sewing you back together after you faced down a man with a Thompson machine gun blazing away at you. If that didn't scare the crap out of you, I don't figure there is much that would." Hal paused and scratched at his chin considering Sheriff Conor Armenta whom he'd known since he was a boy herding sheep with his father in the Red Rock Canyon country two dozen years ago, "unless it's that pretty blonde girl that likes you." Before Con had the wherewithal to respond, Hal continued. His facial expression had suddenly become somber. "I kind of see it like this. You, Judge Tucker, this boy's family, whoever it might be...you folks depend on me to do my best to find answers to a lot of tough questions. It can be really depressing or even sickening if I let it. On the other hand, it can be downright interesting and challenging... if I swallow that lump in my throat and forge ahead. Have you ever thought about the word, funny? It can mean a lot of different things. It can mean humorous or comical in one instance, or weird, strange or even sinister in another. Funny how that works, isn't it?" he concluded dryly.

Hal turned and resumed the course toward his desk as he fumbled for the keys in his pocket. Conor followed in silence. Hal's words of wisdom had struck home and left him somber.

"Take your job seriously, Con"—the old doctor unlocked

the drawer—"but don't be afraid to laugh and smile at life's little quirks and oddities in the process." He handed the heavy envelope containing the buckle to him. "I'll call you when I find something of interest."

* * *

Con returned to the sheriff's office at half past ten.

"You look rather solemn," Hazel greeted as cheerfully as possible when he arrived.

"It's been a rather sobering morning...other than Hal's insatiable sense of humor of course."

"I can't imagine why you'd be gloomy," Hazel mused satirically. "Examining a room full of dismembered body parts. What could be unnerving about that? Sounds downright entertaining to me."

"To you and Hal maybe."

"If it'll cheer you up any, June called a little while ago. I told her I would have you call her when you got back."

As Hazel had suggested, the image in his mind of June Sommers's smiling face instantly lifted Conor's spirits on the otherwise dismal morning. "Thank you, yes, that does seem to help a little." He entered his office and closed the door behind him.

"Robert Westcott, Attorney at Law," the pleasant female voice answered on the second ring.

"Hello. May I speak to Mrs. Sommers, please."

"Why certainly. This sounds rather official," June added teasingly. "May I tell her who is calling.

"Yes, this is official. Tell her Sheriff Armenta is returning her call."

"Let me get her...well, hello, Sheriff. Thank you for getting back to me. I have an errand to run this afternoon and was wondering if you would care to join me for an early lunch before I go?"

"So, you're inviting me out to lunch?"

"I realize that I am being a little bit forward, but I didn't have time to plot a strategy where you would invite me and think that it was your idea to begin with."

"Oh, I see." Conor's mind raced trying to figure a way to maneuver control of the conversation to no avail. "What did you have in mind?"

"Perhaps the Mesquite Café in, say, a half hour."

Con quickly assessed the proposal. His parents owned and operated the modest Mesquite Café. His younger sister waited tables there and almost certainly would attempt to embarrass him in front of June...whom she knew...probably better than he did. "Sure!" he agreed, wishing for a less public alternative. "That'll be great! So, eleven o'clock then?"

"I'll see you at eleven!" June answered almost gleefully as she hung up the telephone.

* * *

Conor opened Hal's envelope and sat the belt buckle in front of him on the desk. It was beautiful in spite of the deep scratch across the center that intersected the mount that had housed a now-missing stone. He wiped most of the dust off with his handkerchief revealing a lustrous shine on the heavy silver. Con had only seen a couple of buckles made like this one before and neither were as large or ornate as this. Indian made he thought...expensive...and probably Navajo. Perhaps a family heirloom of John Doe? How else could an Indian afford such an expensive buckle that would sell to a wealthy tourist for more money than most natives made in a year?

His thoughts turned to having lunch with June Sommers. Mrs. Sommers was a single mother of an eleven-year-old daughter who happened to be best friends with Con's niece. She worked as the secretary for a prominent Las Vegas attorney. Conor had met June at her job when working on a case a few months ago. They were instantly attracted to each other and had begun building a friendship. Well...maybe a little more than a friendship.

Conor snapped himself back from his daydream and pulled the envelope the expressman had given to him from his hip pocket. He glanced again at his name scratched across it. "Andy," he said aloud, shaking his head. Inside the envelope was a small booklet, maybe three inches by four inches, wrapped inside a note written in the same scratchy hand:

Found this in John Doe's pocket. Didn't want to chance it getting wet from the ice. Isn't this the woman who went missing down your way a few months ago?

Good Luck on This One!
Andy

Conor hurriedly opened the booklet. A bankbook from Moapa Valley Bank in Overton. The owner's name and signature accompanied the account number on the front leaf... Katherine Wagner. Con flipped the page. Three years ago, Katherine Wagner opened the account with $76,460. Every month afterward, she had deposited between one thousand

and three thousand dollars, often in quite random amounts. The deposits ended nine months ago. Two months later withdrawals of fifty dollars per month began. There had been no transactions for the last couple of months.

Conor looked up at the clock on the wall. Twenty past eleven. He cursed aloud. Loud enough for Hazel to hear him through the closed door. When he burst through the door, Hazel was already staring at him. "Going to lunch!" he muttered as he ran out the door then quickly returned to grab his hat and disappeared again.

Hazel heard the door of his pickup truck slam and the roar of the engine as he sped off down the street.

* * *

At the screen door of the Café, Con nearly knocked an exiting customer off his feet as they met. With a quick glance, he found June sipping iced tea at a small table near the corner.

"I'm really sorry I'm late," he said as he swiftly removed his hat and sat down across the table from her.

"I thought it was the girl who was supposed to keep the guy anxiously waiting to meet for their date," she commented coyly.

This made Con blush, but he quickly recovered. "Since you reversed the roles by asking me out for lunch, I thought I must be obliged to arrive late."

June blushed in response just as Conor's sister Olivia sat a Coca-Cola on the table in front of him. "Better late than never, big brother. You must think she really likes you to leave her sitting here for a half hour while you're out goofing off."

"It wasn't like that at all," Con stumbled for words. "I just received some new evidence that troubled me. No, interested me. Or maybe bothered me. Intrigued me."

"Isn't he eloquent?" Olivia asked June with a smirk.

"You were right the first time, Olivia. I really like him."

Olivia twirled her index finger around her ear, indicating from beyond Conor's view that June must be crazy. June giggled and took a sip of her tea while shaking her head no.

"What are you going to have, June?" Olivia asked.

"A ham and cheese sandwich, please."

"And you, Mister Johnny Come Lately?"

"Hamburger sandwich, please."

"Coming right up, folks!" Olivia answered and disappeared from the table, leaving the couple to their privacy...to Conor's surprise.

He admired June in silence momentarily. She wore khaki slacks with shoes that laced up to her ankles and a flowered cotton blouse. "You look wonderful today. I don't recall ever seeing you in slacks before."

"I don't wear them very often. I'll have to remember that you like them," she added. "You look pretty snazzy yourself, but I always was a sucker for a man in uniform." June smiled then slipped momentarily into a fond memory of her late husband before regaining her poise, seeing Conor grinning at her response. He had not noticed her brief reverie.

"I am very sorry that I was late."

"You don't have to be. I'm the one who interrupted your morning. What new evidence has you so much at odds?"

"This is absolutely not for public knowledge," Conor told her as he reached into his shirt pocket and handed June the bankbook.

"Oh, my gosh," she barely whispered as she read the name with widened eyes. "Oh, my gosh!" she nearly shrieked the second time, causing other customers to turn in their seats when she read the first deposit. "What about the date?" she asked, regaining her whisper, knowing she had drawn attention to herself.

"Same month she signed over the house," Con told her in a very lowered voice.

"So, Dutch paid her?"

"I don't think so. My guess is, she was hiding the money from him."

"Ooh, oh my."

"Exactly."

"What are you going to do?"

"I'm going out to Overton to talk to the bank."

"That's where I'm going! I have to take some papers for a client to sign. He has a ranch near Logan. I'm a notary."

"What are you driving?"

"Mr. Westcott's Buick."

"The roadster?"

"No, that's Mrs. Westcott's. He has a sedan."

"If we take my car, I can give you a lift. I'll need to also make a stop at the Moapa Trading Post, though. We might be a little late getting back."

"I'll have to ask Joyce to watch April after school until we get back," June replied just as Olivia was bringing their lunch.

"I can watch April when the girls get out of school," Olivia interrupted. "What's going on?"

"It turns out we both have business up in the Moapa Valley," June told her. "If we drove one car, we could kill two birds with one stone, so to speak. But we'll be getting back later than I originally expected."

"No problem, pick her up at my house when you get back."

"We should be back before supper," Conor interjected.

"Says the guy who was late for lunch," Olivia replied. "If you're not back before bedtime, I'll put her to bed with Donna for the night, okay?"

"Okay." Con and June answered nearly in unison.

June and Conor ate their lunch quickly and mostly quietly.

"So, where did you get the bankbook?" June asked.

"A friend sent it to me."

"From where?"

"Milford, Utah."

"You have a snitch in Milford? That's over two hundred miles away."

"Almost three hundred. But he's not a snitch, per se. And he lives in Beaver."

"Well, that explains it." June stared at him, not believing he would leave her hanging in anticipation this way.

Con felt her eyes boring through him. "He's the sheriff of Beaver County."

"So, how did he get it?" she asked in near despair.

"I'd rather not say."

"Rather not say?" she repeated in desperation.

"Not right now."

"What?" she questioned in exasperation as she finished her lunch and wiped her face with a napkin.

"Not on a full stomach."

June was about to unload on Conor for baiting her into a trap of clues, when she recalled Hazel's brief description of how gruesome the case was that Con, Jesse, and Hal were working on.

"Oh," she replied calmly. Then June took a deep swallow followed by a long sip of iced tea.

Conor knew that taste. He was sure June appreciated the drink of tea afterward. "Are you okay?"

"I think so…I will be in a minute."

Olivia came by and filled June's glass from a pitcher she carried. "Are you alright?" she asked, looking at June's pallid face.

"She'll be okay…leave the pitcher."

Color gradually returned to June's face. She took occasional sips of her iced tea in silence watching Con finish eating his lunch. "I feel better now," she finally said. "How can you eat, with all of that…you know…going on in your mind?"

"I've learned to sort of block things out of my head when I need to…it works." He grinned, then added, "Most of the time."

When they stood and left the table, Con went to pay their bill at the counter.

"Is she going to be alright?" Olivia asked her brother as she handed him his change.

"Oh yeah. She just got a little nauseous."

"She's not pregnant, is she?"

Conor turned beet red. "I'm pretty sure she's not. But we're not nearly well enough acquainted to discuss such personal matters."

"Well, you never know. You guys have been pretty friendly lately."

"Not that friendly," he responded and turned away without further comment.

"What was that about?" June asked, as Conor held the screen door for her.

"Just my little sister trying to embarrass me."

"It must have worked," June surmised. "I haven't seen

your face that red since we bought cantaloupes from Mrs. Chavez when we first met."

"She knows how to ask the wrong questions," Con commented as he followed June to Bob Westcott's sedan.

"I will return Mr. Westcott's car to the office. You will pick me up there?"

"In about twenty minutes. I need to stop at the office, then swing by my house to trade vehicles."

"Not later?" she asked with a cynical grin.

"I won't be late."

Conor retrieved the belt buckle from his office and drove home. Minutes later he entered the door of the law office of Robert Westcott. June had her purse over her shoulder and a packet of papers under her arm as she and Westcott stood in the lobby in conversation.

"Good afternoon, Sheriff," Westcott pleasantly greeted him as he turned and offered his hand while June put the papers into a soft leather case.

"Mr. Westcott," Conor answered, accepting it.

"This will work out well for everyone it seems," Westcott commented. "We will see you tomorrow, June."

"Yes, sir," she replied as they walked out the door.

* * *

Conor turned his nearly new Chevrolet coupe onto Main Street and headed north. He accelerated as the street became Arrowhead Trail at the edge of town. Conor enjoyed listening to the quiet, smooth, purr of the six-cylinder engine as they rolled up the graveled highway. The temperature remained moderate in the sunny, early afternoon. June had donned a felt hat that resembled a man's fedora and kept the breeze from the open car windows from tangling her shoulder-length blond hair.

"What are you looking at?" June asked, noticing him staring at her.

"The beautiful woman sitting beside me and thinking how lucky I am to share her company."

"Well," she said, blushing and momentarily at a loss for words. "I think you should keep your eyes on the road, cowboy."

The two sat in silence as they motored up the road. When June looked over, Conor wore a broad grin as he looked straight ahead. She finally interrupted the quiet. "So, what did Olivia ask that made you blush so?"

"Oh, that." His face began to flush again at the reminder. He sat there without continuing for several minutes trying to find a way around telling her the truth.

"Well?" June prodded.

"It's rather embarrassing."

"I'm beginning to gather that."

"She asked if you were going to be okay. I told her that you had just become nauseated and would be fine."

"Well, that's not very disconcerting."

"She asked if you were pregnant."

"Oh!" June startled, suddenly realizing Conor's hesitation. Now, she paused in contemplation wondering how, or if, she even wanted to proceed.

Conor finally began, "I couldn't tell her it was none of her business." He paused again, searching for the right words. "That might make her think there's something going on that wasn't...isn't."

"Implications."

"Yes! That's the word."

"So, what did you tell her?"

"I told her I was sure you weren't, but we didn't know each other well enough to discuss such personal matters."

"Thank you."

"For what? Having a busy body sister?"

"No, for protecting my reputation...for protecting me." She sat thinking again for several minutes. "She really does mean well, you know."

"Olivia?"

"Yes, and she adores you."

"You are talking about my sister?"

"Yes, we have talked a few times."

"About me?"

"More about children...and life in general."

"And me."

"Some." Once again, June paused, contemplating the best way to proceed. "She says that you had a tough time growing up. You worked really hard to help support the family after your father got hurt. She says you always put her and your brother ahead of yourself. Always made sure they had the things they needed while you went without." She paused a moment while Con digested what she had said. "Olivia never grasped what you had gone through for her until she was an adult and had to fend for her own family. By then...by then you two had already established this pattern of picking on each other."

Conor felt betrayed. "So you two sit around talking about me?"

"No more than you talking about me to your guy friends," she retorted.

"I have no friends," Con answered, and the answer shocked him. It was true. All of it was true. Everything June had said was true. And worst of all what he said was true. "I have no friends," he repeated.

"Oh, my God." The words fell from her mouth into the deafening silence ringing in her ears. She could not hear the wind blowing past her from the open car window. She could not hear the tires on the gravel road or the engine humming away as they traveled. The world had stopped around her. "I had no idea," finally escaped her lips. "I never realized." Her thoughts began coming to order. "I, I can't believe it didn't occur to me. I thought I was an observant person. I am so, so sorry. Oh, Conor. I didn't mean to hurt you. Please, please forgive me..." The words trailed off through her tears. The car had gradually slowed to a crawl, and Con pulled to the side of the deserted road and stopped.

"I never saw it myself until just now," he finally said. "I guess I've been so tied up with life since I was fourteen, I never had time for friends. I had Papa and Luis to teach me how to do things then. Now, Hal and Judge Tucker help me learn how to be a better sheriff."

"You grew up so fast in some ways, you never had a chance to grow up in others. No time to make those juvenile friendships that grow into a lifetime. But because of that you have become the responsible, caring, and sincere man who I love." She stopped short. It jolted her. What had she just said? She wiped a reluctant tear from her cheek. She didn't really say that, did she? Did she just tell Conor Armenta that she loved him? What was she thinking? What had she done? One little slip of the tongue, and she ruined everything. The best thing that had happened in her life since losing her husband. The most trustworthy man she had met in a decade, maybe her whole life. Now, he too would be gone.

Conor sat stunned. His head spun like a hurricane of

emotions. He shut the ignition off on the car and opened the door. Was it his imagination, or had it suddenly gotten much hotter outside? He got out of the car and walked back along the roadside for several yards. What did she say? He repeated their conversation since they left town to himself and rolled it over in his mind. They had become short with each other. Almost heated. Then he suddenly realized he had no true friends. Well, not beyond the men he considered his mentors. Then June started crying and apologized, and he told her he had never seen it that way. So, she explained how his adolescence had made him the way he was and…and…and then, did she say that she loved him? Is that what he really heard? The most beautiful, wonderful woman he had ever met in his life. Did she really say that? Maybe he imagined it. Maybe it's the heat. It sure feels hot out here.

He turned around and walked back to the passenger side of the car. June's head was bent down, and she was sobbing again. Conor opened her door. "Are you okay?"

"I will be. I am so sorry."

"Why?"

"For what I said."

Con took her hand and half led, half lifted her from the car. She stood before him with her head still bowed. "About having no friends?" he asked.

Her head remained down. She responded with a nearly inaudible whimper.

Conor gently lifted her chin. "Did you say that you love me?"

She lifted her eyes to meet his. "Yes." She tried to read the look in his eyes. With uncertainty, she added, "I didn't mean to. It just slipped out." She tried to smile.

"Did you mean it?"

She lowered her eyes then lifted them again to meet his. "Yes."

He leaned forward and lightly kissed her lips. "I don't know. I've never felt like this around any woman I've ever met before. I think…I think maybe…I might love you."

June took a deep breath, still looking into Conor's eyes. Then she pulled herself to him and kissed him more passionately than she had ever kissed anyone in her life. When they broke their embrace, a single word escaped her lips, "Yes."

4

At breakfast, Jean Garnier took in Gary and Katherine Wagner's attire. They certainly were clothed to ride. He cautiously made a suggestion. "I am not sure how much equestrian experience you two may have. Might I suggest eating a light meal? We found the rolling gait of the mules on the descent to be very comfortable, but slightly nauseating on a full stomach."

"We have both done some horseback riding in the past, but mules are a new adventure," Gary contemplated. "Thank you for the advice. No need to stuff ourselves and feel queasy."

The foursome enjoyed their breakfast. Gary had to force himself not to over-indulge with the pastries. They were absolutely scrumptious with the strong fresh coffee accompanying them. Bacon, codfish cakes, grapefruit, eggs, and muffins rounded out the meal. So much for a light breakfast, he thought, but they managed to back off just a little before hitting their limits.

At a quarter to six, Palmer wished them all a pleasant journey from behind the front desk as they crossed the lobby to the main entrance. The refreshing morning air welcomed them on the veranda as the first hint of sunlight glinted through the trees.

They were met on the front steps by a man wearing a leather vest and chaps. A broad grin grew on the grizzled face that peered from beneath the well-worn Stetson hat as he held out a gnarled hand. "Name's Emmett," he greeted. "I'm th' guide fer yer' ride down Bright Angel an' Garden Creek. Mules know ther' way. Ain't never slipped a foot yet," he added. "I'm rilly jus' 'long fer th' ride."

Emmett shook each of their hands as they shared names and pleasantries. "You ladies look dressed fer th' part," he said, noting their riding skirts. "Molly an' Bess, th' two black ones er' sweet an' gentle as baby lambs. Buster, th' roan there, he can be a bit fickle sometimes, but ther' ain't a mean bone in his body. Jake, th' buckskin, 's jus' a plain ol' mule. He'll take ye' wherever ye' need t' go an' never complain along the way." He paused a minute to scratch his whiskered face. "That bay over yonder is Mae. I'll be ridin' her. She don' care fer strangers." At that, Emmett took their bags. "Y'all take yer pick an' saddle up. I'll throw yer' luggage on one o' th' pack animals an' come back by to set yer stirrups."

Katherine and Rosalie chose Molly and Bess. Jean and Gary gave them each a foot up. Jean took Buster and Gary the leggy buckskin. As Emmett shortened Rosalie's stirrups and lengthened Gary's, he explained that they each had their own canteen full of fresh, cool water hanging from their saddle horns. Jean and Katherine's stirrups needed no adjustments.

"I'll take the pack string and leadja' t' the trailhead," Emmett said. "I'll pull aside there, ta' let ye' by me. Jake'll wanna lead, so let'm. He'll jus' mosey 'long down th' trail." Looking at Gary's field glasses and Jean's Autographic folding camera, he added, "anywheres 'long the way you folks wanna take a look-see, jus' stop. These mules won't step off th' trail. There's a couple of good rest stops 'long the way an' we'll take a break there...Jake'll letcha know."

With the cluck of Emmett's tongue, Mae led the pack string down the Rim Trail, and the other four fell in behind her without the slightest coaxing. Their passengers' big adventure was underway, but of little importance to them. Just another leisurely stroll down the old familiar trail.

An hour later, they arrived at their first rest stop. Jake led the way to the hitching rail and stopped. After a pause, he turned his eye to his passenger with a somewhat stern glare that Gary interpreted to mean, "this is where you get off now."

Gary dismounted as Jean and their wives pulled up at the rail. He tied Jake securely to the rail and went to help Katherine down just as Emmett joined them with the pack string. Emmett had dismounted, tied Mae to the rail and joined Gary before Katherine was standing on the ground. He eyed the knot Gary had tied Jake with.

"Let me show you a quick little trick here," he told Gary as he tied Molly to the rail with a quick-release knot. "I've heard all kinds of names for this knot, but it's th' best way I know ta' tie a horse...er mule in this case." He showed Gary, and now Jean who joined them, the simple steps of tying the knot.

"Th' way it works, if th' horse pulls back on it, it gets tighter. Th' same time, alls ya hafta' do when yer' ready to leave is pull here." He pulled on the loose end, causing the knot to disappear. "An' there ya' go. Free as a bird."

"I have seen this before." Jean grinned. "At home, they call that a manœud de mangeoirenger. I think that would be *manger-knot* in English."

"Yep," Emmett agreed. "That's what some folks call it here."

"I'm pretty good with knots," Gary stated. "You watch while I try it." He was halfway through the process when he paused to recount the steps.

"Right through there." Emmett pointed, as he watched his student's progress. "Yes-sir-ee. Ya' got it."

As his clients sipped on water from their canteens, stretched their legs, and took in the glorious panorama before them, Emmett commented, "Wer' less'n a quarter mile from El Tovar right here." He looked at the ladies as they gazed above estimating the location of the hotel. "How fer' ya' figger we come?"

"A mile, maybe?" Katherine guessed.

"Purdy near two, a'think." He winked at her. "An' a thousand feet down ta' boot."

Emmett quickly checked over everyone's mounts and asked, "Y'all doin' okay? No problems?"

They all looked around at each other. "I think we are all fine," Rosalie responded.

"Good!" he cheerfully replied. "Le's mosey on down a bit futher."

Jean and Gary again assisted their wives aboard their tall rides. They soon encountered their second set of switchbacks on the trail, and the descent became seriously steeper. They all had been riding quite casually. Now the trail required leaning back significantly in the saddle and supporting their weight on their feet in the stirrups in lieu of their backsides. All were thankful for Emmett's adjustments to their rigging before departure on the trek. Everyone enjoyed their rugged surroundings and the vistas they provided. Though the terrain required a slightly more strenuous ride, they had hardly noticed when more than another hour had passed as they reached the second rest stop.

Gary put his newly acquired knot-tying skills into practice on Jake and Molly, while Jean took care of Buster and Bess. Emmett admired his new apprentices' work as he hitched Mae to the rail. "Good work, boys. Yu'll do jes' fine. I'd ride with ya anywheres," he encouraged, grinning through tobacco-stained teeth as he pulled his canteen from the saddle horn. "Ya' ladies doin' alright?" he inquired after taking a quick pull of water. "Y'all need ta' drink plenty o' water down here. Not a lots alls ta' once, but a lotta li'l sips off'n. It can get hotter'n Hades down here soon as the sun hits th' bottom." He pulled back his hat and stared at the sky. "An' that ain't fer off. Breeze is purdy contrary ta' boot. Kin be plumb comf'terble one minnit an' still as a tomb th' next."

The group again stretched their legs and further absorbed their surroundings. Gary was overwhelmed by the multitude of rocks, cliffs, and spires. Everywhere he looked offered another climbing challenge. Some would offer only a mere jaunt. Others would test the skill of even the most experienced of mountaineers. As the sun began to hit the rocks, what had seemed nearly flat surfaces became a tangled web of shadowed fissures, cracks and crevices. To Gary, every turn in the trail offered another array of obstacles, daring the climber inside him to test his skills.

Emmett interrupted Gary's daydream. "Nex' stop'll be th' Injun Garden. Pay'cus'll have some dinner fixed fer' ya."

"Is Pecos a good cook?" Katherine asked curiously.

"He's a young feller, but th' bes' biscuit-shooter ya' ever saw," Emmett replied.

Katherine was unsure if that was good, but Emmett failed to notice her still questioning gaze. She was unsure whether any further description of Pecos's culinary skills would be helpful, when described in Emmett's unique cowboy vernacular. The group mounted their mules and continued down the trail.

After another series of switchbacks, they were just above a small stream to their left. It cascaded over the rocks in a never-ending series of miniature waterfalls. The trail straightened out and followed the canyon just above the creek. In a short time, they could occasionally spot the copse of trees ahead that marked the Indian Garden. A wisp of smoke appeared sporadically through the leaves.

At half past ten, they rode into the open space of a small meadow. Two mules raised their heads, chewing the native grass protruding from their mouths, and brayed as they drew closer. The rope corral that enclosed them in half of the area became apparent. Pecos's outdoor kitchen nestled among the trees on the far side from the mules. A dog, that seemed to Katherine to be one of the collie breeds, trotted toward them wagging its tail.

"Mornin' folks!" Pecos hollered as he raised up from a pot hanging over the fire and waved with the large spoon in his hand. The tall, lanky young man was dressed in full cowboy regalia right down to his spurs with a flour sack tied around his waist as an apron. He laid his spoon down on a nearby board that stretched waist-high between two trees and supported an array of cooking supplies. Then Pecos approached in long strides to receive them. "Right on time, Emm!" he shouted out to their guide leading the pack mules in behind them.

"Welcome to the Indian Garden," he greeted. "Step down, ladies. We can hitch your mounts to that rail over yonder," he said, indicating a pole lashed to two other trees a short distance away. "Make yourselves ta' home," he told them as they dismounted. They wandered toward the cookfire as Pecos led their mules away, followed by Gary and Jean.

Emmett loosened the girths on the pack animals and released them into the makeshift corral. He then loosened the cinch on Mae's saddle and led her inside the enclosure where he removed her bridle and bit and draped them over the saddle horn so she, too, could graze.

After exchanging names and handshakes Gary, Jean, and Pecos returned to the dining area. The men introduced their wives, and after pleasantries, Pecos handed each of them enameled tin cups, then explained the etiquette of his rustic kitchen. "There's fresh hot coffee I just took off the fire in that pot sitting on the boulder there and cool sweet spring water in that bucket righ'cht yonder." He pointed to the bucket on the end of his makeshift cooking bench. "Help yourselves to whichever ya want. I'll bring your dinner to ya here." Pecos indicated a second board between two other trees mounted at table height. A red checkered tablecloth covered the board and four enameled tin plates sat evenly placed along it. Matching checkered napkins lay alongside each plate with a crude, yet clean, fork and spoon atop each napkin. Four logs cut to the perfect length served as stools for the counter at Pecos's outdoor café.

As his guests took their seats, Pecos brought a small basket full of biscuits, fresh from one of an assortment of dutch ovens. Next came a slab of roasted beef followed by a ladleful of baked beans.

"I know it ain't much, but it's the best I can do out here," he apologized.

"The beans are positively delicious," Rosalie responded after tasting them. "How do you cook food like this in a pot?"

"If you do it right," Pecos began. "When you cover the cast-iron pot over the fire, it becomes a little oven. You just bake in it like any other oven, except the food is in the bottom instead of in a pan inside it. Simple."

"Simple for you," Katherine joined in. "Amazing for us city folks." She smiled. "How do you expect us to eat all of this delicious food?"

"Well, I hope that you enjoy it," he answered. "But leave room for the peach cobbler I've got over the fire. It'll be done in about a half hour."

As the guests enjoyed their meal, Emmett brought their mules to the rope corral and turned them in with the others.

* * *

Katherine and Rosalie dangled their feet in the cool water of Garden Creek while Jean watched Gary climbing a small precipice nearby. The sun had reached the bottom of the canyon. As Emmett predicted, the temperature was rising rapidly. A slight breeze and the surrounding shade kept it comfortable in the meantime.

"Come an' get it!" Pecos yelled as he banged his big spoon on a tin plate.

Katherine and Rosalie shook off excess water and quickly

slipped their stockings on their wet feet and donned their shoes. Gary began his way back down from the cliff. Emmett finished transferring the packs from one of his mules to one of Pecos's animals. The mule had wedged a stone between the shoe and the frog on one of his feet and bruised the cleft.

Four steaming tin bowls rested in their places on the checkered tablecloth with clean napkins and spoons beside them. Two others sat on Pecos's cooking bench. All six bowls were heaped with peach cobbler.

"Dig in," Pecos told them as the guests took their seats. "It's made from dried peaches. I hope ya don't mind, but fresh ones don't make the trip down here very well."

With that, he took one of the bowls from the bench himself and handed Emmett the other.

"Bon appétit." Rosalie toasted the others with a spoonful of steaming cobbler. She took the first bite and looked at Pecos. "You could become a chef in any number of fine restaurants, Monsieur Pecos. How did you learn to cook like this?"

"Mostly by accident." He blushed. "I was the youngest one in the bunkhouse, and none of the other fellas liked to cook. So, they made me do it."

They all laughed and devoured the sweet treat. Emmett had tightened cinches, reinstalled bridles and checked all of the feet on the mules. He thought the lame mule would be better by morning, but exercised precaution before proceeding with the others. At a quarter to twelve, Gary led off as before. The descent had become much more gradual, and they covered the three miles to the river in just over an hour. Taking a short break, they resumed their ride and arrived at the bridge at a quarter past two.

Four men from Phantom Ranch were waiting for them at

the suspension bridge. Each would cover the trail to the ranch four times each way to carry what the four mules had hauled from El Tovar. Emmett made sure that the guests' belongings were included on the first trip. He had sent each of the riders with the canteens from their saddles and instructed them to bring them back full for the return ride.

"I'll meet ya'll righ'cht here at eight thirty tomorry mornin'," he assured them. "Have yer-selfs a nice ev'nin'."

Both women apprehensively studied the bridge as Gary tried to reassure them. Jean also eyed the structure uncertainly. "These bridges are stronger than you could possibly imagine," he told them. "They will bounce with the rhythm of your footsteps. The key is keeping them from bouncing profusely. Walk at a leisurely pace and watch the person in front of you. Try to stay out-of-step with them."

He looked at everyone's faces. Katherine and Rosalie were the most nervous. Jean was anxious, but stalwart. "Leave about three or four paces between you and the person in front of you. Keep an eye on the walkway in front of you, but try not to look straight down." They all still looked uneasy. The packers all had their loads strapped to their backs and waited for the guests' departure.

"You lead off Katherine, and I will be right behind you, then Rosalie and Jean."

Katherine stepped out onto the walkway holding tightly on to the cables on either side. Cautiously moving forward, she anticipated the bridge to move. It didn't.

"You're doing fine, sweetheart," Gary comforted her. "Nice easy steps." When she was about ten feet ahead, Gary stepped onto the bridge. "I'm right behind you, and you didn't even notice. You're doing good."

As they gained distance, Katherine gained confidence and began walking more freely.

"Rosalie and Jean should be right behind us now, and the bridge isn't bouncing, so everyone is doing their part." Gary supported them.

"We're okay," Rosalie chimed in behind him.

Katherine now moved assuredly as they neared the far side. She stifled the urge to run the last ten yards and soon, smoothly touched her feet onto solid ground. When she turned around, Gary had just stepped off the bridge and Rosalie, with Jean, were close behind him. To their surprise, the packers were already past the midpoint of the bridge. Katherine took a swig of tepid water from her canteen and watched them approach.

"We'll go on ahead, folks," the first man said. "Take your time and enjoy the walk. Your luggage will be at the dining hall when you arrive."

When the last packer passed them, Gary said, "Go ahead on. I'll take up the rear."

Katherine now led with exuberance. Rosalie was right behind her. About two-thirds of the way to Phantom Ranch, they met the packers coming back. The men stopped and stood aside as the guests came by.

"Less than a quarter mile," the leader told them as they passed.

* * *

It was dark and amazingly cool when they entered the stone dining hall at three o'clock.

"Good evening, folks," a very pleasant woman of perhaps forty greeted them. "My name is Ada. My husband and I take care of things here at Phantom Ranch. You must be the Garniers and the Wagners," she added as she sat four glasses on a massive table in the center of the room. "Make yourselves comfortable."

Ada disappeared through a swinging door they suspected entered the kitchen as they took seats on long wooden benches on either side of the table. She quickly returned with a pitcher in each hand. "Tea or lemonade?" she asked them. "They're both nice and cold, but we haven't figured out how to get ice down here yet." She laughed a hearty laugh. "Take a few minutes to cool yourselves down." She filled everyone's glasses.

"How did you know our names?" Katherine asked.

"We've known the Garniers were arriving today for several days. Just got word on you two this morning," Ada told her. "We have a telephone, when it works." She chuckled before disappearing again through the back door.

The foursome marveled at the structure of the dining hall. Every bit of it was made of stone except the roof, windows and doors. It had a large fireplace that dominated an entire wall and the floor was made of flat stone slabs that were well fitted together, but not perfectly smooth.

"Your trappings are there at the hearth," Ada told them when she returned. "Supper is at seven o'clock and breakfast at six." She began laying out the system to them. "You'll be staying in cabin number one and number three over here on the creek side," she pointed out. "You can take your pick. There's no locks on the doors, just a latch string. You know how that works?" she asked, looking them over. Gary and Katherine nodded, but Rosalie and Jean looked bewildered. "I'll show you," she said as she led the way out the front door to cabin number one.

"See this string with the loop at the end coming out this hole in the door?" Ada asked.

"Yes," Jean answered as they both nodded.

"Pull on it," she said while pulling the string, causing an audible click. "After you hear that click, push the door open," which she did and the heavy wooden door came open. "If you push too soon, it won't open. And if you pull too hard on the string, it might break, and then you're in a fix."

They nodded understandingly as Rosalie replied with a simple, "Okay."

"Come in here," Ada told them as she led the way inside and closed the door. "The other end of the string is tied to the latch and lifts it open, see?" She showed them the operation of the latch. "When you don't want any unexpected visitors, you pull the string in through the hole in the door, then nobody outside can open the door. If you go to the privy in the night, be sure to put the string back through the door or you'll lock yourself out."

"Got it," Jean replied, and Rosalie agreed.

Gary and Katherine waited outside during Ada's demonstration. "Now," Ada began again. "The privy for these two cabins is right down here below them. Both cabins share it," she pointed out. "There is no bathing facility, besides the creek. What we have is right up here." She led the way a short distance up Bright Angel Creek from the cabins to a solid wooden fence with a gate. Beside the gate was a sign:

BATHING HOURS
LADIES, 4 P.M. TO 5 P.M.
GENTS, 5:30 P.M TO 6:30 P.M.

Ada led the way through the open gate to a small stone patio with a couple of benches and a cabinet with hooks to hang clothing on, a couple shelves, and a cupboard with towels, washcloths, and bars of soap. A large basket stood beside the cabinet. "You can throw your soiled towels and washcloths in there." She pointed, then walked to the edge of the patio where stone steps led to a pool in the creek below a small waterfall. "It's about four feet deep in the middle, and the water is colder than…well, it's really cold. But you get used to it after a bit. You know how the latch string works. You're the only two ladies and same with you two gents. You decide if you want to share your turn or bath separately. It's up to you. Employees have their own schedule."

With that Ada headed back toward the dining hall then stopped and looked back. "See you folks at seven, or a bit earlier if you want a cool drink before supper."

The group discussed hiking up the trail above Phantom Ranch to view the narrow canyon and rock formations at the confluence of Phantom Creek and Bright Angel Creek. As Emmett had warned them, there was no breeze whatsoever now. The air was hot and heavy in this portion of the canyon that some referred to as *The Box*. The pleasant sounds and cool water of Bright Angel Creek flowing behind their cabins seemed more inviting, and they elected to relax by the stream.

Though constantly mesmerized by the lure of the terrain, Gary agreed. He wanted this vacation to offer the opportunity for him and Katherine to rekindle the romance in their lives. In recent times, business had often preempted their personal wants. He suspected she had chosen this detour to the bottom of the canyon to please him. He hoped Katherine would not forego her own relaxation for his preferences.

The sun had already dipped below the crest of the canyon walls. The ladies dangled their bare feet in the cool water of the creek absorbed in conversation. Occasionally harmonious giggles broke out between them, loud enough to be heard over the sounds of the creek and catching their husbands' attention. Jean and Gary relaxed nearby, engaged in their own discussion.

A short time later, Rosalie clamored up the bank to them, shoes and stockings in hand. With a beaming smile, she grabbed Jean's hand. "There's been a change in plans." She giggled as she pulled him to his feet. "Come with me."

Gary watched as they disappeared back toward the cabins. Slightly surprised, but amused, he glanced down at Katherine. She faced him, sitting on a boulder midstream and motioned him to join her.

"What's going on?" Gary asked as he waded barefoot through the stream to join her.

"Nothing frightening," Katherine replied. "You'll see in a half hour."

At the appointed time, Katherine hopped down from her perch. "Our turn," she told Gary as she waded to the bank and picked up her shoes.

Following after her, still somewhat curiously, he began to get the picture. As they walked up the pathway toward the bathing pool, they met Rosalie and Jean. Both were smiling with tousled wet hair.

"Have fun!" Rosalie giggled. "And don't forget the latch string."

When they entered the patio, Gary followed Rosalie's advice. After latching the gate, he pulled the string inside through the hole. When he turned back around, Katherine stood before him, her clothing in a rumpled heap at her feet. She looked at him with a seductive glow.

"Isn't this better than taking a bath with another naked man?"

Gary stepped forward and took her in his arms. "What about the rules?"

"Rosalie and I changed the rules," she whispered as she unbuttoned his shirt.

* * *

The two couples entered the dining hall at half-past five and seated themselves at the table. Ada brought fresh glasses a few minutes later.

"You folks all look refreshed," their hostess commented knowingly as she glanced at the clock on the mantel.

"Yes," Katherine replied, grinning. "The brisk temperature of the water was very invigorating."

Ada returned momentarily with pitchers of tea and lemonade as before. "Holler into the kitchen if you need anything else," she said as she disappeared back through the door.

"It's at times like this that you Americans' choice to abstain from consuming alcohol becomes a bit disappointing," Jean commented. "A cool glass of wine would be splendid right now."

"Or a cold beer," Gary added as he lifted his glass of lemonade to Jean in a toast.

"Men!" Katherine exclaimed to Rosalie with a wink. "I would have supposed the interlude in the bathing pool would have been sufficient to relax them for the evening."

Jean nearly spewed his tea at Katherine's bold implication. American women, he had been told, were much more chaste than Europeans. Rosalie stifled a chuckle as Gary blushed in embarrassment.

The quartet settled into casual conversation in their comfortable surroundings. As they got to know each other better, all were amazed by their similar lifestyles. Somewhat like the Wagner's trucking company, the Garniers operated a successful precision machine shop that served regional coal mining companies and their local bicycle industry. Both couples enjoyed outdoor adventures. Rosalie insisted that Jean's fixation with photography equaled or exceeded Gary's mountaineering addiction. She and Katherine both teased that their husbands were more interested in their hobbies than their wives.

As pleasant aromas began to waft from the kitchen, Ada returned to set their rustic table with fine china and silverware. The group continued to visit as they enjoyed the mouth-watering meal topped off with a scrumptious custard dessert.

The evening swept by rapidly as the couples shared in their newfound friendship. Stars appeared in the dusky sky between the walls of the canyon as they strolled across the yard. They bade each other good night and retired to their adjacent cabins. The hypnotic sound of Bright Angel Creek tumbling over the rocks beneath it carried on the fresh breeze through the open window of Gary and Katherine's cabin.

"I want to apologize," Gary said as he snuggled against Katherine's back on the soft bed.

"What on earth for?" she asked in surprise.

"For being selfish," he answered, recalling his guilty supposition from earlier in the day. "I wanted us taking this vacation to be for you. Not for me. I wanted to pamper you. To show you how much I love you...I think you suggested we take the excursion down here today to please me. In doing so, you forfeited your own happiness. We have spent most of these past years building our business at the expense of our marriage. Most recently, I have spent more time preparing for this climb in Switzerland than I have with you. I wanted to make that up to you. For this to be a second honeymoon of sorts. You have given up so much. You deserve more. I am sorry."

Katherine rolled over to face him. "Part of what you say is true," she began. "But I saw the look in your eyes when Freddy told us about the pack trip down here. I knew that you would love it. I also knew that I could endure it."

"That's what I thought," he interrupted, but Katherine placed her finger over his lips.

"That is what I thought," she continued. "When you and Jean were off exploring at the Indian Garden, Rosalie and I sat by the creek soaking our feet and talking. She, too, had come down here so Jean could take pictures. We were relaxing in the midst of one of the most beautiful places in the world. Birds darting from tree to tree. Somehow it hit both of us that we wouldn't have been here if not for our husbands. We had the two of you to thank for all that we were experiencing. How much we loved both of you." Katherine paused, recollecting her thoughts. "This afternoon, we were talking again. What a romantic place this is. How happy we were to be here and how unromantic it was that she and I would be bathing together. The same for you and Jean. We four were the only guests. The time was blocked out for guests to bathe, so who would care which two bathed with who? She devised the plan, and we did it."

"I'm not sure what to say."

"This afternoon was the most romantic time I have ever

experienced in my life. Tell me that you love me as much as I love you."

He did not answer. He fought back tears and embraced her with a long passionate kiss. "I do," he finally said when they separated. "I love you more than life itself." He kissed her again.

* * *

SUNDAY, SEPTEMBER 9, 1923

At half past seven, the bottom of the canyon lay in heavy shadows. Sunlight would not reach there for some time. Three packers carried everything the group would return to the rim with in one trip. Emmett had all of the mules ready when they got there and packs were quickly loaded and secured. Each of the guests carried canteens that Ada had filled from the icy spring while they ate a hearty breakfast.

"Y'all seem right cheerful this mornin'," Emmett greeted as they stepped off the suspension bridge.

"We've had a good time," Katherine replied.

"Tha's good! Glad ta' hear'ut."

Katherine had barely slipped the strap of her canteen over the saddle horn when Emmett hollered out, "Ready ta' go folks?" Without waiting for a reply, he was in the saddle. "Mount up. It's a long ride ta' th' top."

Jean and Gary gave the ladies a leg up and hurried to board their own mounts.

"I'll lead 'til we leave th' river," Emmett told them. With a click of his tongue, Mae headed out with the four pack mules behind her. Jake followed behind without being prompted.

At ten thirty, they rode into the meadow at the Indian

Garden. The fragrance of Pecos's lunch overwhelmed the woodsmoke from his fire.

"Howdy!" he hollered and waved his spoon when he saw them.

Though the ascent was gradual, the guests were sore from yesterday's ride and slow to dismount. As Emmett rode up, Katherine recalled a question she had forgotten to ask him yesterday.

"Why do they call this place the Indian Garden?"

"They say Injuns yus'ta live down in th' canyon. Hunted sheep, I s'pect. An' grew veg'tables here.

"What kind of vegetables?"

"Corn an' squorsh, I s'pose." At that, he turned to care for the animals.

The couples enjoyed their meal and respite at the welcoming oasis. As they lounged after lunch, Pecos doused his fire with the last of the coffee before cleaning dishes and cookware then stowed them in a large trunk that sat near his cooking bench. He then packed up soiled linens and a few other items onto one of his mules and saddled the other. After getting the mules ready for the climb, Emmett gave instruction to his clients.

"Pay'cus'll draw th' pack animals ba'hind y'all an' I'll take th' lead up out'a heres," he began. "Y'all know how steep th' trail gets. We wanna mak'et easy as poss'ble on th' animals. When it gets steep, stand up in yer stirrups an' leans forwerd. Get yer weight up on ther' shoulders 'stead o' back on ther' haunches. It's easier for them an' more comf'terble fer y'all in th' long run. Y'all okay?" he asked.

With nods of assent from the foursome, he went on, "Le's mount up. Keep a look on me an' foller my 'zample. Ya' ladies foller me, an' gents behind. Holler out if'n ya' need ta' hold up. Pay'cus'll keep an eye on yer tails."

With that he swung into his saddle and waited for the others to do the same. The midday sun had settled into the bottom of the canyon as they pulled back onto the trail for their ascent to the rim. It was low in the sky when they came to a halt in front of the broad stone steps of El Tovar. Even with two significant breaks along the trail in the afternoon, it had been a long, hot day. They smelled of dust and mules and sweat when they entered the lobby.

"Good evening," Palmer greeted them cheerfully as he came to meet them. "I saw your approach and took the liberty of having the maid draw water for baths in your rooms. I hope that you don't mind?" he asked, waiting for signs of approval before continuing. "If you would like to leave laundry by your doors, it will be collected while you dine and returned in the morning, clean and fresh."

"That sounds wonderful," Rosalie replied, enjoying the thought of soaking in a hot bathtub.

Just then, the bellman appeared behind them with their luggage and followed them to their rooms. An hour later the two couples met for supper and again the following morning for a late breakfast. They had become good friends in the short time since their meeting and thoroughly enjoyed each other's company. After breakfast, they strolled along the trail atop the rim east of El Tovar. The same path Gary and Katherine had taken upon their arrival two days earlier. They had seen and done so much it seemed to have been long ago. This time they walked at a more leisurely pace, their anxiety diminished since their initial exposure to the canyon's beauty. The four now ambled along as two couples, hand in hand, in lieu of two ladies and two men. Both had renewed their passion for each other during their trek to the bottom of the vast wonder below them.

Early that afternoon, the porter took charge of the two couples' luggage from the bellman at El Tovar and transported it to the station. Palmer bade them adieu in the lobby and their last stroll at the Grand Canyon took them to the depot where they boarded the train for Williams. On board, Katherine and Gary flipped their seats to face Jean and Rosalie's behind them. They were already well-engaged in conversation when the chug of the locomotive and a slight jolt of their car, indicated their ride had begun.

When the conductor took their tickets, Katherine was reminded of their trip from Williams and began sharing the story of George, the traumatized soldier who lived in a shack in the desert.

This prompted Rosalie to share their experiences with the Germans. The French government had requested Jean keep his machine shop running to support the war effort and things had gone well until the Germans overran their city. They seized nearly all the available food for their military. She and Jean rationed what little they could hoard for several months. Both were suffering mild malnutrition by the time allied forces laid siege to their community and, after a monumental battle with hundreds of casualties on both sides, the allies finally drove the Germans from Saint-Étienne. Two regiments of American infantrymen from Texas were in the battle. When the dust settled, over half of them had been killed.

"We understand firsthand how horrific the war was. Just a few weeks after the battle, the Germans surrendered," Rosalie concluded. "Some say that battle in our little town was a deciding factor in the signing of the armistice."

Four people who had not quit talking for a day and a half suddenly fell silent.

"This is where that man, George, left the train." Katherine finally broke the silence as they passed the remnants of abandoned buildings alongside the tracks.

"Funny," Rosalie replied, staring at the stone skeletons as they passed. "They almost look like some of the bombed-out buildings at home."

"I am sorry, Rosalie. I didn't mean to bring back such terrible memories for you."

"The reason we came to see America was to quench some of those old embers of bitterness," Rosalie continued. "Part of the reason was to rekindle our own fire," she added, looking to Jean and taking his hand lovingly before returning her gaze to Katherine. "You two have been a big part of what happened these past three days. I...we are grateful. A debt that can't be repaid." She turned back to Jean. "No apology necessary."

"About that debt," Katherine responded as she turned and gave Gary a sweet peck on the cheek. "It's already been repaid."

That evening, they all met for one final supper at the Fray Marcus Hotel. Jean and Rosalie would catch a late-night train for New York. There, they would board a steamer to Marseille and only a few more hours by train to Saint-Étienne.

At eleven o'clock, Gary and Katherine hugged and shook hands with the Garniers. The wives exchanged addresses and promised to keep in touch with each other.

"I am sure I can convince Gary to come visit," Katherine told her. "Especially if I drop a hint of some nearby snow-covered alpine peak that needs to be climbed," she whispered with a wink.

* * *

TUESDAY, SEPTEMBER 11, 1923

The next morning Gary and Katherine had breakfast in the Fray Marcus dining room at eight o'clock. The table seemed strangely vacant as they already missed their new friends' company. An hour later, Gary hung their freshly filled canvas water bag from the radiator neck of the Oldsmobile. They soon left a light cloud of dust hanging among the pine trees in the cool morning air as they continued east, resuming their tour.

At half past ten, they rolled into Flagstaff and soon found themselves in the Babbit Brothers Trading Company on Aspen Avenue. Katherine admired the beauty and intricacy in the patterns of a wide assortment of Navajo blankets and rugs on display. The prices were less shocking than she expected, but she still considered them an unaffordable luxury. Her interest in the weavers' artistry did not slip past Gary's notice while he browsed over a selection of turquoise and silverwork. In the end, Katherine purchased a large picnic basket in anticipation of their excursion entering less inhabited regions. Following a quick stop at a market to purchase bread, cheese, and fruit she felt would survive in the new basket without refrigeration, they continued on to Walnut Canyon, where they explored the ancient ruins nestled among the cliffs there.

They chose not to embark down the trail to the bottom of the canyon in the midday heat. A ranger at the monument explained that the residents of the canyon had used the trail to carry water from the creek below up to their homes. Archaeologists, he told them, estimated these people occupied the dwellings about 800 years earlier. After a couple of hours exploring, they drank water from the canvas bag and enjoyed a picnic lunch before heading north.

Dusk found them exhausted as they rolled to a stop in front of the Leupp Trading Post. The proprietor inside the cool sandstone building, offered a simple, but nourishing, meal of lamb and vegetables served with fried bread. After a long day of scrambling among decaying stone structures and hiking in the desert, it tasted delicious.

"Is there any available lodging close to here?" Gary asked as they ate.

"I've a little stone cabin nearby. It has no water, but it's clean and has a bed."

"That would work fine for us tonight," Gary told him.

After they finished the meal, their host brought a lantern and showed them to their domicile for the night. He lit the kerosene lamp that occupied a small table which, along with the bed, filled the small room.

* * *

WEDNESDAY, SEPTEMBER 12, 1923

When they rose the next morning, they saw the rest of the community in daylight. To their surprise, the village centered around an Indian boarding school similar to the one they had seen at Valentine a week earlier.

They wandered over to the trading post and had a morning snack before examining the Navajo-crafted merchandise. Katherine was excited to discover the weavings were much more affordable than they were in Flagstaff where there was a much larger tourist trade. Even then, she still hesitated until Gary urged her to be less prudent and enjoy a few luxuries.

"Darling, we have worked hard our entire marriage. It is time to enjoy a few fruits of our labors."

"I just hate to think that I'm wasting our hard-earned money, dear."

"You aren't," he responded. "I knew that you wanted some of the weavings in Flagstaff to adorn our home when you saw them. These are just as well made, or perhaps even better. We can afford it, and I want you to have them."

She finally succumbed to Gary's coaxing, and they purchased two small matching rugs that, when rolled, would fit into their trunk. When Katherine went to the restroom, Gary hurriedly picked out two larger blankets of similar patterns and colors and quickly hid them beneath some of their belongings then loaded the rugs on top of it all.

When Katherine returned, Gary was back inside looking over a silver concho-style belt buckle.

"Do you like that?" she asked sincerely.

"Yes, I do," he answered, "but I'm not in love with it."

"Would you like to have one?" she continued carefully, not wanting to spoil the surprise if she purchased one for his birthday, only four days away.

"Perhaps, if I find one that I just can't live without," he said. "Right now, you're the only thing that has affected me that way."

Katherine blushed. "I'm very happy to hear that." Then hugged and kissed him a little more seriously than a peck on his lips.

"Excuse me," the shopkeeper spoke after the couple broke their embrace. "I heard you speak of your interest in silverwork."

"Yes?"

"If you're traveling east, I suggest you visit the Hubbell Trading Post at Ganado. Some of the most gifted silversmiths in Arizona live in that area, and Don Lorenzo carries a beautiful inventory of their goods. There are good weavers around there too. The rugs that you bought are from that vicinity."

"Why, thank you," Gary answered. "How far is it?"

"It's about a hundred miles. Mostly pretty good roads. It'll take a good six hours to drive it. Do you have a map?"

"Yes, we do."

"I'll show you the route," he said, "and where to buy gasoline."

They ventured out into new territory before midmorning. Katherine followed their path on the map as they motored down the well-traveled road heading nearly due east. The landscape was similar to much of the Arizona desert country they had already seen. With little deviation in terrain, the various buttes protruding up from the topography provided useful landmarks, they were sure, to voyagers of the past. An hour from Leupp, Katherine spotted Elephant Butte on their left. She felt certain it was the correct landmark from its dark gray stone silhouette in the distance. As they grew nearer, a scattering of saguaro cacti showed like spindly green fingers jutting from its back.

A moment later, Katherine half giggled a stifled snort through her nose. The unusual sound startled Gary enough to rapidly slow the car and turn to see if she was alright. Her face was a vibrant red, and her eyes watered as she pointed to a smaller promontory a mile or so east of the Elephant Butte.

"Nipple Butte," she finally managed to sputter out, straining to contain her laughter. A dry grassy sloped hill rose from below resembling a smallish woman's breast. The brownish outcrop perched atop, looked exactly like a dark nipple pointing excitedly to the sky above it. "It is certainly aptly named," she finally managed as Gary blushed and laughed aloud with her.

A short time later, Castle Butte then Haystack Butte appeared on their right, and soon they arrived at an intersection surrounded by a few buildings, mostly dwellings. A sign read Dilkon. They stopped for a moment at the intersection as Katherine quickly rechecked their route on the map. The road they arrived on was in good condition and well-traveled as was the intersecting road north and south. Their own route continued straight ahead. The road was narrow and rutted from some unknown previous precipitation. Gary and Katherine had only seen two other vehicles since they left Leupp. This road was severely less traveled. They had made good time, thus far driving forty miles in just over an hour. Gary now understood why the man at the trading post had estimated their travel time as he had.

Fifteen miles to the next town, Indian Wells. That was where they planned to buy gasoline. Gary checked the gauge. They had over half a tankful. There was food in the picnic basket and the full canvas water bag hanging from the radiator.

"I sure hope it doesn't rain," Gary verbalized his anxiety. He put the car into gear and continued ahead at a much slower pace. Twenty minutes later, they could still see Dilkon behind them.

"We could almost walk this fast," he muttered under his breath as they crawled along the unimproved path.

"More time to enjoy the scenery," Katherine chided him optimistically.

"Okay, I get it."

"After all," she added cheerfully, "we are on vacation, aren't we?"

Gary readjusted himself into a more relaxed posture behind the wheel. In doing so, he began to observe their surroundings more seriously as he scanned the passing terrain. "It truly is an interesting country," he commented.

Almost as if on command, the hills and buttes Katherine had been identifying in the distance began slowly closing in around them. In doing so, the road gradually wove itself between them. As it continued eastward, the topography evolved into a more mountainous landscape. Time began to pass more quickly, and it was not long before they made a sweeping turn to the north. Bidahochi Butte appeared to their right in the distance, and the community of Indian Wells came into view before them.

Another north–south thoroughfare intersected their course there. Again, that road looked far better traveled than the one they were on.

While Gary refueled their car, Katherine sliced bread and cheese. Accompanied with peaches from the picnic basket and Coca-Colas from the store, they enjoyed a quick refreshing lunch before moseying farther along on their journey.

From Indian Wells, their path skirted south of Bidahochi Butte. Soon they worked their way through the north end of the Hopi Buttes, and from there they could view Twin Buttes a few miles away and straight ahead of them. A mile further, they turned left at the fork in the road and rambled northeast where the road became much improved, and they sprinted into Greasewood, joyful to have escaped the monotony of the unmaintained byway. Grabbing a cool drink at the trading post, they celebrated their success.

The road again continued northeast through Cornfield at

the junction of an even better roadway. Arrows pointed both directions, Klagetoh to the right, fourteen miles, and Ganado to the left, three.

The sprawling village surrounding the old Ganado Mission amazed them both when Gary and Katherine arrived. There was a remarkable commercial area, another Indian boarding school, and a beautiful old stone church.

The J. L. Hubbell Trading Post was quite obviously the major hub of the community. Even late in the afternoon, nearly a dozen individuals, both artisans and patrons occupied the cool dark interior of the red stone building. Men and women of varied ethnicity bartered with the proprietor and his employees in the *Bullpen,* as the main trading room was called.

The mercantile occupied several rooms, food staples and dry goods to supply nearby residents, and the Don provided the widest array of Indian crafts and peltries for tourists. Katherine had never seen so many baskets, rugs, and blankets in one place. There were dozens upon dozens of pottery pieces. She was certain that many of the buyers represented galleries and distributors.

Eventually they found their way into a roomful of display cases. Locked inside them were an uncountable number of pieces of silverwork. There were no windows in the room. Even in the dim light, the cases glowed with reflections of highly polished silver. As they browsed over case after case, both were enthralled. Too many pieces to even look at let alone choose a favorite from. Katherine ultimately focused on one particular case that had several necklaces and earrings of a similar style she really liked.

Gary saw more than a few belt buckles he liked, but none that really stood out to him. They had been browsing for quite some time when they realized the building had gotten quiet. When they started to leave the room, they were met in the door by an elderly man. They startled each other in surprise.

"Excuse me!" the astonished man exclaimed. "I didn't realize you were back here."

"We're sorry," Katherine replied. "We've been looking at jewelry and suddenly noticed the silence."

"We closed up about a half hour ago. I'm just locking up now. I thought I was alone in here."

"We didn't mean to be breaking any rules," Katherine went on.

"No, no. That's quite alright. I'm John Hubbell. I bought this place over forty years ago and have run it ever since." He offered his hand.

"I'm Katherine Wagner," she replied, accepting the handshake. "My husband, Gary," she introduced who still stood behind her in the doorway.

"Let's get out of the doorway," Hubbell suggested. "So, I can shake this lucky man's hand," he continued as he backed into the outer room. "You have a very beautiful and pleasant wife, Señor Wagner," he told Gary as he reached out his hand. "Congratulations, sir."

"Why, thank you, Mr. Hubbell. or should I address you as Don?" Gary asked as they exchanged a handshake.

"It is an honorary title that a few of my friends have bestowed upon me. I am grateful, though unsure that I am worthy of that distinction. I have been called many other, less flattering things over the years." He chuckled. "You may call me John, or whatever else pleases you."

"Thank you. If Mr. Hubbell is suitable, I'm comfortable with that."

"Very well, then," Hubbell continued. "So why is it that

your lovely wife is not wearing any of my wonderful jewelry?"

"Well, sir. To begin with, I suspect the cases are locked. I also suspect I might be shot if I broke into one."

"That would be a possibility, Señor."

He grinned.

"That being said, Mr. Hubbell, I believe she is particularly interested in the case over there," he said, pointing to the one Katherine had been attracted to.

"Very good taste, Señora Wagner. These are all made by one of our finest silversmiths. He lives very near here." Hubbell crossed to the case and stepped behind it. "What in particular pleases you?" he asked as he unlocked the case.

"I like the little ornate bells," Katherine answered as she approached the case.

"Oh, the squash blossoms. Yes, they do resemble tiny bells, don't they," he replied as he pulled a necklace and earrings from the case and sat them on top of it. He then retrieved a nearby desk-lamp and positioned it over them. "They will sparkle in the sunlight, just like that," he said.

"They are magnificent, aren't they," she answered as she ogled them.

"Would you like to try them on? There is a lighted mirror right over there."

"Oh, I couldn't. I'm sure they are far too expensive."

"We are not across the street from the railroad or on Aspen Avenue in Flagstaff," Hubbell answered, implying the Babbitt Brothers might be overpriced. "These are made only a few miles from here." Hubbell may have run a frontier trading post in the middle of nowhere, but he knew how to flatter a potential lady customer and perhaps help loosen her purse strings. He also knew how not to offend her husband in the process, since he suspected everything hinged on his approval. "Please, Señor Wagner." He gingerly lifted the necklace from the display and handed it to Gary. "Would you do the honors?"

Gary stood behind her. Placing the necklace around Katherine's neck, he clasped it. Hubbell anticipated Gary's approval from the moment he pointed out which case Katherine was interested in. Now the trader needed to seal the deal.

"Please, Señora. Take these to the mirror with you," Hubbell added as he handed Katherine the matching earrings.

"I'm not dressed for jewelry like this." She blushed.

"You look fine, dear," Gary urged.

"Well, Mr. Hubbell, Gary would like a silver belt buckle. He has looked your cases over and not found quite what he's looking for. He wants something really unique." Katherine then accepted the earrings and crossed the room to the mirror.

"I will be right back," Hubbell said and vanished through a door at the rear of the room. He returned with a small cloth cinch-string bag that he sat on the counter.

Gary stood behind Katherine admiring the jewelry in the mirror. "Do you like them?" he asked.

"I love them, but we can't afford luxuries like these."

"Wait at least until we find out what the price is. I think perhaps we can."

She left them on as they returned to Mr. Hubbell waiting behind the display case. "They look splendid on you, Señora."

"I do like them, but I am afraid of what the cost will be."

"Just leave them on for the moment, and we will discuss the price shortly." He loosened the string on the cloth bag. "Señor Wagner, what I have here is something very special. It was made by perhaps the finest silversmith ever. He has been gone about twenty years now."

"What was his name?"

"He was Navajo, Señor. Following Diné tradition, I will not speak the name of one who has left us. If you insist, I will write it down for you." Don Lorenzo paused, clearing his throat. He then, almost ceremoniously, took the belt buckle from the bag and handed it to Gary Wagner. "It is sandcast, Señor. One of a kind. There is not another one anywhere in the world like it."

Gary held the buckle beneath the lamp, nearly seized in a trance by its beauty. The artistic design of the silver was like none he had ever seen. As were the blue-green and red stones that adorned it. The silver was shined to an even finer luster than the necklace and earrings Katherine had on. He was totally mesmerized.

Katherine peered over his shoulder at it in awe. She finally found her voice. "What are the stones?"

"The green turquoise is from Persia...I got them soon after I purchased this business. I brought the red coral from California shortly before the artist left us. I am not sure of its actual origin."

"How much for the buckle?" Katherine asked.

"Until now, I have not considered selling it. It has never been on display."

"You have been looking for something unique, darling. This is as good as it gets," she told Gary. She also knew how obvious it must be to the trader how taken they both were by the piece. That tilted the bargaining scale heavily toward Mr. Hubbell.

Gary finally found his voice. "It truly is extraordinary."

"My husband's birthday is in two days," Katherine began.

"I would like to give this to him. I will give you one hundred dollars for it."

It would have been difficult to discern which of the two men were more surprised by Katherine's taking charge of the negotiation.

"Well." Hubbell paused to rapidly assess the situation. Moments before, he felt in control of the barter. Both of the clients' hearts seemed anxious to make a purchase. Even though Katherine seemed to love the necklace set, she had mentioned price more than once. "I am sorry, Señora. I could not sell it for that. I have had it for a long time." He had difficulty reading her face. He had not negotiated with very many women, and he suspected this one was very wise. "I would need one hundred fifty dollars,"

Katherine looked at the floor and slowly turned her head from side to side.

"If you could throw in the squash blossom necklace and earrings? Maybe?" Gary joined into the haggle.

Hubbell said nothing. Katherine mentally glanced at the balancing scale in her mind. She and Gary had tipped the scale toward Hubble by staring blatantly at the buckle. Katherine had, however, jerked Hubbell's thumb from his side of the scale with her opening offer. Don Lorenzo's counteroffer swung the scale back to his advantage, but modestly. Now Gary's suggestion brought it closer to center.

"That would be worth consideration," Katherine agreed, looking Hubbell straight in the eye as she said it.

John L. Hubbell scratched his beard thoughtfully. Katherine Wagner was a worthy competitor at the bargaining table. Her husband had offered a truce, and she had suggested that she might accept the terms...playing poker with this woman would be unnerving if not financially devastating he surmised.

"That is an agreeable compromise," Hubbell offered.

"Then it is done, sir." Katherine offered her hand.

"Yes. It has been good doing business with you, Señora," he replied, accepting. "And you, Señor," he added as he shifted to shake Gary's hand.

The transaction left him somewhat unsettled. The result was good, but he could not say it had been a pleasure. The Don did not often have business dealings with women. When he did it was generally with a single woman. Usually a politically powerful widow. Gary did not seem to be a man controlled by his spouse, but neither did Katherine seem to be subjugated by him. They appeared to contribute equally in their financial affairs and their marriage. Not a common occurrence in Hubbell's experience. To further his surprise, Katherine pulled a roll of cash from her purse and paid for the purchase.

5

W hen he and June reached the railroad trestle between Dry Lake and Crystal, Conor rolled the coupe to a stop in the middle of the road and observed the repairs. A half-dozen, almost white, new timbers and as many new ties stood out against the weathered gray of the rest of the structure. The rail was also new, but too rusty to notice. The raw iron turned the dark reddish brown within a few days of arriving to be stored in the maintenance yard. Even in the dry Nevada desert, the surface aged quickly.

"This is where they found him?" June asked.

"Yes...it's just so strange that he ended up out here," Con adjusted his thoughts from the trestle to the victim. "If it hadn't been for that broken track, who knows when or where he might have ended up."

Conor put the car into gear and gradually accelerated as

they resumed their journey. "Somehow, I need to piece together a very odd puzzle."

"The simplest way to put a jigsaw puzzle together is to start with the border," June commented as they sped up the road toward the Moapa Trading Post. "Once you build a framework, it's easier to fill in the rest."

"I'll try to keep that in mind. I'm not very smart when it comes to that sort of thing," Con replied.

"Oh, I think you are smarter than you give yourself credit for."

"Have you ever been inside a trading post?" Conor asked, changing the subject.

"No, I have not. What are they like?"

"I've only been inside two. One in Arizona a couple of years ago and this one when I was a kid." Con smiled, recalling the time.

"Tell me about them."

"Well, I guess they can be anything from a one-room hogan to very large. The traders buy things the Indians need and barter it for things the Indians make. Sometimes there is cash involved. Sometimes it's just a trade. Goods for goods. They usually keep a ledger and do a good portion of their business on credit."

"So, what made you smile?"

"A memory. Luis Garza brought me up here...to the trading post once. I think I was fifteen...maybe sixteen. I worked for him after Papa hurt his leg."

"All the way up here? Did he drive then?"

"No, we took the train. It was the first time I ever rode on a train. It was exciting. We walked to the trading post from the station. It took a couple of hours. We came to meet an Indian man there that Luis had bought a flock of sheep from. When we got there, Luis bought a burro from the trader, food, a brand-new skillet and dutch oven, canteens, everything we would need for the trip home. All we had with us were our bedrolls. Luis carried a rifle, and I had a shepherd's crook." Conor still smiled at the memory. June waited for more of the story.

"When the man arrived with the flock, he had three herders and four dogs with him. Luis looked the sheep over and counted them. When Luis paid the man, he asked how we were going to get the sheep home. Luis told him we would herd them. 'You and this pup?' the man asked. There were about two hundred I think, but I was young. Maybe it was less. Anyway, Luis told him that I must be a better herder than his men if it took three of them to do a boy's work. The Indian man finally convinced Luis to at least take one of his dogs as a gift.

"We headed for home. Following the river mostly. It took a long time. Two or three weeks, I think. What an adventure."

"It sounds like a lot of hard work, but you are still smiling," June commented curiously.

"The dog didn't speak English." Con burst out laughing, as June tried to comprehend his ironic humor. "She didn't understand a word of English or Spanish," he finally explained when he composed himself. "She only knew whatever language the Moapa herders had spoken to her. She was totally baffled when we tried to instruct her. But she did know sheep. It didn't take her long to figure out what we were trying to do. She was smart and a great herding dog. By the time we got home, she was beginning to learn some Spanish."

"So, why is it we are going there?"

"In hope the trader might be able to identify this." He took the buckle from his pocket and handed it to her.

"It must have been incredible. What happened to it?"

"John Doe was wearing it."

"Oh!" she nearly shouted. Hearing where it came from, she almost wished she had not touched it. But even in its damaged condition, it was almost hypnotically beautiful. "Who made it?"

"I don't know. That's why we're here," Conor answered as they pulled up in front of the trading post.

* * *

June browsed around the trading post. It was almost like a dry goods store, if not for the vast collection of baskets on display. She assumed they were woven by the Moapa. Meanwhile, Con scanned the room as he approached the proprietor.

"What brings you out this way, Sheriff?" the man asked inquisitively, noting Conor was in uniform, but had not driven up in an official vehicle.

"I was in here once when I was a kid. I helped to herd a flock of sheep from here down south of Las Vegas," Con told him.

"When might that have been? I've been here a long time."

"Oh, twenty years ago or more."

"Well, I bought the place in 1900."

"It was after that. Do you know Luis Garza?"

"Yes, I do. John Meriwether," he said, offering his hand.

"I know the name," Conor replied as he shook Meriwether's hand. "I remember. It reminded me of Lewis and Clark in school."

Meriwether burst into a jovial chuckle. "Well, I haven't heard that comparison for a number of years. Back when you would have been here, I might see Luis once or twice a year. I haven't seen him now for, oh, ten years anyway. Maybe longer."

"He and my father are good friends," Con spoke casually. "I used to work for him when I wasn't in school."

"How is he?"

"He's well. Getting old of course. Still ranching. Scaled down a lot from what he used to have. He still lives with no electricity or telephone."

"As I recall," the trader pondered, "Luis was fond of an Indian girl when I first came to this country. She later married one of the local boys. Did he ever marry?"

"No, he didn't. He has no relatives at all that I'm aware of."

"Must be lonely to have nobody as you grow old," Meriwether commented.

Conor had no reply. As far as he knew, the Armenta family was the closest thing to any family Luis had.

"You know most of the Indian tradesmen around here?" Con finally broke the silence.

"All of them, I think."

"Any silversmiths?"

"Not locally. I occasionally get some silver through here that's been traded around some," the old trader replied as he started imagining why the sheriff might have come calling. "I don't have anything right now."

"Would you recognize a unique piece of silverwork if you saw it?"

"Possibly. As I said, I don't get much through here."

"Have you ever seen anything like this?" Conor asked as he retrieved the buckle from his pocket.

"Whew." The trader whistled when he saw it. "That was one fine piece of craftsmanship before it got all messed up. Is it stolen?"

"I don't think so. Have you ever seen it before?"

"No. And I would remember if I had."

"Can you tell me anything about it? I saw a bracelet once that was made kind of like it. They said it was sandcast. Does that make sense?"

"Yessir. This is definitely sandcast silver. The red stones are coral...from the ocean. They've been around in Navajo jewelry for thirty years or more. These blue-green stones are turquoise, but not Navajo turquoise. I had a necklace years ago that had some like this. Somebody told me it was from Egypt or Africa. Someplace exotic like that. I can't remember."

"Who could have made this buckle?"

"Nobody around here. It might be pretty old. And whoever it was, they really knew what they were doing. I'll guarantee, anybody who ever saw this before it got messed up, never forgot it."

"So, if it's not from around here, where?"

"It might be Navajo. I've heard of some really amazing silver-smiths over in the eastern part of that country. There're some good ones down in Mexico too, but this doesn't look Mexican to me. Don't ask me why, just a feeling. To be perfectly honest with you, I've never seen anything of this quality from anywhere."

"Anywhere?"

"Anywhere," Meriwether repeated.

* * *

June was seated in the shade on the porch of the trading post when Con came out. She had purchased a small basket made of finely stripped willow from Mrs. Meriwether while Conor talked to her husband.

"What did you find out?" she asked.

"Luis Garza had an Indian girlfriend thirty years ago," Con answered.

"That's not what I meant...but...really? Luis really had a girlfriend? An Indian girl? Who was she? What happened?"

"Yes, yes, and yes. I don't know, and I don't know. It sounds like he might have even been seeing her when he brought me here to herd sheep back home with him. I know he never saw her then. She married someone else later. Luis has never told me anything about her, so it's none of my business."

"But he is an old and dear friend. You should ask him."

"I may not have many friends, but I do know one thing. The best way to end a friendship is poking your nose in where it doesn't belong."

June became very quiet. She did not want to reopen that wound she had exposed earlier today. They were heading to the ranch where she needed signatures on some documents for Mr. Westcott.

"Yes. You are right," she finally began. "Luis's personal life is not a case. It's not an investigation."

"Thank you," Conor replied.

They drove on in silence for a while.

"What did he say about the buckle?"

"It's made from sandcast silver. The turquoise is from Africa or somewhere. The red stones are coral. He has no idea who made it and only vague suspicions that it may have been made by a Navajo in the eastern part of their reservation. It is extremely rare. Because it is sandcast, there is not another one like it anywhere. And it is the finest piece of silversmithing he has ever seen. He says anyone who saw it before it was damaged would never forget it. He also has never seen it before."

"Wow! That truly makes it unique, doesn't it?"

"Yes, it does. It also means that my John Doe, who I thought was probably an Indian, probably Moapa Paiute, now…is probably not. So much for putting together the edges of the puzzle. The border just got bigger."

* * *

Conor sat in the car under the shade of several cottonwood trees that graced the yard of a large, but not imposing, two-story white house. He penciled notes in the tally book he carried with him of his visit with John Meriwether. He watched June walk to the door and ring the small brass bell that hung from the wide trim surrounding the door. Moments later a tall well-built man about sixty opened the screen door and shook her hand as he stepped out onto the porch. She is beautiful and so graceful, Con thought, as he watched her take a seat near a small table on the porch. June brought out a handful of papers, pen, ink, and blotter from the leather case she carried. She spread the papers on the table and pointed occasionally to one thing or another. Conor went back to his notes.

After perhaps a half hour, he returned the tally book to his pocket and his attention to June and her employer's client. They were obviously engaged in discussion, but even in the quiet stillness of the yard, Con could not hear them talking, let alone discern their conversation. A short time later, the client dipped the pen in the ink and signed, then blotted, a paper before handing it back to June, where she repeated the process. After duplicating the procedure with several other papers,

June sorted through the documents and handed several sheets to the client. She then replaced the cork in the ink bottle and placed the remainder of the papers and writing implements into her briefcase.

They both stood and June, wearing the same pleasant professional expression on her face, again shook his hand before turning to begin walking back to the car. What could this beautiful, intelligent woman possibly see in him, Conor thought. "I sure don't know," he answered quietly to himself, "but I'm beginning to understand what loving someone feels like...and receiving it in return."

Con got out and held the door for June. "That looked like it went well."

"Yes, it did. He was very pleased with the way Mr. West-cott worded a couple of the details. Everything was in order, and he is satisfied with the outcome."

"Now, I get to see what Mr. Banker knows about Katherine Wagner," Conor said as he turned around and headed out the lane.

Con found a place near the bank to park his coupe in the shade. "I don't know how long this might take."

"I think I will visit the dry goods store," June pointed down the street. "If you don't find me there, check the café. Good luck!" she encouraged, then gave Con a quick kiss and sauntered down the street. Conor crossed the street to the Moapa Valley Bank.

"What can I do for you, Sheriff?" the clerk asked as Con entered the door.

"I would like to talk to the manager, if I could."

"Mr. Howard stepped out for a moment. He should be back any time." Before Con could respond, he added, "Here he comes across the street, now."

Mr. Howard came through the door and did a double-take when he saw Conor waiting in the lobby. "I'm sorry, Sheriff." He looked again out to the street. "I didn't see your pickup truck on the street."

"I am driving my personal car today, sir. I didn't want to draw a lot of unnecessary attention."

"Bill Howard, Sheriff," he introduced himself while offering his hand. "What brings you to Overton?"

"Could we talk in private?" Con asked as he accepted the handshake.

"Sure. Come this way." He motioned Con into a private office with dimpled glass in the door. "Please. Make yourself comfortable."

Conor pulled the bankbook from his pocket as he sat down in the chair across the desk from the banker. "What can you tell me about this?" he asked as he handed it to Howard.

His face paled as he opened it and read the name. "Where did you get it?"

"I judge by the look on your face that you recognize it."

"Of course I do. It's one of our bank savings books."

"Do you know the owner of this book...personally?"

"I have met her on several occasions, but I do not know her outside the walls of this building, sir," he answered as he passed the booklet back to Sheriff Armenta.

"Have you seen her recently?"

"No, not for several months."

"Not since she mysteriously disappeared eight or nine months ago."

"That is correct, sir," the banker responded. By now, his face lost all color. Con felt that if he'd seen the man lying down with closed eyes, he would presume the banker dead. That is, except for the droplets of sweat growing on his brow. Growing to the point of releasing periodic rivulets down his face to be absorbed by the starched collar of his white shirt. Bill Howard stood and crossed to a small cabinet against the wall. There he filled a cloudy glass of tepid water from a pitcher that sat on the cabinet. "Would you care for a drink of water, Sheriff?"

"No, thank you," he answered. Howard was not wearing his jacket. When he turned, the back of his shirt was wet from sweat as it ran between his shoulders to the vee in his suspenders. "Are you nervous, Mr. Howard? Afraid, perhaps?"

"Both would be correct, sir."

"About what you have done? Or what I might do?"

"Again, both would be correct."

"What have you done?"

"Nothing illegal, I assure you. It's more what I didn't do, I suppose." He drank nearly the entire glass of water in one gulp and refilled it. Then sat back down at his desk. "I should have called you...I should have called the first time that boy came in...I should have called every time afterward...I was afraid."

"Of the boy?"

"No, not really. Not him...who he worked for."

"Who did he work for?"

"I don't know. I only know that it was bad. I could feel it in the pit of my stomach. But there was a lot of money at stake. A quarter of a million dollars. Without the money that's in her account, I'm not sure we could have stayed afloat this past year. If all that money were withdrawn at once...we'd be broke...not two years ago, mind you, but now? That's a different matter."

"Tell me from the beginning."

"The boy came in—"

"Wait!" Conor interrupted. "What boy?"

"The Indian kid. Jimmy."

"Jimmy who?"

"I don't know a last name. Only Jimmy."

"Did you know him?"

"Never saw him before that day."

"What day?"

"A couple of months after Mrs. Wagner came up missing. It's in the book. The first withdrawal."

"What did he look like?"

"Young. Maybe twenty. Small, but a little bit stocky. Clean. Short hair. Always smiling and pleasant."

"No scars, tattoos? Anything like that?"

"He was missing a couple of fingers. Pinkie and his ring finger. Left hand I think...yes, left hand. Cut off right about here." He indicated the second knuckle on his own fingers.

"What did Jimmy do?"

"He came in with the bankbook and a note."

"What kind of a note?"

"A note from Katherine Wagner. I can nearly quote it. Dear Mr. Howard, I am sorry I cannot come in personally. Consequently, I have no bank slips. Please withdraw fifty dollars from my account and give it to my good friend, Jimmy. He is trustworthy. There will be no problem. Sincerely, Katherine Wagner. P.S. Please send a few bank slips with him also. I may be unavailable for a while."

"And you believed it?" Conor asked. He was incredulous.

"She signed it. I verified it against every signature I had ever gotten from her before I gave him the money. She signed it alright. It's a legal document."

"No signs of duress? No scribbles? Why would she do that?"

"I have no idea, Sheriff. I guessed she was being truthful when she said she would be 'unavailable.'"

"I would have liked to see that note."

"I will get it for you."

"You have it?"

"Of course. It's a legal withdrawal slip. Otherwise, I couldn't have given her...well, Jimmy, the money." Bill Howard left the room and in minutes returned with a file folder. He pulled the note from the file and handed it to Con.

The note was written on a piece of fancy stationery. Parchment, Con thought. The handwriting was smooth and flowing. Nearly as pretty to read as June's. No splotches of ink. It looked like it had been written at a desk and properly blotted. Mr. Howard was right. He nearly quoted it, word for word.

"The other withdrawals?"

"Same handwriting and signature." He took the slips from the folder and handed them to Conor. "All except that last one. I didn't give him the money on that one."

Con looked at the last bank slip. The writing was coarse and signature crude. It looked nothing like the others.

"As you can see, that was three weeks ago. He had the bankbook and that slip. He wasn't in his usual mood. Neither smiling nor talkative. Glum. Apprehensive, maybe."

"What did Jimmy do when you refused the slip?"

"He took the bankbook and left."

Conor began to measure up Bill Howard. The room felt warmer than it had earlier, yet the banker no longer perspired. Color had returned to his face. "Could I have that drink of water now?" Con asked. Howard rose to get it for him. He had calmed down during the questioning. I'm guessing he has told me the truth, Conor thought to himself as he took a cautious sip of the water. It was somewhat alkaline but better than most Nevada villages.

Mr. Howard was more at ease now. Confident that he would not significantly suffer from his possible misjudgment in the past. He thought everything would probably be alright.

"How did Jimmy get here when he came?" Con interrupted Howard's contemplation. "What direction did he come from?"

"He rode a black mule. He came from the south and returned that direction."

"Just rode in, got the money, then rode out?"

"Small town. People don't miss much. Especially when it comes to a stranger. No, he went to the dry goods store on his way out of town. He'd buy a half dozen books and a bag of horehound candy."

"Always the same? Books and candy?"

"Maybe some other little thing. He bought a little bottle of women's lavender perfume one time. Can of peaches another."

"Did it seem odd that he didn't show up last month? Did you notice?"

"Everyone in town noticed. That was part of the surprise when he did finally show up and didn't make any comment about being late. He didn't hardly speak at all actually. Peculiar."

"Curioso."

"What?"

"Nothing, just thinking out loud. Peculiar...in Spanish, curioso." The reminder of the Spanish word brought something else to Conor's mind. He took the buckle from his pocket. "Ever see this before?"

The pallor instantly returned to Mr. Howard's face. "I think so. It was much more beautiful."

"Where did you see it?"

"Jimmy had it on the last time he came in. I got that same feeling in the pit of my stomach when I saw him wearing it. Something bad in the air. He confirmed it with the forged withdrawal slip."

"Did he say where he got it?"

"I didn't ask." He thought for a moment. "There's something else you should probably know about. I'll get it from the safe," he said as he again left the room.

The banker returned with an envelope. "You should see this," he said as he himself studied it again. "You cannot have it, and you cannot open it." He handed it to the sheriff.

Con accepted it and read the inscription on the front. The same graceful script as the note. He turned it over in his hands and returned to the inscription:

Upon my death,
Deliver this envelope to Katie Brumbaugh.

Katherine Wagner

"When did you get this?"

"Mrs. Wagner gave it to me three years ago. She had very explicit instructions as to its confidentiality."

"Katie Brumbaugh. That's her daughter. Right?"

"Yes. She and her husband have a large tomato farm up the valley. Just above Logan. Hard workers. A couple little kids. Good people."

The timeframe of Mr. Howard's receipt of the envelope brought itself to the forefront of Conor's thoughts. He recalled that three years ago Katherine Wagner quietly signed over the deed to the family's small ranch to her son, Dutch. A matter of public record, but certainly not common knowledge. Dutch Wagner sold the ranch to Newt Campbell two months ago. If Mrs. Brumbaugh was not aware of the transfer of ownership three years ago, she certainly was then.

The banker interrupted Con's thinking, "How did the buckle get so beat up?"

The sheriff rose and donned his Stetson. "It got hit by a train," he replied as he walked out the door.

Bill Howard sat in a daze behind his desk. What exactly had he just heard?

6

At seven o'clock, Gary and Katherine Wagner were seated comfortably in Brice and Leanora Campbell's sitting room. This evening was by far not their first invitation to the Campbells' hacienda. They had been friends for several years and often shared supper at either the Campbells' or their own home a mile down the road. Sometimes they ventured down the road into town and dined at one of the restaurants there. This was a celebration. A bon voyage party of sorts. Brice Campbell and Gary Wagner were to embark on a once-in-a-lifetime adventure the next afternoon. They were leaving for Switzerland to climb the north face of the Eiger, a notoriously rugged peak in the Alps.

Leanora Campbell entered the room carrying four champagne flutes on a silver tray, followed by Brice with a magnum of champagne chilling in a silver bucket of ice.

"Good evening, my friends. May the festivities begin," Brice announced as he passed through the doorway.

"Where did you find that?" Gary asked sincerely. Alcoholic beverages were difficult enough to acquire during prohibition, let alone a luxury drink such as a quality champagne.

"I've had it hidden away," Brice replied. "Saving it for a special occasion. This seemed like a good candidate."

Brice expertly popped the stopper and began filling the glasses. Leanora offered the Wagners their drinks as Brice returned the magnum to the ice bucket.

"May I offer the first toast?" Leanora asked. Everyone agreed. "To a successful expedition, encouraged by the youthful aspirations of two not-so-youthful men. May you truly have the-times-of-your-lives." To which she raised her glass to the grinning quartet.

After the clinking of glasses, everyone took their first sip of champagne. Katherine stifled a giggle as she tasted hers.

"Are you alright?" Brice asked her, concerned their guest may have choked. "Is something wrong with your champagne?"

"No. Yes," she stammered slightly. "I am fine, and the champagne is splendid. What tickled me was how much better it is than the last champagne I had. Wouldn't you agree, dear?" She looked at her husband.

"Absolutely." Gary chuckled. "No comparison."

"I am sure Brice is as baffled as I am," Leanora began. "What is so funny?"

"When we were in Arizona, we had the opportunity to stay at the Hotel Escalante at Ash Fork. Katherine had read about it in a magazine," Gary added. "When we ate in their luxury dining room, we were surprised that they served us champagne."

"Was it bad?" Brice asked.

"No. It actually was quite good." Katherine entered in, grinning. "For sparkling cider."

They all had a laugh that began a joyous evening of laughter and celebrations. They talked through supper about the 'good old days' of living in oilfield shacks and working twenty-hour days in the Circle Cliffs of Utah. Gary and Katherine shared numerous tales of their recent adventures in Arizona. As they returned to the sitting room, they told of their meeting Jean and Rosalie Garnier from France and the mule ride to the bottom of the Grand Canyon.

"Oh, my word," Leanora responded. "I haven't been horseback in years. It would have killed me."

"I have barely ridden at all. It was wonderful. You would have been fine, Leanora," Katherine put in. "The views were absolutely breathtaking, and our crusty guide made sure we had plenty of breaks and lots of water." She had almost forgotten. "And the young man, Pecos, who was the camp cook at the Indian Garden? He was unbelievable."

"Really?" Leanora asked, urging clarification.

"He cooked everything in cast-iron pots over an open fire, and it all came out perfect. Roast beef, baked beans, biscuits, pies, cobbler...you just wouldn't believe how good it was. We ate there twice. Going down and coming back."

"And the food at Phantom Ranch," Gary added. "It was as good as we had in any of the fancy restaurants we tried."

"I don't know about that," Katherine joined back in. "The roasted squab at the Escalante was pretty spectacular."

Gary exaggeratedly threw his hands into the air and turned to Brice and Leanora. "It was a tough old chukar they shot out in the sagebrush and poured some sauce over." He winked to the two of them with a grin.

Katherine was miffed at Gary's remark until she saw Leanora break into a smile and knew that he had been teasing her. She slapped him on the shoulder. "You'd eat cold sardines from a can and think it was a delicacy," she threw back at him.

When Gary and Brice turned the conversation toward their climbing expedition, Leanora scolded them. "That's enough of that talk, now. You two are going to make widows of us girls while you go gallivanting halfway around the world for a month or more. Meanwhile, we get to stay home and keep your companies running for you." When she paused a moment, Brice started to attempt wielding off the chiding, but Leanora continued. "You two will talk about how great it's going to be all the way there. Then you'll talk about how great it was all the way back. There are a couple of ladies in this room who deserve some consideration on the last evening before your exodus."

Leanora's point was well taken and both husbands succumbed to more genteel conversation for the balance of the visit. At eleven o'clock, the Campbells bade their guests good night and retired upstairs to enjoy each other's company for the last night in several weeks.

* * *

SATURDAY, SEPTEMBER 22, 1923

Brice and Leanora were late to rise the next morning and relished the breakfast they had on the patio in the courtyard behind their Spanish-styled home. They talked of what a wonderful life they had shared thus far together and how fortunate they had been to have one another. They speculated on their future and vowed to spend less time working and more time appreciating each other's companionship in the years to come.

At two o'clock, both couples were at the station. The men brought trunks containing their personal gear but had arranged with their European counterparts to supply the equipment needed for the climb.

There were hugs and kisses and smiles and tears from all... then Brice and Gary boarded the train as the conductor hollered his, "All abooaard!" and they were off.

* * *

TUESDAY, OCTOBER 2, 1923

At a quarter 'til eleven, Agnes Spencer tapped on the door-frame into Gary Wagner's office. "Mrs. Campbell is on the line for you, Katherine."

"Thank you, Agnes," she replied as she laid down the letter she had just opened and picked up the telephone. "Hello, Leanora. How are you?"

"I'm just fine. Would you like to join me for lunch today?"

"What a great idea, I've been so busy with Gary being gone, I've hardly eaten a decent meal. Where?"

"The Nevada at noon?"

"Perfect, I shall see you there." She returned to the letter, postmarked Boston, four days earlier.

Dearest Katherine,

Brice and I have spent today scurrying around Boston like a couple of mice running from a cat. We have seen Paul Revere's House and been to Bunker Hill and a dozen other places we've heard about since childhood. Oh, The Old North Church should also be near the top of the list. "One if by land or two if by sea," and all of that. Sorry, if I sound sarcastic, I should not be. It was great to be outdoors today, after being cooped up on the train for so long and has been fascinating to see all of this.

Such a different world than Phantom Ranch only a few weeks ago. The scenery was incredible, but nothing as beautiful as you standing before me at the bathing pool. The most romantic moment in my life. A vision that will never leave my memory for as long as I live. I love and miss you dearly. I wish it had been you that I shared today with. Perhaps our next adventure together should be a visit here to spend a few days, instead of a few hours enjoying the city.

We set sail in the morning on the S.S. Bellingham...within spitting distance of where the patriots threw the tea into the harbor I would suppose.

With All My Love, Gary

When Katherine stepped through the door of the restaurant at the Hotel Nevada, Leanora sat at a table across the room, smiling and waving what appeared to be a letter, presumably from Brice.

Katherine retrieved Gary's letter from her purse as she crossed the room and waved it back at Leanora. "So, they've conspired to make us both miss them instead of being jealous that they are having fun, instead of working like we are."

"So it seems," Leanora answered as the two women exchanged their mailings.

The waitress refilled Leanora's glass with iced tea and filled a second for Katherine, assuming the nod from her suggested she also would like some. The ladies quickly absorbed the messages of the other's spouse. Katherine noted that both had similar information and likewise, messages of loving and missing them. Brice's letter was not nearly as suggestive as Gary's, she thought, unless he and Leanora had some secret code they used that no one else would understand.

"Okay, deary." Leanora stared accusingly at the younger woman across the top of the letter in front of her. "What happened at the bathing pool? I don't recall you mentioning it at supper the other night."

Katherine flushed to a bright crimson and took a drink of her tea while preparing a reply.

"So, I see," Leanora responded before Katherine could perjure herself. Then both women giggled knowingly before continuing on to enjoy their lunch together.

* * *

MONDAY, OCTOBER 15, 1923

"There's a young man here to see you, Mrs. Campbell," the receptionist announced nervously as she stood in the doorway of Brice Campbell's office. Leanora sat behind the desk.

"Thank you, Susan. I will come out." She stood and followed her into the main office. A thin boy of perhaps fifteen stood fidgeting near the front door. He wore a dark-colored, flat-topped cap with a bill. Like the ones some railroad conductors wore. When he turned, it said 'Western Union' across the front. It halted Leanora Campbell in her tracks. He held an envelope and a notebook in his hand.

"Mrs. Brice Campbell?" His voice cracked as he asked.

She swallowed and took a deep breath. "Yes."

"I have a telegram for you, ma'am." He handed her the envelope. "Would you sign here please?" he asked as he pointed to a line in the notebook and offered her a fountain pen. Leanora sat the book on the edge of Susan's desk and, taking a pen from its holder there, dipped it in the inkwell and signed the book beside the *Mrs. Brice Campbell* printed on the line. The line above read *Mrs. Gary Wagner* accompanied by Katherine's signature.

Leanora Campbell's face was ashen white when she turned and handed the notebook back to the messenger. Without a word, she turned with the envelope in her hand and began walking toward the door to the inner office. Her pace increased to nearly a run as she crossed the threshold and closed the door behind her. Tears of fear streamed down her face as she propped her back against the inside of the door. She composed herself enough to continue to her seat behind the desk and shakily opened the envelope.

LAUTERBRUNNEN, SUI.

MRS. CAMPBELL,

BRICE HAS BEEN CRITICALLY INJURED IN AN ACCIDENT. HE

HAS BEEN TAKEN TO THE HOSPITAL IN BERN.

JOHANN BERGER

Leanora knew the name. Johann was the Austrian mountaineer leading the climb of the Eiger. She laid her head on the desk and sobbed uncontrollably. Her worst fears were being realized. Brice had left on this foolhardy escapade, and now he was hurt and might die before she could arrive there to be by his side. Her anger momentarily overcame her dread and ironically gave her the reprieve she needed to regain control of her senses.

Leanora preferred to tell her daughter, Amelia of the situation in person rather than a telephone call. Besides, she would need to see her son-in-law about how to obtain a passport before she could do anything more. Since their marriage, Amelia has acted as her attorney husband's secretary in order to save money toward purchasing a family home of their own.

Leanora called Katherine.

"Wagner Trucking, may I help you?"

"Katherine Wagner, please."

"I am afraid Mrs. Wagner cannot come to the telephone right now."

"Agnes?"

"Yes."

"This is Leanora Campbell,"

"I'm sorry, Mrs. Campbell. She's locked the office door and won't answer when I try to talk to her."

"I will come over there."

"Thank you."

Wagner Trucking was only a few minutes away from Fremont Construction.

"Susan, I'm going to Wagner Trucking," she told her receptionist as she headed out the door. "I may not be back."

Minutes later she arrived at Wagner Trucking.

"Hello, Agnes. What happened?"

"She received a telegram, opened it, read it, and without a word, went in there, closed the door and locked it. She's not answered when I've tried to talk to her through the door. I can hear her crying sometimes."

Leanora crossed to the door of Gary's office and knocked loudly. "Katherine? It's Leanora."

No answer.

"Are you okay?"

No answer.

"Do I need to call Sheriff Baker to break the door down?"

She waited. She could hear movement from inside. The door opened, and Katherine handed a wadded piece of paper to Leanora...it was the telegram. Leanora unfolded it as she followed Katherine into the office, and Katherine closed the door behind them.

LAUTERBRUNNEN, SUI.
MRS. WAGNER,
GARY HAS BEEN KILLED IN A FALL. HIS BODY IS BEING RECOVERED AND WILL BE TAKEN TO WIDMER LEICHEN- HALLE IN INTERLAKEN.
JOHANN BERGER

Leanora wrapped her arms around the again-sobbing woman.

* * *

WEDNESDAY, OCTOBER 17, 1923

At two o'clock in the afternoon, Amelia and Robert Westcott stood on the platform with Amelia's mother as she waited to board her train. Little shade could be found for relief from the sun. They huddled in the doorway of the station.

"I am so nervous," Leanora attested.

"Don't worry, Mrs. Campbell," Bob Westcott reassured her. "I talked to the passport office in Salt Lake City on the telephone. They have everything ready to issue an emergency passport to you in the morning. You have your photograph and identification with you, right?"

"Yes, it's right here." Leanora showed him the envelope she carried in her purse.

"Good! That's all you will need. Your train will arrive there early in the morning. You can take a cab to get your passport and your connection to Boston won't leave there until late in the afternoon. You will have plenty of time."

"Okay." Leanora nodded. "How I wish your brother could have gone with me," she told Amelia.

"He will meet you at the station in Cheyenne. If the train is on schedule, you'll have time to visit," Amelia told her. "If not, at least a cup of coffee, maybe."

A moment later, the conductor stepped down from the passenger car onto a small portable step then to the platform. There appeared to be a half-dozen other passengers crossing the rough wooden deck toward the conductor. Robert had checked Leanora's trunk in with the agent earlier, and they had seen it loaded into the baggage car. He now picked up her small carpetbag and escorted the two ladies toward the conductor.

"Why do you still use that dirty old thing?" Amelia reproached her mother about her antiquated luggage.

"It was your grandfather's...and I like it," Leanora replied haughtily, resulting in a broad grin from Robert Westcott.

Amelia kissed her mother's cheek, and they both began to cry as they hugged each other goodbye. Robert gave Leanora a warm hug and held her arm as she climbed the steps up to the little platform at the front of her car. She turned at the top of the steps to receive her bag and scarcely had a hand on it when the conductor hollered his, "All abooaard!" and tossed the little portable step at her feet.

A blast of air signaled the release of the brakes, and the train began moving just as Leanora found her seat. She quickly waved to the *children* through the open window as they waved back to her from below. They rapidly disappeared from her sight. She put her handkerchief to the corner of her eye to dry a lingering tear. Suddenly overwhelmed, she covered her face and wept freely into it in silence. Leanora was a strong-willed woman and soon regained herself. She lowered the kerchief and looked around the car. Either the others had not noticed her lamentation, or they discreetly avoided her glance.

The past two days had been a whirlwind of emotion. Gary Wagner was dead, and Brice had fallen. Perhaps by now, he had succumbed to his own injuries. Sorrow, fear, anxiety, anger...yes, anger too...all rushed through her entire being. Why had these grown men determined it so necessary to exploit their very lives on such a dreadful venture? She stared out at the endless desert that blasted like a furnace back into her face through the open window. She could not ignore it, so she defied it. Daring it to make her cry again, she turned and faced it straight on.

Gradually, Leanora Campbell returned to reality. Had she dozed off? She must have, though she still sat very upright in her seat. How much time had passed? They wound through a shadowy canyon. The sun had not set but did not reach the bottom. It was cooler now, but not cool enough to warrant closing the window. She felt calmer. Peaceful.

* * *

WEDNESDAY, NOVEMBER 7, 1923

A drizzling rain fell through cool, late-morning air onto the concrete platform as Leanora stepped off the train in Bern. The sky was gray and dismal. It suited her mood. She was thankful at least for the versatile wool cape she wore to travel. It could serve as a blanket or a pillow as necessity arose. Or as today, for its intended purpose as a cloak.

A sandy-blond-haired man standing beneath the awning near the station started toward her. Rather tall, he crossed the distance quickly in a graceful stride. He wore a dark-green wool fedora that looked soft and comfortable. His broad shoulders were not disguised beneath the oversized flannel shirt he wore, and his suspenders looked overextended as they stretched across his barrel-shaped chest. His sleeves, rolled up to the elbow, strained around large forearms that reminded Leanora of a man who had worked for her father when she was a girl. Her father had told her that the man acquired his massive hands and forearms from many years of swinging a hammer against a hand drill in the coal mines of Wales before coming to America. The weathered features of the man approaching her belied his youth. Leanora suspected he was barely past thirty when he spoke.

"Mrs. Campbell?" he asked with a thick Germanic accent.

"Yes?"

"Johann Berger," he replied as he doffed his hat, seemingly impervious to the rain that, without a jacket, rapidly dampened his shirt. "I am at your service, madam. I have my car and can drive you wherever you wish, the hospital, your hotel…have you eaten? Perhaps a restaurant?"

"The hospital first. How is Brice? Can you tell me what happened?"

"Your husband has broken his back, multiple fractured vertebrae. He also has four broken ribs, a broken leg, and a concussion. When he's conscious, he can move his feet and toes, so they believe he will be able to walk once he heals. Brice is in a lot of pain, and the doctors are keeping him sedated to the point of unconsciousness most of the time."

"What happened? How did he fall?"

Johann began telling the story, amid getting Leanora and her baggage to his car. He spoke English quite well, and she had little difficulty understanding him.

"There were six of us. Three pairs and each pair accustomed to climbing together. I led off with my climbing partner, Jakob Kohler, second. Since Gary could speak some French and both of the Frenchmen could speak some English, Gary was fourth in climbing order. Brice was third. Adrien LeBeau and Xavier Fortin followed in the fifth and sixth positions.

"Everything was good on the first day. We all worked together and made great progress. Middle of the second day, Xavier smashed his thumb. Though it looked nasty, he assured the rest of us that the pain was minimal, and he would not slow us down. He traded places with Adrien so he would have a climber behind him. He communicated well with Gary, and we continued without problems. A storm came in that night. The surface completely iced over, and fog engulfed the mountain. Xavier's thumb turned black and froze overnight. The beginning of the third day, we discussed our dilemma and elected to begin our descent.

"By noon, Xavier had nearly lost consciousness. We wrapped him in blankets and a tent like a mummy and lowered him down in stages. We changed our order. I led. Brice second. Gary followed Brice, and he and Adrien lowered Xavier between them. Jakob was last.

"A couple of hours later, a piton pulled out of the ice between Adrien and Xavier. Adrien called out to Gary to brace himself and Gary to Brice. When the rope between Adrien and Xavier scraped across the jagged rocks, it cut in two. The whole weight of Xavier's body hit the piton nearest Gary, and it, too, pulled out.

"Gary hollered, 'Hang on, Brice!' I heard him.

"Brice's foot got tangled in the rope between him and me. That may have saved his life. When Gary fell, still tied to Xavier, they dropped about six meters. The rope broke between Gary and Brice. Gary and Xavier plummeted to their deaths. Gary screamed..."

The narration paused for several minutes as Johann drove silently toward the hospital. The burly man stared straight ahead, and Leanora caught the glimpse of a tear as it rolled down his cheek.

Johann cleared his throat and continued. "When the rope broke, there was one piton between Brice and me. His foot was tangled in the rope, and he fell about ten meters when he hit the end of the slack in the rope and jerked me into the piton. The piton held, but when Brice hit the end of the rope, it slapped him into the face of the mountain. Hanging by his foot, he was unconscious or perhaps dead. I did not know. I was helpless. I could not move with his weight holding me tightly into the piton against the face. I could not see them, but I called to Jakob and Adrien. They did not hear me.

"I weighed my options. If Jakob and Adrien did not come, I would be forced to cut Brice free. It was the first time in all my years of climbing that I feared for my life. I waited.

"It seemed a long time, but probably not. The fog shifted for a moment, and I saw movement above me to my left. I called out. It was Adrien. The fog had moved back in between us, but he had seen me. Help was coming.

"Jakob and Adrien climbed down to Brice, still hanging upside down. They said he was alive and began working to get both of us out of the predicament we were in. That being accomplished we prepared to bivouac for the night.

"Brice had only regained consciousness for a few moments during the night, and his speech was incoherent. The weather was better, and we bundled him up, much the same as we had done with Xavier."

As they pulled up in front of the hospital, Johann concluded the story. "The three of us got him off the mountain on the fourth day. That is when I telegraphed you and Mrs. Wagner," he concluded, then climbed out and rounded the car to open Leanora's door for her. There was no braggadocio in Johann's story or tone. She was certain of its authenticity.

* * *

THURSDAY, DECEMBER 13, 1923

Brice and Leanora Campbell sat side by side in silence as the train rolled westward across the plains of Minnesota. Half sedated with laudanum, Brice drifted in and out of sleep. Leanora stared blankly through space at the bleak midwestern plains. A strong north wind blew snow across the scene outside the window of their car. Ghostly cyclones surrounded telegraph poles that dared to interrupt its path. The landscape seemed nearly flat. It reminded Leanora of home as she watched through the center of the glass encircled by heavy frost growing to rippled ice framing the opening. Home, not Las Vegas, where they lived now. Wyoming, where she was born...and lived until not that many years ago. The country-side looked much the same as it would outside Cheyenne this time of year. She would verify that in a couple of days when they passed through there.

Leanora longed to be home. No longer Wyoming, but home now. Relaxing in the sunny courtyard of their hacienda near Las Vegas. It seemed so long since she sat outside in the sun. She had been gone for two months. Journeying to Switzerland where she spent most days sitting beside her husband in his hospital bed. Then caring for him, semi-crip-pled, as they crossed western Europe by train then steamed across the Atlantic, and again by train, traversed half of America to spend another month of multiple surgeries at the Mayo Brothers' hospital in Rochester, Minnesota. Now Brice was well on his way to recovery. His pain had diminished significantly and mobility improved greatly. And after surviving what seemed a never-ending series of obstructions, they would be home before Christmas.

7

At half-past six in the morning, Sheriff Conor Armenta strolled into the office and filled a cup with coffee. Hazel had already arrived and sent Dottie, the night dispatcher, home for the day.

"You're here early," Conor commented cheerfully.

"Not much going on at home. Frank has been staying out at Boulder City since they started working seven days a week," she commented dryly. "He manages to make it in on Friday nights to drop off his paycheck and dirty laundry."

"That should be encouraging."

"Dirty laundry?" she questioned sarcastically.

"No, that he brings you his paycheck."

"Oh, I guess so."

"I'm sure many of his coworkers cash their checks at the first saloon they come to and their wives never see any of it."

"You're probably right. He is a good man. I should be more

appreciative," she contemplated. "But it sure is lonely with him working way out there."

"Still better than being at home and not working," Con reassured her.

"Very true," she agreed. "Oh, I almost forgot. Hal called yesterday afternoon. He's finished with his autopsy. He wants you to come over to the morgue first thing this morning."

Conor went into his office and shuffled through the disarray of papers and notes scattered on his desk. He doubted Hal would be at the morgue before eight. He sorted the papers into three piles. Nothing accomplished, but it looked more organized.

He turned to yesterday's *Evening Review* that he brought from his front porch this morning. The headline read, "John Doe Hit by Train Sunday Near Crystal." The column was not much more informative than the headline other than mentioning the body being mangled beyond identity. Well, the newspaper doesn't know any more than we do, Conor concluded.

At a quarter to eight, Conor drove to the morgue. He found Hal in his office.

"Good morning, Con," he greeted, grinning with pride. "Grab yourself a cup of coffee and a chair."

Conor filled a cup and set it on the corner of Hal's desk as he seated himself in the well-worn chair across from the aging doctor.

"I had to cut the glove off that left hand," Hal began, wanting to build suspense into the story he would weave for the sheriff. "Nearly destroyed the glove, but I saved the pieces if we need them for evidence. You will never guess what I found."

"Let me try." Conor scratched his chin as if in thought.

"The victim was missing his pinkie and ring finger. Previously amputated. Close to the second knuckle."

Hal sat staring at Con. His mouth gaped open in disbelief. "How on earth? Who told you? I never told a soul, but someone told you. They had to. Who was it?"

"Someone told me," Con began, trying desperately to keep from smiling in victory, "that someone else was missing a couple of fingers on their left hand."

"It wasn't me, so who was it?" Hal demanded, almost in anger.

"It's a long story. I'll fill you in, but I know you have more," Conor encouraged, hoping to reinflate Hal's ego that he had just blown to smithereens.

"He had beef steak, corn, and potatoes for supper not more than an hour or two before he died. I'd be willing to bet that it was sirloin steak, corn on the cob, and a baked potato along with an ill-gotten beer, if you care to make a wager, Mr. Smartass."

Con was surprised by Hal's sarcasm. He had not intended to rile his old friend. "You figured all of that out from his stomach contents?" he asked in amazement.

"The first part. The rest was the special in the downstairs bar at Dutch's Oasis on Saturday night."

"How did you find that out?" Con asked.

"I've got my own sources, too, you know," Hal responded with pride.

"So Dutch could be who scared him," Conor thought out loud.

"Scared who?" Hal asked. "John Doe?"

"Well, him too, but the guy who told me about the missing fingers was scared of John Doe's boss. Now we know who that might be."

"You're jumping to conclusions. Just because the guy had supper at the Oasis doesn't mean Dutch killed him. We both know that Dutch was in way over his head on that moonshine deal a couple of months ago. It could be any one of a number of lowlifes who frequent that place. There's more. I know how John Doe was killed," Hal added. "Follow me."

When Hal got up and crossed to the door, Con knew they were headed into the morgue so Hal could show him something. He was glad he hadn't eaten breakfast. Hal walked to a nearby table. Something round lay beneath the towel on the table. Con suspected John Doe's skull. Hal quickly flipped the towel from the face-down head, confirming Conor's suspicions. Hal slipped on surgical gloves. Parting the black hair at the back of the neck, Hal pointed out the small bump at the base of the skull.

"That's where the spinal cord enters the cranium," he said before moving the part about an inch above it revealing a purplish quarter-inch dot surrounded by a black smudge. "That's the entry point. Killed him instantly. There's not a single drop of blood outside the wound." Hal waited a moment as the pallid sheriff swallowed that acidy taste that had risen again in the back of his throat. "His brains were like ground pork, but I mushed around in there until I found this," he said as he removed a petri dish from under the edge of the towel and rattled its contents before handing it to Con.

Conor knew that Hal was intentionally presenting the evidence as graphically as possible. Getting even for his own earlier grandstanding. He accepted the dish as nonchalantly as he could muster and looked inside at a substantially misshapen bullet.

".25 caliber," Hal commented flatly. "More than enough at the range of a quarter-inch or so judging by the powder burn."

"You're right." Con nodded in agreement. "That looks more like the mark of a professional hitman more than a small-town hustler like Dutch." Conor contemplated the evidence, then added, "I need a good photograph of the buckle."

"What are you going to do?"

"Put it in the *Evening Review*," Con answered. "Maybe someone will recognize it."

"And maybe that someone is a hitman," Hal added.

"That too."

* * *

WEDNESDAY, JUNE 4, 1930

Again, Con arrived at the office at six thirty. And again, he poured a cup of the fresh hot coffee Hazel had already made before his arrival.

"Good morning, Hazel. Sleep well?"

"Good morning, Sheriff. You have a man in your office, waiting to see you."

"What about?"

"He would not say."

Conor entered his office. A native man Con guessed to be in his early twenties sat in the chair in front of his desk. Conor rounded the desk and sat his coffee cup down before taking his seat.

"I'm Sheriff Armenta," he announced. "You needed to see me?"

The younger man fidgeted in his seat. "Yes, sir."

"What about?"

"I know the owner of the buckle," he said. "The one in the newspaper."

"And who might that be?"

"Jimmy Garza."

Conor nearly lost his footing on the office floor. "Jimmy who?" he asked, wondering if he had misunderstood. His old family friend, Luis Garza, was the only Garza he had ever heard of.

"Garza, sir," the young man repeated as Con walked to the door and closed it.

"And what is your name?" Con asked as he returned to his desk and sat down.

"Lonny, sir. Lonny Tido."

"How do you know this belt buckle belonged to Mr. Garza?"

"I seen it. Seen him wearin' it."

"When?"

"All the time. Every time I seen him."

"Do you know Mr. Garza well?"

"Sure. Since we were kids. His name was Pete back then."

"Pete Garza?"

"No. Jimmy Pete."

"Does Jimmy have any identifying marks? Tattoos? Scars? Or a mole somewhere, maybe?"

"Is Jimmy the guy who got hit by the train?" Lonny asked.

Conor was unsure how much information he was willing to share with this young man. He wanted Jimmy's murder to be kept secret for as long as he could. "I suppose that's a possibility," he finally answered. "Are you sure this is the same buckle Jimmy wore?"

"I'm sure," Lonny nearly shouted. "How'd it get all smashed up?"

Lonny was getting annoyed, and Con did not want to lose this young man's trust as a material witness in a murder case.

Conor remained cool and calm. "I don't know. What you saw in the newspaper is exactly the way I found it." Con spent a moment carefully choosing his next question. "You're sure Jimmy had no scars or tattoos?"

Lonny drew a deep breath. "He got his little finger and the one next to it cut off in a saw when we were fourteen," he answered calmly. "His left hand."

"You're sure," Con stated, more than asked, but awaited confirmation.

"I was there," Lonny stated. "I seen it happen."

"Your friend, Jimmy," Conor proceeded softly. "He is dead."

Lonny Tido sat in the chair silently staring at the floor. His shoulders began to shake, almost imperceptibly. He was weeping.

"Can I get you anything?" Con asked him. "A glass of water? Coffee."

"Coffee," Lonny answered past the frog in his throat.

Conor picked up his cup and left the room. Closing the door behind him, he left it slightly ajar. He felt Hazel watching him as he crossed the room to the coffee pot. He did not glance her way. Con refilled his cup and stared at the blank wall above the pot as he silently sipped his coffee. The border of his puzzle had grown larger. Who was Jimmy Garza? An unknown relative of Luis? Or maybe the name is just a coincidence. In his experience, Indian men seldom showed their feelings. It represented a sign of weakness he supposed. Lonny Tido clearly mourned the loss of his friend. Con refilled his coffee cup then filled another and returned to his office. Closing the door behind him with an elbow, he gave Lonny the second cup. The young man held a red bandanna in his other hand.

"You, okay?" Conor asked.

He nodded his head. "Yeah."

"How long have you known Jimmy?"

"My whole life. We're cousins. Or stepcousins, I guess. Rayno Pete is my uncle. My mother's brother."

"How long has Jimmy had the buckle?"

"A couple of months, I guess. I saw it once before that."

"Do you know where he got it? It's pretty unusual."

"An old woman gave it to him. He was taking care of her."

"How did he take care of her?"

"She stayed in a house out in the desert. He just kind of watched over her. Kept her company. Made sure she was okay. She cooked food for him and read stories to him. He really liked her. He liked the buckle too, and she let him wear it to town once. She told him that he could have it when she went back home."

"And that was about two months ago?"

"Yeah, something like that."

Conor paused in his questioning to catalog the conversation in his mind. He opted not to take notes to avoid intimidating his witness.

"Where is this house at?"

"He never really said. I kind of think it's over by White Basin somewhere."

"Did he mention water?"

"That's one of the things he did for the woman. Brought water from the spring."

"Did she pay him to stay there?"

"No, her son who lived here in town. He paid Jimmy to look after her."

"And Jimmy never mentioned her name?"

"Nope."

"Or the son's either?"

"No. He was kind of secretive about the whole thing. Said he got paid real good though."

Those secretive kinds of jobs often do pay well, Con thought to himself. Especially if the work is illegal. Like kidnapping some wealthy woman and holding her prisoner. Why? Not for ransom. The person who would be targeted for ransom was paying him to do it. And the prisoner paid him too. Conor tried to make sense of it without conclusion. He changed the subject.

"You said Jimmy Garza's name used to be Jimmy Pete. When did he change it?"

"When we were twelve, they sent us to the Indian School at Fort Mojave. When we got there, the White woman called our names. When she called, 'Jimmy Garza,' no one answered. She looked right at Jimmy and called it again. When he still did not answer she came over and hit him, then asked him, 'Are you Jimmy Garza?' Jimmy said, 'I'm Jimmy Pete.' She said, 'Your birth certificate says your father's name is Garza. You are Jimmy Garza.' When Jimmy tried to tell her otherwise, she hit him again. He was Jimmy Garza after then."

"You said you saw it when Jimmy lost his fingers."

"They were teaching us to be cabinet makers at the school. One day Jimmy was cutting a board on the table saw, and it jammed. When he was getting it free, he slipped, and his hand hit the saw. There was blood everywhere. The teacher was mad and yelling at Jimmy, then he took him to the doctor, and they sewed him up."

"How long were you at the school together?"

"'Til we were eighteen."

"That's a long time."

"Six years. Never got to see our families. Not even once in

six years. We were supposed to forget we were Indians. Become White men." His demeanor changed, and he smiled but almost sneered. "But they sure called us stupid Indians every time they tried to beat it out of us."

Con was aghast, but he had heard stories like this before. "It must have been hard for you. Alone."

"We always had each other," Lonny responded. Sounding positive as he spoke, a tear rolled down his cheek.

Not anymore, Conor thought...and he was sure Lonny thought the same thing.

"More coffee?"

Lonny shook his head.

"So, you know Jimmy's parents? Who are they?"

"Rayno and Tomanie Pete. They live up at Acton."

"Thank you for all of your help, Lonny," Con concluded. "We may never have found out who Jimmy was without it. I need to ask that you keep this to yourself for a couple of days until I can notify his parents. I don't want them to read his name in the *Evening Review*."

"I won't tell anyone, sir."

"Thank you," Con replied sincerely. "Is there some way I can get a hold of you if I need to?"

"Ernst Steinberg's Furniture Shop."

"I guess the trade you learned at the Indian school helped out some after all."

"Helped some ways. Hurt in others."

"I think I understand," Conor answered. He offered Lonny his hand as they stood. "I am sorry you lost your friend."

* * *

At ten forty-five, Con laid his fourth dull pencil beside the notepad on his desk. He had nearly filled it. It started with his interview of Lonny Tido. Then continued by transferring notes he had made in his tally book while waiting in his car for June near Logan. After completing that task, Con realized he had failed to record his conversation with Mr. Howard, the manager of the Moapa Valley Bank.

Sections of border for the puzzle began to fit together. Now he wanted to start connecting them...but too many pieces were still missing. The coroner would have his report later today. He needed more.

"I'll be out the rest of the day," he told Hazel as he donned his Stetson and walked out the door.

* * *

The county sheriff's pickup eased down the road into Luis Garza's hard-packed ranch yard. Proceeding at a pace slow enough to not raise dust, it rolled to a stop with a slight complaint from the brakes before the picket fence that surrounded the small house.

"Buenos dias, amigo," Conor greeted with a satirical smile as he climbed out of the truck.

"Buenos dias," Luis replied, lifting his glass of water in a toast as he sat in the shade of the front porch. "What brings you all the way out here?"

"How are your sheep?" Con asked the old friend.

"Nobody's shot any more of them since you cleaned those moonshiners out of the canyon," he motioned Con to a well-worn kitchen chair identical to the one he sat on.

"That's good to hear." Conor took his seat. "How are you otherwise?"

"I'm good. How's your papa?"

"He's fine. Says he's coming out to see you, but he works too much. Never has any time."

"What about that nice pretty girl?"

"June?" Con blushed. "She is pretty and very nice. I like her a lot."

"You should marry her. Start a family. Before you get too old."

"Yeah, maybe. That would be good." He nodded in agreement.

"What about you? Were you ever married?"

"Sort of. Long time ago."

"Do you know a Jimmy Garza? Is he family?"

Luis stood up abruptly, walked into the house and slammed the door without a word. Con waited. Through the open windows, he could hear Luis's feet shuffling across the bare wood floor inside the house. The old man mumbled under his breath, but nothing Conor could make out. Finally, the door opened.

"Who told you about him? Your father?" Luis's volume increased. "All the years I've known him." He was reaching a crescendo. "I thought I knew him better than that."

Con had known Luis his entire life. He had never seen him angry. Conor answered in a calm, steady voice. "No one told me anything. I just heard about a young man from Moapa named Jimmy Garza. Who is he?"

"He is Jimmy Pete."

"Then who is Jimmy Pete?"

"He is my son. He is younger than you. He should be twenty-two now."

"Why have I never heard about him?"

"It was a long time ago. Things were different then."

"You need to sit back down, Luis. I need to talk to you."

Luis returned to the chair he had been sitting in when Con arrived. "Is he in some kind of trouble?"

"He is dead, Luis. I don't know any better way to tell you. He died Saturday night. I just figured out who he was this morning."

Luis was visibly shaken. He slumped in his chair. "We were not close. He came to see me when he was eighteen. When he found out I was his father. His mother sent him to meet me."

"Can you tell me what happened? Why he didn't live with you?"

"His mother is Tomanie Pete. She was Tomanie Pahgoroo. Moapa Paiute. Her father was a shaman, Tomah Pahgoroo. We met one summer when you were a little boy. I was grazing my sheep up near the reservation. She was young and beautiful. Much younger than me, twenty years younger. But love does not know age. And we fell in love. Very much in love. We were married in a tribal ceremony. We spent the late summer and fall together. Then I had to bring my sheep back here for the winter. Her father would not allow her to leave the reservation for the winter, so she stayed up there."

"That must have been terribly difficult," Con tried to be consoling. Luis was fighting back tears, and it was difficult to discern if they were tears for Jimmy, or for his mother. Maybe both.

"It was hard being apart. I rode the train every month to see her. The second month she told me she was with child. That I would become a father in the spring. I began building this house for her and our child. It helped me through the loneliness.

"In the spring, I drove my sheep back there, and we were

together again. Tomanie lived with me in my sheep camp as we grazed our band across the desert. She took care of me and our camp. I took care of her and our band of sheep. In early summer, Jimmy was born. We took him to the Indian agent, and he filed the papers for a birth certificate. In the fall, we were to come here. To our house that I built for us. When we were leaving, her father came with the chief and other men and told us that Tomanie and Jimmy were members of their tribe. That I was not. They pointed guns at me and drove me away and forced Tomanie and Jimmy to leave with them."

"What happened then? What about your marriage?"

"When I got the flock home, I came back to see her, but was refused by her father. John Meriwether, at the trading post, got word to her, and she snuck away with the baby to meet me in secret. We did this every month. For four months. When I got to the trading post on the fifth month, Meriwether told me she had been caught returning to her father's home the last time I had been there. He beat her pretty badly and threatened to kill Jimmy. She would not be coming to see me.

"I drove my sheep up there a few weeks later but kept away from the reservation. In the middle of a moonless night, men came and shot up my camp with rifles and shot into my flock of sheep. They killed twelve of them. I hid, and they didn't find me in the darkness. I didn't stay in my camp at night after that. I slept nearby, but away from the sheep. A few nights later, they came back and shot things up again. They killed nearly all of my sheep and this time, one of my dogs.

"The next night, Tomanie came to my camp. She called to me in the darkness, and I crept closer and closer to her until I was sure she had not been followed. Then I revealed myself to her. We spent the rest of the night talking. She convinced me to take my sheep south and not come back, or her father and his allies would eventually kill me."

"You never heard from her again?"

"A couple of months later I got a letter from her. She told me the chief had dissolved our marriage, and the tribal council arranged for her to marry Rayno Pete. She told me he was a good man and would take care of her and Jimmy."

"And you stayed away."

"Yes, mostly."

"You still kept in contact?"

"About a year later, Rayno Pete came here."

"Here to the ranch?"

"Yes. He brought Jimmy with him. He was almost two. Rayno is an honorable man. He had raised Jimmy well. I played with Jimmy that day. And cried when he called Rayno Daddy." Luis could not hold back the tears any longer and wept uncontrollably for several minutes. "You won't respect me after seeing me crying like a baby," he began again when the tears subsided.

"I will respect you even more now, knowing what you have gone through all these years."

"Do you remember riding the train to Moapa and herding a flock of sheep back here with me?"

"Yes, I do. It was very exciting for me. I had never ridden on a train before."

"Do you remember the man that I bought the sheep from?"

"Sort of. He gave us a dog."

"That was Rayno Pete. The whole thing was an act, to make everyone believe I bought the sheep from him. He actually gave us those sheep, and the dog. That was his gift to replace my sheep and my dog that Tomah Pahgoroo and his men had killed. That's what he came to tell me when he brought Jimmy to see me a couple of months earlier. The truth be told, he gave me nearly twice as many sheep as I had lost."

"And you never saw Jimmy again until he was eighteen?"

"I saw him when he was twelve. I saw Rayno and Tomanie then too."

"What did Tomanie say?"

"She told me that Tomah died two years earlier."

"That's all?"

"They were sending Jimmy to the Indian School at Fort Mojave. She introduced Jimmy to me as an old friend of his father's. Then told him that his father and me knew each other very well."

"Then he came to see you six years later."

"At the school, they told him his name was Garza, not Pete. I don't know if he put it all together then that I was his father, but when he got home, he was eighteen. His mother sat him down and told him the whole story. Then sent him to meet me again.

"I told him I was proud of him for graduating from the school and not running away, like so many of those kids do. And how sorry I was that I hadn't been a better father for him growing up. He said his mother had told him what happened, and that if I hadn't left, his grandfather would have killed me and had threatened to kill him too. He didn't blame me."

"Then I tell you he is dead."

"How did he die, Conor?"

"I hoped not to divulge that until I had it all figured out myself. He was murdered."

* * *

THURSDAY, JUNE 5, 1930

For the third morning in a row, Hazel was already at the office when Con arrived. Before he could say good morning, she spoke.

"You have another visitor."

"Who?" he asked as he poured himself a cup of coffee.

Hazel nodded toward his office. "She's in there."

"She?" he verified.

"Yes, she."

The woman's back was to him sitting in front of his desk. As Conor rounded the desk to his chair, she began to stand. "No," he told her. "Please, don't get up."

The woman was younger than him, by as many as ten years he thought, but her face was weathered from working outdoors day after day. The kind of work that makes a young woman old before her time but outlives her city-dwelling counterparts from fresh air and hardy living. This woman reminded him of Juanita Chavez, an old friend of his parents who worked side by side with her husband raising fruit and vegetables they sold in Las Vegas. At the same time, Mrs. Chavez fed three meals a day to her growing family, rearing four children to adulthood in the process. Con's own mother lived a similar life, for that matter. Always working alongside his father.

Conor knew the lady in front of him, though he had only spoken with her once for any length of time. "Mrs. Brumbaugh, isn't it?" he asked, presenting his hand to the woman who stood before him after ignoring his offer to remain seated. She shook his hand vigorously with a firm grip. The hand was not soft. Though rough and calloused, he imagined it to be tender when consoling one of her young children with a skinned knee or bumped head.

"Katie," she said. "Yes, Katie Brumbaugh."

"What brings you here today, ma'am?"

"The buckle. The one in the newspaper. I know whose it is."

"Please sit down. Can we get you anything? Coffee?"

"Yes, coffee would be nice."

Con stepped toward the door. "Hazel? Could you bring Mrs. Brumbaugh a cup of coffee, please?" They both sat down as Hazel placed a steaming cup of coffee on the edge of Conor's desk in front of the visitor and returned to her desk.

"What can you tell me about the belt buckle?" Con asked.

"It is, was, my father's. My mother bought it for him while they vacationed in Arizona shortly before his death. It was a birthday present. She wore it in his memory on his birthday every year afterward. She must have been wearing it the night she disappeared. It hadn't been found among any of her belongings."

"That is very interesting. Have you heard anything from or about your mother since her disappearance?"

"No, I haven't. Dutch says she's off on a frolic with her latest boyfriend somewhere and not to worry about her. I don't believe him. Mother was never that kind of person."

"Dutch hinted at a similar scenario to me when I spoke to him a couple of months ago. Though I don't recall ever meeting your mother, I tend to agree with you. It doesn't sound likely to me either." Con rolled Katie Brumbaugh's suspicions of her brother and the evidence around in his mind. He carefully worded his next question. "Is your mother the kind of person who would give an expensive gift to someone she felt was loyal to her?"

"Yes, I could see her doing that. Are you referring to the buckle?"

"Just considering the possibility."

"I doubt she would ever give the buckle to anyone. That vacation with my father just before he died is her dearest memory of him. She told me, more than once, that they fell in love all over again on that trip. The buckle has kept those memories alive for her."

"If Dutch's theory is right, she may have fallen in love with someone else."

"I've measured that prospect too. I certainly wouldn't blame her. She's still a young woman, though I sometimes find it difficult to think of her in that way. I just can't imagine her not telling anyone before leaving on an extended trip. It's not as if some likely man disappeared along with her."

"Not from around here anyway," Conor added. "Perhaps she may have sold the buckle if in desperate need of money. Maybe escaped a kidnapper in some remote location and needed the money to further her escape. As I recall, at the time she disappeared, her purse and several hundred dollars were found in her bedroom. Not likely she would have had much additional cash in her pocket."

"Your second scenario sounds much more plausible to me, but she would have to be totally destitute." Katie Brumbaugh was an intelligent woman. This new possibility intrigued her. "How did you get the buckle?"

"It's evidence in another case I'm working on."

"Tied to Mother's disappearance?"

"I'm not at liberty to say right now, but I will let you know if anything turns up."

"How did it get so beat up? That buckle was beautiful."

"I'm sure it was. Perhaps a silversmith can repair it."

"You didn't say how it got damaged."

"Any history of what has happened to the buckle would be conjecture on my part. For now, I would not like a guess to be considered fact."

The disappointment showed on her face. "I think I understand," she resigned herself to accept the circumstances. She knew it had something to do with her mother's disappearance, but what?

"I am sorry to be secretive regarding this, Mrs. Brumbaugh. I am your ally, and I hope you consider me one. What we have discussed here should not be repeated. I need to find answers to many of these questions myself, before I can share them with the public."

Conor truly was sorry. The woman had been honest and sincere with him, and he could not quite return that at the moment. He would have liked to confide more in her, shown her the bank book, and heard her opinions on the contents. He would like to know her feelings about Dutch selling their parents' estate. She clearly did not trust him. More than anything he would like to know the contents of the letter in the safe at the Moapa Valley Bank.

The visit produced more questions, but one new answer. He finally knew for certain where the buckle came from.

* * *

When Conor drove to the Garza ranch, Luis awaited him on the front porch. Clean shaven, he wore a fresh white shirt and red bandanna. As he stood, he placed a nearly new Stetson on his head of a crease more commonly worn twenty years earlier. Con could not recall ever seeing it before. They met at the gate and shook hands without exchanging words. Luis climbed into the passenger seat of the sheriff's pickup as Con returned behind the wheel. They headed toward Las Vegas enroute to Acton, a community along the railroad north of Moapa.

Luis was quiet, and Conor did not try to engage him in conversation. Luis had asked to accompany him and was wrapped in his own thoughts…and grief.

"Pull into the Moapa Trading Post," Luis finally spoke, when they neared Moapa. "Meriwether will know where they live."

When they arrived, Con started to get out of the truck. Luis grabbed his forearm with a firm grip. "Wait here," he said and went into the building.

Fifteen minutes later, Luis returned to the truck. "Head to Acton, I'll show you where to turn."

As they approached Acton, Luis pointed ahead down the road. "Turn there by the red mailbox," he told Con. "The white house right up here," he added.

When they pulled in the drive, Rayno Pete was working on something near a shed beside the house. He stopped and watched Conor get out of the truck. When Luis climbed out, Rayno dropped what he was doing and ran to the rear of the house. A moment later, Tomanie Pete appeared at the door. As she stepped onto the porch, Rayno followed behind her. Luis crossed in front of Con and removed his hat, as did Con simul- taneously. Both Luis and Tomanie stopped a few feet apart, staring at each other. Conor was amazed. In her midforties, she was a handsome woman. She must have been beautiful when she captured Luis's heart.

"It is not good news, that brings me to see you," Luis said, choking back the frog in his throat.

"What is it, Luis?" She paused. "What has happened to our son?" she finally managed before bursting into tears. She nearly collapsed to her knees as Rayno caught her in his arms and, holding her up, guided her to an old sofa that adorned the porch. Con stood ready to do the same for Luis as he stood, with head bowed...quietly weeping.

Rayno stood beside his wife, now seated on the couch with her elbows propped on her knees and her face buried in her hands.

"Sit," he told Luis. Almost a command. "Sit down beside her." He pointed to the couch.

Luis lumbered shakily to the seat beside the love of his life. The mother of his son. The two people dearest to him in all his life. This person with whom he had been denied. He held his hat on his lap and stared down at it.

"What has happened?" she asked again faintly.

"He is gone," Luis whispered. "Gone from us forever."

"How?"

"Someone has killed him."

"The evil man he worked for?"

"I do not know," Luis answered and looked at Conor.

"I don't know either," Con responded. "I'm trying to find out."

Tomanie reached out and took Luis's hand. She inched closer and hugged his hand in both of hers to her chest. "It isn't your fault," she told him. "Jimmy told me when he came from seeing you that you felt guilty for not being a good father to him. It's not your fault."

Rayno stood beside her with his hand on her shoulder. He

loved her. Always had. There was no jealousy in him. He knew that Tomanie cared for him. They had been married for twenty years. They had taken care of each other and together cared for Jimmy for all those years. But her heart still belonged to Luis. It probably always would.

8

Katherine Wagner welcomed Brice and Leanora Campbell home from Brice's extensive treatment with open arms. She had met them at the train the previous day along with their daughter, Amelia and her husband Robert Westcott. Brice was pale and walked with a cane. Both of them looked exhausted. Katherine invited the Campbells and Westcotts to supper at her home this evening and all had accepted. She had been depressed as the holidays approached, not looking forward to spending her first Christmas in over twenty years without her husband. Meeting Brice and Leanora had invigorated her. She didn't have a tree, but had spent the prior afternoon and into the evening decorating her home as festively as possible.

She rose early this morning and drove to the Nevada Meat Market where she picked out a beautiful rack of ribs to bake a standing rib roast. She returned home to spend the rest of the morning making sugarplums. For the first time in months, she felt like living. She could hardly wait for her guests to arrive.

* * *

FRIDAY, AUGUST 7, 1925

In another month, the two-year anniversary of Gary and Katherine Wagner's Arizona vacation would begin. Katherine glowed remembering every detail of the romantic adventure. The problem that always arose when reminiscing on the bliss of those two weeks was the reminder of the tragedy that followed five weeks later. Katherine had repeatedly interrogated Brice Campbell on every detail of the events that took place on the north face of the deadly Eiger. He did not relish discussing the disaster, but had always been honest and truthful about it with her. She felt no reason to distrust him. Her son, Dutch, disagreed.

Dutch Wagner convinced himself that Brice Campbell's inexperience as a mountaineer and advancing age had somehow caused his father's death. He did not believe the account of the incident Campbell related to his mother. In Dutch's eyes, Brice Campbell had killed his father, and Campbell's version of the story was a coverup for his own ineptitude. Dutch loathed him for it. Nothing his mother could say or do would ever change his mind.

Katherine really didn't care very much what Dutch thought. She was repulsed by his choice of business. She had given him a substantial share of Gary's life insurance money to purchase an upscale restaurant. He used the money instead to open a soft drinks saloon and brothel in the seedy Block-16 district of Las Vegas. Hardly the kind of place she would patronize. Not that she was a proponent of temperance, but Katherine was certain he sold illegal liquor there also.

Since Brice's recovery, he had been very helpful to her with making business decisions. Katherine had always been involved in managing Wagner Trucking, but Gary was the brains when it came to operations and revenue. Brice had been a good mentor, and she could already see improvements in productivity and profits over the previous year that she ran the company by herself.

Leanora had been a dear friend and confidante in other ways. Every few weeks, Leanora had called or just showed up at the office to go to lunch together. It always offered a pleasant diversion. Leanora was a decade older than her and much more sophisticated in many ways. She had discretely urged Katherine into becoming more professional in both appearance and demeanor. Fellow patrons at various lunchtime venues may have disagreed on their maturity occasionally, if their attention was suddenly drawn to an outburst of girlish giggles from the ladies' sharing in some intimate quip.

Tonight however, Katherine would host Brice and Leanora Campbell for supper to show her gratitude for their help and appreciation of their sympathy this past year. At a quarter to seven, a robust rap brought Katherine to the front door. She greeted her guests with hugs and good wishes and escorted them to the sofa in the living room and disappeared into the kitchen. Moments later she returned carrying a tray with three glasses and a pitcher filled with iced tea. She sat the tray on the coffee table in front of them and perched on the edge of a chair across the table.

Taking a glass of tea for herself, she said, "I'd like to propose a toast."

"Sure," Brice responded.

"Go ahead, Katherine," Leanora added, remembering the toast she had made when there were four of them. Two long years ago. Dreadful years. Her eyes welled up, but she managed to keep them from spilling over.

"To my friends. My very, very dear friends...who have helped me survive these past two years...and helped me realize again that life is worth living. Thank you." She paused, wanting to say more, but found no words. "I guess that will do. Cheers."

They raised their glasses and clinked them lightly together. "Cheers."

The trio moved to the dining room and shared an enjoyable meal with pleasant conversation. Afterward, Brice stepped outside to smoke his pipe while the two ladies cleared the table. Katherine put leftovers in the refrigerator while Leanora prepared to wash dishes.

"Leave them in the sink, Leanora," Katherine insisted. "I will do them in the morning."

"Are you sure?"

"I'm sure."

They then returned to the living room and refilled glasses with tea.

"How are you doing, Katherine?"

"I'm doing fine."

"No, really," Leanora repeated. "How are you really doing?"

"Fine most days," she began. "I want to go there. See where it happened."

"Where? Switzerland?"

"Yes, the Eiger. I wrote to Johann Berger. Gary had his address."

Leanora was nearly speechless. "What did he say?"

"I've not heard back yet."

"How long has it been?"

"Two months. It should have been long enough."

"Yes," Leanora agreed thoughtfully. "I met him in Bern. Or he met me, I should say. A very nice and sincere young man. He chauffeured me around Bern for most of the first week I was there. I think he will reply."

"We should go together," Katherine blurted out.

"No," Leanora answered tersely. "I don't want to go back there."

"Have you seen it?" Katherine asked. "Did you see the mountain? The Eiger? Did you see where it happened?"

"Yes. I saw it when I went to Interlaken. I will never go back there. All that is there is memories. Bad memories. Days and days and days of bad memories."

"I'm sorry, Leanora. I didn't mean to upset you. I will go alone."

"Perhaps Dutch would go with you," Leanora suggested.

"No. Dutch would not make good company. He's become deplorable. He has that awful...that awful place."

"His soft drink saloon?"

"You know what it is, don't you? Where it is?"

"Well, I suppose." Leanora thought for a minute. "I suppose that I do," she finally answered, blushing ever so slightly.

"Besides," Katherine continued. "I have never told anyone this, but...he thinks Brice was the cause of his father's death. We know that's not true and don't mention it to Brice, but he will not listen to me. He's obsessed with it."

"Who is obsessed with what?" Brice asked as he came up behind Katherine. Neither woman had heard him enter.

"Katherine," the quick-thinking Leanora jumped in. "She's obsessed with seeing the Eiger. She's going, no matter what. You should accompany her." The sounds coming from her mouth raced away faster than her thoughts could catch up. "A male escort would be perfect. I would feel much better knowing she was safe."

Katherine was aghast. Unable to respond.

"Well," was all that escaped Brice's lips.

All three were silent. The two women shared the sofa, and Brice eventually picked up his glass of tea and made his way to the chair Katherine occupied earlier.

"When were you planning on going?" he finally asked.

Katherine thought for a moment. "Soon, I think. Before the weather gets bad."

"That would be good, I suppose," Brice replied as he stared into nothing, trying to wrap his brain around the whole concept. Planning, transportation, logistics of traveling halfway around the world with the widow of his best friend. Leaving Leanora alone again. They had not really been able to get their own lives back together.

"There's a lot to think about," Katherine offered.

"Yes," Brice agreed. "Yes, there is."

The conversation eventually picked up as each of them slowly warmed up to the idea. Leanora finally spoke on the subject all three were trying to avoid.

"I think you both need it," she began. "You both need closure. You both loved Gary. He's been gone nearly two years, and neither of you has fully accepted it. Maybe this will help you both."

They all further hedged around the subject until Leanora finally concluded, "We all have time to think about this, but not too long. We should be going," she said as she prepared to leave, "but both of you need this. You need to do this for your-selves and also for Gary."

Brice stood and worked his way toward the door.

"Next Friday," Leanora told Katherine. "Supper. Seven o'clock. Our house. Final decisions then. Do you have a pass-port, Katherine?"

"No, I don't."

"Talk to Robert. He'll tell you what you need and make the arrangements."

Leanora, who had initially spoken quickly to evade the subject of Dutch's animosity toward Brice, began weighing the possibility. As she began analyzing the prospect, she realized how the excursion may benefit both her husband's and Katherine's mental states. She had all but reached the final verdict for them.

* * *

SATURDAY, AUGUST 8, 1925

Even though she was late getting to bed, Katherine woke early. It was still dark. She went into the kitchen, filled the sink with water and began washing last night's dishes. The house was cool and dark. Gloomy and depressing in her judgment. She had left the windows open last night, and the morning air smelled clean and fresh. She made coffee.

Still in her cotton nightgown. Katherine walked out onto the patio with her coffee and sat down in the large wing-backed rattan chair that Gary had loved. Katherine hated it. The chair was big, awkward, and too heavy to move around easily on the uneven stone surface. But it was comfortable. She snuggled into the big cushions with her feet wedged into the corner and sipped her coffee as dawn broke over the eastern sky. Faint aromas of lingering desert blossoms slightly outweighed the insignificant mustiness of the upholstery. Wrens flitted about the wild desert brush. As it grew lighter out, they chattered and sang more and more. No cares, Katherine thought as she listened to them. She finished her coffee without noticing and watched as the sun rose a half hour later without moving. The wrens began quieting down, and as another half hour passed, they could not be seen. A new day had dawned.

She went inside and dressed in casual slacks and one of Gary's plaid cotton shirts. Far too large for her, she rolled up the sleeves and tied the front tails together at her waist. With minor alterations she could make it into a dress she thought absently.

Katherine walked to the garage and opened the doors to reveal the Oldsmobile coupe Gary had bought for her before their trip to Arizona. The dove-gray body looked fine, but the dark maroon fenders showed a coating of dust from the road to town. She climbed behind the wheel and made her way to town.

As she drove, thoughts of Gary's funeral strolled across her memory. Leanora had made arrangements and shipped Gary's body home from Switzerland when she was there. The casket arrived on the train and arrangements were made. She buried him seven weeks after he had been killed. A worthy group gathered in remembrance. Her children were there, no grand-children yet. The memory paused for a moment. She consid-ered the consequence, her grandchildren would never meet their grandpa, not in this world, anyway. The memory strolled on to employees and former employees. There were a few business associates, several from Fremont Construction.

Robert and Amelia Westcott. There were no other friends. They had none beyond the Campbells she could think of, as she turned the car into the cemetery.

A large sedan sat beside the lane. Near Gary's headstone, a tall man stood with a fedora in hand and head bowed. She parked behind the other vehicle. The man did not look up as she left her car and climbed the slight rise to the graveside.

"Paying your respects?" she asked as she stood beside him.

"Asking his blessing," Brice answered. "It is an awkward circumstance that Leanora has proposed."

"Only as awkward as we make it, Brice. We are both adults, and Leanora has given her blessing."

"Yes, but how does he feel about it?" Brice nodded to Gary's headstone.

* * *

FRIDAY, AUGUST 14, 1925

By the time Friday rolled around, it had already been confirmed that Brice Campbell and Katherine Wagner would travel to Switzerland together. Supper at seven o'clock became an opportunity to discuss final details of the voyage. They planned to leave for Salt Lake City on Monday. There, Katherine could secure her passport. Robert Westcott had made the arrangements. Much as he had for Leanora two years earlier.

Since Gary and Katherine's trip to Arizona, she had corresponded by mail with Rosalie Garnier who, with her husband Jean, they had met at the Grand Canyon. In lieu of departing from Boston, they would steam from New York to Marseille. From there they planned to travel by train to Saint-Étienne for a short stopover visit with Jean and Rosalie. Katherine telegraphed a brief message to Rosalie estimating the day of their arrival. They would probably be there before the postal service could deliver a letter. From there, their journey continued by train on to Interlaken, Switzerland...and the Eiger.

Leanora endorsed the arrangement completely. Katherine was somewhere between apprehensive and excited. Brice's level of anxiety could not be measured.

* * *

MONDAY, AUGUST 17, 1925

At ten o'clock, Brice and Leanora pulled up in front of Katherine Wagner's estate in Brice's sedan. The low-slung, ranch-style stucco home with a red tile roof suited its surroundings. Invisible from the road, it nestled peacefully in a little hollow of desert. Less luxurious than their own home, the Wagners' was far above average by Las Vegas standards, yet casual and comfortable.

Katherine met them at the door. Brice had delivered their trunks to the depot earlier this morning and now carried Katherine's valise as he followed the ladies back to the car.

They reached town intentionally early. Brice parked in front of the station, and they walked across the park to the restaurant at the Hotel Nevada. They were seated by a window with a clear view of the station. At eleven o'clock, Brice chose to order a hearty breakfast while Leanora preferred lunch, ordering a salad.

Katherine was about to order a salad also when Brice

chimed in. "You'd better fill up. The food on the train won't be nearly as pleasing as here."

"If that's the case," she told the waitress. "I'll have the ham steak with mashed potatoes and green beans."

Brice could not hold back a stifled chuckle.

"Well, you said to fill up," Katherine exclaimed.

"Oh, no," Brice replied, still grinning. "You're just fine. It's just that Leanora would never have taken me quite that literally."

Leanora slapped Brice's shoulder somewhat playfully at the remark. The incident helped relax them all. Conversation became light and cheerful as they enjoyed their meal. They had finished their brunch and were sipping coffee when the train pulled in from Los Angeles.

"No need to hurry, Katherine," Brice told her, pulling his watch from his pocket. "We have nearly an hour before our departure."

A short time later, Brice paid the tab and escorted the ladies toward the station. As they continued ahead, he stopped at the car and gathered he and Katherine's luggage. While Katherine and Leanora seated themselves on a shaded bench, Brice paced up and down the platform.

"Are you alright, dear?" Leanora asked him.

"Yes. Yes, I'm fine."

"Are you sure?" she clarified. "You seem awfully nervous."

"I'm fine," he paused in his pacing. "It's just not too often that a man's wife escorts him to the train in order to send him off on a two-month excursion with a nice-looking woman."

"Is that what's bothering you?" she scoffed. "Katherine has been our friend for nearly twenty years. Besides, if you remember correctly, this was my idea."

"That's another thing…" he began, but was interrupted by a long, sharp blast from the train's whistle.

Leanora rose and embraced her husband. "Don't be nervous. Everything will be fine, and I will watch after things while you're gone." She then kissed him long and passionately. "Now that will need to hold you for two months," she reminded him with a wink and a giggle.

She then turned to Katherine and hugged her. "You relax, too. You need this. It will be good for you." She hugged her again and added, "You have nothing to worry over either. Agnes will take care of business for you. I will check in with her occasionally. Just in case."

Brice grabbed up their luggage. Within minutes they had found seats in the passenger car and were waving through the window as a blast of air escaped the brakes, and the engine began its chug, chug away from the platform.

* * *

SATURDAY, SEPTEMBER 5, 1925

After their quaint conversation at the restaurant before their departure, Katherine and Brice became aware of how little they knew each other. They had been friends for a long time, but associated as couples often are by way of two men and two women. After nearly three weeks of excursion and much of that time spent alone together, they had become very comfortable with each other. Katherine recognized for the first time that she had not spoken privately to a man, any man since Gary's death. She also acknowledged to herself that she missed male conversation and companionship. She and Brice had become truly dear friends in the short time of their journey.

The two stood on the deck in the cool morning air watching the approach to Marseille. As the port drew closer, Katherine shivered in the breeze. It brought back memories of the morning she and Gary crossed the Colorado River on the ferry two years ago today. Brice wore a light jacket and put his arm around her shoulders to warm her. She turned to face him and slipped her arms beneath the open jacket and around his back. When she looked up, he was looking into her eyes. She pulled herself to him and closing her eyes, she kissed him... ever so gently on his lips. He did not recoil or pull away. She opened her eyes briefly. His face was an inch away from hers. His eyes were closed. She raised slightly on her toes and kissed him again. More passionately. His arms gradually encircled her. Then slowly contracted around her waist. The kiss became more intense. She was no longer chilled. She was warm. Warm clear down into the core of her soul. When their lips separated, she was gasping for breath. She pressed her cheek against his and softly kissed the neck that touched her lips.

Her legs were quivering as she gradually loosened her arms around him. She did not open her eyes. She was afraid to look at him. He relaxed his embrace just enough that she turned around to face the railing. His hands now held her sides just above her waist. She held onto the cold steel rail to steady herself, then opened her eyes. They were nearly to the port. Tugboats approached to greet them and carefully tend them to the pier.

* * *

Throughout the day, neither mentioned the improprieties of the morning's episode nor encouraged repeating the event. Jean and Rosalie Garnier met Brice and Katherine in front of the Saint-Étienne station at four-thirty. After a short introduction, Jean grabbed their luggage and pointed them toward his red Citroën Torpedo parked at the curb.

The Garnier home was on the far side of the metropolitan area which seemed similar in size to Salt Lake City. Jean and Brice engaged in casual conversation. Business since the war being the primary topic. Jean, a machinist, was somewhat familiar with the types of equipment Brice's construction company operated. His own company sometimes contracted to make parts for the manufacturers of similar machinery in France.

A half hour later, Jean brought the car to a stop in front of a comfortable-looking two-story home near the outskirts of the city. He sat their bags at the foot of the staircase.

"We will show you upstairs after supper," Jean commented as he directed them to the salon. "Would you care for a glass of wine? Or a brandy, perhaps?" he added, looking to Brice.

"I will take the wine," Katherine said. "It is so seldom I have had any recently."

"Brandy sounds wonderful to me," Brice answered.

Rosalie seated Brice and Katherine on a casual settee. She found her own place in one of two club chairs as Jean brought their drinks from the kitchen.

When they had drinks in hand, Jean offered a toast. "May you both have a fruitful journey."

As he accepted the toast, Brice puzzled over Jean's choice of words. Perhaps there was a slightly different interpretation in Jean's translation from his native French. It did not strike him as inappropriate necessarily, just unusual.

The pleasant conversation and drinks continued. As the clock on the mantel struck seven, a modestly plump woman appeared from the kitchen. "Si cela vous plaît de vous retirer dans la salle à manger, je commencerai à servir le dîner," she announced.

Brice and Katherine shared equally bewildered glances.

"She's ready to begin serving supper," Rosalie explained. "We're having clapassade for the main course. Do you like lamb, Brice? I remembered how Katherine enjoyed our supper at the Ranch Fantôme."

"Phantom Ranch," Katherine clarified. "At the bottom of the Grand Canyon."

"I almost put that together, but had forgotten where I had heard of it. To answer your question"—he turned to Rosalie—"yes, I enjoy lamb."

They moved into the dining room, where glasses of both water and wine accompanied each place setting. The table was not large. Jean held Rosalie's chair at one end of the table and moved toward the other while Brice seated Katherine to Rosalie's left and took his place across from her. He was unsure of the proper etiquette and hoped he hadn't done anything embarrassing.

Conversation continued as the woman who had appeared earlier brought course after course of what both Katherine and Brice considered a sumptuous gourmet meal. Remarkably, they did not feel overstuffed. Supper had lasted over two hours, leaving ample time for the digestive process between the variety of dishes. Now they sat quietly sipping coffee from dainty cups on the otherwise empty dining table.

"It is so wonderful that you've been able to comfort one another these past two years," Rosalie began as she softly took Brice's left hand in hers and lightly tapped his wedding ring with her thumb. "That you both loved Gary, and now you have each other."

Brice did not pull his hand away nor deny the implication of the kind of a relationship he and Katherine did not share... or did they? He looked across the table to Katherine. Her face flushed, but not from embarrassment. She looked away, staring blankly past him as she caressed her own wedding ring with her right hand...with suddenly a new sensation.

"I have seen that look on her face before," Rosalie continued.

The comment startled her, causing Katherine's attention to snap toward Rosalie.

"No?" Rosalie asked.

Katherine's face turned a brighter shade of crimson. She did not offer an answer.

Jean, seemingly oblivious to the recent conversation, spoke to Brice. "So, you are returning to the Eiger," he commented. "The Ogre," he went on. "That is what the Germans call it. Did you know that?"

By this time, Jean had pulled Brice out of his trance and almost sent him into another. "Yes, I have heard that before. L'enfer dans le ciel. Or something like that. That's what one of the French climbers called it. Hell in the sky, Gary told me. That's what it meant. The Frenchman never made the descent either. Gary died trying to save him."

Jean and Brice's conversation also caught Katherine's attention. A tear escaped her eye and raced down her cheek.

"I am sorry," Jean tried to backpedal. "I, I did not realize. I am no mountaineer, but I know enough to have recognized that Gary was a very good one. Excuse me, please." He rose from the table and left the room.

The dining room was silent. Katherine raised her napkin to

dry her face. She took another sip of wine as Jean returned to the room with a handful of photographs.

He handed them to her. "These are for you."

She looked down. The first was Gary climbing a nearly sheer face at the Indian Garden. She handed it to Brice. The next dozen images were all of Gary at Indian Garden. There were photos of her with Gary. Photos of them riding their mules. Photos of her on the bridge, crossing the Colorado River in terror as Gary coached her from behind. A photo of her and Rosalie soaking their feet in Bright Angel Creek with sunlight glinting on their hair. A close-up of the same photograph of her and Rosalie discussing the men they loved.

"That is the look." Rosalie broke the silence. "Is that the look I saw before?"

"Yes. I think it might be."

The conversation recovered for a short time. Katherine was nearly exhausted from the rollercoaster of emotions she experienced today. When Rosalie suggested they retire for the night, the thought of curling up in bed wrapped in the security of warm covers sounded oh so welcoming. Jean led the way up the staircase then Rosalie. Katherine followed as Brice carried up their luggage behind.

At the top of the stairs, Rosalie opened the door to the right. "This is your room," she said. "The bathroom." She pointed across the hall. "Jean and I are at the end of the hallway. Do not hesitate to knock on our door if you need anything. Bonne nuit."

"Good night," Katherine answered in scarcely a whisper.

Brice Campbell stood behind her in silent shock.

"We're in here," she said softly.

When Brice came through the door, she closed it behind him. He sat their luggage on the bed. Katherine opened her valise. Retrieving a cotton nightgown, she placed the valise on the floor and stood silently looking down at the bed. Brice found his pajamas and also put his bag on the floor. He then went to the door and shut off the light. Quickly, he redressed into his nightwear and climbed into the bed. Katherine carefully removed her clothes and laid them on the bureau. Brice could not help but notice her nakedness in the moonlight that entered through the window. He watched, mesmerized as she slipped her gown over her head and let it fall over her body. Cautiously, quietly, she crawled into the bed and eased onto her side facing away from him.

Brice lay on his back, staring into the darkness at the ceiling. His thoughts raced through the day. Katherine's kiss on the ship this morning. Rosalie's supposition of their intimacy, maybe even marriage. Rosalie knew nothing of Leanora or their marriage. She saw his ring, Katherine's, what else would she think? And her reference to Katherine's "look." What was that about? Was Katherine in love? How could that be? He was attracted to her. More than he would like to admit, to be truthful. Why hadn't he just told Rosalie that she was mistaken? Why hadn't Katherine? He rolled the images over and over in his mind. It seemed as if for a long time.

"Brice?" Katherine asked softly so as not to rouse him if already asleep.

"Yes?" he queried.

"Hold me."

* * *

WEDNESDAY, SEPTEMBER 9, 1925

The brief train ride from Interlaken to Grindelwald was scenic to say the very least. As breathtaking as the Grand Canyon but in an entirely different way. The overbearing presence of the Eiger drew closer and closer. Katherine envisioned a gigantic broken tusk protruding from the jaws of the Alps surrounding it, irritating its neighbors with the nagging throb of dentalgia. The labels Jean and Brice discussed a few nights ago sent a shiver through her. She slipped her arm through Brice's. In a new level of intimacy, she snuggled into him.

Johann Berger greeted them at the outdoor café Brice had chosen for lunch. The mountaineer was as young and virile in appearance as Leanora had described him.

"It is good to see you, Johann," Brice hailed as they vigorously shook hands. "This is Gary's wife, Katherine."

"It is an honor to meet you," he offered as he gently shook Katherine's hand. She felt like a small child as his massive fist engulfed hers.

"And you," she replied, unsure quite how to respond.

"You look well, Brice," Johann offered as they sat down. "How is your back?"

"Better," he answered. "Still painful. Especially when things are still and quiet. At night I occasionally allow myself to be overcome by it." He tried to change the subject. "Is this your first trip back here?"

"No, I have been here many times since..." He did not finish his response.

"Climbing?"

"Not since the day we brought Gary and Xavier off the mountain." He paused and turned to Katherine. "The day I telegraphed you." He looked away from them, understanding perfectly Katherine Wagner's need for this visit. "We have our demons."

They all sat in silence for several minutes until a waitress came around with coffees and took orders.

"Can you tell me what happened up there?" Katherine looked toward the Ogre.

"After we have eaten," Johann replied. "While we ride the train to Jungfraujoch, the top of Europe."

After lunch, Johann had begun telling of the tragic events of their climb as the trio walked to Grindelwald Station to board the train. Brice offered no additions to the account except when Johann sought verification.

They boarded the Jungfrau Railway and began the slow ascent upward. Much of the rail line passed through a series of tunnels penetrating the Eiger that protected it from the year-round snows that impacted the high elevation. A portal at Eigerwand Station looked out over the ominous north face.

When Katherine saw the vertical monstrosity closely, she could hardly believe these two men, her husband, and three others would attempt such a trial.

"Insanity," she muttered. "You were all out of your minds."

"Yes," Johann agreed. "Foolish." The most experienced and renowned member of the fated expedition regretted making the deadly attempt, his demon. A young man, he would regret it the rest of his life.

It was late evening when they returned to Interlaken Station and bid their farewells.

Brice held out his hand, but Johann walked past it and embraced him. "We are forever bonded by this catastrophe my friend. Auf Wiedersehen."

"Goodbye."

Johann turned to Katherine and hugged her so tightly she

could scarcely breathe. "I am so sorry for my contribution to your loss. Please forgive me."

"Thank you. I do not blame you in any way," Katherine managed to whisper. "Maybe now we both can find peace."

Johann bid a final adieu and waved as he climbed into his car. Katherine and Brice turned and began the walk to their hotel. As Johann passed out of sight, Katherine wrapped her arm around Brice's waist inclining him to reciprocate, placing his arm around her shoulder. They shared a quiet supper in the hotel restaurant, then took the elevator to their suite.

* * *

THURSDAY, OCTOBER 1, 1925

Joseph Mariano looked out of place when he stepped off the train in his Chicago attire. Dutch Wagner spotted him easily and crossed the platform to meet him.

"Mr. Mariano?" Dutch asked as he approached.

"Joe." The man smiled as he reached out to him.

"Dutch Wagner. Welcome to Las Vegas."

"Thank you," Mariano replied as he squinted slightly from beneath his black fedora onto the sun-soaked walkway. "It's a bit warmer here than I expected."

"How long are you in town for?" Dutch asked as they walked toward the station.

"Long enough to check out your operation and make a recommendation to my boss. So I guess that depends on what I see." His voice and demeanor were friendly and congenial. The pistol and shoulder holster that bulged beneath his jacket this hot day were not.

"I think you will find my business pretty well run, Mr.

Mariano." Dutch was lightly clothed, but began to perspire profusely as they stood beneath the awning of the depot.

"Let's hope so," Mariano commented in the same amiable tone.

Just then, Dutch caught a glimpse of movement out of the corner of his eye. He turned to see Leanora Campbell crossing the far end of the platform to meet someone. His eyes followed her path. Looking ahead of her, he saw his mother and Brice Campbell exiting the train. Joe Mariano followed Dutch's gaze.

"Someone you know?" he asked.

"My mother," Dutch answered, "and a business associate of hers."

Mariano chuckled. "More than an associate, I'd wager."

"What do you mean?"

"I rode the train with them all the way from Chicago. Deluxe private cabin, holding hands as they took strolls during stops, a rather extensive kiss when he held her chair in the dining car...a little more friendly than most of *my* associates."

"Is that right?" Dutch nodded as he watched them from the shadows of the station, and his blood pressure rose.

"But we are out west here," Mariano added. "Maybe folks are just friendlier here than I'm accustomed to."

"Friendly, but not that friendly."

* * *

TUESDAY, OCTOBER 6, 1925

Brice Campbell stepped into the office of Fremont Construction at seven thirty with the briefcase full of files in his hand that he had taken home to work on last evening.

"Good morning, Susan," he greeted the receptionist as he headed toward his private office.

"Good morning, Mr. Campbell. You have a visitor waiting to see you."

Brice stopped dead in his tracks. "Who would be here before we've even opened for business?"

"Dutch Wagner, sir."

"What on earth for?"

"He didn't say, Mr. Campbell."

Brice Campbell could not imagine what Dutch Wagner could possibly want. Leanora had paid a rather large invoice to Wagner Trucking over a week ago and well ahead of the due date. He reviewed the paperwork himself last night. Brice had never dealt with Dutch on anything.

"Thank you, Susan." Brice reassessed his appearance and continued to his office.

Dutch sat slouched on the leather sofa in Brice's office. He flicked ashes from a rather large cigar into the potted plant beside him as Brice walked in. "Sorry," he said, seeing Brice. "I didn't see an ashtray."

Brice ignored the comment. "Hello, Dutch. What brings you in this morning?"

"Just a little matter of a favor," Dutch answered.

Brice turned and closed the door. "What kind of favor are we talking about, Dutch?"

"The kind of favor where you don't ruin your high and mighty reputation and have to leave town."

"Dutch, really. What on earth are you talking about?"

"Your little indiscretions, Brice."

Brice tried to ignore the snide tone of this snot-nosed brat.

After all he is Gary and Katherine's son, he thought. If not for that, he would backhand some respect into him. But there is that. Gary was, above all else, a gentleman. How could Dutch have become this?

"I haven't a clue what you're talking about, Mr. Wagner."

"I'm talking about your little honeymoon trip to Europe. The problem is, your wife stayed here taking care of business, while you romanced my widowed mother to see, of all things, where you killed my father."

"You don't know what you're talking about. Your father's death was an accident, and I had nothing to do with it, besides—"

"I've heard your lame account of the *accident*," Dutch interrupted, screaming. He jumped to his feet as he hissed the last word. "You've brainwashed my mother with your lies, but not me." Surprisingly, his voice became calmer. "You will never convince me."

"If you don't believe me, perhaps you should ask your mother what the leader of the expedition told her while we were in Switzerland."

"Some other little worm you've paid to retell your contrived story?"

Brice visualized Johann Berger tearing Dutch's tongue out of his foul mouth for the slander it was spewing, without breaking a sweat. And he could do it. But he wouldn't. Not Johann, whose strength was beyond normal comprehension. He did not have a violent bone in his body.

"Nothing you are saying makes any sense, Mr. Wagner. I think it's time for you to leave."

But as Brice moved toward the door. "What about the deluxe private cabin you shared with my mother on the train?" Dutch took a seat in a leather chair across from Brice's desk. "What about the cute little strolls you took holding hands at the stops? How about the two of you kissing in the dining car?"

"And where did you hear all of this?" Brice snapped back in dispute of the accusation, even though he knew it was true.

"A colleague of mine happened to be on the same train last week. I was at the station when you and my mother got off, and you almost ran to hug and kiss your waiting wife, as if nothing at all had been going on." Brice was speechless. Like a schoolboy caught stealing his best friend's lunch, he was ashamed. He tried desperately not to show it.

"After a few hundred dollars in cables," Dutch continued, "I also discovered the two of you shared the Ambassador's Suite in the hotel at Interlaken for the several days you were there. It cost me dearly, but it was worth it." He had Brice Campbell exactly where he wanted. "Now you will pay for it."

"So, what's the favor?" Brice prepared to concede to this slimy imp.

"The favor is, I don't tell everyone in this town and everyone you do business with what a disgusting piece of trash you are."

Brice coolly controlled his indignation. "And in return?"

"In return, you will never see my mother again."

"That will be a bit difficult, since this company and Wagner Trucking do a substantial amount of business together."

"Alone."

"Since your mother and my wife are good friends, no more evening get-togethers? Wouldn't that cause suspicion if the normal socializing were suddenly to cease?"

"Intimately." Dutch was becoming impatient.

"That's all?"

"And you hand me one thousand dollars. Right now."

"That's absurd! That's extortion!"

"In the circles I do business in, that's called 'hush money.'"

"I won't pay it."

Dutch pulled his watch from his pocket. "Your wife should be arriving at the V.F.W. about now for the meeting of the Ladies Auxiliary. I can be there in ten minutes. After she rushes from the building in embarrassment, the rest of those gossips will begin talking. By noon, half the town will know, and by tomorrow morning, it will be old news. She's a smart lady. Within a month, she'll be the wealthy divorcée who owns Fremont Construction Company, and every good-looking bachelor in Clark County will be lined up at her door."

Brice reached into his top left desk drawer and brought out his checkbook.

"Cash," Dutch added.

Brice got up and walked to the safe in the corner of the office. From where Dutch sat, Brice blocked his view as he unlocked the safe. Dutch could not see the contents past the partially opened door, as Brice removed the cash. He latched the door and spun the dial before standing. Brice stood across the desk from Dutch and handed him ten one-hundred-dollar bills. Dutch took the money and stuffed it into his pocket without looking.

"Is that all?" Brice asked.

"No. From this day forward, Wagner Trucking will have a twenty percent advantage on every contract they bid to you. Whatever the lowest bid, add twenty percent, and that is what you will pay my poor, widowed mother for the service."

"Are you finished?" Brice asked, repulsed by the entire situation.

"See you next month."

9

Tomanie Pete turned to Sheriff Armenta. "Do you know the man Jimmy worked for?"

"I'm not sure," Conor answered. "Do you know his name?"

"No. He is evil. He sells women and liquor."

"How long did Jimmy work for him?"

"A year, I think. First making whiskey. Then…I never really figured it out. Sort of guarding a woman. Like a prisoner. Then more, kind of taking care of her."

"Did you know who this woman was?"

"She was his boss's mother. It was very strange. The boss is evil. The devil is in his heart."

"Did Jimmy tell you why this woman was a prisoner?"

"To keep her away from her boyfriend. His boss hated the boyfriend. He told Jimmy the boyfriend had killed the boss's father, then seduced his mother. Mr. High and Mighty, his boss called him."

"What happened to the mother?"

"Jimmy still took care of her the last time he came here."

"When was that?"

"A few months ago."

"Did he tell you where this woman was?"

"Out in the desert. Somewhere south."

* * *

"Do you know of any water in White Basin?" Conor asked Luis as they drove toward Las Vegas.

Luis Garza looked off in the direction of the basin as he contemplated the question. "Only when it rains."

"You used to graze sheep up here?"

"West of here mostly. White Basin is east."

"Yeah, I know. When we drove the band of sheep from the trading post, we stopped for a couple of days at a spring. Where was that?"

"Further east. East of White Basin. Bitter Spring. The water isn't very good, but it's the only place to drink for a long way."

At Crystal, Con turned off the main road and headed southeast on a scarcely traveled road through the Muddy Mountains. From there, use of the road diminished completely except for occasional traffic to a dozen borax mines scattered over fifty square miles of inhospitable geology known as White Basin. Heading east across the basin, Con stopped at a high spot along the road and retrieved his field glasses from the glove box. Climbing into the bed of the truck for better elevation, he scanned every nook and cranny in search of any sign of habitation or water without success. He repeated the process at every opportunity until the road turned south and cut between the ends of Bitter Ridge and West Longwell Ridge into the Bitter Spring Valley.

"Satisfied?" Luis asked him. "I told you. There isn't any water out here until you get to Bitter Spring."

Con failed to comment and continued southeast on the road to the spring.

"This is it. Bitter Spring," Luis told him.

"I remember it," Conor acknowledged. "Still looks the same. No shack or cabin," he concluded, looking over the surroundings.

"We rested them here. Two or three days until they filled up on water. Then we moved them on south," Luis remembered.

"No other water?"

"Some, here and there on this side of East Longwell Ridge." Luis pointed off toward the north from where they stood. "There is a sort of bench in the slope as it runs along the ridge here. There are some springs on it," he added, trying to put it into proper perspective for Con. "When we drove the sheep, we followed the river down from Moapa and trailed them up the road out of there through Bitter Wash to here."

Con analyzed his clues. Lonny Tido thinks Jimmy watched after the mystery woman in a cabin or a shack near White Basin. If he is right, there is a spring nearby. And by what Bill Howard at Moapa Valley Bank told him, it is probably within a day's mule ride of Overton.

"So, if there's a spring out here that few people know about, it might be out there?" Conor clarified, looking toward the bench Luis described.

"Maybe," Luis answered. "You're looking for the woman?"

"Yes. Someone killed Jimmy five days ago. If the woman has been out here since before then, probably locked in a shack, she could be in pretty rough shape by now. I think this should be the first place to look."

"I think so too." Luis nodded. "How are you going to get there?"

"One of Paddy's horses."

* * *

Con had a lot to do tomorrow. He felt an urgent need to get moving early. It was nearly midnight when he dropped Luis off at his ranch.

"I'll let you know when Jimmy will be buried," Conor told him. "It'll be a few days."

"Be careful, Conor. The last time you went hunting someone on horseback, you got shot."

An hour later, Con pulled in at his house. He began locating some of the gear he would need over the next few days, while awaiting his adrenaline to subside enough to allow him to sleep. He finally forced himself to bed and lay awake trying to make a mental checklist of all the things needing to be done before leaving. One item kept finding itself at the top of the list, call June. He finally drifted off to sleep, with her his last conscious thought.

* * *

FRIDAY, JUNE 6, 1930

Conor woke early with little sleep. Luis's last words filled his mind. He dressed in a plain khaki shirt in lieu of the white uniform shirt he normally wore and tucked his badge into his vest pocket. Pulling the Winchester 94 from his closet, he checked it before covering the rifle in a blanket along with two boxes of cartridges beneath the seat of his pickup. He loaded his bedroll, canteen, and jacket into the bed of the truck. Then a partial side of bacon, cheese, jerky, and fry bread joined his gear before covering it all with a small tarp.

He returned to the house and looked at the clock on the mantel as it struck six. Con sat down in his favorite chair. He picked up the telephone beside it and dialed.

"Hello?" came the sweet feminine voice from the other end of the line.

"Good morning," Conor replied cheerfully. "Did I wake you?"

"Heavens, no," June answered. "It is early though. Is everything alright?"

"I'm going to be gone for a couple of days, so I won't get to see you this weekend."

"Where are you going?"

"Out north of here."

"In the desert? What are you looking for?"

"Katherine Wagner."

"You know where she is?"

"Maybe." He didn't want to consider the odds. "I have an idea of a general area to look over."

"I will miss you."

"Me too. I've been trying to figure out how to get an invitation to Sunday dinner, but nothing has come to me. Looks like I'll miss out anyway."

"Leave the psychology to the ladies." She kept a chuckle to herself, but Con could hear the smile in her voice. "Next Sunday then. I have a whole week to plan it."

"I accept."

"Please, be careful."

"You know that I will. I have extra incentive now, looking forward to Sunday dinner with you." Some of the cheerfulness left Conor's voice. "I'll call you as soon as I'm back. Monday or Tuesday probably."

"I'll be waiting," June replied with apprehension in her voice.

"Don't worry," Con tried to sound stern.

"I won't." They both sat silent for a moment, neither wanting to say goodbye.

"I'll call you," he finally managed.

"Bye," came the soft voice from the other end of the line in return.

"Bye."

Conor found his seldom-used hunting knife in the top drawer of his dresser. He knew he didn't need to, but checked the blade for sharpness. He had learned his lesson at fourteen about failing to keep his knife blade honed. It had never happened again. He pulled the 1911 Colt automatic from its holster on the belt hanging from his bedpost. It, too, was clean and fully loaded. There were no empty loops in the cartridge belt. He added the knife to the belt and buckled it around his hips. Snatching his Stetson from the back of a kitchen chair as he passed, he donned it and walked out the door.

* * *

At a quarter to seven, Conor rounded the corner a half block from the sheriff's office just in time to see Hazel enter the door. Jesse Slater's patrol car sat angled in at the curb. He pulled in beside it.

When he walked in, Dottie Dickenson, the night dispatcher, along with Jesse and Hazel had the coffeepot, and a fresh bag of doughnuts beside it, surrounded. Jesse must have brought the doughnuts, he deduced. When he entered Dottie and Jesse both turned toward him with a mouthful of powdered doughnut. Each had half a doughnut in one hand and a cupful of coffee in the other. Both had expressions of surprise on their faces behind the white powdered rings encircling their lips.

"Are either of you seeing anyone right now?" Con asked, causing them to look at each other in even more amazement. Then he added, "Right now, you look perfect for each other."

They both looked at Conor in confusion then back at each other as he went to his office.

"Jesse?"

"Uh, yeah, Sheriff?"

"Don't run off. I need to talk to you."

"Got it, Sheriff."

Before Con could return for coffee and a doughnut himself, Dottie had escaped out the door at the end of her shift. He poured himself the end of the pot of coffee and helped himself to a doughnut.

"You bring these?" he asked Jesse, holding up the doughnut.

"Yessir."

"Hope you don't mind," Con added as he took a second bite and a sip of the coffee.

"Oh, absolutely. I mean, I brought them for everybody," Jesse stammered, still not quite sure what to make of his boss's earlier statements. "Help yourself. Have as many as you like."

"Thank you," Conor replied as he watched Hazel make a fresh pot of coffee. "You make the coffee too?"

"Why, yes, I did," Jesse replied proudly.

"Watch Hazel next time she makes a pot," Con added as Hazel plugged the pot back into the wall to brew. She turned to Con with her motherly scolding eye for chastising his pupil.

Conor rolled his eyes at her and turned back to Jesse. "You know where Bitter Spring is?"

"I've heard of it, but no," he answered, unaffected by Con's earlier criticism. "Up north somewhere, isn't it?"

"Yes," Con beckoned Jesse to the large map of Clark County on the wall. "Here is Bitter Spring," He pointed on the map. "I am going to search for a possible hidden spring at every hint of water drainage from there to Overton."

"Why are you looking for a spring?"

Conor looked to Hazel. "You both know how to keep an investigation confidential. This particular conversation is not to leave the three of us in this room."

"Yes." Hazel nodded as she answered.

"Got it," Jesse agreed.

"John Doe?" Con waited. "Is Jimmy Garza."

They both looked at Con in shock.

"He was Luis's son. I'll fill in all the blanks on that later. Jimmy has been a guard of sorts over Katherine Wagner for the past few months. She was, or is being, held prisoner somewhere out there. There is a building of some kind and a spring nearby. I've narrowed it down to that specific area as the most likely location. Unfortunately, the only person who knew for sure where it was, is dead. Not counting whoever he was working for. If Jimmy left Mrs. Wagner locked up out there somewhere, she's been at least six days with whatever food and water was left for her. Finding her is urgent. Probably a matter of life and death."

Conor turned to Jesse. "I will leave my brother's truck near

Bitter Spring. He will have my pickup for emergencies until I get back. If you see someone besides me driving my pickup, don't shoot him. I'll be gone at least two, maybe three, days. In the meantime, you're in charge, Jesse. No big ordeals, just float along until I get back. If you haven't heard from me by Tuesday night, come looking for me and be ready for anything. If something urgent arises that you need to make a major decision on, bring Judge Tucker into the circle to help with the process. For now, it's just business as usual. Does everyone understand?"

"Yes, Sheriff," Hazel answered.

Jesse took the indoctrination very seriously. "Got it, Sheriff. Any decisions beyond routine, hold until you get back. If it's urgent, call Judge Tucker and ask for assistance."

"Exactly," Con confirmed. "Go ahead with your work. I'll be leaving shortly."

After Jesse left, Hazel came to Con's office door. "I know you have a dozen other things of greater importance on your mind." She hesitated. "You realize that Dottie and Jesse have been seeing each other, don't you?"

Conor was somewhat stunned. "So my earlier comments were both in, and out, of order."

"So to speak, yes."

"I had no idea. I just…I hope I didn't interfere in any way."

"I'll let Dottie know that your comments were purely innocent. She'll keep Jesse calm." Hazel thought for a minute. "Part of the reason I've sometimes come in early lately is so they can go have breakfast somewhere before Jesse goes on duty."

"You and Jesse can bring Dottie into the circle, and your husband too, for that matter. I don't believe in keeping secrets between couples in a relationship. June knows what's going on."

"I'll fill Dottie in. Frank couldn't care less."

Con grabbed his hat and prepared to leave.

"Con." Hazel's face reddened, realizing she had not addressed him as sheriff. "Please be careful. One person has already been murdered. We don't need more."

"I'll do my best, Mother," Con answered and kissed her on her forehead.

"Speaking of Mother, go see her before you leave town."

"Yes, ma'am."

* * *

Conor pulled up in front of the Mesquite Café at a quarter past nine. The breakfast crowd had significantly thinned out. He hung his hat by the door and took a seat at the counter.

"Coffee or Coca-Cola, big brother?" Olivia asked as he sat down.

"Coffee."

"Where's your uniform? Too busy to do laundry?"

"Troy Steam Laundry does my uniforms," Con replied. "All my laundry for that matter."

"Well, you have your gun, so you must be on duty."

"Yes, I'm going out of town for a few days, so I decided to stop in before I left."

"Where to?"

"Working on a case I'm investigating."

Olivia's mind was moving too fast to realize he had evaded her question. "Ham and eggs are on special."

"Perfect."

"Coming right up," she answered as she turned toward the window into the kitchen and hollered his order to their father.

Their mother came over from serving a customer's breakfast on the far side of the room. She gave Conor a peck on the cheek and sat down beside him as Olivia poured his coffee.

"Where've you been? I was too busy to say hi when you were here for lunch Monday. I did get a minute to talk to June before you got here though. She is such a nice girl."

"Yes, she is, Mama." Con blushed as he thought to himself. She's nice and pretty and smart. And for some unfathomable reason, she loves me. And I am in love with her.

"...so, where are you going?" His mother was asking when Con realized he had been ignoring his mother and sister's conversation.

"Working on a case," he answered.

"Where?" she repeated.

"I can't say."

"Why not?"

"I'm working on a case."

"What kind of case?"

"A sheriff's department case."

"Well, that doesn't tell me anything."

"Exactly. It's business, and not your business."

"Okay, I get it."

"Thank you."

Conor savored his breakfast as he ate. This would be the last decent meal he expected for several days. A half hour later, he put on his hat and gave his mother a hug on his way out the door.

* * *

At noon, Con drove into his brother's ranch yard west of town. Patrick came from the barn as he pulled in. He eyed Con's apparel when he stepped out of the pickup truck.

"You look like you're needing a horse," he said, scratching a few days' growth of whiskers on his neck. "Again."

"You're getting quite perceptive in your old age, little brother," Conor responded. "I might have a job opening for you at the sheriff's office."

"No thanks. I like it here just fine. The last time I loaned you a horse, you got yourself all shot up. I'm lucky our mother didn't skin me for helping to get you hurt."

"You might be right, Paddy."

"You want Bob?" he asked.

"And your truck."

"You're leaving me afoot?"

"No, you'll have my sheriff's pickup if you need it."

"What if somebody shoots at me? You're not too popular with the moonshiners around here, you know. Especially after your buddies burned up forty or fifty grand worth of merchandise a couple of months ago."

"That should have made the others happy. For a while, anyway. Less competition. Besides, the department knows you might be driving it. So, if anybody shoots at you, feel free to shoot back."

"Jeepers creepers, that's comforting to know," Patrick retorted, shaking his head. "Bob is in the little pasture behind the house. Bring carrots?"

"Of course. I'm getting smarter too." He chuckled.

"Where you going?"

"Bitter Spring."

"Good thing I shod him last week. It's gets pretty rocky around there."

An hour later, Con had his gear transferred to Patrick's Model-T stock truck. He added a saddle and bridle from his brother's tack room along with a rifle scabbard, saddlebags, and two lariats.

As he brought Bob around the house, Patrick came from the spring with Con's canteen and a canvas water bag filled with fresh water.

"That water's not very good up there," he said. "Figured you'd want to have some from here."

"Thanks," Conor replied as he walked Bob up to the rear of the truck. Without hesitation, the horse leaped the three feet up and into the bed. "There's just not too much to dislike about this horse," Con commented, referring to how easily he loaded. Bob stood peering ahead over the cab.

"I know, that's why I wasn't going to let you use him that first time. Now you won't ride any of the others. You're spoiled," he added. "By the way. The truck needs gas."

"Of course." Con chuckled. "It'll be full when you get it back, Paddy."

"When?"

"By Tuesday, I hope."

"Don't get yourself killed, Conor," Patrick said as he hugged his brother. "Or my horse either."

* * *

The sun began to set as Conor drove off the side of the road and came to a halt near Bitter Spring. He unloaded Bob and picketed him near the spring. Then, finding some dry mesquite, he rustled up a small campfire. Positioning the saddle for a pillow, he rolled out his bed and the spare blanket he'd wrapped his rifle in earlier. Just before dusk turned to dark, he cut three slabs of bacon from his supply. He found a suitable green branch on a singleleaf ash tree near the spring to sharpen one end for a roasting stick. In the flickering light from the fire, Con unbelted his Colt and hung it from the horn of the saddle.

As the sky darkened, his fire burned down to coals, and Con roasted his skewered bacon over the glowing embers. He half laid and half sat on his bed eating his supper. He supplemented the bacon with a chunk of his mother's homemade cheddar cheese and a round of fry bread. When finished eating, he took a drink of marginally cool water from his canteen and added a little more mesquite to his fire. As the light grew from the replenished fire, Conor pulled off his boots and found his way between the blankets of his bedroll. The small branches of mesquite were quickly consumed by the flames and soon joined the dim red coals beneath them.

The moon had yet to rise as Con stared into the starlit sky above him. Would a city girl like June see the beauty of the stars, far from electric lights to subdue them? As the moon rose above the eastern horizon a coyote called in the distance. Would June appreciate the wildness of sleeping on the ground in the desert on a night like tonight? Taking in a long deep breath of fresh air, Con suddenly realized how tired he was. He had scarcely slept the previous night. His thoughts of June melted into nothingness.

* * *

SATURDAY, JUNE 7, 1930

A gold line over the Black Mountains to the east signified the beginning of a new day. Conor sat up in the semi-darkness and wiped the sleep from his eyes. He could make out the faint outline of Bob sleeping on his feet near the spring, likely prepared to bolt at the first scent of danger. Con pulled up his socks and shook out any unwanted visitors in his boots from overnight before slipping them onto his feet. He stamped his feet firmly into them, then strapped on his pistol.

Con checked for any signs of life in the remaining coals of last night's fire. They were cold. Finding his lamb jerky, he tore off a narrow strip. Slowly, he began to chew on it until his salivary glands became active enough to begin softening it. As it began to get light out, he located his supply of carrots and wandered toward the spring. When Conor approached, Bob's head snapped in his direction with ears forward.

"Good morning, partner. You ready to stretch your legs?"

Bob nickered as if in agreement. As Con reached to his neck for some vigorous rubbing, Bob's nose was stuck on his vest pocket and the half carrot inside it.

"You think I brought you something, do you?" Con continued to stroke the horse's neck and shoulder with one hand as he gave him his treat with the other. Leading Bob to the truck, he dropped the picket rope on the ground. Bob stood there as Conor shook out the saddle blanket and laid it across his back. When he turned and picked up the saddle, Bob remained patiently waiting as Con swung it over the blanket.

"Dang, you're a good horse, Bob," he told him as he tightened the cinch.

Con strapped the scabbard, which now held his Winchester, to the saddle. Then came the saddlebags which were now filled to capacity with food, his field glasses, and extra ammunition. Bob looked suspiciously back at him, which reminded Conor of the carrots still on the seat of the truck. He shook out his blankets, then carefully rolled them tightly inside his rain poncho and strapped them atop the saddlebags.

Two lariats and the picket rope were tied to forward saddle strings, and the water bag and canteen hung from the saddle horn.

He stepped back and looked over his rig one more time. It seemed like a lot of gear, but he expected to be out here two to three days and needed to be prepared for anything that might arise during that time. Satisfied with his equipment he stepped into the saddle. And crossed the Bitter Spring Wash.

With the broken ridge to his left, Con headed north. In less than a half mile, he came to the first dry wash coming from the ridge. He turned west and followed it. The wash narrowed where it cut through the ridge but remained passable on horseback. He continued on for another half mile to where the wash began in a small valley. Con scanned the surrounding hills. No spring. No sign of a dwelling. He turned around and rode back through the cut then turned north out of the wash.

Three-quarters of a mile later, he came upon the second wash and repeated the process. This time the wash continued through the broken ridge for a mile. All the way to the foot of East Longwell Ridge before dissipating. Once again, he scanned the hillsides and found nothing. He returned again through the broken ridge and proceeded north for a half mile to a third wash. It was nearly identical in geography as the second one.

When he reached the fourth wash, the broken ridge had merged into East Longwell Ridge. The wash ran a quarter mile up to the foot of the ridge and ended abruptly beneath the nearly vertical four-hundred-foot-high face. There were no springs or dwellings on the next ten washes. All had the same physical characteristics. Here the East Longwell Ridge came to an end at the Muddy Mountains.

To Conor it all looked the same, except that the face of the mountain turned eastward. In his estimation, they had covered about seven miles in a straight line. Possibly three times that distance the way they had traveled. The sun was high in the sky. Luis had said there were springs along this way, but he hadn't located any yet. Perhaps they had gone dry since the last time Luis crossed this country, twenty years ago or more.

Bob had barely broken a sweat and showed no signs of weakening, but it was getting pretty hot out. He would give it another hour. If they didn't find water by then, he would fill his hat from the water bag for Bob to get a drink, thus ruining a nearly new fifteen-dollar Stetson. They continued on and investigated five more washes without promise.

On the sixth wash, he found a spring producing a decent flow of water right at the base of the mountain. There were a dozen small trees along the little rivulet that flowed some twenty yards before disappearing into the sandy wash. Con sampled the water. A little alkaline tasting, but not too bad. He loosened Bob's cinch and tied his picket rope to a tree near the water and large enough for the horse to get some shade. He removed the bridle and bit and hung them from the saddle horn so Bob could comfortably browse on the clumps of grass there.

The proximity of water and shade made the air at least ten degrees cooler than it had been a quarter mile down the wash. Con procured a piece of cheese and more lamb jerky from the saddlebags. With canteen in hand, he found a comfortable place in the shade and took a break.

With bodies replenished by food and water for both horse and rider, their mission continued. A half hour later, they made their way up another wash. A small underground stream there surfaced intermittently. Abundance of vegetation near the foot of the mountain looked promising to Conor, though the source or a dwelling eluded him. He urged Bob to make his way through a cut into the face of the mountain. After winding its way north and east for a mile and a half, the wash concluded at yet another dead end in a small box canyon. Returning, Con followed the stream down from where he first encountered it. A half mile below, it vanished into the sandy bottom of the wash and did not resurface. When he reached a point where he could see the road and the Virgin River below, he scanned the area with his field glasses, again finding nothing he could identify as a dwelling.

He rode back up the wash. A quarter mile below where he had last seen water flowing, a dry tributary joined the wash from the east, Con followed it. The limestone outcropping known as Blue Point loomed five hundred feet above the base of the mountain in the distance. It marked the east end of the Muddy Mountains, a reference for Conor identifying how far he had advanced on his expedition. Increasing plant life in the bottom of the wash suggested the nearness of water to the surface. Bob occasionally grabbed a mouthful of the tall native grasses as they passed.

A rivulet of water soon appeared near the center of the wash and grew gradually into a small stream. Before long, Con discovered it actually branched off from a much larger stream that ran to the southeast as far as he could see. The sound of running water drew Con to the source of the creek where it emerged from a rock bluff at the base of the moun-tain. He dismounted to test the water. When he dipped his hand in to taste it, the water was warm, over a hundred degrees he suspected.

"This must be Rogers Spring," he determined to himself.

"I've heard about it, partner," he told Bob who helped himself to a drink. "Just never been here."

He surveyed their surroundings. The bluff already shadowed the location and dusk would soon follow.

"A good place to camp, I expect," he muttered to Bob and himself.

Conor found a dry level area nearby and removed Bob's bridle and saddle. The horse's back was wet with sweat. Con laid the saddle blanket upside down across the top of an Arrowweed bush and rubbed Bob's back briefly with his bare hands.

"We don't have a brush," he told the horse as if he would understand. "But shortly, I'll do what I can with some grass."

He led Bob toward the creek, planning to picket him in the abundant grass, within reach of the water. When they got into taller grass, Bob balked and pulled back against the rope.

"What's the problem, old boy?" Con asked. As he turned around, Bob had dropped to his knees. He continued laying down, then rolled back and forth several times on his back in the tall grass. "Couldn't wait, huh?" he asked as Bob regained his feet and shook himself vigorously. He gave him the carrot he'd retrieved from the saddlebags and patted and rubbed him profusely before driving the picket pin into the soft ground.

Conor set up his camping spot and rolled out his bed. He scrounged up a substantial bunch of firewood from among the trees along the creek and built a small fire. With plenty of daylight still in the sky, Con analyzing his setting. It wasn't often a fellow had the occasion to take a hot bath in the desert. He ventured near the source of the water rushing from beneath the rock and found a small pool about ten feet across. He hung his belted Colt from a nearby branch. Stripping naked, he waded in and sat down among the rocks in a couple of feet of nice warm water. He had no soap but enjoyed the pleasant soak for long enough to wrinkle the skin on his fingers and toes.

Bob looked at him quizzically when Con climbed from the pool. The warm desert air nearly dried him by the time he reached for his clothes. He dressed, and on the way back to his campfire, sharpened two willow sticks. The dry wood had burned more quickly than he anticipated, or perhaps he lingered too long in the pool, whichever, he needed to re-stoke it in order to cook his supper. Slicing slabs from the side of bacon, he skewered them on his sticks and set them aside, awaiting his inferno to subside to roasting temperature.

As shadows disappeared with the setting sun, Bob let out a soft nicker. Slightly different from his usual tone. It drew Conor's attention to the gelding. His head pointed straight toward the spring with ears bent forward attentively.

Con slid his Winchester from the scabbard and as quietly as possible checked the action for a cartridge in the chamber. He stealthily eased his way toward Bob who momentarily turned one ear his direction then returned his full attention to whatever was at the spring. Con gently rubbed the horse's neck and whispered to him.

"What is it you see or smell out there, boy? A mustang coming for water? Or maybe a puma or lobo, huh?"

Conor caught a glimpse of movement right near the pool he had soaked in. He eased the hammer back on the rifle and began to raise it, ready to fire. "A big cat checking a remnant of human scent?" he questioned himself. A loud thump and sudden movement nearly scared the wits from him until the massive curl of horns caught his attention. Silhouetted against the lighter rock behind him stood a desert bighorn ram staring straight toward him.

Slowly, Con released the air that he'd held in his lungs for what seemed an eternity in one long, drawn-out breath. Then returned the hammer on his rifle to the half-cock safety position. As Con returned to his again-smoldering campfire, he stopped to rub and pat Bob in thanks for his attentiveness. Whether or not the horse understood the reason for his praise made little difference to Conor. He deserved it.

He fumbled in the darkness to again rekindle the fire. He ate cheese and a round of fry bread while he waited for the flames to shrink once more to embers. He finally squatted on his haunches carefully holding his sticks of bacon a few inches apart, moving them slowly above the coals. Drops of grease dripped sporadically onto the cinders causing them to pop as they emitted tiny bursts of bluish flame when the melted fat incinerated.

When finally cooked, Con burned his fingers and his tongue on the sizzling bacon. He took a quick swig of tepid water from his nearly empty canteen. It helped. He slung his pistol from the saddle horn and pulled off his boots. The dim glow of lingering coals was barely visible in the night when he climbed between his blankets. Resting his head on the saddle for a pillow, he gazed into the moonless night. As he reviewed the events of his first day's search, a shooting star sped across the sky above him.

"I wish to find Katherine Wagner," he said aloud. "Before it's too late."

The streak of light extinguished itself in the midst of his thought.

* * *

SUNDAY, JUNE 8, 1930

Morning broke over the oasis-like atmosphere of Rogers Warm Spring. Conor shook out his boots and stamped his feet into them. Taking a carrot from his saddlebag, he walked toward Bob and the creek that flowed from the spring. Giving Bob half the carrot, he put the other half in his vest pocket and began rubbing the horse's neck. Talking to Bob as he petted and rubbed, he started out gently then more briskly. He worked his way over the horse's shoulders, back, sides and legs to eventually give him a complete and vigorous rubdown. After checking all four feet, he gave Bob the rest of the carrot and continued his way to the spring.

Con laid his hat beside him on the bank as he kneeled and dipped his entire head into the warm water. He scrubbed his face with his hands. As he rose from the bank, he shook the dripping water from his head before running his fingers through his hair and replacing his hat.

Leading Bob to the campsite, he chewed on jerky as he saddled up and packed his gear. He started in the direction of the spring with his empty canteen then changed his mind. Refilling the canteen with the much more palatable water from the water bag, he estimated there was enough to repeat the process at least once more before resorting to the more mineralized water of the nearby area.

Bob had grazed well overnight on the grass near the creek, and Con felt confident the horse remained in good condition. "Well, partner," he said as he stepped into the saddle. "You'll have plenty of water available for a while, and we'll make sure you've had your fill when we leave it."

They followed the creek as it meandered down the gentle slope toward the Virgin River. Vegetation was plentiful as it split and rejoined forming multiple small islands. Two miles downstream, the slope became steeper and the creek remained in one channel. Conor could follow its course in his field glasses to the road below and the river beyond. He found no sign of a dwelling.

Turning back upstream, Con stayed on the east bank. After a quarter mile, he followed a dominant dry wash tributary north. His instinct served him well, and in less than a half mile, they followed an intermittent stream that continued to grow in size. In another quarter mile, the stream had become continuous and the vegetation denser. Con soon found the source. The stream seemed to appear from nowhere. It simply rose up from the sand and ran down the wash. After giving Bob a chance to drink, they continued on. What could barely be considered a wash quickly flattened out and disappeared. Another uninhabited spring.

Conor pointed Bob north, and they passed Rogers Spring a quarter mile to their west. Soon after, they reached another predominant wash coming straight east from the Muddy Mountains. When they entered the cut into the mountain, though blocked from view, he suspected they were within a few hundred yards of Rogers Spring. Con's optimism heightened as he anticipated the possibility that a sister to Rogers Spring might surface on the opposite side of the bluff. His hopefulness began to diminish as the cut through the mountain continued for a mile. It only widened slightly then as he continued to follow the dry creek bed for another mile before the next cut that was too craggy to chance injuring Bob. It appeared highly unlikely to Con that Jimmy Garza rode his mule through it on a regular basis.

As he emerged from the mountain, Conor noticed a glimpse of vegetation downstream from where he had entered the wash. He continued toward it. Sure enough, a spring surfaced from the dry creek bed about a mile from the mountain. The water was sufficient enough to sub irrigate perhaps ten acres of desert before disappearing back into the sand. Con followed the wash until it plunged into a narrow crevice down a steep hill toward the river below. Again, he could spot nothing in his field glasses that looked habitable.

When they returned to the spring, he loosened the cinch of Bob's saddle and hung his bridle from the horn. Con let him drink and graze. He slung his canteen over his shoulder, gathered a chunk of cheese and a handful of lamb jerky from the saddlebag, and sought out a place in the shade to shroud the noonday sun. Leaning against a boulder, he gazed across the landscape watching heatwaves dance across the desert floor. He and Bob had covered over ten miles this morning in search of the elusive cabin and Katherine Wagner. He doubted they were much over a mile from Rogers Spring right now. He allowed himself to doze off for perhaps a half hour and woke in a sweat. The sun had overtaken his place in the shade as it strolled across the sky. A scattering of feathery clouds began to appear above, but did little to abate the scorching sun.

Conor stood and swished a sip of water around in his dry mouth before swallowing it. He tightened the cinch and exchanged his canteen for the bridle dangling from the saddle horn. Bob readily took the bit in his mouth, and Con soon swung his leg over the saddle to resume their hunt. Though he'd never seen it from this perspective, Blue Point rose from the desert a mile away to the northwest. Blue Point Spring should be at its base and the Valley of Fire beyond it. He remembered as a teen hearing about an attempted irrigation project planned from the spring a decade earlier. If the farmers from St. Thomas thought it feasible to build ten miles of irrigation ditch from the spring, it must be of substantial supply. They headed that direction.

Blue Point Spring turned out to be a warm water spring like Rogers Spring, but to Con's surprise, was much smaller. There were large shrubs surrounding it and the creek that ran from it, but no substantial trees. He followed the creek downstream where it soon split. Conor took the branch to the right which meandered southeast for about a mile before disappearing into the sandy wash. As before, he continued until the slope increased, and he could see the road and river below. Con turned north and intersected the other branch in a quarter mile. It, too, was dry at this point, but soon showed water that gradually increased in volume as he followed it back to its source.

As Con rounded Blue Point and continued following the foot of the Muddy Mountains, he noticed the light feathery clouds seen earlier thickened into taller cumulous formations. As he entered the mouth of the Valley of Fire, he found two dry washes about a half mile apart. He followed each up to the base of the mountain. Neither offered up a spring at its source.

A bolt of lightning struck the top of Blue Point, and the instant clap of thunder caused a momentary jump from both horse and rider. Bob's hair stood on end from the electricity in the air, but he did not waver. A curtain of rain roared across the red rock formations that gave the valley its name. Conor fumbled with the ties of his bedroll, hurrying to procure his poncho before he became soaked by the approaching deluge. He slid into the poncho and climbed back aboard Bob just as the first spatter of massive raindrops hit him. He scanned the area through the growing downpour in search of shelter among the array of rock formations.

The only likely candidate came from across the valley, and

Con pointed Bob toward it. The outcropping quickly disappeared in the deluge. Using the direction of the encroaching
storm as his only landmark, he urged Bob through the torrent.
Fifty feet ahead, a steep bank once marked the edge of a wide
wash that ran down the center of the valley. A narrower,
deeper wash cut its way through the floor of its ancestor forty
feet farther away and against a taller bank on the far side. As
Bob slid down a game trail to the intermediate level, Con
spotted it out of the corner of his eye.

The weathered gray boards on the walls of the small shack
looked black when soaked with rain. The runoff from the
nearly flat tin roof looked like a waterfall breaking over a
natural dam in a river. As Conor neared, he slipped the loop
from the hammer of his Colt and kept a hand on the grip as he
guided Bob with the other. A lean-to had been added to one
side of the shack that served as a stall. Con leaned forward
over Bob's neck, and he ducked as he rode in under the edge
of its roof. He dropped Bob's reins and grabbed the horn as he
slipped from the saddle, not relinquishing the hold on his
pistol as he did so.

Balls of nickel-size hail now joined the rain in a raucous
clatter on the tin roof. Con's Stetson had grown two sizes in
the soaking rain. His jeans were drenched from the knees
down and clung to his skin when he moved. Water ran from
the seams of his boots as he put weight down on them when
his feet hit the hard-packed floor of the stall. He slid the Colt
from its holster. Keeping it concealed under the poncho, he
eased back the hammer and cautiously rounded the corner to
the front of the shack. The only window was on the far side of
the door. He stood aside from the door, partially protected
from the weather by a narrow overhang of tin on the roof, and
beat as hard as he could against the door with his free fist.

"Anybody home?" he hollered as loudly as he could. He waited as he counted a minute without response.

He hammered again. "Sheriff Armenta," he yelled. "Open up!" He counted off another minute.

If anyone moved inside the shack, he could not hear it through the storm. Cautiously, he reached for the doorknob, careful to leave as little as possible of his body exposed in the frame of the doorway. He twisted the knob. It turned freely in his hand. The rain-swelled wood caused the door to pop open as soon as the latch released it.

His heart raced as Conor carefully peered into the shack. From where he stood, he was looking into a cooking area. A small cookstove and a homemade Hoosier cabinet stood against the far wall. In front of those stood a small table and three chairs. The door blocked his view of anything more. A rusty shovel leaned against the front of the shack. Con crossed quickly to the far side of the door. He drew his pistol from beneath the poncho and with his free hand, pushed hard and swiftly on the door. It swung freely and banged against the wall as it smacked it. Had anyone been standing behind it, it could not have done so.

Con leaped into the shack, ready for anything. There was no sign of habitants. The room was clean and well-kept. A single bed that doubled as a couch sat against one wall of what otherwise served as the living portion of the main room. The blanket and pillow on the bed were neatly made up. A rocking chair with a side table and a kerosene lamp also graced the area behind the door. A second, larger kerosene light hung from the ceiling in the center of the room, and a makeshift bookcase of crates were nailed to the wall near the chair. They held fifteen or twenty books. Conor guessed the room to measure perhaps ten by twenty.

A doorway at the end opened into another room that seemed much brighter. A double bed positioned between two small windows dominated the eight-by-ten room, and a crude dresser sat at the opposite end. A mirror hung from the wall above it. Yellow curtains hung at the sides of the windows, and pale-yellow wallpaper had been applied to the uneven, rough walls. A patchwork quilt adorned the bed, and a woman's clothing hung from a half-dozen nails driven into the wall.

"Katherine Wagner's dresses?" Con asked himself aloud. Everything was neat and clean, as he suspected Katherine Wagner may have liked it. A flash of nearby lightning illumi-nated the windows. Something odd drew Con's attention to them. He pulled back the curtains. Bars. Iron bars. Someone had bolted iron bars over the windows. Conor's heart sank. Another flash of lightning drew his attention to the far side of the bed. A large trunk sat opened, an assortment of clothing strewn from it. He then realized the two blankets piled on the bed were probably also from the trunk. They were the only things out of place he'd seen in the shack. He looked again at the open trunk.

"I know this trunk. It was dark, but I've seen it before."

Con looked closer at the labels from various destinations in Europe. He had seen this trunk outside of Las Vegas two months ago...in Katherine Wagner's garage. He looked around the room again. Then returned to the door into the room. There was a hasp installed above the doorknob.

"This was Katherine Wagner's prison," he muttered to himself.

Another flash of lightning brought his attention to the floor beside the bed but quickly returned to darkness. Too dark to see clearly. Con went to the stand beside the rocking chair and lit the lamp. Returning the chimney, he adjusted the wick for the brightest light. In the bedroom, he set the lamp by a beautiful little Navajo rug near the bed. A dark, purplish-black patch covered an area nearly a foot across. He was certain it would be blood.

"Oh, Mrs. Wagner," he muttered. "Oh, no."

10

SATURDAY, SEPTEMBER 14, 1929

The evening skies grew darker as Dutch Wagner drove his sedan out Pine Canyon Road toward his mother's house. Actually, it was his house, he reminded himself with a smug grin. He had blackmailed her into signing the estate over to him two years ago, threatening exposure of her romantic relationship with Brice Campbell. Dutch got the house but had not thwarted the affair. He had an inside source that kept him informed of their monthly trysts at the Hotel Nevada.

No lights came into view from the house as he rolled down the long drive. Dutch began spinning demented thoughts in his twisted mind. Perhaps she had gone to have supper with her spinster assistant, Agnes, from her pathetic little trucking company. It was his father's birthday, and she was sentimental about such maudlin things. After all, Brice Campbell had

murdered him six years ago and faked the accident in Switzerland to cover up the crime. All just to seduce his naïve mother.

Dutch's hatred of Brice Campbell soon overtook any
compassion he had for his mother. He pulled up to the house
and left his car running with the headlights aimed at the front
door. It was unlocked as he had suspected.

"Stupid bimbo," he muttered to himself as he turned the
lights on in the living room. He strode from room to room
looking for her...just in case. Turning on the light in each, he
found them clean and tidy before returning them to darkness.

"She must really be bored," he mumbled. "Nothing better
to do than clean house." When he reached her bedroom, his
mood became more sour. A long sheer negligée lay on the bed,
and another hung from the corner of the full-length dressing
mirror. She was out with Mr. High and Mighty. He was certain
of it.

Dutch went back to his car and parked it behind the
garage. He opened the side door and switched on the light.
The Auburn that Campbell had given his mother occupied the
far stall. The near stall was empty. She drove the Oldsmobile.
He shut off the light and retrieved a bottle of whiskey from his
car before returning to the house. It might be a long night. He
could wait.

The clock in the living room struck eight as he walked in.
He found a glass in the kitchen and carried it with his whiskey
as he turned off the lights. The light from the bedroom guided
him down the hall. Dutch sat the whiskey and the glass on the
nightstand. His mother's rocking chair sat beside it where she
liked to read before going to bed. He went to the door and
switched off the light. Then he stood in the darkness waiting
for his eyes to adjust to the dim moonlight entering through

the window. He poured a glass of whiskey then sat down in the rocking chair.

The clock struck nine when Dutch's glass of whiskey was half empty. He refilled the glass as the clock struck ten. He continued to seethe and slowly sip his whiskey. At a quarter past eleven, he heard the rumble of the Oldsmobile's V-8 coming down the drive. The slight squeal of brakes indicated the car stopping while his mother opened the garage door. Then she pulled into the garage, and the engine became silent. With a slight creak of hinges, the doors closed. In just a moment or two, she would face him, he thought with satisfaction.

The front door opened and closed. He could hear her light footsteps on the clay-tiled floor. A light came on down the hall. Water ran for a few seconds. *She's getting a drink in the kitchen*, Dutch thought to himself. The light went out, and footsteps came down the hall. He heard her use the bathroom and flush the toilet in the darkness. He snickered to himself as he invaded her privacy. A few more footsteps and…suddenly the room drenched with light. So instantly bright it blinded him.

"What?" Katherine shrieked. "What the hell are you doing in my house?"

"*My* house," Dutch slurred as he staggered to his feet. "Don't you remember?"

"What are you doing here?" she repeated in the same tone.

"I came out here on my dad's birthday to tell you I need *my* garage to store merchandise. You'll have to park your cars elsewhere." He took a step closer imposing his superiority over her. He noticed Katherine wore his father's belt at the waist of her skirt. "I see you wore Daddy's buckle to celebrate while you're out whoring with…"

The liquor on Dutch's breath repulsed her, but Katherine

Wagner was not intimidated. She slapped him as hard as she could. "Drunk or sober," she screamed. "You don't talk to me that way!"

He stood there stupefied for a full minute as she glared at him.

Then he hit her. She did not see it coming. A devastating backhand that landed squarely on her right cheekbone, fracturing it. The gaudy ring he wore on his right middle finger cut her face, but she did not feel the trickle of blood escape from it. It felt as though someone blindsided her with a ten-pound ham, sending her flying like a ragdoll. The room spun in slow motion for what seemed forever. She landed unconscious across the bed in less than a second.

✱ ✱ ✱

SUNDAY, SEPTEMBER 15, 1929

Katherine Wagner awoke with a jolt. She lay on her side in total darkness. Her hands were tied behind her back and ankles tied together with a tether that connected them to her wrists. A strip of cloth, pulled through her mouth and tied tightly at the back of her neck, allowed her to breathe but not much else. The right side of her face ached profusely, and her left cheek ground into a hard floor, she thought. It smelled musty and dirty. There was a rumbling sound beneath her head. The floor almost seemed in motion. Katherine suddenly realized she was in the trunk of a moving car.

"Oh God," she pleaded aloud, trying not to cry. "He's taking me out into the desert to kill me."

She tried to shift her cramping legs and arms ineffectively within their restraints. It brought to her attention that her hands were numb. She began clenching and releasing her fists in an effort to revive circulation in them. The road became rougher and the near-constant bounces and jolts slammed her aching face and body against the floorboards of the trunk. Then the car came to a stop, and the engine went silent.

"Sal," a muffled voice hailed. "What brings you out here?"

"Brought you a present," a gruff voice answered.

A car door slammed shut and another opened, then closed.

"I've got plenty of food," the first voice said. He sounded young.

"You'll need more," the gruff voice responded. Sal, she thought. Whoever he is.

She could feel the heat of the sun radiate from the steel above her. It was daylight, she thought. The still air inside the trunk heated rapidly. She heard a loud, almost crunching sound of the latch, and the lid sprang open above her. Her right eye failed to open. Light was barely visible through the left with her face planted into the floorboards.

"Holy smoke!" the young voice exclaimed. "Who is she?"

"Dutch's mamma," Sal replied. "She's your prisoner for a while. He ain't too happy with her right now."

"What happened to her face?"

"He slugged her. Like I said, he..."

"Yeah, I guess not," the young voice interrupted before Sal repeated his previous comment.

"Sit that box of groceries down and give me a hand."

A moment later, she heard the click of a switchblade knife, and her feet, still bound together, suddenly broke free from the tether. They sprang automatically to straighten themselves, only to stop abruptly when they hit the edge of the trunk. Sal's large coarse hands grabbed her and dragged her from her cave. Then, with the young one's help, he manhandled her over his shoulder and hauled her into a nearby shack. When he threw her down on her back onto a bed, she thought her arms would break beneath her. Then he rolled her over and quickly clasped a handcuff to one wrist as the switchblade clicked again, and her hands were free. Before she realized in her half-conscious state what happened, her shoulder wrenched with mind-numbing pain, and Sal clasped the other end of the cuffs to the bed frame.

He tossed the key to the handcuffs to the young one. Shaking his finger at him, Sal gave his limited orders. "Don't let her loose except to go to the outhouse. Hold this on her when you do," he told the young one as he tossed a snub-nosed .38 to him. "If she tries anything, kill her."

Katherine was shocked into a more aware state of consciousness by Sal's blunt command. These were the kind of men her son worked with. He was their boss, she suspected. These were his orders. Kill her if she tries to escape. Dutch's mental state had continually deteriorated since Gary's death, she had observed. He had become more and more obsessed with his terribly mistaken notion that Brice Campbell had caused the accident. And now it had come to this.

The gruff one, Sal had gone to the car, and the young one brought in the groceries. The door of the shack remained open. She heard a car door open and close then Sal reappeared in the door and threw a stuffed-full pillowcase on the floor.

"I almost forgot," he said. "There's some clean clothes for her. Dutch said you could watch her change if you want," Sal gave a menacing chuckle. "The more humiliated she is, the better he'll like it."

"How long is she going to be here?"

"Until she forgets her boyfriend," Sal said.

"Who is that?"

"Mr. High and Mighty. That's what Dutch called him. See you in a couple of weeks."

"Sure," the young one replied.

He watched out the door as Sal started the car and drove slowly away. Katherine watched him through her left eye. Her right hand was free now, and she cautiously touched her damaged face. Even the faintest contact was excruciating. She could not hold back her wincing groan.

The young one snapped around to look at her. The look on his face was softer than she expected. He crossed the room to a rickety old Hoosier and poured water from a pottery pitcher into a slightly misshapen tin cup. He pulled the pistol from his waistband and laid it on the table in the cooking area as he carried the cup toward her.

"I won't hurt you," he said gently as he sat the cup on an upended crate that served as a nightstand. He sat down beside her and reached behind her neck, lifting her hair to untie the gag in her mouth.

"It's too tight," he said. "I'll need to cut it. Try to sit up if you can," he told her as he went back to the Hoosier and found a rather menacing-looking knife.

"I'll be careful. I know it must hurt, but I'll have to get my fingers under it to keep from cutting you."

Katherine looked at him and nodded in understanding. Whoever the young one was, he was not mean or cruel like Sal was...and Dutch had somehow become. Her left eye welled up, and a tear ran down her cheek. Her right eye had done the same, but she did not feel it. The young one worked two fingers beneath the tight cloth just below her left ear. She groaned in agony as it pulled even tighter into her swollen face. She would not allow herself to scream at the young man helping her. He cautiously sawed at the fabric over his fingers.

"This material is very strong," he muttered almost to himself. "It reminds me of the silk stockings my mother had once, back when I was little."

The gag gradually loosened as he worked his way through the layers of fabric. It finally fell free, and the young one pulled it from her mouth as gently as he could. He handed her the cup of water.

"My name is Jimmy."

* * *

Jimmy Garza untied Katherine Wagner's feet and refilled the tin cup twice. Much of the water dribbled from her swollen lips down the front of her blouse. Jimmy started a small blaze in the little stove by the Hoosier, took a large enameled coffeepot and disappeared out the door. He returned carrying the brimmed-full pot by the bail, splashing water as he walked, and sat it on the stove.

"Are you hungry?" he asked.

Katherine nodded.

"Do you think you can chew?"

She cautiously worked her jaw, then nodded somewhat hesitantly.

"I've got a ham at the spring. I can cut some into little pieces. You like ham?"

Katherine tried to smile. Jimmy noticed the left corner of her mouth raise slightly. Her forehead wrinkled some, and she nodded. He took the butcher knife and went to the spring. When he returned with a thick slab of ham, the smoky aroma filled the room. Katherine's stomach growled. An unladylike sound, she thought and tried to hold her abdomen with her free hand to silence it. She realized then, there was nothing ladylike about her in her present circumstance. Jimmy probably thought her to be no better than the girls who worked the upper floor of her son's disgusting establishment. He brought a tin plate with a plentiful serving of diced ham mounded on it. A thin slice of bread accompanied it.

"Try it," Jimmy said. "If you can't chew it, suck on it. It will get soft enough before long to swallow."

She took a piece of ham and forced it between her lips into her mouth. It hurt to move her jaw, but she managed to slowly chew it.

"Fank you." She succeeded in muttering the first words since Dutch had hit her.

The sound of her voice startled Jimmy. "You're welcome." He smiled back at her. He wanted to be pleasant. The horrific bruising on her face was sickening, but he did not want her to deduce that from his behavior. Jimmy had heard from his coworkers that she was rich. He had no idea what events had brought her here, but it must be akin to a nightmare for her. He would show respect as best he could within the limitations of Dutch's orders.

Jimmy made himself a sandwich with the balance of the ham he had brought in and sat it on a battered chair at the table to eat it. He'd filled a second cup with water and washed down a large bite of the sandwich after barely chewing it.

"When the water gets hot, I'll doctor your face," he told her. "I don't have much to work with, but I'll do my best."

"'Kay," she said and nodded.

Jimmy wolfed down his sandwich as Katherine continued slowly with her own. He procured a large bowl from the Hoosier and sat it on the makeshift nightstand. Bringing the coffeepot and a towel, he filled the bowl with steaming water.

"This will probably hurt, but I don't know no other way,"

he told her as he dipped the towel in the hot water and wrung the excess from it.

"'Kay," she answered again with a nod.

As gently as he could, he began washing her bruised face. She occasionally winced but did not pull away. As he worked on the gash left by Dutch's ring, he talked to her.

"This should probably have stitches," he said as he washed the cut below her right eye. She flinched when the cloth crossed the hard bump at the end of it. "I don't have anything to sew with and wouldn't know where to begin if I did." Jimmy continued to carefully wash her face, keeping the towel wetter to rinse the wound as best he could. He crossed the room and returned with a nearly full quart of liquor.

"Dink?" Katherine asked.

"Me, no." He chuckled. "You've heard what they say about Indians not holding their liquor? That's me." He grinned at her. "I don't drink."

The left side of her mouth raised slightly. Jimmy knew she was trying to smile back at him.

"Dink?" she repeated and tapped her chest while managing to raise an eyebrow.

"Sure!" Jimmy acknowledged and poured an inch into her cup.

He watched as she held the cup and inhaled the smell of it. Raw whiskey she surmised and took a small sip. As she swallowed the harsh liquid, it burned all the way to her belly and took her breath away causing her to cough. A condition which made her face and much of her head explode in pain. She set the cup down, taking slow deep breaths of air. The whiskey churned in her mostly empty stomach. She did not wish to contemplate vomiting in her current state and managed to overpower the impulse. Katherine picked up the bread and tore it in two, stuffing half between her swollen lips. Jimmy watched her and waited.

"Waddo," she said, holding the cup to him.

"Water?"

Katherine nodded.

Jimmy took the cup from the table that he had drank from earlier and filled it from the pitcher. Katherine took a mouthful, tongued the bread and water into mush and swallowed. Then she repeated the process. After that made it down and stayed there, she stuffed two or three more cubes of ham into her mouth and began patiently chewing.

"Are you doing okay now?" Jimmy asked.

"'Kay." She nodded.

Jimmy poured whiskey over the towel and prepared to wash the cut and abrasions on Katherine's face. "This is going to sting like hell," he told her as he reached toward the gash below her eye. He squeezed whiskey from the towel into the open wound. She closed her eye and mouth as tightly as she could and gritted her teeth, but she could not hold the mournful moan from escaping her nose, nor the tears from running down her cheeks as Jimmy flushed the lesion with whiskey. When he finished, sweat beaded on her brow, and she gasped for breath. Jimmy took the damp towel and wiped her entire face with it. The whiskey felt cool as the alcohol evaporated from it on her skin.

"I have nothing to use for bandages. When you've finished eating, you can lay down on the bed, and I'll cover your face with a damp cloth to keep the flies from pestering your injuries. The dry air will be better for healing anyway."

She nodded and continued to eat. Jimmy sat at the table staring out the doorway. Dutch had told him to stay here for a couple of weeks to keep an eye on the place. By then, they could get the rest of his moonshine still, spare parts, and supplies moved to their new location eighty miles south of here. He had already been here for a month. Now he had a new job to do. He turned toward his pledge. He watched her and refilled her water as she painstakingly ate the ham.

"Awd-aws," she said as she took a drink to wash down the last of the ham.

He looked bewilderedly at her.

"Awd-aws," she repeated and tapped her chest then pointed toward the door.

"You need to use the outhouse?"

"Yeff." She nodded.

"Yes, ma'am,"

"Kaffrine."

"What?"

"Kaffrine," she repeated and pointed to herself.

"Your name is Katherine?"

She nodded.

"Can you walk, Katherine?"

"Yeff."

Jimmy took the pistol from the table and put it in the Hoosier. Then moved to the bed and unlocked the cuff from Katherine's wrist. She rubbed it momentarily then, taking hold of the metal tube of the headboard she had been secured to, she pulled herself to her feet. She was weak, and every muscle of her body ached, but she would walk herself to the outhouse. She moved toward the open door, and Jimmy followed a few paces behind her. As she stepped through the open door, the glaring afternoon sun nearly blinded her.

"To your right," Jimmy said from behind her.

She glanced around and headed in the direction of a small

wooden structure fifty feet away. It sat in the partial shade of a scrubby tree at the end of a well-beaten path.

As she began to walk, the sharp bray of a mule only a few feet away gave her a start. If in better physical condition, she was certain she would have jumped half out of her skin.

"That's Toohoo," Jimmy said from the door. "My transportation."

She patted his nose briefly as she walked past his stall beside the shack and continued to her destination. It surprised her when she opened the door, not to reek excessively. It had evidently been lightly used in recent times.

"Go ahead," Jimmy told her from several feet away. "There's only one door, and I can see it fine from here."

When she entered, the luxury of a roll of toilet paper hanging from a nail surprised her. The tin of lime in the corner to periodically cover your evidence helped explain the lack of foul odors. For a privy, it was remarkably pleasant. Through the cracks between the boards, she could see Jimmy complacently waiting. When she exited, he stood in place until she passed, then followed her back to the shack.

As she sat down on the bed, she picked up a portion of the cloth that had bound her. The negligée she had left in her bedroom when she had gone out the night before.

"Queen quose?" she asked.

"What?"

"Quose," she repeated and shook her skirt.

"Clothes. Yes." He picked up the pillowcase and handed it to her.

When she began to take the clothing from the pillowcase, she soon realized that Dutch had gone through her closet and handpicked the most revealing attire she owned. Right down to her undergarments. He clearly wanted to shame her. How had he become so vile? She was exhausted. She did not want to deal with this. Not now. She needed to feel clean. Or cleaner. And rest.

"Can I wass fings. Yado?"

"Wash your clothes?"

"Yado, Maw-wo?"

"Later? Tomorrow? Yeah, sure."

Katherine put the clothes back into the pillowcase and unlaced her shoes. She latched the handcuff around her wrist and laid down on the bed. Jimmy rinsed the towel in water and laid it over her face.

Katherine Wagner slept.

* * *

WEDNESDAY, OCTOBER 9, 1929

A month had passed since Katherine's arrival at the little shack near the mouth of the Valley of Fire. Sal had brought food two weeks ago. Another of Dutch's lackeys arrived with more groceries yesterday. There had been no change in orders from the boss.

As guard and prisoner became more accustomed to each other, and Katherine's face began healing, conversations grew more relaxed. In the first two weeks, an old fallen-down tool shed nearby offered materials for Jimmy to build a partition at one end of the shack. An iron grate left from the still and bolted over the window sufficed for bars, should his prisoner attempt to run away. With a salvaged hasp on the door, he now had an effective cell that provided both security and privacy for his inmate. If she somehow escaped, Jimmy was certain Dutch would kill him without any remorse.

Most of the time, his prisoner had been complacent. She seemingly accepted her misfortune without complaint, presuming it all would end soon enough, and she could return to Las Vegas, her home, and her freedom. She, however, slipped into a deep depression a week ago and did not eat for several days. Jimmy liked Katherine and also felt dreadfully sorry for her. He tried to remain cheerful and respectful through it all. Consequently, he did the best he could to make her living arrangement as comfortable as possible.

She had full use of the only bed, and Jimmy had slept on the floor since her arrival. He knew of an abandoned homestead a couple of miles away. After providing her a trip to the privy and making water available, he secured her in her room and made an exploratory trip there today. He found several useful amenities and made plans for their removal. First on his list was a twin bed. He doubled the cotton mattress over and tied it over his mule's saddle. Then disassembled the frame and lashed it on top. It was a precarious-looking arrangement, but stayed in place as he led Toohoo back to the shack.

When he arrived, Jimmy released his prisoner. He had hidden the pistol many days ago, seeing little need for it as long as he could keep watch on his captive. She followed him outside.

"I was a bit selfish on my first trip," he told Katherine as he began unloading the bed.

"You deserve it," she told him, smiling. "It hasn't seemed fair to me that the convict has a more comfortable sleeping arrangement than the warden."

"You never said anything about it."

"I was the one being selfish." She actually giggled slightly. "I didn't want to lose my bed."

Jimmy beamed. "That's the first time I've heard you laugh," he said. "It's nice."

Katherine helped him assemble the simple steel bed frame against the back wall of the main room. Jimmy carried in the mattress. When he rolled it out onto the frame, a blue-gray enameled pot rolled off and clanged when it hit the floor. Katherine picked it up and flushed. It was a chamber pot. She stood staring at it in her hands.

"For you," Jimmy said as he placed the lid on it. "A little less embarrassing sometimes, maybe."

"This was very thoughtful and kind of you, Jimmy. Thank you." She carried it into her room and slid it under the bed. When she returned to the main room, Jimmy was making up the bed with his blankets from the floor.

"Were there any books?" Katherine asked.

"I didn't see any."

"A book or two would be nice," she said. "I enjoy reading. Do you read, Jimmy?"

"I learned how at Mojave. I don't like it much," he scratched the scant whiskers on his chin. "There are some other things at the homestead that we could use. I'll look for books when I go back."

"You can spend longer next time." Katherine snickered. "I now have a commode."

Jimmy grinned as he nodded his head. "Tomorrow."

* * *

THURSDAY, OCTOBER 10, 1929

When he arose the next morning, Jimmy unlatched the door to Katherine's makeshift cell and knocked on it to let her know he was up. He started a fire in the small cookstove and grabbed the water bucket on his way outside. Jimmy picked up the mule's bucket on his way past the lean-to and proceeded to the spring, filling them both. On his return, Katherine met him halfway.

"I'll get breakfast," she told him in passing as she went to retrieve the supplies. "Can you bring the knife in to slice the bacon in a few minutes?"

"Sure," he told her. Katherine had assumed the cooking duties within a few days of her arrival. She enjoyed having something to do and did a much better job of it than he could. Like the pistol, he kept the butcher knife hidden outside of the cabin.

Jimmy's refrigeration system was simple. It consisted of a large crate that had once contained distillery parts. He partially submerged it in the narrow stream that flowed from the spring before dissolving into the sandy bottom of the wash that hid the weathered structures from open view. The crate had a hinged door that could be accessed by wading in the cool, calf-deep water. The cracks between the boards in the crate allowed ample flow of water to pass through while still being tight enough to discourage entrance by scavengers. A shelf installed a few inches above the water level gave ample room to store cured ham or bacon as well as cheese and butter.

He covered the whole thing with a double layer of canvas tarp whose shade and insulation kept the temperature inside within a few degrees of the water that flowed beneath it. A few large stones held everything in place. The system, though somewhat inconvenient, sufficiently kept his semi-perishables from spoiling for two or three weeks in mid-summer and longer in the early days of fall.

Katherine returned to the shack with the rare luxury of a

half-dozen eggs cradled in the flour sack she had tied around her waist as an apron. A side of bacon held beneath her other arm completed her cargo. The coffeepot already sat warming on the stove, and the butcher knife was placed on the table when Katherine stepped through the door. Jimmy was back outside, busy in his morning routine. He fed Toohoo a handful of oats and a scrap of hay, then began splitting a fresh supply of firewood for the cookstove. Kathrine sat breakfast on the table as Jimmy dropped an armload of wood near the stove.

They barely spoke as Jimmy devoured the meal. "I'll look for books," he told her, as he wiped his plate clean with the last biscuit.

"That would be wonderful. I will hurry with the dishes, so you can get going before it gets too hot out," she told him as she cleared the small table.

Jimmy emptied the bucket into the dishpan and picked up the butcher knife as he walked out the door. A few minutes later, Katherine put the last of the utensils in the Hoosier cabinet as Jimmy carried the brimming bucket in and sat it on the bedroom floor with the dipper.

"I think you're all set," Katherine told Jimmy as she handed him a not quite empty flour sack.

"Where did these come from?" Jimmy asked as he discovered four biscuits in the bottom of the sack.

"I hid them from breakfast so you could have something to eat if you get hungry before you get back."

"What about you?" he asked as Katherine retreated to her room.

"Oh, I saved a couple for myself too." She smiled as she closed the door for him to slip the bent spike through the hasp and secure her inside. She heard his footsteps cross the uneven board floor of the cabin and the outer door close. A moment later there was a faint creak of leather as he stepped into the saddle and the soft sound of hoofbeats on the sandy soil diminishing into the desert. She watched out her window but saw no sign of Jimmy or Toohoo. Katherine surmised the homestead must be another direction.

*   *   *

As Jimmy led Toohoo across the wash, the mule's unstable cargo shifted. The small dresser escaped its restraint and tumbled down the bank to halt at the bottom, but not before emptying one drawer and ejecting the second all together. Scarcely two hundred yards from the cabin, Jimmy re-secured the remaining freight and continued on in the midday heat. At the shack, he unloaded a rocking chair and carried it into the main room. He then pulled the spike out of the hasp on Katherine's door and knocked.

"I'm back," he announced a moment before the door opened.

"What did you," she began to ask. "A rocking chair!" Katherine exclaimed, spotting the newly acquired furnishing. "It's beautiful!"

"There's more." Jimmy beamed as he returned to Toohoo with Katherine on his heels.

She helped keep things from falling as Jimmy untied a salvaged window and a kerosene light designed to hang from the ceiling. Jimmy leaned the window against the front of the building and went inside to find Katherine standing on a chair, hanging the light from the rafters. When she turned toward him, her scarred face showed her elation.

"Are you pleased?" Jimmy asked, returning her smile.

"I'm beyond pleased. I am thrilled."

"Wait 'til you see the rest."

"The rest of what?"

"What I brought from the homestead."

Her puzzled expression displayed her unasked clarification.

"We lost part of our load crossing the arroyo. Follow me," he added as he grabbed the mule's reins and headed back on the trail.

Katherine spotted the beat-up little dresser first, then an array of miscellany scattered down the far embankment. Jimmy uprighted the dresser, and both began collecting the plunder and putting it into the two drawers. Katherine looked like a little kid in a candy store. She picked up a hairbrush and hand mirror, then two issues of *Collier's National Weekly Magazine*. There was an assortment of kitchen utensils and a box containing a pen, ink, and stationery. Another small mirror to hang on the wall was cracked but still usable. Then she saw her scarred face for the first time. She barely recognized the person looking back at her. She started to cry but managed to suppress it and continue working.

Suddenly she spotted the ball of clothing. A dress, then another. They looked close to her size. In the center of the ball were lady's undergarments. As she shook the dust from a camisole and held it up to look at it, Jimmy commented, "I'm not sure what some of that stuff is, but I figured you would."

When she turned toward him, he blushed and quickly looked away.

"Thank you so much," she told him. "They will all wash up. You are so thoughtful."

Jimmy thought he saw her wipe away a tear from her cheek as he put the refilled drawers back into the dresser. He then laid the chest on its back and lifted it across Toohoo's saddle. Katherine balanced it there while he tied it down.

* * *

Katherine began the afternoon washing her newly acquired wardrobe and spreading it across the tops of several nearby bushes to dry. She then prepared the most elaborate meal she could muster with their supplies to thank Jimmy for his generosity. Her laundry dried quickly in the sun, and she brought it inside. While her fresh peach cobbler baked in the dutch oven for dessert, she dragged the washtub with water left from washing into her room and took a bath. She donned clean underclothes and a flowered dress, then brushed her hair for the first time in a month. It was not long ago she would not have considered it such a luxury.

Ham steak accompanied with biscuits, beans, and fried potatoes made up the main course for supper. Jimmy's eyes lit up when she scooped large servings of cobbler for each of them to complete the feast. The sun had fallen below the mountains to the west as they finished eating, and Katherine washed dishes afterward, allowing Jimmy to relax with a cup of coffee in the shadows outdoors. As the main room darkened, she lit the overhead light. The large shade reflected the glow to illuminate all of the small room. When Jimmy came in, Katherine sat in the rocking chair poring over the October 8, 1927, issue of *Collier's*.

"There's a story in here you might like," she told him. "It's the first installment of Zane Grey's novel, *The Water Hole*." She held the magazine up to show an image of a Native American adorning the cover.

"I saw that when I found it," he acknowledged.

"Would you like to read it?"

"I don't read big words very good."

"I could read it to you."

"Would you?"

"I'd love to."

Jimmy sat on his bed leaning against the wall behind him. An hour later, he had not moved as he hung on every word Katherine recited of the tale to her audience.

* * *

FRIDAY, OCTOBER 11, 1929

The next morning, Katherine began the conversation over breakfast.

"We're near the Valley of Fire, aren't we?"

Jimmy suddenly became wary. "Why do you ask?"

"How long would it take to get to Overton?"

"Why?"

"I have a bank account there. I could give you a note for the banker, and he would give you money from my account."

"Why?" he repeated, suspiciously.

"You could buy a couple of books for me and anything else you like for yourself…" She paused momentarily as Jimmy analyzed the possibility. "…and you could keep the rest."

11

SUNDAY, JUNE 8, 1930

Conor returned to the main room of the cabin. He felt sure that Katherine Wagner had been at least held captive, if not murdered behind the adjacent partition. The roof seemed to be withstanding the rain as another flash of lightning brightened the room. The clap of thunder that followed led another deluge of hail reverberating even louder on the tin overhead.

A handful of matches lay beside the lamp by the rocking chair. Con struck one and lit the light that hung from the rafters. With the storm raging outside, he felt sure that no one would be returning soon, if ever. He put to use the ample supply of firewood and kindling piled next to the cookstove and started a small blaze in it.

He made his way back out to Bob through the torrent. He unsaddled the horse and slung the saddle across the top rail that divided the stall, then hung the bridle from the horn and laid the damp saddle blanket atop it out of the weather. An empty bucket lay on its side at Bob's feet. Con filled it from the waterfall coming off the roof and set it in front of the horse. On closer examination, he noticed the floor of the lean-to was riddled with mule tracks. A brush full of black hair hung from a nearby nail.

"Jimmy's mule," Conor said to Bob as he began to brush him down. "I doubt anyone will mind you using it."

Con made two trips to bring his gear inside the cabin. On the second, he slid the rail across Bob's enclosure and filled his canteen and water bag with rainwater flowing from the roof.

Once inside, he pulled off his poncho and hung it with his Stetson by the door. The cabin offered the only sensible place to wait out the storm and spend the night, but Con vowed to himself to make every effort not to disturb any possible evidence. He had already left his own fingerprints on the lamp and the chimney of the hanging light when he lit them. He looked around him. Somewhat relieved, aside from door-knobs, he did not think he had touched anything else with a smooth enough surface to find prints. He eyed the coffee pot and package of ground coffee on the Hoosier. As nice as a hot cup of coffee sounded right now to the still-dripping sheriff, he refrained and left them untouched.

He stoked the fire in the cookstove as full as he felt safe and began drying his gear. He first removed his Winchester from its wet scabbard and laid it across one end of the table. He hung his gun belt from the back of one of the chairs away from the heat and unrolled his bed, draping it across the rest of the table and turning it closer to the heat. He hung his boots from a rafter above the stove and after wringing much of the water from his socks, laid them across the woodpile close to the fire. Assessing the rest of his attire, his jeans were soaked to the middle of his thighs, but the rest of him was pretty dry. He stripped to his underwear and laid the jeans across the back of the second chair and moved it close to the stove.

Conor commandeered a cast-iron skillet and sat it on the stove, then sliced bacon from his saddlebags. Steam rose from his wet blankets and clothing as he warmed himself from the stove and his supper began to cook. By the time he had eaten, his jeans and socks were warm and dry. Heat from the stove had overpowered most of Con's chill from the rain, but his feet were still cold. The warm socks were comforting when he redressed.

As day turned to night, Con re-stoked the fire and sat back on a kitchen chair with his feet near the stove, resting atop the woodpile. The overhead lamp provided adequate light, so he pulled out his tally book and pencil and began to write. As he made notes, the lightning passed, and the rain subsided to a calmer yet steady din upon the roof.

He laid out his bedroll and folded the spare blanket for a pillow before the stove. After setting his Colt close at hand, Conor turned down the light and climbed between his bedding on the uneven board floor. As he lay contemplating the fate of Katherine Wagner, the sound of the rain diminishing to a faint patter overhead lulled him to sleep.

MONDAY, JUNE 9, 1930

Con awoke to the sun shining through a small window in the front of the shack. It shocked him to have slept so long. The exertion from dealing with the storm had evidently been more strenuous than he realized. The coals in the stove had long disappeared, and he felt no need to start a fire. His boots were dry but curled and slightly shrunken in the process. He still managed to force his feet into them and knew they would conform themselves to their previous shape soon enough. Con belted on his Colt and peered through the window. There was no sign anyone might be watching the domicile. He gathered two portions of carrot from the saddlebags and opened the door. Still cautious, he stalked to the lean-to.

As suspected, Bob had fared the storm well. The bucket of water remained half full and the horse eagerly ate the carrots while Conor rubbed his neck. He led the horse out and picketed him among several nearby clumps of grass that were beaten down from yesterday's hail, but not beyond consumption. Wrens flitted about the brush and scrubby trees, chirping and singing in the damp morning air as Con commenced investigating the vicinity.

He chewed on a piece of jerky while examining the remains of a shed that had been reduced to a pile of lumber and rubble. Then he continued on up a well-worn trail to a spring. The water was cool but tasted strongly of alkali. An improvised larder contained a moldy slab of bacon and equally rancid cheese and butter. Broken and discarded parts of a distillery lay decaying amid the surrounding vegetation. Any tracks that may have remained in recent days were obliterated by the storm.

He followed the stream from the spring a short distance before it sunk into the sandy soil. The remnants of a small wash below it led to the main wash that had seemingly grown in size from a flash flood in yesterday's storm. A trickle of water remained running down the center of its bottom. Also, something red at the bottom looked strangely out of place.

Con began scanning the bank for a route down and soon found one.

Slipping and sliding on the still-damp trail, he skated his way to the foot. He then worked his way upstream, searching for the red object. He spotted it, but as he neared, his heart sank. A red, beaded moccasin. In good condition. Much too small for Jimmy Garza to wear. It could belong to a child...or a woman. He had already picked it up when the realization struck him. He stacked three rocks in its place and pushed a long stick into the wet sandy soil beside them to mark the spot. When he returned to the trail, he put the shoe inside his shirt and using both hands, he scrambled back up the embankment.

When reaching the top, Con scanned the terrain upstream for any formation that might seem a likely source of the moccasin. Nothing stood out to him, and he assumed it may have washed a substantial distance in last evening's high water. Thankfully, his boots were softening up as he walked. He brought Bob back to the cabin and began loading his gear. Twenty minutes later, he swung his leg over the saddle and began his search.

As he worked his way along the crest of the bank, he followed an intermittent game trail that occasionally disappeared in yesterday's erosion. He stopped often to scan the wash with his field glasses on a lookout for any clue. A half mile upstream, the wash had widened and become shallow. There it forked and Conor followed the tributary to his left toward the foot of the Muddy Mountains. He rode up the bottom studying both sides as he went. In less than a mile, indications of enough water flow to carry the moccasin dissolved. Returning to the main wash, he continued upstream. Remnants of a road now shown along the sandy bottom where highwater had not erased the two parallel trails.

In another half mile, a second tributary entered from the left, and Con pointed Bob up the bottom of it. After a mile the streambed became boulder strewn and again, offered even less evidence of enough drainage to carry the shoe downstream.

Back below, the main channel became narrower for a few hundred yards. As it continued from the west, the road became more clearly visible along its south bank. Where the wash widened back out, the road cut across a bend in the creek and then crossed it just as a larger tributary joined in from the right. Conor followed it through his field glasses to the Old Arrowhead Trail a half mile to the north. The branch of the stream continued beyond where the mouth of Fire Canyon clearly became its source another half mile beyond. For now, he stayed on the main wash.

Five hundred yards farther, the third tributary from the left side entered the main stream. Deeper and narrower than the others, it ran from the southwest between a low ridge of forty to fifty feet in height on its left and a small butte on the right about twice that high. As Con assessed the drainage, he glimpsed movement a dozen yards above the fork. He rode toward it. A white cotton sock, caught on a twig nearly in the center of the little side stream waved in the slight breeze. He dismounted for a closer look. Finding it invigorated him. The lacy fringe at the top of the sock sent a chill up the back of his neck in the warm midmorning air.

Back in the saddle, he left the sock dangling from its snare and urged Bob ahead. He eased his way along, careful to miss no clue. Directly below the butte to his right, the waist-deep channel made a bend to the left. A Navajo blanket protruded midway in depth from the bank on the right. Shifting sand from last night's flood exposed an arm-length portion of it. Something was wrapped inside the blanket. He was afraid he knew what held it, pointing straight out from the bank. Con stepped down from Bob. Staring straight ahead, he took a deep breath and dropped Bob's reins. Methodically, he took eight steps toward the blanket, then kneeled down just within his reach.

He took another deep breath and slowly let it out. Shakily, he pushed the blanket back toward the bank. Two feet stuck out from it. A dark blue dress or skirt came to mid-calf above them. One wore a red beaded moccasin. The other was bare. The bare foot appeared partially mummified. The body had been buried in the dry desert for at least a few weeks. He pulled the blanket back over them and stood up.

On closer examination, a layer of stones a foot deep were buried over the body. After the rain, the sandy soil above showed no sign it had ever been disturbed. The grave was probably completely disguised from the curiosity of any random passerby...even before the rain. Six feet due west was a large black boulder. Every other nearby rock was red. An unmarked headstone? Someone had painstakingly buried her. Her feet facing the rising sun. A layer of stones protecting her sleep from intrusion of coyotes or lobos exhuming her. He was certain the corpse belonged to Katherine Wagner. Who would have taken such care of honoring her in death? Jimmy Garza? Jimmy Garza. Preparing her for the spirit world.

Conor unrolled the poncho from his bedroll. Carefully, he used it to wrap several layers of the heavy oilcloth around the exposed feet and legs. He bound it securely.

"I hope that will keep the scavengers from bothering you," Con uttered. "At least 'til tomorrow," he added, then stepped into the saddle and trotted north, staying out of the wash and off the little road.

As he crossed the Old Arrowhead Trail a quarter mile west of the Fire Canyon Wash, Bob had already fallen into his ground-eating comfortable lope. He slowed slightly in a few places when they entered the mouth of the canyon, but kept a steady pace. When the canyon made its sweeping turn west, they climbed up through the draw continuing north. Crossing the saddle at the west end of Baseline Mesa, they maintained their northerly course across the silica-laced desert to Overton Ridge. After cutting through Overton Ridge at Kaolin Wash, they followed the wash down to hit the road three miles south of Overton and cantered into town.

* * *

Con tied Bob in the shade near the mercantile where he had parked his car a week earlier. He loosened the horse's girth and slipped him a carrot then crossed the street, and at four p.m., Conor walked through the door of the bank. Bill Howard leaned against the doorframe of his office talking to his clerk when the sheriff entered.

"Good afternoon, Sheriff," he greeted as he came toward Con with his outstretched hand. "What can I help you with?"

"Can we talk privately?"

"Come in." Howard motioned to his office and closed the door behind him. "I didn't see your car."

"I rode in."

The answer caught the banker off guard. "Rode?"

"Horseback."

"From where?"

"Bitter Spring initially, but about fifteen miles south of here today...maybe a little farther."

"Where's your horse?" he asked as he filled a glass of water for the sheriff and motioned to the chair in front of his desk.

"In the shade by the mercantile."

"What brings you here?" Mr. Howard continued in wonder as he took his own seat.

"Well, first I need a telephone," Con began.

The banker turned the modern rotary telephone on his desk around to face the sheriff. "Would you like me to leave?"

"No. Some of this concerns you too. We will talk about that in a few minutes," he said as he dialed.

"Clark County Sheriff's Department," Hazel answered cheerfully.

"Hello, Hazel. This is Con."

"Where are you?"

"Overton. Is Jesse around?"

"He's out right now."

"Okay. Here's what I need you to do. Have Jesse and Hal meet me at daylight tomorrow morning at John Clark's grave. It's in the Valley of Fire. If Jesse doesn't know where it is, Hal will. Tell them to bring shovels. Are Ben and Whit on the board tomorrow?"

"Yes."

"Have them come too."

"Why are you digging up John Clark? Didn't he die about fifteen years ago...and don't you need a Court Order? Should I call Judge Tucker?"

"We're not digging up John Clark. Katherine Wagner is buried about a mile from there."

Hazel gasped but said nothing for a moment. "Anything else?"

"I found the cabin where Mrs. Wagner was being held captive too." Conor ran through a list of mental notes he carried in his head. "Tell them to bring plenty of water...and food too. It'll be a long hot day. And don't tell anyone where they're going or what they're doing."

Hazel read her notes back to her boss.

"You've got it," Con noted. "I'll see you Wednesday."

"Yes, sir," Hazel answered and hung up the telephone.

* * *

Bill Howard sat pale-faced, staring blankly across the room. Returning from semi-consciousness, he asked the sheriff, "Should I deliver the letter?"

"Not until the coroner has made positive identification. I'll call you, and we'll travel out together to the Brumbaugh's farm."

"Sure," he agreed.

"The case has progressed considerably since we spoke last week. Jimmy was Jimmy Garza. Turns out he was related to a close friend of my family. His parents live north of Moapa. The buckle he wore belonged to Mrs. Wagner. I don't know how he got it. He may have stolen it, but I doubt it. I'm not sure what will become of Katherine Wagner's bank account," Con concluded. "I suppose that will depend on her will."

"Actually, she named Mrs. Brumbaugh as the sole beneficiary on the account," Howard replied. "As soon as a death certificate is issued, the funds will be allocated to her."

"We should have something in a few days. I will try to bring it with me when we visit the farm."

"That should be fine," the banker resolved, still in a daze from the events of the past half hour.

"Could I make a personal call from your telephone?" Conor asked.

"Certainly." Howard stood and went to the door. "I'll be in the lobby."

* * *

April answered the telephone on the second ring. "Hello?"

"Good afternoon, Princess. Is your mother home?"

"Sure is, Con. I'll go get her."

As he listened, he heard the screen door slap closed in the background. A welcome voice came on, "Hello, sweetheart."

Con was momentarily dumbstruck by the greeting. "Well...hello," he finally managed.

June continued as if she had not noticed the pause. "Where are you?"

"Uh, Overton."

"Any luck?"

"Yes. I'm pretty sure I found Katherine Wagner's grave."

"Oh. I'm sorry. That's not the news I was hoping for," she responded sincerely.

"Me either," Conor answered, then reviewed his endeavors of the last few days. "Hal and Jesse will meet me in the morning with two other deputies," he finished.

"I miss you. When will you be home?"

"Late tomorrow night, I think. It will be a long day."

"Call me when you can so I know that you are home and safe."

"I will. I may wait until morning if it's very late."

"Okay. Good evening then?" she asked.

"Yes, I have a long ride ahead of me yet," Con replied.

"I love you."

Again, another declaration that struck him. "I think that's what I'm feeling about you too," he answered. "It's new to me. I've never experienced this sensation before."

"I fell in love with April's father a long time ago. We were young, but I knew what it was when it happened. It was not infatuation. It was love." June paused to choose exactly how she wanted to proceed. "I am older now. More mature. A mother...yet...I've not known this amazing emotion before either. The intensity is beyond my wildest dreams. I truly do love you, Conor. I know it. I am sure of it."

"I...I don't know what to say."

"You don't have to say anything. I know by your actions and the respect you show that you care about me. I don't want to embarrass you or make you uncomfortable. If you don't want me to say it, tell me, and I won't. I don't want you to feel obligated to say something you are not sure of. I don't want to scare you. And very most importantly, I don't want to lose you."

"I...I'm fonder of you than anyone I've ever known in my entire life. There. I said it. I got it out. I usually get tongue-tied just thinking about it."

"Thank you. You have no idea how good it feels to hear that from you...you need to go. You have an important, and often dangerous, job to do. Don't think about me while you are working. Keep your mind clear. Instead, think about me when you go to bed tonight...I love you," and she hung up before he could stammer through another difficult discourse.

* * *

When Conor opened the office door, the bank was closed. Bill Howard sat at the clerk's desk going over a ledger.

He looked up at Con. "Everything okay?"

"Yes. Sorry I took so long. I guess I got lost in the conversation."

"Oh, that's quite alright. It gave me a chance to check some paperwork without interruptions. Your wife?"

"Lady friend."

"The pretty blonde who was with you last week?"

Con blushed. "Yes, that's her."

"Congratulations. I hear that she's very nice."

"How's that?"

"Clerk at the mercantile spoke to her while you were in here. Small town, you know."

Conor nodded and grinned. "I've been on bacon and jerky for almost four days now, anyplace open to eat this time of day?"

"Shamrock Café down the street on the left."

"Irish?"

"Assuredly." Bill Howard grinned, knowing of the sheriff's Irish heritage.

"I think I saw it when I rode in. How about somewhere to water my horse before I leave town?"

"Muddy River across the tracks is probably the easiest."

"Thank you for your hospitality, Mr. Howard." Con extended his hand.

"Anytime, Sheriff."

"I will call you soon, sir, and we can deliver that letter to Mrs. Brumbaugh."

"I am very curious as to its contents," Howard commented.

"You're not alone." Con donned his hat and walked out the door.

* * *

Conor took Bob to water then tied him with his picket rope to a tree in the vacant lot behind the café. There, he could browse on dried grass while Con went inside. A young Native American girl greeted him when he entered the empty eatery and sat down at the counter. He ordered lamb chops from the menu posted on the wall behind the counter and a Coca-Cola. She brought the Coca-Cola while the cook prepared his supper. As he waited, the girl wiped down the already clean counter out of boredom and engaged in nonchalant conversation. Con fully understood from his sister how waitresses could pick up local gossip just by keeping an attentive ear to daily chitchat.

"Have you worked here long?" Conor asked.

"About two years," she replied.

"Did you live around here before that?"

"Over at Moapa."

"An Indian kid about your age has been living down south of here. He's from Moapa too. Name's Jimmy. You know him?"

"Jimmy Garza?" the waitress verified.

"That's him," Con answered, somewhat surprised.

"I know him. He comes in sometimes. Likes his Coca-Cola, like you." She grinned a bit sarcastically.

"Yep," Con agreed, chuckling as he smacked his lips. "I'm guilty. I like the sweet stuff. Never got enough cookies and candy as a kid, I guess."

When the cook hollered from the kitchen, the waitress got his order and sat it in front of him. She went back to the kitchen and returned with a bowl of chili for herself.

"My name's Dellis," she offered, a bit flirtatiously, as she took a seat at the far end of the counter.

"Nice to meet you, Dellis," Conor replied, intentionally refraining from sharing his own name. "Jimmy been around recently?"

"He came in about three weeks ago, I think it was. Had lunch. Said he left his mule over at Sam Quail's place for a few days and was hopping the freight train to Las Vegas."

"Does he do that often?"

"No. Maybe once every couple of months." Her face reddened visibly beneath her dark complexion. "Too many white-eyes, he says."

Now Con blushed. "Yeah, I can understand that." He waited a bit trying to keep his questioning casual so as not to cause suspicion. "Was he doing all right when you saw him?"

"No, actually not." She thought about it for a minute before answering, continuing, "He was sad. The woman he was taking care of died."

"What from?"

"He didn't say. She was kinda old I think...anyway, her son made Jimmy bury her. He didn't like doing that...I think he really liked her. I remember he would buy little presents for her sometimes when he came to town."

"I don't know Jimmy except through family. Sounds like he's a nice guy."

"Not just a nice guy, a really good guy."

"Glad to hear it," Con replied appreciatively as he stood. "Don't need a slice of pie to satisfy that sweet tooth?"

"Not this time." Conor patted his stomach. "The lamb chops were more than enough."

For the first time, Dellis noticed his gun belt. "Are you a deputy or something?"

"Yeah," Con answered and quickly changed the subject. "Great food, Dellis."

She returned his smile at the sound of her name and seeing him drop enough money on the counter for the meal plus a comfortable tip.

"I'll be sure to stop back by next time I'm up here." He took his hat from the rack by the door and walked out.

As he tightened the cinch on Bob's saddle, Con noted his Winchester still in its scabbard. He regretted his carelessness to have left it in plain sight for a little over two hours while at the bank and café. In a small town like Overton, most definitely someone noticed its presence. On the other hand, everyone in town would have noticed if he carried it around with him. At least no one stole it.

12

TUESDAY, JUNE 10, 1930

Sheriff Conor Armenta sat astride Bob atop an oblong knoll. They were fifty feet higher than the Old Arrowhead Trail below them. He had made a cold camp shortly after midnight a mile to the north near the mouth of Fire Canyon and been in the saddle for nearly an hour. The slightest hint of gray appeared in the sky behind him as he scanned the darkness up the Valley of Fire to the west. First, an approaching pair of headlights appeared, then another. In less than a minute, the first set of lights disappeared and a moment later the valley returned to total darkness.

"That'll be them," he told Bob and turned the horse to work his way eastward down the hill to the grave of John Clark. Con recalled Clark's demise. He had been traveling by buckboard from California to Salt Lake City a decade and a half earlier. Evidently searching for water along Fire Canyon Wash, he died of apparent thirst there. Little had he known he was only a couple of miles from the same spring the moonshiners used just a few months ago. Where Katherine Wagner had been held captive.

The sun lit up the tops of the brilliant red ridges and bluffs that gave the Valley of Fire its name. John Clark's grave remained in shadow from the peak of a conical formation of stone south of Elephant Rock. Con stood in the middle of the road chewing a piece of lamb jerky when the sedan delivery with Coroner painted on the side rounded a turn in the road a quarter mile away. The car that followed bore the star of the Clark County Sheriff's Department on the door.

"Hello there, stranger," Hal greeted as he stepped from the car. "I allowed an hour to drive from the trestle to here. Road's not so good anymore...nor my memory. This place is a little farther out than I recalled too."

Conor grinned. "I haven't been waiting very long."

"I didn't even know where it was," Jesse admitted as he came near carrying a Stanley vacuum bottle. "Had your morning coffee yet?"

"No, I had a cold camp."

Jesse pulled the cork from the bottle and began filling the steel cup. "Dottie made it," he commented. "Not me."

"Thank you," Con replied, taking a sip. "First I've had since Friday."

"So, you found Katherine Wagner's grave?" Hal asked.

"I believe so. It's about a mile from here. You should be able to drive about halfway there. It's down this road." Con indicated the dim trail down the nearby wash. "Sunday's rain may have washed it out a bit. I'll lead the way."

"Good morning, Sheriff," Whitney Ellis hailed as he and Bennett Neilly walked up. Jesse had ridden with Hal, and the other two followed in the patrol car.

"Glad you two guys are here," Conor welcomed. "We'll have our work cut out for us."

"We're ready," Ben replied.

"I know that neither of you have much experience with investigations. Jesse has a little," Con began. "From this point on, if you see anything that looks out of the ordinary, bring it to either Dr. Martin's or my attention before you touch it. We are investigating a probable murder. The smallest thing could turn out to be a key piece of evidence. Keep your eyes peeled."

"Yes, sir," Whit answered, and Ben nodded.

"Got it," Jesse chimed in.

"You're driving down this remnant of a wagon road behind me. I'm walking my horse ahead of you, scouting for obstacles. Take it slow and easy."

Con mounted up and headed down the side road. When they got to where their road crossed the main wash, he halted them.

"Wait here," he told Hal. "We're going this way." He pointed up the wash. "Let me see if you can drive part way."

Conor rode a couple hundred yards up the wash as Hal and Jesse watched him, then turned around and came back.

"You can back your delivery up to where we leave the main wash. It's too narrow to turn around. The tributary we follow from there isn't drivable."

Jesse got out to guide him, as Hal prepared to back the sedan delivery up the wash.

"Leave your car here and bring whatever you brought with you," Con told Ben and Whit. "It's close to a half mile from here."

Con rode past Hal as he cautiously backed his way up the wash. At the fork, he stopped and dismounted. Dropping Bob's reins, the horse began grazing on the ricegrass growing in the wash. The coroner's car came to a halt just as the two deputies walked up carrying shovels and two water bags.

"How did you find this place?" Jesse asked, scanning the vast valley.

Conor reached into his saddlebag and brought out the moccasin he had found. "Exhibit A," he said. "I found that about a mile and a half down the wash. Fresh after Sunday night's flood." He handed the shoe to Hal. "I already picked that up before I discovered it was evidence." He looked at Ben and Whit. "I marked the spot," he added before turning back to the coroner. "Grab your camera."

He walked toward a small white piece of cloth waving slightly in the breeze on a twig a few yards away. The others followed.

"What's that?" Ben asked.

"Exhibit B," Con replied. "A sock."

The two deputies looked at each other, then at Jesse just as Hal walked past them with a sophisticated-looking camera hanging from a strap around his neck.

"Eight paces," he said aloud as he reached the sock. "That's thirty-two feet for me." Hal scribbled something in his notebook as he kneeled down and photographed the sock. Then carefully he untangled the lace fringe of the sock from its snare and slipped it into a cotton sack. He penciled B on a manila tag, put it in the bag with the sock and handed it to Whit. "Put that in the back of my car with the other bag. Then unload the stretcher."

"Jesse, grab a half dozen more evidence bags from the front."

"Got it," he replied and returned to the car.

As Hal took two photos of the drainage they would soon

enter, he winked at Con while the sheriff picked up the waterbags and hung them from Bob's saddle horn.

"They'll learn fast on this case," Conor commented to Hal out of earshot of the others.

As Ben and Whit pulled the stretcher out of the back of the delivery, Hal called to them. "Lay those shovels on the stretcher along with the bags. They'll be easier to carry that way."

Con stepped into the saddle and spoke to Hal. "Just follow the wash. You can't miss it. It's about a half mile. Just below that butte on the right." He rode on ahead.

"Jesse," Hal said, "you follow Con and keep a close eye out for anything he might miss from horseback." He turned to the other two who had hardly spoken a word that he had noticed. "You two boys follow behind me with the stretcher. Keep the chatter to a minimum. I'm counting."

"Yes, sir," they replied almost in unison.

Jesse walked ahead with longer strides and soon was thirty yards in the lead. At one hundred paces, Hal paused momentarily to make a hash-mark in his notebook and scuff a mark in the soil. He did the same at two and three hundred paces. Suddenly, a shot rang out from ahead. The report startled all four as it rent through the quiet morning air.

"Forty-two," Hal said aloud as he stopped and quickly raised his head just in time to see two large vultures take to the air in the distance ahead. "I guess we know how far it is now, huh?"

"Hell of a way to find out," Whit added, his heart still racing with adrenaline.

"Yep," Hal replied. "Forty-six."

"Forty-two, sir," Whit corrected, then bit his tongue.

"Just checking, deputy. Didn't rattle you too bad," Hal added. "Forty-two," and continued up the wash.

* * *

Con and Jesse were carefully unwrapping the feet of the corpse when Hal marched up.

"Six hundred seventy-two," he said as he stopped adjacent to them. "Much damage?" he asked as he made notes.

"Only to my rain poncho," Conor replied. "When I found the feet and legs exposed from the sand yesterday, I wrapped them in it to avoid that very possibility. To my surprise, it worked."

"How long do you think she's been dead?" Hal asked.

"Just from what I have learned from you? Three to six weeks is my guess. The feet and legs are beginning to mummify from being buried in the hot, dry, sandy soil. No rain that I know of for several weeks until Sunday afternoon and night."

Hal took several photographs of the site. At least one included what Con suspected was intended as a nondescript headstone. Two or three closeups of the layer of stones atop the body. Ben and Whit arrived with the stretcher moments behind Hal and watched intently as the coroner began his assessment. He took more pictures as he rolled back the blanket exposing the extremities.

"Okay, fellas," Hal began. "Take turns. Two at a time. Don't hurry. When you get down about eighteen inches, you should hit this layer of stone." He pointed it out on the bank. "Be extra careful when you start getting close, just in case. We can't risk damaging the remains. This is absolutely crucial. Go ahead and get started."

Con and Hal leaned against the far bank beneath the shade of a clump of rabbitbrush and observed the younger men at work.

"I think you're right," Hal said. "About a month. Maybe a little longer. I'll be able to get a closer estimate with an autopsy."

"Did you notice the black rock on top of the bank?" Conor asked.

"Headstone," Hal answered. "Feet facing the rising sun to welcome the new day in the spirit world. Layer of stones to protect against scavengers. All things not out of character for many of our Indian friends."

"Paiute?"

"I'm not well schooled in Paiute traditions specifically," Hal considered. "Nor any other tribe, for that matter."

"Keep in mind our most likely mortician," Con mentioned.

"The Paiute kid."

"Jimmy Garza. The teachers at Mojave tried to beat the Indian out of him, but at the same time he might have been exposed to other traditions, too. A young Indian, untrained in ancestral rituals."

Hal mulled over the possibilities. "Probably just doing what he thought should be the right way."

"Exactly."

At that moment, the distinct clink of a shovel striking stone sounded.

"Stop!" Hal interrupted the excavators. "With your hands from here on out."

"Are you sure?" Ben balked.

"I'm sure," Hal answered. "One little slip of a shovel between two stones could be detrimental to the entire investigation. You can dig out individual stones and pitch them away from the grave. When we have the outline of the body, you can dig down halfway around her. Then we can all get a hold on the blanket and lift her straight up. Once she's on top of the soil, we'll slide her out this way and put her on the stretcher."

"Yes, sir," Ben answered as Jesse and Whit had already begun following Hal's instructions.

Rocks and handfuls of dirt began to fly from the hole as all three deputies were able to work at the same time closer together. As the last of the rocks began to disappear, they uncovered a wide board that covered the head and torso. Jesse called Con and Hal to have a look.

"It seems like he didn't want to hurt her with the rocks, so he put the board over her face and body to protect her," Conor surmised.

"Never seen anything like it," the grizzled coroner agreed. Con thought he heard a frog in the old man's throat as he said it and turned away. The display of tenderness had finally penetrated the thick hide of the man who could stomach anything.

"You're almost there, boys," Con added. "Keep up the good work. Slow and easy."

A few minutes later, they could clearly see the outline of the body. Carefully working their way around, they pulled up on the sides of the blanket until it could easily be lifted out. With two on each side and one at her head, the group raised her from the grave and to the stretcher positioned beneath her feet. Hal took photographs of the blanket-wrapped body on the stretcher.

"Let's see who we have here," he said as he leaned over to pull back the blanket over her face. His momentary lapse of compassion a short time ago had quickly been retaken by years of less than pleasant exposure to the more gruesome aspects of his career. "Well, the right side of her face is bashed in, and the rest is pretty shrunken from mummification, but this is Katherine Wagner. I don't know her well, but I've seen her enough times. This is her."

Conor peered over his shoulder trying to visualize the face being fuller. "I believe you're right, but I hope we can get a more positive identification."

"Joe Anderson took her appendix out a couple of years ago," Hal remembered. "That'll narrow the field considerably."

"Maybe dental records?" Con asked.

"We'll find out."

Her eyes were closed, the coroner noted as he photographed her exposed face. Then he proceeded to pull the rest of the blanket back. She wore a navy-blue cotton skirt and matching velvet blouse with a purple silk sash. An unbleached wool, Navajo-style shawl covered her shoulders and a silver squash blossom necklace and earrings decorated her neck and ears. The hands crossed over her chest revealed a wedding ring. The distinctive gold ring with two small diamonds set side by side adorned her left hand.

"There can't be too many rings like that one," Con observed.

Hal took more photographs and wrote down a series of notes, occasionally glancing back at the corpse. He then rewrapped the blanket around her.

When he rose up, Jesse appeared stoic. Neilly and Ellis both looked queasy.

"Get yourselves a drink of water," Conor told them as he brought a water bag from Bob's saddle horn. "Which one of you is carrying the shovels?"

"I will," Jesse volunteered.

The sheriff traded the water bag for his canteen and handed it to Jesse. "You'll probably want that before you get back to the cars. Stay together. Pretend that's your sick grandma on the stretcher. Slow and easy. Take plenty of breaks and trade off if you need to."

Hal was a couple hundred yards down the wash when Con climbed on Bob to catch up to him.

"You doin' all right?" Con asked as he rode up alongside him.

"Sure," he answered, wiping his bandanna across his forehead as he walked.

"Drink?"

"Why not."

Con paused and handed him a water bag. Hal took a big swig. Rinsing his mouth, he spit most of it out. Then took a second that he swallowed.

"I'll leave the water at the cars," Conor told him as he received the bag from Hal. "It's probably close to two miles from the cars to the cabin. Straight down the main wash. I'll continue on to make sure the road isn't washed out anywhere. I should be at the shack when you get there...if you don't see me beforehand."

"We'll be along." The old man waved his hand as the sheriff rode ahead.

* * *

When Con rode into the yard at the cabin, he stopped at the spring to let Bob have his fill, then led him into the stall and unsaddled him. He picked up Jimmy's brush and gave the horse a thorough rub down before picketing him with access to food, shade, and water. The sound of squeaking brakes drew Con's attention to the two approaching automobiles.

"We made it," Jesse announced as he and Hal climbed out of the coroner's car.

"It's nearly noon," Conor announced. "Other than some blood in the cabin, there's little chance of running across much that's very gruesome. You fellas feel like eating now?"

"I could eat," Jesse chimed in as he glanced toward Whit and Ben.

"I'm ready," Hal announced.

"Me too," Ben agreed.

Whitney Ellis, the eldest of the three deputies, had yet to fully recover from dealing with Mrs. Wagner's corpse. "I'll just look around some."

"Remember the rules, Whit," Con reminded as he wandered toward the cabin.

"Don't touch anything?"

"Yep." Con followed along to retrieve some jerky from his saddlebags. He returned to find the threesome in the shade of a scrub oak tree.

"I brought an extra ham sandwich," Hal announced as he held out the contribution wrapped in waxed paper to Con. "... if you're gettin' tired of jerky, that is."

"Never happen," Conor replied, accepting the doctor's gift. "But I've been a bachelor long enough to not turn down a free meal when it's offered."

The two old friends both chuckled in understanding.

"Hey, Sheriff," Whitney called from the end of the cabin. "What do you make of this?"

Con wolfed down the sandwich as he returned to the cabin. He took a drink from his canteen to wash it down with as he passed the stable to join the deputy. Ellis stood beside a pile of firewood neatly stacked against the cabin.

"What'd you find?" Con asked.

"First I saw this." He pointed to a rusty layer of steel sandwiched between two well-worn pieces of wood making up the hilt of a knife. It lay wedged into the woodpile about a foot above the ground. He got down on his knees. "Then I found this." He pointed into a space beside the knife.

Conor joined him and peered into the hole. "It looks like the butt of a pistol," he assessed.

"That's what I thought," the deputy agreed.

"Grab your camera, Hal," Con called to the trio beneath the tree.

"I thought it was lunchtime," Hal grumbled as he lumbered to his feet.

"It was," the sheriff answered, holding back a snicker. "Now it's over."

"For a guy who just got a free lunch," Hal complained as he joined them. "You sure can be a pain in the neck, Con."

Whit could not stifle his laugh.

"And you agree?" Conor stared at Ellis.

"So, what have you got here, deputy?" Hal quickly interrupted, giving Whit an escape from Con's chiding.

"A knife and what looks like a pistol, sir." Whit kneeled back down. "Right here." He pointed.

Hal joined him peering into the stack below. "Good find," he commented as he snapped a photograph. "It's too dark back in there for the pistol to show up, and the flash won't work there either," Hal instructed. "Start down through the stack. Be mindful of anything else in there and stop as soon as that gun is visible so I can take a couple more pictures."

He dug down through the heap and discovered a snub-nosed .38 revolver and a butcher knife. Hal took another picture.

"Things unlikely to end up there by coincidence," Con mused. Picking up the revolver with his bandanna, he checked the cylinder. "One empty chamber and five unfired rounds." Looking down the short barrel, he found what appeared to be an insect nest. "Looks like a spider nest in the barrel. That doesn't mean the gun couldn't have been fired three or four weeks ago, but it definitely leaves room to question the likelihood of it." He called to Jesse and Ben to bring evidence bags.

"Jesse," Conor addressed after the knife and gun were safely tagged and bagged, "You and Whit keep looking around out here. Ben, come inside with us."

Con led Hal and Ben into the cabin and waited without comment as they began to look around.

Ben made his way to the door of the second room. He saw the bars over the windows, then looked back at the doorjamb and the hasp. "A cell?" he asked cautiously.

"It sure looks like it to me," Con answered.

Ben went on into the cell. Hal and Conor followed. The sun filled the little room with bright yellow light reflecting from the wallpaper.

"Kind of nice actually," Ben commented.

"I thought so too," Con agreed.

He made his way toward the open trunk. "That's a big ol' steamer."

"It was in Katherine Wagner's garage two months ago," Con told him.

Hal's head snapped around. His eyes met Conor's with a fiery glare, but he made no comment. Ben continued with his careful examination of the room when the stain on the small

Navajo rug by the bed caught his attention. He kneeled down to see it better. But did not reach to touch it. "Blood?"

"I think so," the sheriff agreed. "What else do you see?"

"A mirror and hairbrush there on the dresser. A couple of dresses hanging on the wall. A bigger mirror hanging there." He nodded toward it and continued to scan the room. "Everything looks neat and pretty clean except for that stain…and all the stuff out of the trunk."

"Now then, why would someone who kept this little room so neat and tidy, then throw half the stuff out of that trunk onto the bed and just leave it?" Con asked him.

"Somebody else, did it?"

"Exactly," Con blurted out with enthusiasm. "You hit the jackpot! Now who do you suppose would have done that?"

"The killer," Ben answered with fervor. "The killer would leave a mess."

Conor encouraged Neilly's thought process. "Why not just walk out?"

"Jimmy Garza," Hal spoke up. "Jimmy Garza would dig through the trunk knowing Mrs. Wagner had a nearly new Navajo skirt and blouse. Everything right down to her earrings."

"And a Navajo blanket to bury her in. His boss made him bury her," Con added.

"How do you know that?" Hal interrogated.

"Waitress in Overton told me."

"She just offered that information up. Out of the blue?" he asked incredulously.

"Almost. She told me that Jimmy was upset the last time she'd seen him because the woman he was looking after died, and his boss made him bury her."

"If Jimmy Garza dressed her up in all of her Navajo finery

to be buried in, why doesn't she have the fancy Navajo buckle on?" Hal asked accusingly.

"She promised he could have it when she went home," Con answered.

"Meaning, home. Pine Canyon Road."

"I imagine that was her intention. Not how it turned out."

"And where did you learn that, Sherlock Holmes?" Hal asked sarcastically.

"Lonny Tido. Jimmy's best friend. One of the witnesses who identified the buckle. Jimmy had told Lonny that a few months ago."

The room was silent. Hal did not reply.

Bewildered by the conversation, Ben finally asked, "How do you guys know all of this stuff?"

"Investigation," Hal answered.

"And some conjecture," Conor added. "You did a good job inspecting the room, Ben. I don't recall you missing anything I found when I entered the room. Good work."

"Speaking of conjecture." Hal's glare returned to meet Con's eye. The sheriff knew it was time to explain his knowledge of the trunk.

"Ben, keep looking around the rest of the cabin. I've got to show Hal where I found the moccasin."

Hal followed Con out the door. Halfway to the wash, Conor heard him clear his throat behind him. He stopped and glanced around to see Jesse and Whit looking around the spring.

"So," Hal began. "How did you come to the conclusion that trunk was in Katherine Wagner's garage two months ago? Just driving by out there? The gate was open, so you drove on up to the house? Someone, say, Dutch maybe...he's standing in the garage maybe, with the door wide open, and you just happened to notice this exact trunk there when you two are chatting...about...say, the weather, maybe." Con could feel Hal's eyes boring holes through him. "Is that how it went, Sheriff Armenta?" He paused, waiting for Conor's response. "The truth, the whole truth, and nothing but the truth. Is that right, Sheriff?"

"Not necessarily," Con finally managed to get out after taking a long deep breath.

"I'm not Judge Tucker, necessarily. So, just how, necessarily, did the circumstances arrive that you would happen to know that a particular trunk, that is now at an alleged murder scene, was in the victim's garage, not necessarily nearly eighty miles away not necessarily about the same time that Brice Campbell not necessarily offed himself?"

"I saw it there," Con answered, staring down both barrels of Hal's glare.

"When?"

"The night after Campbell's suicide."

"Night. Say, seven, eight o'clock?"

"One or two o'clock."

"You drove out there in the middle of the night and broke into Katherine Wagner's garage?" Hal was beside himself. "What if somebody saw you? What were you thinking?"

"Nobody saw me. Nobody could see me."

"You're the invisible man too?"

"I traded my pickup for Dottie's runabout. I drove out to Paddy's and rode Bob unshod to the Muleskinner's Rest. I left him about a hundred yards away from the fence behind the house. I rode back to Paddy's, drove Dottie's car back to the station and drove my pickup home before Hazel got there the next morning."

"Why would you take a chance like that?"

"I didn't want to tip off any suspects by getting a search warrant to investigate the place."

"What were you looking for?"

"After you left the Campbells' place, I tracked Brice to the back of the Wagners' place. When I drove back to town, his tracks were at the gate where he'd let himself out and back in again the night before."

"Conjecture," Hal muttered, all of his fury escaped him.

"Exactly."

Hal seemed to have forgotten his notion of Conor breaking into the garage. Con felt no need to remind him.

* * *

As they stood on the bank above the deepest portion of the wash, Con pointed out the miniature cairn of rocks and the stick below that marked where he found the moccasin. He left Hal and Jesse in charge of the investigation and collecting evidence, including the trunk, right down to the bottle of perfume and books Jimmy bought at the mercantile in Overton.

Conor saddled Bob up for the ride back to Bitter Spring. He had a dozen miles ahead of him, followed by fifty miles of questionable roads back to Las Vegas. He still needed to fill Paddy's truck with gas there and another twenty miles out to his ranch. He looked up at the midday sun, then at his watch. One-thirty. He led Bob to the spring for one last fill of water then stepping into the saddle, he rode back by the cabin.

"We've had a good day, gentlemen. Not a word to anyone about anything that's gone on out here today. I'll see you in my office at eight o'clock in the morning," He looked over to Hal. "I'll stop by the morgue afterward."

13

The sun shone brightly in his open bedroom window. A slight breeze moved the curtain hanging over it. Conor looked for his watch just as the clock in the living room began to chime seven times. A shave and sponge bath would have to suffice this morning. He did not have time to fill the bathtub.

The sheriff walked into the department office with a sack of doughnuts at a quarter 'til eight. Jesse and Whit stood by the coffeepot. Each had a cup of coffee in one hand, a doughnut in the other. Con sat his bag down on the table beside two others that preceded it and filled a coffee cup.

"Good morning, Sheriff," Whit greeted cheerfully. "What time did you get in?"

"Around two," he answered as he selected a doughnut from an already opened sack. "And you two?"

"Ten, Sheriff," Jesse replied for both of them.

At that moment, Ben entered the door with a bag of dough-nuts in hand. "Good morn..." he began as he spotted three more bags on the table.

"Mornin'." Con raised his cup in a mock toast. "Looks like we all had the same idea this morning."

"And not enough time for breakfast," Ben added with a grin.

Armenta and his three deputies refilled coffee cups, chose a second doughnut and entered his office, closing the door behind them. Conor rolled his chair out from behind the desk. He offered it to the deputies beside the other two chairs, then perched himself on the corner of his desk.

"What happened out there after I left?" he asked the group in general.

After a twenty-minute discussion, Con surmised the rest of their day had been uneventful.

"Okay," he concluded. "I need reports from each of you on my desk by noon. We've already discussed most of what we found yesterday, but I want them written individually. No comparing notes."

"Yessir," Jesse replied, and the others agreed.

"And," Con began. "I can't stress enough how critical this investigation is. Keep this entire case, everything you know or suppose, under your hats until I say otherwise. We can't afford to tip off a murderer with what we've found. I trust each of you, or you wouldn't have been chosen to be involved. Don't give me reason to question that confidence."

The trio departed to go about their duties.

"Anything I need to know about?" Conor asked Hazel.

"Dr. Martin's autopsy report on John Doe is on your desk

along with all of the deputies' reports since Thursday. In reverse chronology, of course."

Con sighed as he crossed the room to refill his coffee cup and return to the weeks' worth of paperwork on his desk. He began by extracting the envelope containing Hal's report from two-thirds of the way down through the stack. He started to read. Cause of death, gunshot wound to the head. Entrance, base of the skull three-quarters of an inch above the foramen magnum. Exit, none. Bullet appears to be .25 caliber. Time of death between eight and eleven p.m., Saturday, May 31, 1930.

The rest of the report gave descriptions and distribution of multiple body parts found at the scene. Con picked up the telephone and dialed the *Las Vegas Evening Review*.

"Is Stanley Olsen in?" he asked the female voice who answered the telephone.

"He's in with the editor. Can I ask who's calling?"

"Sheriff Conor Armenta."

"Please hold on for just a minute," she answered. Con heard the sound of hurried footsteps receding into the distance after the familiar clunk of the receiver being dropped on the hard surface of a desk. A shuffling of larger feet approached and…

"Yessir, Sheriff. This is Stan," the young man's voice greeted excitedly. "What can I do for you?"

"Can you come by my office in about a half hour? I've got some information on our train victim."

"Yeah. I sure could. I'll see you shortly."

When Conor hung up the telephone, he glanced at the clock. Eight forty-five. He called Robert Westcott's office. June answered.

"Good morning, Mrs. Sommers."

"Well, good morning, Sheriff Armenta. What can I do for you today?"

"How about joining me for lunch?"

"Is there a catch?"

"Nope. Eleven thirty at the Mesquite?"

"Should I just wait until noon, or will you actually be there on time?" she mocked him after his late arrival to their last lunch date.

"I'll be there."

"As will I."

"Are you smiling?"

Con's question caught her off guard. "Well...yes. As a matter of fact, I am."

"I can hear it in your voice."

"And you?"

"Yes, definitely. I think I've been smiling a lot lately."

"Me too. I love you, Conor."

Still unprepared to hear that declaration, Con stammered, "I'll see you soon," and hung up.

When he looked up, Stan Olsen entered the outer office. Conor glanced at the clock. Five minutes 'til nine.

"A short half hour," he offered without getting up from his desk.

Stanley crossed the room, smiling. "I was free. I can wait if you'd like."

"No, you're fine." Con stood to shake the reporter's hand. "Come on in. Have a seat."

Stan pulled his notepad from his pocket and sat eagerly awaiting what information the sheriff had to share.

Con glanced at Hal's report. "His name was Jimmy Garza, sometimes called Jimmy Pete. He's the son of Luis Garza and

Tomanie Pete. His mother is the daughter of an old shaman, Tomah Pahgoroo, who died a few years ago."

"Luis Garza. Isn't that the old man whose sheep were getting shot down toward Searchlight a couple of months ago?" Stan asked.

"That's him," Conor told him.

"Any connection to the sheep thing?"

"No, he and Jimmy hadn't seen each other for a couple of years."

"Okay."

"He was twenty-two years old and lived in Acton. His mother and stepfather, Rayno Pete, live in Acton too. He had friends in Las Vegas and was known to ride the rails. It appears he may have fallen from the train on Saturday night on his way home from here."

"Is that it?"

"For now. He'll probably be buried at Moapa, but I don't know when. I'll let you know after I talk to the family again."

"It must have been awful," Stan muttered. "Getting run over by a train like that."

"Quick," Con offered. "He probably never knew what hit him."

* * *

The ring of Conor's bootheels echoed down the empty hall of the morgue. He peered through the window in the door to the right marked CLARK COUNTY CORONER'S OFFICE in large gold letters. It was vacant. The same bold lettering adorning the solid door across the hall read PRIVATE. Con went in. Two men wearing lab coats both looked up when he entered.

"Good morning, Con," Hal greeted cheerfully. "I called Joe in to verify the appendectomy scar."

"There was a slight complication when I performed the surgery," Dr. Anderson began. "I removed a cyst on the bowel near the appendix. I believed it to have been the true source of Mrs. Wagner's pain. Not appendicitis as I'd originally diagnosed." He paused for a moment returning his gaze to the open abdomen in front of him. "Even with the decomposition." He looked back up to meet the sheriff's eyes. "...there's no question. This is the body of Katherine Wagner."

"You're sure," Conor replied. More so a statement than a question.

"Positive."

"There's something else," Hal interrupted the sheriff's thought. He rolled the corpse onto one side and raised the curly auburn hair from the neck. A small patch of dried blood matted the hair at the base of the skull.

"Jimmy missed this when he cleaned her up for burial," the coroner told him. "There's a bullet hole beneath it."

"Same size?"

"Real close," he answered. "I'll have to open the skull to retrieve the bullet. Should I go ahead or wait?"

"I doubt it will be necessary, but can you disguise it if her daughter wants to see the body?"

"It'll take a little longer to do, but I'll plan it that way," the old doctor agreed. "...just in case."

"Where's Jimmy Garza?"

"On a gurney in the cooler. All the pieces in the general vicinity of where they belong."

"I met with the *Evening Review* this morning," Con announced. "I didn't tell them the cause of death, only that it

looked like he fell off the train. I'm hoping the killer will think
he covered his tracks. Committed the perfect crime."

"My lips are sealed, Sheriff Armenta," Hal agreed.
"Always have been and always will be. Nothing wrong with
being vague." His chuckle grew to a belly laugh. He glanced
toward the other doctor. "Your secret is safe with us." He
turned back and winked. Con felt Hal's wry grin suggested a
recollection of his midnight ride to the Wagners' Muleskinner's Rest.

Joseph Anderson agreed. "Everything I hear or do here is
strictly confidential, Sheriff."

"You have photographs of the wedding ring?" Conor
asked.

"Yes. Why do you ask?"

"Can you give it to me?"

"Yeah, give me a minute," Hal answered.

"I need to make a call. Can I use your office?"

"It's open."

Con sat down at the coroner's desk. Picking up the telephone, he rang the operator. "This is Sheriff Armenta. Can you
connect me to the Moapa Valley Bank in Overton?"

* * *

He hung his Stetson on a hook by the door of his parents'
Mesquite Café at ten past eleven. The lunch crowd had yet to
begin arriving. Two ladies sipped iced tea as they chatted at a
table near the counter of the otherwise empty room. Olivia
prepared his usual Coca-Cola at the fountain as Con seated
himself at the corner table.

"You alone?" she asked as she set his drink in front of him.

"For a little while," he answered.

"Enchiladas on special," she offered.

"I'll wait."

Olivia returned to her work behind the counter, preparing for the noon rush. Maggie Armenta peered through the order window from the kitchen and spotted her son alone at the table. She came out to visit with him. As she stopped at the counter to pour herself a glass of iced tea, June Sommers came in the front door. Conor stood to hold her chair as June came toward him. She strode straight to him, wrapped her arms around him, and kissed him passionately. The room fell silent. The two ladies near the counter stared, as did Olivia and Maggie.

"I have missed you, Conor," June uttered when she broke the kiss.

"You're early."

"I've not seen you for a week…and so are you."

"Anxious," he replied as they still held their embrace. "And hungry." He gave her another short kiss.

"Me, too," she replied. "And happy," she added as she accepted the chair.

"That's her," Con heard the ladies whisper from across the still room. He ignored it as he took his seat across the table.

"Small town," June whispered to Con. She squeezed his hand as she stared into his warm brown eyes.

Conor could not help returning the stare. Her gorgeous smile, the sprinkle of freckles across her nose, and the glistening blue orbs that welcomed him. He was in love. He knew it. Olivia's voice broke up his trance.

"Would you like iced tea?" she was asking June.

"I have this taste for Coca-Cola today," she answered as she licked her lips.

"Wonder what caused that?" She grinned. "We're about to

get slammed," she told June. "Enchiladas on special. I'll take your orders when I get back."

A moment later, she set June's Coca-Cola on the table. "I'll have the chicken salad sandwich," June told her as Olivia took her little pad from her apron pocket.

"Enchiladas for me," Con added.

"Coming right up," Olivia confirmed as she walked away, stuffing her pencil behind her ear.

As they ate their lunch, Con touched on the highlights of his trip into the desert without mentioning names to be over-heard in the busy café. He told her Dr. Anderson had made a positive identification this morning, and he would be driving to Overton this afternoon. But mostly, he talked of the ride, peaceful solitude, finding springs, sleeping beside a campfire while staring at a starlit sky...then he said it.

"I love you, June Sommers. I know it now for certain."

The proclamation took her breath away. She sat momen-tarily in silence absorbing the feeling that welled from inside her. A tear rolled down her cheek.

"What's wrong?" he asked, fearing he had spoken out of turn, said too much, too little. He did not understand women. Their emotions. They scared him. It embarrassed him.

"Nothing. Nothing is wrong at all." She smiled through the tears that now flowed freely down her face. "I have hoped and prayed that you felt for me how I have felt for you for quite a while now. Almost since the moment we met. After April's father died, I never thought I would love someone again. Never thought I would be loved again. I am truly the happiest woman in Las Vegas. Maybe on earth."

"You're a wonderful woman, June Sommers. A wonderful mother. I only hope I can live up to half your expectations."

"Conor, you have already exceeded my expectations."

At that moment, Con became aware that the café was unnaturally quiet. As he glanced around, June came to the same realization and followed his gaze around the room. Both of their faces glowed bright red as dozens of pairs of eyes watched and listened in silence.

"Well, kiss her, Sheriff!" came a loud male voice from somewhere in the crowd.

He stood up, pulling June to her feet with him...and did just that.

14

The brown Chevrolet coupe rolled smoothly up the highway toward Moapa. Conor's right hand rested on the gearshift. June's left hand rested on his. They both shared in the newly realized bliss of their love for each other. June took the afternoon off from work at the last minute in order to join Con as he attended to duties in the northern part of the county. His sister Olivia had again offered to take care of April after school, so they could have time alone together.

They turned off the main highway near the trestle where Jimmy Garza's body had been found and followed the Old Arrowhead Trail eastward through the Valley of Fire. Not too many years had passed since this had been the main route to Utah from Las Vegas. Less maintained than the newer road, the Valley of Fire offered the kind of scenic desert grandeur that Con loved and wanted to share with June. Time did not allow them the opportunity to stop and take in most of the vistas, but Conor pointed out landmarks and things he would like to show her on a more leisurely tour in the future.

They turned left toward Overton when they reached the road along Muddy River. Con pointed out the location across the valley where the ancient Indian ruins known as Lost City lay. They would be submerged beneath the waters of the reservoir when Hoover Dam was completed. He promised to bring June and her daughter there before that happened. They rolled to a stop in front of the Moapa Valley Bank at a quarter 'til three.

June accompanied him when Con entered the bank.

"Good afternoon, Sheriff. I have everything in order," Bill Howard announced.

"Mr. Howard, June Sommers," Conor introduced. "June's a legal secretary and notary should the need arise. June, William Howard. The bank manager."

June offered her hand, and Howard accepted. "My pleasure, Miss Sommers. Pleased to meet you."

"We will follow you to the Brumbaughs', Mr. Howard," Con continued. "When we arrive, I will notify Mrs. Brumbaugh of Mrs. Wagner's death. When appropriate, I will ask you to present the letter."

"Very well," the banker answered. "My car is behind the bank. I will meet you out front."

They followed Mr. Howard's sedan. Just before crossing Muddy River at the outskirts of Logan, the sedan made an angled turn to the right and headed due north on a country road. A mile up the road, he turned left and soon pulled up before a modest two-story house among a grove of cottonwood trees. As Con pulled his coupe alongside, Mr. Howard climbed out of his car and donned his suit jacket.

"This is it, Sheriff."

"Nice place," Conor observed.

"Rightly so," Howard agreed. "From what I've heard, they have a pretty successful tomato farm."

A slight breeze through the trees offered a pleasant respite from the afternoon heat on the warm spring day. Con climbed the steps of the front porch with June and Mr. Howard a few feet behind him. He held his hat in his left hand as he approached the entry. The front door stood open behind the screen door. A cast-iron bell hung from the casing. He rang it.

"Mommy, somebody's here," a small voice called out from somewhere inside.

"I heard, Augie," a woman's voice responded, followed by approaching footsteps. They stopped suddenly as Katie Brumbaugh came into Con's view.

"Sheriff Armenta." She finally spoke as she dried her hands on her apron. With a slight quiver in her voice, she continued. "You need to see me?"

Conor cleared his throat. "Yes, Mrs. Brumbaugh, I do."

A small boy of perhaps three or four clung to her dress. As she neared the door, she saw June and Mr. Howard standing on the porch behind him. "Augie," she said as she patted the little boy's head. "Go back to the dining room and play with your tractor while I talk to these people. Okay?"

"Okay, Mommy," he answered as he scampered off around the corner.

"Who are these people, Sheriff?" she asked through the screen door.

"Mr. William Howard of the Moapa Valley Bank in Overton and Mrs. June Sommers, a legal secretary and notary from Las Vegas."

"Please be seated." She indicated a group of wicker furniture on the porch as she opened the screen door. "I think I need to sit down myself."

Visibly shaken, Con offered his hand at her elbow. She accepted it as she settled into a rocking chair. He took a seat facing her.

"I found your mother's remains on Monday," he began in a soft, calm voice. "The coroner made a positive identification this morning."

"Are you sure?" she asked as a tear ran down her suntanned cheek.

"Yes, ma'am," Con answered. "Dr. Anderson recognized the scars from a surgery he performed two years ago. There was a unique procedure that would leave no doubt they belonged to her." He reached into his shirt pocket and found the wedding ring. He handed it to her. She burst out sobbing. "You know this ring?"

"Yes," she sobbed. "It's hers...the two diamonds represent me and my brother. Our father had it custom-made for her when we moved back to Las Vegas from Utah."

"I'm very sorry, Mrs. Brumbaugh." Conor heard June trying to stifle a sniffle behind him.

"How did she die?"

"She was murdered."

"By the Indian who stole the buckle?"

"I don't think so...and she probably gave it to him or intended to." Katie Brumbaugh looked at him questionably. He went on. "The Indian's name was Jimmy Garza. After talking to several people who knew him, he seems to have been a very kind young man. It appears that your mother was kidnapped. Initially, Garza was assigned to guard her. As time progressed, he seems to have become more of a friend. He bought her books. A bottle of perfume for Christmas. She probably gave him money. I think he tried to make her as comfortable as possible under the conditions."

"I doubt she would ever give that particular buckle away."

"Much of what I'm telling you is conjecture based on circumstantial evidence. His cousin in Las Vegas said that Jimmy wore the buckle when he went there a few months ago. Jimmy obviously admired it. Who wouldn't? He told his cousin that the woman he was taking care of said she would give it to him when she went home."

"I don't know what to think," she said, shaking her head in confusion.

"Though I'm sure you have contemplated many 'what ifs' since your mother's disappearance, this is still a lot to take in. Unfortunately, I need to investigate your mother's murder as well as the murder of Jimmy Garza..."

"What?" Katie interrupted. "He was murdered too? I thought he got hit by a train!"

"That's the impression I've been trying to imply without stating it. I'm hoping most people come to that conclusion before I make any announcements. I just released his name to the newspaper this morning. I've intentionally been vague regarding the cause of death."

"What killed him?" she asked. Her thoughts ran rampant in a senseless fury trying to make sense of it. Anything. Any connection with whatever had happened to her mother.

"I don't think I should tell you right now," Con admitted, trying to keep from adding to her present distress.

"Confidential?" she concluded. "I won't tell anyone."

"Yes," he answered. "But that's not why."

"What then?"

Conor held back trying to decide if he should release these specifics. "Jimmy Garza was shot in the back of the head with a small caliber bullet at the precise location to cause the most damage and instant death." He said it as quickly and clearly as possible. He did not want to stumble over the words. "In all practicality...he was executed."

Katie Brumbaugh and June both let out a simultaneous gasp.

With a mixture of fear and anxiety in her voice and intensity in her eyes, Katherine Wagner's daughter pushed the sheriff harder. "And my mother?"

"The same," Con answered flatly.

"Who? Who could?" She could not complete the question or the thought.

"I hope you can help me answer that question," Con replied, then turned to the banker. "Mr. Howard."

William Howard sat in a daze staring blankly at the Brumbaughs' home. The sheriff's voice snapped him back to reality, or whatever you could call the lurid fantasy that embroiled him.

"Yes, Sheriff." He reached into his inside jacket pocket, pulled out the envelope and handed it to him.

Conor looked at the red wax seal then turned it over in his hand, already knowing the inscription on the other side.

Upon my death,
Deliver this envelope to Katie Brumbaugh.

Katherine Wagner

He held it out to her. Her hand shook uncontrollably as she reached for it.

"Can I have a cookie, Mommy?" a small voice asked from behind the screen door.

Katie Brumbaugh nearly jumped from her skin. Her hand jerked back as if touched to a flame. Con dropped the envelope. He did not see June or Bill Howard's reaction.

"Yes, dear," she answered. Instantly reposed and as calm as if she were enjoying a relaxing moment of rest in her rocking chair from hours of physical labor. "Just one. Use the stool, Augie. Don't stand on a chair...and put the lid back on the jar when you're finished."

She turned back to the visitors and blushed. "He will take two, eat the first one as quickly as possible, then savor the second."

Conor smiled at her. He marveled at her composure. A complete bundle of nerves suddenly soothed to nurture her child. He picked up the envelope and handed it to her. She read the inscription, recognizing her mother's handwriting immediately. She broke the wax seal and opened it.

May 9, 1927
My Dearest Katie,

If you are reading this, my life has ended. I probably died tragically.

I have no idea where to begin, except the beginning.

A few weeks before we lost your father, he and I went on our only vacation. A second honeymoon, so to speak, though we had never had a first one. He had just bought our new Oldsmobile recently. We chose a trip by car to Arizona. On the first morning, before sunup, we crossed the

Colorado River on the ferry east of Searchlight. As
we stood by the railing watching birds skimming
the water for insects in the predawn light, I shivered in the cool breeze off the water. He wrapped
his arms around me to ward off the chill. That
moment of tenderness warmed my heart and my
soul. We fell in love all over again through those
days and enjoyed a renewed passion we had
somehow lost in our twenty-five years of marriage.

I'm sure you are already aware of most of
this, but two years ago I asked Leanora Campbell
to accompany me to Switzerland. I wanted to see
the mountain that had captivated your father so
deeply that he lost his life attempting to climb it.
She declined. She didn't wish to relive her own
trauma of Brice's fall and hospitalization there. To
both her husband's surprise and mine, she
suggested that he and I make the trip together.
She wanted Brice to face his own demons of the
Eiger and hopefully relieve some of his sleep-
lessness.

After much apprehension, he and I finally
agreed with her. Surprisingly, we realized on the
train to New York that we hardly knew each other.
He and Gary were close, as were Leanora and I,
but not as couples particularly. By the time we
reached Marseille, that had changed. We'd spent

nearly every waking hour for the past three weeks together and become the friends we should have been for several years.

We stood at the rail near the bow of the ocean liner as it approached the harbor. The cool breeze brought a shiver. Brice opened his jacket and partially covered me as he put his arm around me. The memory of your father's arms around me on the Searchlight Ferry swept over me. I turned to face Brice and slipped my arms inside his jacket. I closed my eyes and kissed him, half dreaming it was your father and half knowing it wasn't. We embraced for several minutes. Brice returned the kiss. It took my breath away.

When the horn of a tugboat blasted me back to reality, I turned away. Neither of us mentioned our transgressions throughout the day. My feelings were inexplicable. My legs were shaking. I was both ashamed and excited. That evening, Rosalie Garnier noticed Brice's wedding band, then mine. She suggested that we were helping each other heal from our loss of Gary, implying we were married. I waited for Brice to deny it. He didn't...nor did I.

Two hours later, the Garniers escorted us to a shared guest bedroom. We changed into our night-clothes in the darkness. I climbed into bed, laying on my side with my back toward him. I laid awake remembering how it felt that morning to embrace a man for the first time since your father's departure and to feel his embrace in return. I felt ashamed that I should have romantic feelings toward his best friend. Wondering what Brice thought. How he felt. I spoke quietly so not to disturb him if he'd already fallen asleep. I asked him to hold me. He turned and snuggled up against me. We made love.

We shared our bed for the rest of the trip. The next three weeks were surreal. Almost as if I were living in someone else's body. I was sleeping with my late husband's best friend. Torn between loving another woman's husband and rapt with guilt for dishonoring your father's trust...and my own.

Once we were home, everything returned to normal for a time, other than the incessant disgrace I felt every time I spoke to Leanora. A month later, I met with Brice on a matter of some work Wagner Trucking was doing for Fremont Construction. At the conclusion, Brice told me that Dutch had discovered details of our illicit encounter in Europe. Almost immediately after our return, Dutch blackmailed him into paying hush money, lest he humiliate us and his family by spreading the news of our infidelities. The second payment would come due in a few days.

Fear of disclosure should have petrified me. For reasons I cannot explain, it excited me. The smoldering flame of a few weeks ago suddenly became fanned to a new inferno. For a week, I tried to contain it, drowning it for hours in my bathtub, smothering it beneath my pillow at night. Instead, the forbidden desire flourished. I reserved the suite at the Hotel Nevada for Friday night and sent Brice a note asking him to meet me there at seven o'clock. He did.

The following Monday, I accumulated every dollar I could without your brother's knowledge. I deposited it into a savings account at the Moapa Valley Bank in Overton. Your name is listed as the sole beneficiary. I have added to it as I have been able to.

Brice and I have continued to see each other every few weeks since that time. Leanora and I have become distant. In my shame, I cannot face her. Neither can I stifle my desire for her husband. I am addicted to him.

Your brother blames Brice for your father's death though nothing could be further from the truth. I met the Austrian who led the expedition.

Brice had nothing to do with the Frenchman and your father's fall. Dutch loathes him.

A few days ago, Dutch showed up at my office. He somehow found out about my meetings with Brice at the hotel. He is enraged beyond sanity. He screamed despicable names at me that I'm sure others heard through the door. He also brought with him a transfer of the deed to my home. He demanded that I sign it over to him. I refused. He choked me until nearly unconscious. It terrified me. He literally would have killed me. I signed it.

I am so sorry. I always intended to leave you an inheritance. I am solely to blame. In my foolishness, I have cost you and my grandchildren everything I owned.

Please tell Leanora that it is my fault. I fell in love with her husband. Brice did nothing wrong. He comforted his best friend's widow. He still loves her. He has told me so many times.

Call the sheriff. Dutch has killed me.

With all my love,
It's all that I have left,
Mom

Katie Brumbaugh did not say a word. She handed the letter to Sheriff Armenta. "You need to read this."

When Conor finished reading the letter, he held it in his hands, staring at it. "This letter divulges a lot of information. It answers questions. Confirms many theories."

He looked up at Mrs. Brumbaugh. She stared off blankly into the trees surrounding her home. "May I have Mrs. Sommers copy this for me?"

"Sure," she said. "Come with me, Mrs. Sommers. You can use the dining table."

"You can call me June."

"I'm Katie."

The ladies passed through the door into the house. They had disappeared around the corner by the time the screen door banged against the jamb as the spring pulled it closed.

"I believe this concludes your services, Mr. Howard."

"What about the letter? What did it say?"

"A lot about circumstances that led up to her death. She told about the savings account at your bank and the beneficiary. She named her killer. The rest of it is mostly personal."

"Who? Who killed her?"

"The man you suspected."

"Who was it?"

"Jimmy's boss."

Soon after Bill Howard drove away, Katie Brumbaugh appeared through the screen door. "Would you like a glass of tea?"

"Yes, thank you."

"Come in. You can join your companion in the dining room while she transcribes the letter."

June sat at the table, diligently copying the letter into short-hand while Augie played at her feet with a toy tractor. By the time Katie Brumbaugh brought the tea, June had completed the task.

"Done," she announced as she separated the pages from the pad of paper. "You owe me one, Conor."

"If I had taken on that task, we'd be here half the night… and only I could read it."

"And only I can read this. I guess we are even."

"Yes, ma'am."

"You two act as if you're married," Katie Brumbaugh commented. They both blushed, but neither commented.

Con drank his tea quickly as June finished the glass she had sipped on.

"I will need a little information about your mother for the death certificate," Con asked Katie as they sat at the table.

"Of course. What do you need?"

Conor noted in his tally book Katherine Wagner's date and place of birth, maiden name, parents' names, and other data the state required. "I am so sorry to have brought you such sorrow, Mrs. Brumbaugh," Con offered as he stood. "Then to bother you at the same time with more questions. I hate that I have put you through all of this. And I thank you for sharing the information in this letter, it's very helpful."

"Please call me Katie," she replied. "The news you brought me today? I suspected as much. It's both bad and good." She held up the letter in emphasis. "Now maybe she can conquer her own demons, in peace."

As they moved toward the door, Katie suggested in the tone of a newly found friend, "Gus will be coming in soon. I would like you to meet him, Sheriff."

"I would wait, but we have another stop to make in Acton, and I'm afraid it's getting late."

"Acton?"

"Jimmy Garza's parents," Con replied without further explanation.

Katie nodded. As she walked them to Conor's car, Gus Brumbaugh rolled into the yard in an old farm truck. He bailed out of the truck and strode toward them. A gangly suntanned girl in bibbed overalls hurried to keep up behind him.

"I didn't know we had company, Kate," the grinning giant remarked.

"Gus, this is Sheriff Armenta and his friend, June."

"Is anything wrong, Sheriff?" he asked as he held out a hand that seemed the size of a small ham. "Something to do with Gary's buckle?"

"Yes, sort of," Katie replied before Con could retrieve his hand from Gus's massive palm. "I'll tell you about it after supper."

"Good to meet you, Mr. Brumbaugh," Con added.

"Call me Gus. Every time I hear Mr. Brumbaugh, I look around for my dad."

"Gus then." Con nodded. "I'd love to stay and get to know you and your family better, but we really should be going," Conor added as he held June's door.

"Understand," Gus said as he stood beside Katie, a head and shoulders taller than her. "I don't get away from this place much, but you're welcome to stop by anytime."

"Obliged," Con answered as he climbed into the coupe, and they drove away.

"I do not envy your job, Conor," June remarked as they drove toward Moapa. "Today was clearly difficult, telling Katie her mother had been murdered and still needing information from her. You handled it very well, I think."

"Thank you. I never quite know how I'm perceived by others." His expression showed how much he appreciated her support. "I was grateful for your being there too. I think it naturally makes most women apprehensive when approached by men in this kind of setting. I thought your presence helped calm her." He paused a moment, then added, "Not to mention, copying the letter."

"You know that I am happy to do that sort of thing."

"I didn't intend for you to be my personal assistant when I asked you to join me today."

"Would you like me to stay in the car on your next stop?"

"You'd miss the chance to meet Luis's former wife."

"You know that your sister and I are both dying to see the woman who could lure Luis from bachelorhood."

"I couldn't deny you the opportunity to one-up the biggest gossip in Las Vegas now, could I?"

"And you know that you're the one who truly gets the honor of that accomplishment."

"Oh, and it's such a grand distinction. I couldn't think of anyone I'd rather share it with than you."

June chuckled, then kissed her finger and touched it to Conor's cheek as they sped on up the road.

* * *

At half past six o'clock, Con turned into the drive of the Petes' home. Rayno Pete heard them pull in and opened the front door of the small house as Conor and June climbed out of the car.

"Come sit down, Sheriff. Miss..." He motioned to the furniture on the porch. "I'll get Tomanie."

"Are we interrupting your supper?" June asked.

"No. We just finished. She's washing dishes."

"Can I help?" she offered.

Rayno pointed her to the door. "It's the sheriff," Rayno told Tomanie as he followed June in.

Tomanie was startled to meet June face to face when she turned around drying her hands.

"Let me help you finish these up," June offered cheerfully. Before Tomanie had a chance to reply, June was elbow-deep in the kitchen sink. They worked side by side in silence for a few moments.

"I am June Sommers," she said. "A friend of Sheriff Armenta...and consequently, Luis Garza."

Tomanie stopped working. "I am Tomanie Pete. Luis and I were married. We had a son."

"I just learned that recently. I'm sorry to hear about your son...I had no idea Luis had been married. Conor told me."

Tomanie turned in curiosity at the strange name.

"Sheriff Armenta," June clarified.

They finished the dishes in relative silence. As they dried their hands, Tomanie said, "Let's go see what he wants."

Conor and Rayno sat in chairs facing each other when the ladies came through the screen door. "You want Simon to do the ceremony?" Rayno asked Tomanie as she and June seated themselves on the old couch where Tomanie and Luis had sat during Con's previous visit.

"Yes."

"The coroner has completed his autopsy," Con said. "He can deliver Jimmy's remains somewhere up here if necessary. Otherwise, whoever you name can receive them in Las Vegas."

"Simon can come to Las Vegas. He has a truck," Tomanie replied.

Conor had his tally book in hand. "What is Mr. Simon's first name?"

"Simon Pahgoroo. My big brother. He's a shaman like my father was," she answered.

"I will come with him," Rayno announced as Con scribbled notes.

"Let me know when and where he will be buried so I can tell the newspaper and Luis." Con asked.

"Moapa Paiute Indian Cemetery. Probably Saturday," Rayno answered. "I will know when we come."

Conor and June pulled out of the Petes' driveway.

"She's beautiful," June proclaimed.

Con nodded. "Yes, she is. She and Luis are still clearly in love with each other."

"Are you sure?" she asked in shock.

"It's a long story...and complicated. I'll tell you as we go. Right now, lack of planning on my part leaves us without supper," Con admitted. "There's nowhere I know of in Moapa to eat. Look in the glove box."

June did as he instructed and began shuffling through the contents. "What am I looking for?"

"A small paper bag...maybe."

"This?" She held up a little brown bag like she usually sent April's lunch to school in.

"Aha!" Conor exclaimed. "That's it."

June peered inside. "What is it?" she asked, unable to distinguish the contents peering into the sack.

"Lamb jerky."

"Cowboy fare." She giggled as she reached inside.

"Sheepherder cuisine," Con corrected, laughing.

"Well, there's four pieces," she confirmed, holding them up for his approval.

"That's enough. Depending on how dry it's gotten, we might still be chewing when we get to town."

He chewed off a bite of jerky and began chewing to moisten and soften it. Then he began the story of Luis and Tomanie's romance as Luis had shared it with him. Afterward, he told her how they had held hands and the look on each of their faces as they suffered their bereavement together...and Rayno Pete's compassion and understanding.

* * *

THURSDAY, JUNE 12, 1930

Conor entered the sheriff's office at ten 'til seven. June sat beside Hazel's desk with a cup of coffee chatting with her.

"You're here bright and early," he greeted when he saw her.

"Her or me?" Hazel asked a bit mockingly.

"June, this time," he answered. "Her presence is what surprised me."

He poured himself a cup of coffee and was thankful he chose not to buy doughnuts today as he helped himself to one from the bag and a half left from yesterday. "To what do I owe this pleasure?" he asked June as he pulled up a chair in front of the desk.

"I was not sleepy when you dropped me off last night, so I transcribed the letter into longhand for you before I went to bed," she responded. "I thought you would want it today, so I brought it by."

Hazel's expression did not belie her surprise that the sheriff had kept his girlfriend out late on a weeknight. "It's on your desk...the top of the pile you left yesterday," she added.

Con scowled at Hazel. "I get the hint, mother. That's part

of the reason I came in early myself." He rose to confront the mission.

"The deputies' reports from Tuesday are about a quarter of the way down," Hazel's comment drew another glare.

"Will it distract you if I sit in your office while you work?" June asked. "I have time. Mr. Westcott will not be in for another hour."

"Yes, it probably will distract me," he answered. "Come on in."

Hazel smirked as Con held a chair in front of his desk for June. She started to remark on his placement of the chair so as not to obstruct the view from behind his task at hand but thought better of it. They left the door open.

As Conor knew, the job was much less overwhelming than Hazel suggested. He had made a good start on it yesterday morning. Most of the reports were simple as he scanned through them. Some required a little more scrutiny and fewer still needed questions clarified. Reports regarding the Garza and Wagner homicides he laid aside for further review and inclusion in the appropriate case files. Other than an occasional comment between them, the room was quiet, and the hour passed quickly.

"I need to be going," June announced. "I will have my own catching up to do today."

Con walked her to the main entry and gave her a quick goodbye kiss.

June embraced him. "I love you, Conor," and returned with a much more fervent kiss.

"I hope you have a pleasant day, darling," Con told her, and she was out the door.

When he turned to go back into his office, he was met with Hazel's blank stare and gaping mouth from behind her desk.

"Is something wrong?" he asked her as seriously as he could. "Are you okay?"

"Uh, no...I mean, yes...uh, everything is fine." She looked down at her desk and tried to look busy. "...I just..." She never completed the response.

Barely able to force a straight face, Conor tried not to hurry as he reentered his office and closed the door behind him. He could only imagine the conversation that would arise between the matronly mother hen and her chick when Dottie arrived at work this evening.

"That'll keep them guessing for a few days," Con mumbled to himself as he gathered a pile of reports and took them out to the main office.

"These are ready to be filed," he told Hazel as he set them on her desk, then returned and again closed his door.

Con picked up the telephone and dialed Hal.

"Coroner," he answered.

"Con. Simon Pahgoroo and Rayno Pete will probably be in today to pick up Jimmy Garza's body. You can sign it over to them."

"Sure thing."

"Anything new on Katherine Wagner?"

".25 caliber slug. I'm no expert, but under a microscope, it looks identical to the one I found in Mr. Garza. I've got them carefully separated and well-marked."

"Anything else?"

"Mrs. Wagner has a broken right cheekbone and a nasty scar over it. Healed about six months at the time of death. Which, by the way, was about six to eight weeks ago."

"So, you're about done with the autopsy?"

"Finished up yesterday evening. I have Joe's report in a

sealed envelope on my desk. I'm completing mine right now. I'll drop them both by your office before noon."

"That'll be great, thanks."

He hung up the telephone and dialed Leanora Campbell.

15

THURSDAY, JUNE 12, 1930

When Sheriff Armenta traveled out Pine Canyon Road, newly constructed barbed wire fences surrounded Newton Campbell's property as he drove past. Longhorn cattle dotted the rolling hills of Newt's and his mother's adjoining estates. He continued on to Leanora Campbell's hacienda. As Conor strode across the courtyard, an unusually cool midmorning breeze welcomed him. The pleasant aroma of mint growing near the door added to the appeal of the patio. Leanora Campbell came to the door when he knocked. Though nearing sixty, the recent widow carried an air of attractive grace.

"Please come in, Sheriff," she invited pleasantly as she stepped aside. "You know the way to the sitting room. Would you care for coffee? Perhaps iced tea?"

"The tea sounds nice, thank you."

She beckoned her housemaid to bring it. "Have a seat, Sheriff Armenta."

"I noticed cattle grazing by the road as I drove in," Con commented.

"One of Newt's hobbies," she explained. "I know you did not drive all the way out here to talk about cattle, Sheriff. What is it that you would like to discuss?"

"This information is not public knowledge," Con began and paused for her response.

"I understand."

"We found Mrs. Wagner's remains on Monday."

"Oh...my goodness! Poor Katherine." She was quite obviously surprised and shaken. "Do you think Brice..." She stared inquiringly at Conor but could not bring herself to complete the question.

"Oh, no. Quite the contrary," Con stammered slightly. "I'm sorry, Mrs. Campbell. I didn't mean to imply...I didn't consider..."

The maid entered the room and held a tray before him with two glasses and a pitcher of iced tea. He accepted one of the glasses and took a sip while she offered the tray to Mrs. Campbell, then sat it on the coffee table between them before leaving the room.

"No. It's nothing like that at all," he managed as he regained his composure. "Mrs. Wagner had left a letter with the Moapa Valley Bank in Overton a few years ago. She instructed the bank manager to deliver it to Katie Brumbaugh upon her death. He and I delivered it to Mrs. Brumbaugh yesterday."

Leanora Campbell sat poised. Looking at nothing. Thinking. She took a sip of tea and turned her gaze to the sheriff.

"What did it say?"

"Mrs. Wagner told her daughter of her relationship with Mr. Campbell. She said how Dutch had blackmailed Mr. Campbell. She told of Dutch abusing her both physically and verbally and how Dutch had forced her to sign her property over to him." Con waited, but Leanora Campbell made no comment. "She said that she couldn't bear to face you in her shame."

"You want the ledger."

"Yes, ma'am." He thought about it for a minute as did Leanora Campbell. "If we proceed with this, there will be consequences."

"That is what I am considering."

"There's a lot to consider. Shortly after I arrest Dutch Wagner on extortion charges, all of Las Vegas, and probably most of Nevada, will know about Mr. Campbell and Mrs. Wagner's indiscretions."

"I doubt that will really affect me very much."

"The earthquake will be over when we get a conviction. The aftershocks might reverberate for years. What about your daughter? And don't forget your son-in-law."

"What does Robert have to do with it?"

"He's a prominent attorney. Didn't he make the arrangement for Mrs. Wagner's passport so she could travel to Europe with your husband? And he filed the transfer of deed on her property when Dutch wrested it from her. Gossip travels swiftly. Rumors of conspiracy could run rampant."

"I had not considered that."

"Newt could be implicated, too. He bought the Wagner estate. Not to mention a car that Dutch obtained title to by other rather dubious means."

"I will need to talk to the children before I make a decision,"

"You should. I need to talk to Judge Tucker, but I think with Mrs. Brumbaugh's letter and testimony, we have a good start. With the ledger and your testimony added, we should have a strong enough case to put Dutch away for quite a while. I didn't discuss any of this with Mrs. Brumbaugh yesterday. I had already dropped enough bombshells on her for one day. But she will have this same decision to make. She has two small children to consider. A classmate's parent making an unsubstantiated accusation at the supper table can quickly grow into cruel hazing in the schoolyard the next day."

"How soon do you need to know?" Leanora asked him.

"A few days, I suppose," Con replied as he stood. "The sooner the better."

She walked Conor to the door. "I will have your answer by Monday."

"Thank you," he replied and turned to walk away. He had taken a half-dozen steps toward his pickup truck when Leanora stopped him.

"Sheriff," she beckoned. "I almost forgot that I had a question for you also."

He turned back toward her. "What can I do for you?" he offered.

"When you were in the garden…with Brice." She wished for a better way to ask. "Did you find a pipe?"

"Like a water pipe?" he asked curiously.

"No," she replied, smiling at the misconception. "A smoking pipe. Kind of small and curved. It was Brice's favorite because it fit well into his pocket. We haven't found it."

"No, ma'am. We sure didn't see it," he answered, somewhat puzzled.

"We've looked about everywhere. All through the house. His car. At the office. Even in Newt's car. He always had it with him," she commented. "He must have lost it when he fell that night...well, thank you."

"You're welcome," he responded. "Sorry I couldn't help," he added as he turned away.

"I will call you," she replied with a slight wave of her hand.

* * *

As he drove back to town, Conor pondered over Leanora's question and her comments about Brice's pipe. If you had both a revolver and a pipe in your pocket, how could you lose one when you fell off a fifty-foot cliff, and not the other...probably separate pockets.

* * *

"Two men came in a little while ago to talk to you about Jimmy Garza's remains." Hazel looked at her notes. "Pete Rayno and Simon Pahgoroo."

"Rayno Pete," Con corrected her.

"I sent them over to the morgue."

"How long ago?"

"Maybe twenty minutes."

"Thanks." Con turned around and headed back out the door.

When he walked down the hallway, he could hear Hal talking to the two men in his office. "Sorry I missed you gentlemen at my office," he apologized when he walked in.

"We just finished up the paperwork, Sheriff," Hal announced.

"Thank you, Dr. Martin."

"Sheriff, this is Tomanie's brother, Simon Pahgoroo," Rayno introduced.

The shaman held out his hand, and Conor shook it. "You're a shaman?"

"Yessir, Sheriff. Jimmy will be buried according to Paiute tradition."

"I'm not familiar with the ceremonies or things like that," Con began. "It seems Jimmy tried to perform some sort of ritual when he buried the woman he had watched over."

"How so?" Pahgoroo asked.

Con and Hal proceeded to describe the clothing and jewelry Katherine Wagner wore. How her feet faced the rising sun. That she was wrapped in a Navajo blanket and how she had been covered with the stones and the board.

"She was a White woman?" the shaman asked.

"Yes."

"It sounds like he did the best he could remember. He must have cared a lot about her."

"That's what we figured," Hal concluded. "Unfortunately, Jimmy's body is horribly mangled and dismembered. I don't know what you'll need to do in preparation."

"I will take care of it," Pahgoroo answered.

"You bring a casket?" he asked.

"Yes."

"That will be best." He got a cart for the casket and wheeled it to the entry. "Bring it right down the hall," he told them. "I'll get the door."

Conor stood aside in the doorway to Hal's office as the two men rolled the casket past him, then followed down the hallway to the cooler. The small body of Katherine Wagner lay beneath a sheet on a gurney to one side. Jimmy's gurney stood in the middle of the area. Hal lifted the sheet from the far side for Simon Pahgoroo to see. He shook his head, then took it from Hal's hands. Pulling it aside, he exposed Jimmy's naked, fragmented body. Rayno Pete bent over and grabbed his knees, vomiting. Con helped him down the hall to the restroom. After rinsing his mouth and washing his face, Rayno looked at Con, embarrassed and ashamed of his weakness.

"You told me," Rayno said to Conor. "I had no idea."

"We can wait in Hal…Dr. Martin's office."

When they passed the door of the cooler, Con glanced inside to see Hal assisting Simon as he prayed over Jimmy in Paiute and moved the body parts into the casket.

In Hal's office, Rayno Pete wept. "I'm sorry," he said.

"Don't be."

"I am weak and ashamed."

"It's a terrible thing to see someone like this that you love," Con tried to console him. "It's hard for me too, and I've seen lots of awful things in my life…and I never knew Jimmy. Since I discovered he was Luis's son, it has also been even more difficult. I am sorry."

"You know Luis well?"

"He and my father have been best friends for as long as I can remember. He gave me my first and only rifle when I was fourteen. I still have it. I worked for him from the time my father sold our sheep until I was eighteen and went to work in the gypsum mines. I thought I knew him well, but I never knew he had been married and had a son until a few days ago."

"You're the boy who came to the trading post with him?"

"Yes."

"I remember you." Rayno smiled.

"I remember the dog you gave us."

"She was a good dog...and still young."

"She was smart." Conor laughed. "But she didn't understand English or Spanish, and we didn't speak Paiute. We were finally beginning to understand each other by the time we made it home with the sheep."

Rayno laughed aloud. "I never knew."

"Luis had her for many years," Con reminisced. "Possibly the best dog he ever had."

Rayno became serious. "Luis is a good man, Sheriff."

"He says the same of you." Con paused, unsure whether he should continue. "He told me what happened. About Tomanie and her father. Where the sheep we herded back from Moapa came from. He told me you made a good father for Jimmy. It's too bad you couldn't be friends. You would make great friends."

"Moapa Paiute Indian Cemetery. Eleven o'clock, Saturday," Rayno said and looked away.

He occasionally wiped his face but never spoke again or looked toward Conor. When Hal and Simon pushed the casket down the hall, Rayno took over for Hal. As they lifted the casket into Simon's truck, he spoke to Simon in Paiute. Simon replied in Paiute in a kindly tone. Con had no idea what they said.

"Thank you, Sheriff." Simon shook Con's hand and climbed into the truck.

"You are welcome."

* * *

When Conor returned to the office, he telephoned the *Evening Review*. He told Stan Olson about Jimmy's funeral. Stan said he would make sure an obituary would be published right away. Con went back to his paperwork. When finished, he reviewed everything he knew about Jimmy Garza and Katherine Wagner. All of the evidence strongly suggested they were killed by the same person. If Katherine Wagner predicted correctly, her son Dutch was the murderer. Con thought so too, but nearly all of the evidence was circumstantial. He looked at the clock. Four p.m. He dialed Robert Westcott's office. June answered.

"Have plans this evening?" he asked.

"What did you have in mind?"

"I thought we might introduce April to Luis."

"On a school night?"

"I need to go out there tonight. We'll be home early. I promise." Conor only heard silence on the line. "Are you there?"

"Supper will be on the table at five o'clock sharp."

"Five fifteen?"

"Okay. Don't be late."

"Promise."

Con left the office and drove home. He shaved and took a bath then splashed foo-foo juice, as his niece Donna called it, on his face. He brushed his teeth, put on clean clothes and headed for the door at four forty-five. Then retraced his steps, grabbed his gun belt and nearly skipped out the door. He rolled the belt around the holster, then slid it beneath the seat of his car and climbed in. Hazel's car was gone and Dottie's runabout took its place when Con rolled up in front of the Sheriff's Department. Jesse's patrol car sat beside it.

"Perfect," he said as he climbed the stairs two at a time.

"Glad to have caught you both here," he said as he burst through the door.

Jesse sat at Hazel's desk possibly filling out reports and Dottie at hers. Both of their eyes were wide with surprise.

"What is it?" Dottie asked as innocently as possible.

"I had the funniest feeling that a whole new wave of rumors was about to be unleashed regarding my relationship with a certain secretary for an attorney here in Las Vegas."

"I wouldn't know what you're talking about," Dottie replied, trying very hard to suppress a grin.

"Well, that's good, because if such a thing were to start making the rounds, I might be inclined to start my own rumor about you two." He grinned sardonically, pointing his finger back and forth between them as he exited.

Not a word had escaped Jesse's mouth as he stared after Conor with his mouth open. Dottie was wide-eyed and beet red.

"What was that about?" Jesse asked her.

She quickly filled Jesse in as she dialed Hazel's number. When she finished sounding the alarm, Dottie became aware of the lingering scent of aftershave lotion drifting across the room from where Con had stood near the door.

The chocolate brown Chevrolet coupe with black fenders rolled to a stop in front of June Sommers's home on South Third Street at ten after five. April awaited his arrival from the porch swing.

"Hi, Con," she nearly screamed as he stepped from the car.

"Hello, sweetheart. How was school today?" he asked as she ran down the steps to hug him.

"It was okay," she answered cheerfully. "Michael threw up on Betsy after lunch."

"How interesting," Conor answered as they climbed the

steps together. "I had a similar experience about that same time today."

"Someone threw up on you?" she asked, wrinkling her nose.

"Not on me, near me," Con clarified. "But let's not talk about that right before supper."

"Okay," she replied agreeably. As they walked through the door, she hollered to the kitchen. "Mamma, Con's here. Someone threw up on him today."

Conor stood inside the front door, shaking his head as he hung his hat on the tree. June appeared around the corner from the kitchen.

"I hope that is not repeated anytime soon," she said amusingly.

Con stood in awe when he looked at her. Her face glowed. She wiped her hands on the apron she wore over the flowered summer dress she had worn to the office. The aura was dream-like, her smile welcoming. What would it be like to come home to her every night he wondered? She met him halfway across the room. April blushed and giggled when they kissed.

"What is so amusing?" June asked her. She giggled again, then scampered into the kitchen.

June held their embrace. She loved the masculine feel of his chest against hers. He smelled of soap and shaving lotion. She breathed in his essence, wishing she had had the opportunity to freshen up for him and feel more feminine when she got home. She did not see herself as Con perceived her, the most cultured and sophisticated woman he had ever known. Truly a lady in every respect.

"Hope I'm not late," he told her, looking down to her in his cowboy boots.

"You are right on time," she whispered into his ear as she

nuzzled his freshly shaved neck. "I am sure that April is setting the kitchen table right now."

Momentarily, she broke the hold and led him by the hand, almost whimsically, into the kitchen. As suspected, April had set the table and taken her seat. June pulled out a chair.

"Please be seated, monsieur," she joked as she went to the stove. "Leftover ham and potato salad along with fresh sweet corn. Hardly French cuisine, but the standard fare in this kitchen." She laughed.

"Definitely better than stale jerky, and it sure smells good," Conor complimented.

"So do you." She smirked.

"A bit of Donna's last Christmas gift, when I shaved." Con smiled as he rubbed his chin.

June brought the meal to the table, and they began filling their plates. "Would you say Grace, Conor?"

"Well, uh, sure I guess," he said, taking both of their hands as he bowed his head. "Dear Lord, thank you for bringing this wonderful family into my life. Please give healing to the Garza, Pete, and Wagner families as they grieve. May this meal you have provided us nourish our bodies as your heavenly spirit nourishes our souls. Amen."

"Amen," the ladies followed.

"That was lovely, Conor, thank you," June commented seriously, still holding his hand. "Thank you for coming into our lives too. I feel we have been blessed."

The meal began quietly. June finally broke the silence. "You said you needed to see Luis tonight. It could not wait until tomorrow?"

"Jimmy Garza's burial is Saturday morning in Moapa. Papa will pick up Luis after they close the café tomorrow, then bring him to spend the night at their house and go to Moapa Saturday."

"Who will run the café on Saturday, then?"

"It'll be closed."

"I see." She thought for a minute. "Why not take Luis yourself?"

"I was hoping you would go with me."

"Oh, of course," June answered, somewhat surprised to be included in such a personal event for Con's family. "I would be honored."

They ate their meal, and Conor helped June clean up fairly quickly. April took her favorite spot in the rumble seat, and they sped down Charleston Boulevard toward the Searchlight Highway a few minutes past six o'clock. June sat in the front with a plate of ham and potato salad for Luis in her lap. They talked casually about the events of the past few days and the conversation rolled around to Con's meeting with Leanora Campbell that morning.

"That explains Mr. Westcott closing the office early today," June commented. "He said he had a family meeting to attend this evening."

"Sounds like Mrs. Campbell isn't wasting any time."

"Evidently not," June agreed.

When they rolled into Luis Garza's yard, he sat on his porch drinking a glass of lemonade. It looked to Con as if he'd aged ten years since seeing him last week.

"Buenos noches, tío," Conor greeted when he stepped from the car. "We brought someone we'd like you to meet."

"Who would that be?" he asked as he stood and walked to the sagging gate of the picket fence surrounding his house.

"My daughter," June offered cheerfully as she stepped out

of the car with her plate of food. "And we brought you supper if we are not too late."

Con helped April down from the rumble seat while June sat Luis's supper on the table on the porch.

"I haven't eaten yet." He smiled as he tottered to follow her.

She was shocked to see how frail Luis had become in such a short time since she had last seen him.

"Have you been eating at all?" she asked accusingly as he sat down.

"I haven't had much appetite lately." He really liked her, but scowled at her chastising, then returning to the grin, he added, "But I don't cook as good as you."

Con had never seen Luis around any children except himself and his siblings decades ago. He had no idea what reaction to expect when he brought April to the porch.

"This is April," Conor told him. "April, this is Uncle Luis. He and my papa have been friends since before I was born."

"Wow," she exclaimed, looking Luis in the eye. "That's a really long time."

"Yes, it is," Luis replied between bites. "Has anyone ever told you you're just as pretty as your mother?"

"No, not exactly," she shied away slightly.

"Well, you are," he said. "And I'm pleased to meet you." He held out his hand. She blushed as she shook it.

"Do you like dolls?" he asked her.

"Sure!" she answered.

"Well, I have one you can play with. If you go through that door, there's a sofa under the window to your right. She's sitting on the back of the sofa. You can bring her out here to play with."

The screen door banged as April dashed into the house.

Luis chuckled as he continued to eat. April was back in a moment with a rather dusty Raggedy Ann doll.

"You'll need to shake some of the dust off of her before you get that pretty dress dirty," Luis told her. "She's been sitting there for quite a while."

"Is she your daughter's?" April asked as she slapped dust from the doll.

"No, she belongs to Conor's niece. She's a couple of years younger than you."

"Donna?" April shrieked. "She's my best friend. We're in the same grade. She's two months older than me," she babbled with excitement.

"Well, maybe she is." Luis chuckled. "I haven't seen her in quite some time."

"I could take her back," April offered. "I would give her to Donna for you. I see her almost every day."

"I'm sure you would, sweetie. And thank you. But why don't you just tell Donna where her doll is so she can come pick her up."

"Okay," April agreed cheerfully. "I'll see her tomorrow."

"That will be good. You tell her I miss her, and she and her mom should come visit."

"I will."

Conor and June kept out of the conversation as they marveled how cheerful it seemed to make Luis to visit with her. It brought back memories to Con of his boyhood when he and Luis would banter back and forth about rustlers and bandits in the sheep camp.

"Uncle Luis?" April questioned. "Don't you get lonely out here all by yourself?"

"Oh, sometimes I suppose," he fielded the question. "But it's my home, and I've lived here for a very long time."

"Don't you have kids?"

The question stopped him cold, but he cleared his throat and answered before June was quick enough to divert the conversation.

"No, sweetie." He choked back the frog in his throat and a tear escaped down his cheek. "Not anymore...and no grand-children."

"April," June interrupted. "Go out to Conor's car and bring me my purse, please."

April rushed down the step and across the yard.

"I am so, so sorry, Luis," June muttered as tears poured down her face. "She has no idea...she doesn't know what has happened. Hurting you, oh my, I never dreamed she would ask that."

"She is beautiful," he said, trying to regain his composure. "And so sweet." He turned to June. "I never got to share with my own son. I won't have grandchildren...she's just like her mother. I bet you were a beautiful child. Perhaps you and Conor will have children together," Luis rambled just as April handed June her purse, and Con nearly fell out of his chair. June hoped April had not heard Luis's comment thus opening up a whole new line of questions for the young inquisitive mind.

"Perhaps," she answered without looking toward Con.

April returned to Raggedy Ann and played mindlessly on the porch. Luis finished his supper, and June took his plate into the house to wash it. Conor moved his chair closer to Luis and spoke softly.

"You know that we aren't married...or even engaged for that matter," he told Luis.

"Why not?" Luis asked in a normal tone, either unaware of Con's attempt at discretion or ignoring it. Con wasn't sure.

"You should marry her," he said flatly. "I told you before. It's plain to see you are in love with each other. And you adore the little girl as she does you. What are you waiting for? To lose her? To lose the only one you will ever love. Live in lonely misery while some other man has her and your son? The son who doesn't even know who you are until he's grown and then is murdered before you ever had the chance to tell him you loved him?" he yelled at Conor. Tears streamed down his face. His shirt was soaked by them. Con had never seen him angry in his entire life. He was beyond angry. He was furious. And bitter. A bitterness that had eaten away a decade of his life in only a week. A lifetime of bitterness that suddenly over-flowed. Con started to speak, but found no words.

April sat silently in her chair staring at them. June stood behind the screen door listening.

Luis spoke in a normal tone. "You are the only son I have ever had, Conor. Jimmy never knew me. And you were forced to become a man when you were only a boy. Your mother saw it, but could do nothing about it. She used to send stick candy when you were out herding sheep. Remember?"

"Yes."

"Grow up, Conor. That little girl knows more about love and loneliness than you do. And so does her mother. Figure it out. It's that pain in your gut that's been driving you crazy these past months. Marry that woman and have children with her before it's too late and you grow old and lonely and angry like me."

He reached into his pocket, pulled out a cheroot and struck a match. Con had not seen him smoke in over twenty years. He leaned back and blew smoke rings. April returned her attention to Raggedy Ann. June came out and moved her chair beside Conor. She reached through his arm and held his hand.

They watched the sun drop below the hills on the west side of the valley.

"Luis?" Con finally queried.

"Yes?"

"Jimmy's burial is Saturday. The day after tomorrow. Papa will pick you up after the café closes tomorrow. You'll spend the night with them, and they will take you to Moapa the next morning. There will be a shaman. Tomanie's brother."

"Simon? I know him."

"June and I will meet you there."

Luis took June's free hand in his. "You heard what I said?"

"Yes."

Luis did not reply to her. He called to April, "Sweetie?"

"Yes?" April answered as she looked at him.

He beckoned her with his hand. "You can take the doll to Donna."

"No," she said. "I will tell her. If she doesn't come for it, I will play with it when I visit you." She went into the house and placed it where she had found it.

16

Deputy Whitney Ellis sat behind Hazel's desk at eight-fifteen filling out a report when Sheriff Armenta entered wearing a jacket and string tie.

"Sheriff," he acknowledged when Con walked in.

"Anything I need to know about, Whit?"

"Dottie left an envelope on your desk. Someone dropped it by last night for you."

Conor went to his office and opened the envelope. The note was simple and to the point.

> Sheriff,
>
> The answer is Yes.
> I had lunch with Katie today.
> You should hear from her soon.

Leanora C.

"I'll be at a funeral in Moapa today," he told Whit. "Call Jesse if you need help."

* * *

"Hi, Uncle Con!" Donna McLeod yelled as she and April waved from the yard of June's neighbor. Con returned the gesture as he climbed the steps of June's porch and knocked on the screen door.

"I'll be right out," June called from beyond Conor's view.

A moment later he heard the approach of high heels on the wood floor. She soon appeared from around the corner across the front room. June wore a navy-blue short-sleeved dress, lace gloves, and a hat with a half-veil covering her eyes.

"How do I look?" she asked as she opened the door.

"Stunning," he answered, staring.

"You look pretty good yourself," she commented as she looked him straight in the eye with her heels on.

"Is it all right to kiss you?" he asked, feeling almost afraid to touch her.

She reached one arm into his jacket and pulled herself to him, then kissed him. "Does that answer your question?"

"Mm, yes, I think so. Maybe I should verify it, though." He kissed her again.

They waved again at the girls playing next door as they walked to Con's car.

"It surprised me to see Donna here," Con commented as he held June's door.

"Joyce is watching both of them so Stuart and Olivia can go to the funeral also."

Con paused a moment, somewhat surprised Olivia would be attending.

* * *

When Conor and June drove up the road into the cemetery at ten thirty, a dozen cars sat near a group of people congregated a hundred yards away. Con recognized his father's sedan and Stuart's as they walked past them. June had no trouble negotiating the hard-packed trail to the gravesite in her heels.

Tomanie and Luis sat on wooden folding chairs holding hands. Rayno Pete stood behind his wife with hands on her shoulders. Luis wore a black pinstriped suit Con had not seen before and the hat he'd worn to the Pete family's home last week. He sat at attention staring straight ahead...into another world. Tomanie bowed her head and did not look up. Conor could not tell if Rayno bowed his head also or if he watched Tomanie. Maybe both.

Olivia and Stuart stood with their son David next to Juan and Maggie Armenta. A young Paiute man broke away from a group he was talking with and came toward them. Con recognized him. Lonny Tido. The girl following a few paces behind him also looked familiar. Then he placed her. Dellis from the café in Overton.

"I'm surprised to see you here, Sheriff." Lonny held out his hand. "Thank you for coming."

"Luis Garza is an old family friend," Con told him, then introduced Lonny around.

"My sister, Dellis," Lonny introduced her.

"So, Sheriff," Dellis began accusingly. "You told me you were a deputy."

"Or something, I believe you put it," Conor countered. "And Jimmy was someone who came into the café a few times."

"He did come into the café a few times,"

"And I'm a deputy...or something," Con retorted. "I guess we're even."

"Even," she concluded with a meager smile.

"Your family looks a bit out of place here," Lonny commented.

"We aren't familiar with your ceremonies, but want to pay our respect to Jimmy and his family."

"We sent his spirit off last night at the big sing. It started at sundown and went 'til early this morning. That's the main thing. Now we will bury his body," Lonny instructed. "It's pretty simple."

"Who all is here?" Con asked him, looking around the crowd.

"The Petes and Pahgoroos mostly and a few Tidos," he answered. "And of course, the Garzas," he added, looking around Conor's family.

"Are these folks yours too?" he asked, looking past him.

Con turned around to see Gus and Katie Brumbaugh walking up the trail behind him. "No," he said. "She's the daughter of the woman Jimmy took care of."

Lonny looked puzzled.

"The woman with the silver buckle."

"Ohhh." Lonny nodded his head as he watched them approach.

"I'm sure she and her husband are also feeling a little awkward."

"Excuse me, Sheriff," Lonny said as he walked over to greet them.

Conor studied Lonny's conversation with the Brumbaughs beyond his hearing. He and Gus had shaken hands and now Katie Brumbaugh was hanging on every word Lonny spoke.

"Who's that old man?" Dellis interrupted Con's observations.

Con returned his attention back toward the path. He did a double-take as he saw Hal Martin puffing his way up the low hill under the bright sun.

"Dr. Harold Martin," Conor told her, causing June to snap her gaze toward Con's object of attention. "He's the coroner. Known me since before I was born. In all those years, I've only known him to attend one funeral. His wife's."

"Why is he here?" Dellis asked.

"There was something about the way Jimmy buried the woman with the buckle, it touched him. He talked to Rayno and Simon for quite a while when they came to get Jimmy. I don't know what was said."

"Spirits," Dellis replied, then turned and walked back to the group she and Lonny had been talking to earlier.

As Dellis Tido walked away, her brother joined her and the Brumbaughs stopped to stand beside Con and June.

"Sheriff," Gus greeted just as Simon held his hand above the casket and began to sing.

Conor nodded to Gus and all attention became focused on Simon Pahgoroo. Hal wandered past them and worked his way through the crowd into a position as close to the shaman as he could get. The song was in Paiute, and Con could see by their faces that few of those his own age or younger understood the language. Like Jimmy and Lonny, it had been beaten out of them at the Indian school. The song was sad. Con could feel it, even though he didn't comprehend the words. Luis's arguments returned to him. He held back tears, understanding for the first time that Jimmy had truly lost it all. And he might have taken Luis with him.

"I will do better," Conor unintentionally said aloud. Mesmerized by the shaman's song, he stared into infinity. His blunt realization drew a bewildered look from June when he spoke. She reached and took his hand. Drawing him back to reality.

Simon had finished singing and began a long oration. Speaking in his native tongue. There was sadness in his eyes. When he finished, Simon Pahgoroo stood in silent prayer for a few minutes. Then spoke in English.

"Many of you don't understand the language of our fathers," he began. "I will tell you in English."

Simon started telling how Jimmy had gone to the Indian School at Fort Mojave to learn how to be a White man. "He came home," Simon said. "Then went to work for a White man. An evil White man, but Jimmy didn't understand the difference. He thought he was doing what the people at the school had taught him."

Simon went on to tell how Jimmy came to guard a White woman. "They became friends, and he learned from her. He learned that good and evil to Indians were still good and evil in the White man's world. When she died, Jimmy tried to remember the old ways and bury her correctly. He probably sang over her, though he didn't know the words. He did everything he could to send her spirit off. Today we do the same for him."

When Con turned, he saw Katie Brumbaugh's face buried in her husband's chest. Hal was sitting on the ground. Someone helped him to his feet. They were lowering the casket into the grave. Luis was hugging Tomanie. They were crying. Rayno was on his knees behind them, hugging them both. Con took June into his arms, closed his eyes and held her for what seemed a long time.

When he opened his eyes, people were leaving. Hal had walked past them without comment. A mound of dirt covered the grave. Simon Pahgoroo helped the trio, Rayno, Tomanie and Luis to their feet. Katie Brumbaugh approached Tomanie and spoke to her. Tomanie reached up and embraced her. Rayno and Luis shook hands, then hugged each other. Then Rayno steadied him and began walking with Luis toward Juan and Maggie who were halfway there to meet them. The McLeod family had gone. Rayno Pete and Gus Brumbaugh arrived simultaneously beside their wives huddled together. Rayno and Tomanie stood arm in arm beside the grave while Simon stood nearby. Gus helped Katie back toward Conor and June.

"Sheriff Armenta," Katie said. "The evil White man is Dutch. He caused all of this. The answer is yes."

17

Sheriff Connor Armenta sat in the chair across from Judge William Tucker's desk as the judge pored over Conor's copy of Katherine Wagner's letter to Katie Brumbaugh. He had already looked over Brice Campbell's ledger marked "Dutch" on the cover in Campbell's handwriting. Brice Campbell had also made every entry in the book himself. Tucker finished reading the letter.

"They were lovers? All those years, and no one suspected it?" He could hardly believe his eyes. "And Leanora Campbell and Katie Brumbaugh will both testify against Dutch... knowing full well what it will do to both families' reputations?"

"Yes, no, yes, and yes."

"What?" the judge asked incredulously.

"They were lovers. Leanora Campbell figured it out several

years ago. They will both testify, and both fully understand the consequences."

"Well," the judge began.

"Robert Westcott and Newt Campbell will most likely also testify...and there's this." Con handed Tucker the bank book.

"Where'd you get this?"

"Out of Jimmy Garza's jacket pocket. Or I should say that Sheriff Andrew Neilson of Beaver County, Utah, got it out of Jimmy Garza's pocket."

"What the...I thought he got hit by a train."

"No one ever said that," Con explained. "I implied that, but actually said it looked like he fell from the train."

"Same difference," the judge scoffed.

"Not if somebody shot you in the head and tied your body up in the brake linkage of a boxcar with twine."

Tucker thought about it a moment. "So how did his jacket get to Utah and how do you know it was his?" he interrogated.

"Only half of the jacket made it to Utah. His right arm was still in it tied to the brake linkage of the boxcar. The twine didn't break."

"That's a little disgusting." Tucker turned up his nose. "So, how did the kid end up with the bank book?"

"He was making withdrawals for her. The last five or six in the book."

"Where was she during all of this?"

"In a cabin in the Valley of Fire."

"Where is she now?"

"In the cooler at the morgue."

"Dead?" the judge asked, instantly realizing how stupid the question was.

But Conor answered, "Yessir," without comment.

"How long?"

"I think Hal estimated six to eight weeks. I can check the autopsy."

"The kid killed her?"

"I don't think so."

"Why not?" Tucker pressed the sheriff to substantiate his theory.

"It appears that Jimmy liked her. He bought her gifts. And he buried her very respectfully. Then there's the cause of death. Gunshot wound to the head. Same caliber. Hal thinks the same gun. We'll need a ballistics expert to verify it."

"And no murder weapon?"

"Not yet."

"And you think Dutch did it?"

"Correct, but Hal would say I'm jumping to conclusions because I don't like the guy."

"Even with the letter? He still thinks it could be someone else?"

"Well, I know that it could be someone else. It's possible. And Hal doesn't know about the letter."

"So, what do you want from me?" Judge Tucker asked.

"Your blessing, I guess," Con answered. "An arrest warrant and a promise that bail will be set high enough to keep Dutch in jail until the trial." Con thought about it a minute. "Is there a way to freeze the assets of Wagner Trucking and the Oasis pending the trial?"

"An arrest warrant for two counts of extortion? Search warrants for Wagner Trucking and Dutch's Oasis? Between the ledger and the real estate, we're looking at over two hundred thousand dollars. That should suffice for bail. We'll let the lawyers worry about the assets," the judge summarized. "I'll have the warrants delivered to your office in an hour. I'll hold on to the ledger, bank book, and letter as evidence. I want the original of that letter as soon as you can get it to me."

* * *

SUNDAY, JUNE 15, 1930

June and April accompanied Conor to morning mass at the Joan of Arc Catholic Church. They walked the block and a half from June's home to the service. Luis also accompanied Con's family. June hugged him and kissed his cheek. He blushed but hugged her back. April and Donna hurried to arrange positions on the pews the group shared, allowing the girls to be seated together.

It surprised June that other than the speaking of Latin, the service did not differ that much from that of the Episcopal Church she and April usually attended. After the service, Father O'Malley showed her added attention and pumped Con's hand so vigorously it was almost painful. They visited for a few minutes on the lawn outside afterward. The Armentas and McLeods departed in their separate automobiles while Conor and June strolled hand in hand with April between them to her home.

"I have an errand I need to run," Con admitted, standing on the porch with his hands around her waist.

"On Sunday?" June questioned in disappointment.

"I won't be that long." Con squirmed. "I'll be back in plenty of time for dinner. My mouth has been watering for weeks now in anticipation." His expression helped dissuade her discontent.

Her smile began to return. "Two o'clock," she insisted.

"We can spend the entire evening together," Conor encouraged. "I won't be late." He pulled her close and kissed her. "I love you, darling."

"Promise?"

"Promise."

* * *

A little past noon, Dutch Wagner sucked on a cigar and sipped a Bloody Mary as he sat behind his desk nursing his hangover. The star he drew over yesterday's date on his calendar marked a milestone in his perceived accomplishments. The burial of Jimmy Garza. The culmination of his troubles with the pesky Indian who knew too much. He had corrected that problem and celebrated yesterday's event with a hard night of drinking. He drew another long pull on his cigar and blew the smoke into the rancid gloom of his dark office on the main floor of Dutch's Oasis, the hallmark of his lurid career.

* * *

MONDAY, APRIL 15, 1930

Dutch drove to the shack two days after Sal delivered his mother's trunk there. He had to get the trunk out of her garage. Newt Campbell was moving into her house that week. When he saw how Jimmy had fixed up the shack for her, he was enraged. In his tantrum, he blurted out that Mr. High and Mighty was dead, and Katherine became hysterical. She fell onto her knees next to her bed, bawling uncontrollably over her lost lover. Dutch walked up behind her. He grabbed her by her long curly hair, shaking her and yelling obscenities.

"Shut up your sobbing, you worthless whore," he sneered as he poked his little pistol against the back of her head.

"Dutch!" she screamed. "Please don't kill me!"

He pushed her head between her knees into a fetal position.

"PLEEEAASE!" she begged.

He pulled the trigger.

"What have you done?" Jimmy exclaimed in fear and horror.

"Bury her where no one will find her," Dutch ordered him as calmly as if nothing had happened. He got into his car and drove away.

* * *

SUNDAY, JUNE 15, 1930

In hindsight, Dutch could still not believe the Indian had guts enough to walk into this office wearing his father's belt buckle and tried to blackmail him. He threatened he would tell the sheriff all that he knew. All about the whiskey and Dutch killing his own mother and where she was buried. He wanted a hundred dollars, like it was a fortune, to hush up and go back to Moapa forever.

Dutch looked at the rug in front of his desk, remembering where Jimmy had stood. How Jimmy had begged for his life, just like his mother had. How he held him down by his short black hair with his head between his knees. How the disgusting little Indian crapped his pants in fear just before he pulled the trigger.

"Tell that bumbling sheriff," Dutch scoffed as he refilled his empty Bloody Mary glass with whiskey. "You got your wish. You went back to Moapa...forever."

He had pulled off the perfect murder. More than once.

As Dutch chuckled to himself pompously, Leanora Campbell handed the ledger with his name on the front of it to Sheriff Armenta at her front door.

* * *

MONDAY, JUNE 16, 1930

A little past noon, twenty-four hours after he received the ledger, Conor Armenta sipped on a bottle of Coca-Cola. He sat behind his desk rehearsing in his head the coming arrest of Dutch Wagner. The two warrants lay in front of him. Jesse, Ben, and Whit would be here any minute.

When the three deputies arrived, Con shuffled them into his office and closed the door.

"What's up, Sheriff?" Ben asked.

"We're going to arrest Dutch Wagner." He looked for a reaction from the trio. Each had their attention focused on Con waiting for instructions.

"I don't think Dutch is nearly as tough as he thinks he is, but he has a squad of goons for bodyguards and bouncers that might be. The place should be quiet this time of day. Each of you will carry shotguns as well as your sidearms." All three nodded with understanding.

"Whit, you will drive your car up the alley and post yourself near the back door. Use your car as cover between you and the door. Stop anyone who comes out. If they don't stop, shoot them."

"Yessir." Whit swallowed before he answered.

"Jesse, you will ride with me. We'll pull up right out front. I will go in the front door and cross the room to Dutch's office. You'll wait at the front door until I get to the office, then post yourself near the end of the bar where you can use it for cover if necessary."

"Got it. After you go to Dutch's office, I go to the bar and stand ready," Jesse repeated. A surge of adrenaline hit him remembering the last mission when he backed up the sheriff.

"Ben, you drive Jesse's car. Wait down the block until Jesse enters the Oasis, then pull up behind my pickup. Just like Whit in the back, use the car for cover and stop anyone who comes out."

"Yessir, Sheriff," Ben established. "I understand."

"What are we waiting for?" Jesse asked in anticipation.

Just as Conor started to answer there was a soft knock on the door. He held up his index finger to the deputies and opened the door.

"I just got the strangest call, Sheriff," Hazel began. "A woman said, 'Tell him he's in his office,' and hung up."

"Thanks, Hazel."

He turned to Jesse. "That's it."

* * *

Conor waited down the street as Whit pulled into position. Then he proceeded to the front door. When Con pulled up out front, Sal ran out the back.

"Hold it there, big fella," Whit announced as he pumped a shell into the chamber of his shotgun. "Just move over into the shade there and find yourself a comfortable-looking place to lay down on your belly and rest."

With raised hands, Sal moved slowly into the area indicated and carefully laid down on his stomach. Whit cuffed him behind his back. And checked his waistband for weapons. Not too concerned with Sal's access to other areas, he ordered. "Just lay there nice and quiet. Take a nap, if you'd like. I'll be right over here watching you."

The room was empty. As Con walked past the bartender, he told him. "Set up a glass of iced tea for me at the end of the bar, would you?"

The bartender poured a glass of tea and sat it at the end of the bar, then watched Conor as he walked past and up to Dutch's office door. When the bartender turned around, Jesse kept his right hand on the grip of the shotgun laying across the bar.

"Thank you," he said and nodded as he took a sip of the iced tea with his left.

Con looked behind him and saw the nose of Jesse's car pulled up behind his pickup. Through the open front door, the barrel of Ben's shotgun became barely visible across the hood.

Con placed his right hand on the butt of his Colt and opened the door suddenly with his left.

"Sheriff!" Dutch exclaimed as he nearly jumped to his feet. "I didn't hear you knock."

"I didn't," Conor announced as he pulled the search warrant from his pocket

"I have a search warrant for this place and Wagner Trucking." He handed it to him.

"We're in the city of Las Vegas," Dutch stuttered slightly. "Isn't that out of your jurisdiction, Sheriff?" He tried to reassure himself without looking at the paper.

"I'm the sheriff of Clark County, Nevada," Con told him with authority. "I have jurisdiction everywhere in this county except the Moapa Indian Reservation. I have jurisdiction there too, if I'm pursuing the suspect of a crime committed outside the reservation."

Dutch backpedaled. "What are you looking for?"

"Anything I want. Anywhere I want."

"I don't understand," Dutch stammered. "I run a perfectly legitimate business here."

"You'll understand soon enough," Con said. "Let's start with that safe there." He pointed to the wall safe behind Dutch's desk.

"That's private. The contents of that safe are strictly personal."

"That warrant doesn't provide an exemption for personal. Open it."

"Uh, I don't, uh, remember the combination."

"You'll remember it quick enough, or I'll have somebody in here with nitroglycerin to blow the door off it. Take your pick."

Dutch turned around and began spinning the dial between glimpses over his shoulder.

"Don't fret about me," Conor told him. "I'm not very good with numbers. I won't remember the combination. Oh, and by the way, step back so I can see both of your hands when you open it."

Dutch turned around and to one side, then reached with his right hand to turn the handle and pull the moderately heavy door open. The compartment was small, without a shelf. Two tall stacks of greenbacks sat atop a ledger. The ledger was cocked up on one side. Con leaned over to see what was under it in the dimly lit room. It wasn't the pistol he hoped to find, but appeared to be the briarwood bowl of a pipe.

"I almost forgot to tell you, I've got another warrant here."

He pulled the arrest warrant from his pocket with his left hand and held it out to him. As Dutch reached for it, Con continued.

"Gary D. Wagner, Jr., you are under arrest for one count on the felony extortion of the late Brice Campbell and one count on the felony extortion of the late Katherine Wagner."

Dutch's face paled and his hand dove into the pocket of his trousers. Before he could get ahold of the little pistol, he heard the ominous click of the hammer being pulled back on Armenta's 1911 Colt automatic. He looked up into the barrel of the .45 only a few inches from his nose.

"I hope that's the .25 Automatic that killed your mother and Jimmy Garza," Conor said calmly. "My day would become so much more satisfying."

A LOOK AT BOOK THREE:
SONS OF THE TEXAS STAR

HOLLYWOOD GLITZ, RIVALRIES, AND A DEADLY SHOT IN THE DESERT SUN.

In the heart of Las Vegas, the buzz of Hollywood invades a small desert town as Unified Stars Studios rolls into Clark County to film their latest talkie, a high-profile adaptation of the best-selling novel *Sons of the Texas Star*. The book's success, reminiscent of Owen Wister's *Virginian*, sets the stage for a blockbuster, starring cowboy superstar Matt McCoy and his twin brother Mark. The film's dramatic tale of twin brothers battling over a family ranch is poised to captivate audiences nationwide.

But what begins as an exciting production soon turns into a nightmare. During the filming of the climactic scene, where the brothers are meant to shoot it out, a fatal twist occurs. A live round is slipped into Mark McCoy's revolver instead of a blank, and Matt is found dead in the grand foyer of a luxurious hacienda.

Sheriff Conor Armenta must navigate the glamorous yet shadowy world of Hollywood's burgeoning film industry to uncover the truth behind Matt McCoy's murder. As he delves deeper into the glamorous facade, the truth behind who really killed Matt—and why—is far more sinister than any cinema illusion.

AVAILABLE NOVEMBER 2024

ABOUT THE AUTHOR

Jefferson Glass grew up near the Klamath Indian Reservation in the ranch country of southeastern Oregon. Influenced by the stories found in his grandfather's collection of Zane Grey novels, his young imagination went wild in these rural surroundings. At an early age, he often hiked with his dog over countless miles of public land that bordered his family's property. The only rule was to be home by suppertime. As a teenager, his wanderlust gave way to working the hayfields of a nearby ranch.

In 1981, Jefferson moved to central Wyoming where he began his writing career. He has written numerous articles on Western history for *Annals of Wyoming*, *True West Magazine* and WyoHistory.org. His non-fiction books, *RESHAW: The Life and Times of John Baptiste Richard* and *Empire: The Pioneer Legacy of an American Ranch Family*, won a Western Writers of America Spur Award and a Will Rogers Medallion Award respectively.

Jefferson began research in 2020 on his Conor Armenta Mystery series, set in 1930s Las Vegas. While exploring Clark

County, Nevada, and surrounding areas, he and his wife stumbled across Kanab, Utah, where they purchased a home and relocated. The magnificent view of The Grand Staircase-Escalante out their back door is certain to inspire years of future writing.

www.ingramcontent.com/pod-product-compliance
Lightning Source LLC
Chambersburg PA
CBHW011421010726
47494CB00011B/2437